MW01127307

The Lure of a Rake
Heart of a Duke Series

For more information about the author:
www.christicaldwellauthor.com
christicaldwellauthor@gmail.com
Twitter: @ChristiCaldwell
Or on Facebook at: Christi Caldwell Author

For first glimpse at covers, excerpts, and free bonus material, be sure to sign up for my monthly newsletter!
Printed in the USA.

Cover Design and Interior Format

The Lure of a Rake

Heart of a Duke

THE SERIES

USA TODAY BESTSELLER

CHRISTI CALDWELL

Other Titles by
Christi Caldwell

SINFUL BRIDES
The Rogue's Wager
The Scoundrel's Honor

THE THEODOSIA SWORD
Only for His Lady

DANBY
A Season of Hope
Winning a Lady's Heart

BRETHREN OF THE LORDS
My Lady of Deception
Memoir: Non-Fiction
Uninterrupted Joy

DEDICATION

So much goes into the creation of a book. I often say, it takes a village. From beginning to the literal and figurative end, there is plotting and writing and revising and editing.

To my editorial team, Sandra Sookoo and Scott Moreland. Thank you for your brilliance. Be it phone calls or emails or late night Facebook messages, when I absolutely must talk to someone about my story, you're always there. Cedric and Genevieve's story is for you.

PROLOGUE

London, England
1813

MAYHAP THEY WON'T FIND ME here.
    Lady Genevieve Farendale sat in the corner of the schoolroom with her knees drawn to her chest. The hum of quiet in the darkened room was faintly calming.

She laid her tear-dampened cheek upon the soft satin fabric of her ivory wedding dress. Mayhap, they'd know the last place to look for an eighteen-year-old young lady on her should-have-been-wedding-night would be in a child's schoolroom.

The door opened. "Genny?" Her just fourteen-year-old sister, Gillian, stuck her head inside the room and scanned the darkened space. The girl hesitated and Genevieve held her breath, hoping her sister would turn on her heel and leave. "Are you in here?" Gillian called out again and stepped inside. The door closed with a decisive click.

She should have known better. Especially given the rotted turn of events that day where invariably, nothing went right—at least for her, anyway. For one moment born of cowardice, she contemplated saying nothing. But this was Gillian; devoted, loving, and all things kind in a world that had proven how elusive those sentiments were. "I'm here," she said quietly, discreetly brushing her hands over her tear-stained cheeks.

Squinting in the dark, Gillian located Genevieve with her stare. Then, with an uncharacteristic guardedness, she wandered closer. She came to a stop, hovering beside her older sister. "Are you all right?" There was a singsong, almost haunting quality to her words.

For her sister's benefit, Genevieve mustered a smile. Or she tried. She really did.

Gillian's eyes formed round moons. "Oh, dear," she whispered, sailing to the floor in a noisy ruffle of skirts.

With the hell of the day whirring around her mind, Genevieve wanted to yell for her to leave. She wanted to snap and snarl and hiss and demand Gillian allow her to her misery. "What is it?" Alas, she'd never been able to yell at her loving sibling.

"You are crying."

"No, I am not." She *had* been crying. Well, sobbing, really. The noisy, ugly kind of sobs producing tears that left a lady with a hopelessly red nose and bloodshot eyes. Nothing really pretty about those tears. Now, she'd not a single drop left to shed.

Gillian leaned forward and peered at her. "But you were," she insisted, worry filled her usually hopeful, cheerful tone.

With a sigh, Genevieve stroked the top of her sister's head. "But I was."

Capturing her lower lip between her teeth, Gillian troubled the flesh. "Is it because of your wedding?" The inquiry emerged hesitant.

It was because her heart had been ripped from her chest in the most public of ways. Her honor and virtue had all been thrown into question by the very same man she'd loved. Alas, one couldn't say all of that to a young girl still untainted by life. Genevieve searched for words.

"I overheard Mother and Father," the girl supplied.

"Ah." For really, what else was there to say? What, when she didn't truly wish to know what, was being discussed between her previously proud mama and papa? Her mother was a leading Society matron, who prided that position above all else. Her Papa loved…well *nothing*, except his title and power.

"You are not getting married then?" Her sister's question pulled her back from her useless musings. For even a girl of fourteen, who could not know the precise details, at least registered the ramifications and knew—Genevieve was ruined.

Tears welled once more. Unable to form a reply, Genevieve opened her arms and Gillian threw herself into them. Closing her eyes, Genevieve took comfort in the slight, reassuring weight of her sister's small form. She dropped her chin atop her sister's head and blinked back tears.

"I do not understand why he would not marry you," Gillian whispered.

"Because…" Because he was a cad. A liar. A blackheart.

But the truth was, she didn't know *why* the Duke of Aumere had jilted her. With a missive delivered by his closest friend, no less. That note that had been turned over to her parents.

Her stomach churned. Words that threw aspersions upon her character and marked her a whore. Lies. All of the words, lies. But it mattered not. When a duke whispered, everyone listened, and ladies were ruined.

And Genevieve was well and truly ruined.

Footsteps sounded in the hall and both girls looked up. The door opened and their mother stepped inside. In her fingers, she carried the same damning piece of vellum she'd raged over in the return carriage ride from the church. With sure, determined footsteps, she entered deeper into the room and Gillian hopped quickly to her feet. Genevieve, however, moved with a greater reluctance. "Moth—"

"Gillian," their mother snapped.

The girl looked back and forth between mother and daughter, indecision in her eyes. Genevieve mustered a smile, gave her sister's fingers a slight squeeze and said, "Go."

Eyes lowered, Gillian skirted the seething marchioness and took her leave, shutting mother and daughter alone.

She tried again. "Moth—"

"What have you done?" her mother's clipped words shook with fury.

What had she done? The more apropos question would have been; what had *he* done? Or why? How? Anything was surely more appropriate than "what have you done?" Squaring her shoulders, she held her mother's furious stare. "I did nothing."

Her mother brandished the page. "You've done nothing?" she squeaked. "You lay with the duke—"

"I did not lie with anyone," she bit out. She'd had but two kisses from the man who'd been her betrothed and those were brief, chaste ones upon her lips. Never anything more.

Her mother scoffed. "Are you calling the duke a liar?"

She stiffened. Is that the way of this coldly reserved world they lived in? A mother would believe lies upon a page over her own daughter's words? "I am."

Her mother's broad nose flared and she studied Genevieve. Fury burned from within her eyes. Then, she quickly smoothed her features. Of course, one must never show emotion. How shameful for her mother to drop that mask for even a sliver of a moment. "You are ruined."

Yes, she was quite ruined. Beyond marriageable. What happened to women such as that? Rumored virtue-less, may as well, in fact, be truly without virtue. What happened to those ladies? A panicky laugh built in her chest.

"You cannot stay here."

That decisive, emotionless statement snapped her back from the precipice of her silent ramblings. "No," she agreed. There had, however, been something oddly comforting in the schoolroom. A peace. A quiet. The schoolroom had been the one place she'd felt accomplished. She'd earned the praise and pride of her nursemaids and governesses. Of course, on the day of her greatest failure, this place harkened to the time in her life when she'd done right. Genevieve made to step around her mother, when the woman shot a hand out, and wrapped it around her forearm. "I am leaving," she said with a frown, wincing at her mother's painful grip.

"Not this room, Genevieve."

A pebble of dread knotted in her belly. Perhaps it was the events of the morn. Perhaps it was the shock of betrayal. And yet, she could not make sense of those decisive four words. "I don't understand."

"Surely you see that you cannot remain here. You will be a visible blight upon your sister's future. As long as you are here, people will talk and whisper. But your sister is young enough that she might make a respectable match in four years."

Did her mother truly believe her absence would make all of that go away? It was madness. Her mother spoke as though, in leaving, Genevieve's very existence would be forgotten. By the firm set to her mother's mouth, she knew. She'd be banished to the country.

She smoothed her shaking palms over the front of her rumpled wedding dress. "Very well," she said, proud of the steady quality of those words. But inside, she was shaking with equal parts rage and hurt betrayal—first her betrothed and now her mother. Was there loyalty, anywhere? "We will return to the country and when we return—"

"Not us," her mother put in impatiently. "*You* need to leave."

A dull humming filled her ears. She shook her head. *No.*

"Yes." The marchioness took a step closer.

She imagined living in a world away from Gillian and tears flooded her eyes. Even though she'd so often deliberately needled her sister through the years, those bothersome sibling behaviors were now gifts she'd not give up. Ice traveled along her spine. Her teeth clattered noisily and she hugged her arms close. "Wh-where would you send me?" she croaked as the reality of her mother's cold disdain stole the last of her logic. Her mother sought to snip her from the fabric of the family as though she was nothing more than a bothersome thread dangling from an embroidery frame.

"Your grandfather's property in Kent." Her mother pursed her lips. Rumored to be as frigid and unyielding as a winter freeze, her parents would send her there. "I do not hold you entirely to blame. I attended Mrs. Belden's when I was young." She peeled her lip back in a disappointed sneer. "Perhaps you would have been best served by attending that institution. Instead, we indulged you with lax governesses and nursemaids." She gave a flick of her hand. "Regardless, the mistake was mine for allowing you to remain here with those who encouraged your flights of fancy. Now we are to live with those circumstances."

We. A familial equation Genevieve no longer fit within. She turned her hands up and managed but one word. "Please." The entreaty emerged garbled and hoarse.

Her mother scowled and ignored the outstretched offering. "Would you be so selfish as to steal your sister's right to a respectable marriage?"

Guilt sliced at her heart. Even though it wasn't her fault. Even though the duke's words were all lies. They belonged to a Society where women had no voice and certainly one that would never be believed against a duke. And yet, for that, she would be sent away and never again see Gillian. She let her arm fall to her side.

"I cannot leave," she whispered.

"Of course you will," her mother said with a matter-of-factness that froze her on the inside. "For Gillian, you will." Then, turning on her heel, she started for the door.

A burgeoning panic clogged Genevieve's throat. "Wait," she managed to cry out, as her mother gripped the door handle. "When can I return?" Her body trembled with the force of terror spreading through her.

Her mother cast a look over her shoulder. "Why, when your sister makes a respectable match." On that sure pronouncement, the marchioness left, closing the door behind her.

And just like that, the thread was cut.

CHAPTER 1

London England,
Spring 1818

As Lady Genevieve Farendale stepped through the front doors of the lavish London townhouse, she wondered just exactly how parents decided going about ending an imposed exile on one's daughter.

Was it a certain number of days or hours? Or was it something more arbitrary? As simple as waking up one day and realizing that there was, indeed, a fabric of the family missing that needed to be restored. Given their remarkable absence from her life all these years, she'd venture it certainly wasn't the latter.

Whatever precipitated the reinstatement into one's family, however it had come about, five years had been the amount of time. Five years of remaining in the country while her family spent the Seasons in London. Five years of no letters or words. And five years marked the end of her penance. Penance for an imagined crime.

"My lady?"

Genevieve blinked at the butler, Dunwithy. Time had left wrinkles at the corners of his rheumy eyes and upon his cheeks. And yet the spectacles perched on his slightly crooked nose were the same. Odd, a servant should be more a member of the household than the marquess' oldest daughter. The man stared expectantly at her, startling her into movement.

Wordlessly, she shrugged out of her modest cloak and turned it over to his waiting hands. Other servants, unfamiliar, young footmen rushed forward to collect the trunks and valise. Of course, they would not have been in her father's employ all those years ago. As such, they'd not remember the shame of that long ago day.

"May I show you to your chambers, my lady?" the butler offered.

With the servant's question echoing through the soaring foyer done in Italian marble, she looked about. What had she expected? A warm, familial greeting from an abjectly broken mother and father who pleaded her forgiveness? An exuberant reunion from the younger sister, whom she'd not spoken to in years?

"My lady?" the butler urged again.

How long had she remained silent with no one but her ancient grandfather? He was now given to sleeping his days away and leaving her to her own thoughts for company. And so, she lifted her head and followed behind the butler. As she began the long walk to her once familiar rooms, one of the liveried footmen stole a sideways glance at her and then quickly looked away. A dull flush marred his cheeks.

Her lips twisted in a bitter, humorless smile. So they'd heard the whispers, too. What had they heard exactly? Tales of the shamelessly wanton lady who'd spread her legs for her betrothed and the gentleman's friends? That had been a popular one bandied about. In fact, it had been the one that had found her standing alone at the altar with a collection of intimate guests looking on. Or mayhap it had been the rumor spread that she'd slept with her betrothed's younger brother. That had caused quite the stir among the gossips…and even the non-gossips.

The thick carpets muffled the sound of her footfalls. As she walked, Genevieve passed her gaze over the familiar in some ways, altogether different in other aspects of her *home*. The gilt frames bearing the proud Farendale ancestors remained fixed in the very spots they'd always been. Those pompous bewigged lords stared down their long Roman noses. However, the wallpaper was different. Pale satin, that harkened to the country skies of Kent, and as much as she'd thought she despised her banishment and abhorred the country, she'd been wrong. So wrong. A hungering gripped her to go back to that remote estate where she could paint and write and sing and simply *be*—without any of the whispers and only the servants for company.

But alas, it was not to be. Because as time had proven once before, the dream of simplicity was all imagined. Proper betrothals; broken and shattered. The allure of anonymity, ended in one six-hour carriage ride.

"Here we are, my lady," the butler murmured and opened the door.

Genevieve tugged off her gloves. She lingered in the doorway. "Thank you. That will be all," she said dismissively, her voice hoarse from ill use.

Relief flared in the servant's eyes. He backed away and rushed down the hall with a speed reserved for a man twenty years his junior. She hovered in the doorway. Passing her soft leather gloves into one hand, she brushed the other over the doorjamb.

Five years. It had been five years since she'd last stepped foot out of these chamber doors. One thousand, eight hundred and twenty-five days to be precise. Her throat worked and she damned the weakness that came rushing back from simply being in this godawful place. But she'd braved isolation from her family and Society. Endured cruel whispers and lewd offers. Given all that, stepping inside her bedchambers really was rather insignificant. Willing her legs into movement, Genevieve forced her feet over the threshold. Her breath caught and she looked around.

From the pale pink of the wallpaper to the floral Aubusson carpet, in this room, time stood still. She wandered over to the canopied bed and trailed her fingertips along the ivory coverlet. Why, even the upholsteries were the same. The only thing that had been missing from this nauseatingly cheerful room—had been the girl who'd slept within these walls. Setting her gloves on the rose-inlaid side table, she perched on the edge of the mattress and passed her gaze about. It collided with the only splash of green in this pink and white space.

Shoving to her feet, her legs carried her unbidden over to that rounded, porcelain perfume bottle. With numb fingers, she picked up the piece, a gift given long ago, and liquid sloshed around inside. She fixed on the bucolic couple painted within the center of the bottle; a loyal love knelt at the feet of his sweetheart—their happiness forever suspended in time. How singularly wrong that any piece of *him* should remain in this room when she'd been sent away. Genevieve tightened her grip about the fragile piece; her knuckles whitening.

A tentative rap sounded at the door and she yanked her head up. "Enter," she called out, quickly setting the bottle down.

The door opened revealing her maid, Delores—the one loyal figure she'd known these years. "Hullo, Lady Genevieve."

She mustered a smile. "Delores." The foolish part of her soul where hope still dwelt had believed Gillian or her mother would be there. Yet, why should they? For the time that had gone, Genevieve may as well have been a stranger. Time had marched on. They'd lived their lives, and she…well, she had lived hers.

Delores gave her a small, encouraging nod. "His Lordship has summoned you."

Genevieve's weak attempt at a grin faded. *Already?*

"Yes, Lady Genny."

She gave her head a shake, not realizing she'd spoken aloud. Genevieve nodded. "I'll be but a moment," she assured the young woman who nodded and then backed out of the room, closing the door behind her.

Genevieve stood there a long moment with the porcelain clock atop the mantel marking the passing seconds. Nothing her parents had ever done had ever been without purpose. The lavish wedding celebration they'd planned for their eldest daughter to the sought after Duke of Aumere. The abrupt and lengthy exile of that same daughter. Of course, her return would have been driven by some motives which could only be a product of her father's wealth, power, or title. Nervousness twisted in her belly and she fixed on the passing ticks of the clock.

With the powerlessness in her existence these years, and even in this impending meeting with her father, there was something so wholly empowering in keeping that same faithless, shameful parent waiting. She sighed. Alas, all good moments came to an end. Time had taught her that in spades. Squaring her shoulders, Genevieve stalked over to the front of the room and, unhesitant, opened the door. Silence reigned in the corridors.

But she'd wager the remainder of her sanity that servants laid in wait, holding their breath and listening for that long-overdue meeting between father and daughter. Stepping outside, she picked her

way along the carpeted halls, onward to an office she'd been summoned too many times to remember. She'd been summoned there
as a girl who'd earned his displeasure for her scandalous sketches
and paintings. And again as a young woman who'd secured the
match of the Season and, for a fleeting moment, earned his pride
and approval.

Then there had been the last meeting in that dreaded office. The
meeting when her father, the person who'd helped give her life,
had spat at her and pledged to never let her set foot in these halls
again. Genevieve reached his office and came to a stop. She stared
at the silver handle.

When she pulled that door open, she would reenter a world
she'd never again wanted to be in. It would be like ripping open
the bandage on the darkest mistakes of her foolish youth, and the
resentments and pain she'd managed to bury these past five years.

She firmed her jaw. She'd been called whore, liar, and wanton
these many years. But no one would ever dare call her coward.
Genevieve knocked once.

"Enter."

Even as she'd been expecting it, she jumped. That thunderous
boom had not been diminished by time. It still carried the weight
of power and strength it always had. Genevieve pushed the door
open and stepped inside.

He didn't even deign to look at her.

She stood there, much like the recalcitrant child summoned to
these rooms years and years earlier, awaiting the scolding to be
laid out. Those were times when governesses and nursemaids had
failed to tame her. She stood there…as though she'd never been
gone. *Look at me. Look at me and acknowledge me after five years. Tell
me you were wrong.*

Her father tossed down his pen and picked his head up. But for
the faint dusting of gray at his temples and several wrinkles on his
high, noble brow, there was no hint of aging. He was the same man
who'd so easily shipped her away. "Genevieve," he called out and,
jolted into movement, she pulled the door closed.

No need to give the servants easy access to the gossip about the
Farendale whore. "Father," she said and came forward. She did a
quick look about for her mother. Of course, she'd not bother to be
here. Why should she? She'd had her other perfectly unscandalous

daughter to worry after. The muscles of her stomach tightened and she hated that she should care still about their disregard. Without awaiting permission, Genevieve moved to the leather winged back chair in front of his desk and sat. "I trust you are well?"

Her father's mouth tightened. "The scandal has not gone away," he said without preamble.

"I am also well. Thank you for asking," she said deliberately needling. By the vein bulging at the corner of his eye, she was one wrong utterance away from one of his notorious diatribes. "The scandal? Which scandal do you refer to?" And yet she'd always been hopelessly troublesome.

He opened and closed his mouth several times. "*The* scandal," he bit out.

Genevieve inclined her head. "Ah, yes. Of course." She paused and gave a solemn nod. "*My* scandal." She drummed her fingertips on the arm of her chair until he pointedly glared at her hand and she stopped mid-movement.

"You would be so flippant," he said in frosty tones. "You speak so very casually without a regard for the fact that Gillian is gossiped about." The marquess banged his fist on his desk. "Not a single suitor."

A frisson of guilt unfurled inside for the sister who'd be so marked as an immoral creature, all because of Society's opinion of her. "I am sorry," she said softly and folded her hands on her lap. She studied the interlocked digits. With but four years separating them, Gillian had been her loyal friend; albeit a young one. She'd lain upon Genevieve's coverlet and pleaded for tales of the balls and soirees she'd attended and the suitors who'd earned a dance.

And now, by her father's account, Gillian had never known those perceived thrilling moments herself because of Genevieve's scandal. That hungering to return to the obscurity of the countryside filled her and she launched her appeal. "I do not see how my being in London will serve to benefit Gillian. I can only serve as a reminder. Would it not be best if you allow me to return?" *Please. Please let me go.* Was there really much life for her in Kent, though? A voice needled at the back of her mind. Was that the future she dreamed of? One in which she was the detested, shameful child without any control of her future and fate?

Her father folded his arms at his chest and eyed her contemplatively. "We have tried purging your memory from Society. The whispers have only persisted because of your stay in the country. Speculation of a…" His cheeks turned a mottled red. "Child."

"Ah, of course," she said dryly, while inside she seethed with a gnawing fury. Her stay in the country? That was what they should call it? Not, the banishment forced upon her, but rather, a stay? She remained silent, wishing him to state his piece so she could be gone.

"No," her father said at last. "We've tried hiding our dirty secret." Which would be her. She was that dirty secret. "To no avail. The only thing we did not do…" She went still. Oh, good God, no. "Is face it head on." No. No. The litany ran around her mind.

Genevieve gave her head a slow shake. "I do not understand," she said with a calmness she did not feel. All the while praying that the long travel and fatigue muddled what he truly meant.

"You need to be reintroduced into Society." That handful of words conjured a foreign beast removed from its natural habitat and reinserted into its proper home. *Then, is that not how my own parents see me?* "Society needs to see you are a proper lady now. Once Society's fascination with you has died, then your sister can resume a normal life and find a suitable husband. It worked for the Moore chit after *she* was jilted and it will work for you."

The least of import to that speech pertained to a young lady she did not know. For with the long-case ticking loudly, she stared unblinking at her father. That was his plan? Thrusting her back into the scornful world which had sharpened their claws on her once hopeful, whimsical self? She gave her head a shake. "No. That will not work." For so many reasons. Too many to even enumerate. "Furthermore, who would marry me?" she blurted, interrupting him, just as he made to speak. No one. No one unless he was truly—

"A desperate gentleman," her father supplied. "One who requires a wife." With cool, methodical movements, he pulled open his desk drawer and withdrew a note from inside. He laid it on the table.

Even as she did not want to know what was contained on those pages, Genevieve craned her head and quickly skimmed the page.

Lord Tremaine?

She knew that name. Her mind muddled through. How did she know that name? Genevieve froze. Lord Tremaine, one of Father's friends from his Oxford days. Widowed twice, with a bevy of daughters. She shook her head. Surely he was not suggesting…? Surely…?

"Tremaine's wives never birthed him an heir." The muscles of her stomach tightened reflexively. "He will be arriving in London within a fortnight to assess your suitability."

"My suitability?" she choked out. As though she was a bloody broodmare.

He continued as though she'd not spoken in horrified shock. "He is not opposed to marrying a girl with a scandal, as long as she can be a proper wife and bear him an heir," he said, tapping the page. "He'll overlook your sins and restore this family to respectability."

As the shock of his words abated, a healthy, seething rage built within her. "*My* sins?" She shook from the force of her fury. Layering her hands to the side of the chair, she gripped it to maintain calm. Yes, she had been a flirt. A shameful, wicked flirt. If she could go back and not be the coquette who'd seduced with her eyes, then she would have happiness, a family, and stability. But that had been the extent of her crime. She'd never been the whore the *ton* whispered of. Nor the liar her betrothed and his bastard of a brother had proven themselves to be.

"You are to conduct yourself with dignity and honor and proper decorum," her father went on. He peeled his lip in a sneer and raked a hard stare over her, and she sank back under the force of the revulsion there.

As much as she despised herself for caring, how could a daughter not feel shame at such open loathing?

"You will wear colorless skirts."

Did he truly believe she gave a jot about the fabric of her gown? "Would you have me don white or ivory?" she asked in a smoothly emotionless tone as she angled her chin up.

Either he failed to note or care about her mocking response, for he continued as though she'd not even spoken. "I'll not have you batting your lashes at rakes and rogues. When you go out, you are to take your maid and a footman. When you attend *ton* functions, you are to sit primly on the sidelines with the matrons." He ran through his perfunctory list with such precision her head spun. "You are not to attract any notice, whatsoever."

Why, he thought her incapable of proper behavior? Despite his ill-opinion and her own flirtatious ways years earlier, Genevieve, in five years, had buried that spirited part of her soul. She had carefully crafted a reserved, proper figure in her stead. Then, her father would have had to speak to her through the years to know as much. "Am I permitted to take meals with the family? Or am I to be confined to my room, then?" There was, however, still the matter of her loose tongue.

The marquess pounded his fist hard the desk, rattling the crystal inkwells and she jumped. "By God, this is not a matter of jest," he thundered. "You have forever marked this family. The least of what you can do is make this right, as much as you are able, for your sister." And the fight was sucked out of her. "Is that understood?"

She sat there trembling; not unlike the same girl she'd been five years earlier. *Do not be that girl. Not anymore.* Except, for the pleasure Genevieve found in exerting herself over her father, she loved her sister more. "Abundantly, my lord," she bit out. Her father would order her return to London, with neat plans to order her life and bind her forever to a gentleman. Given the oppressiveness she'd known at her own father's hands, did he truly believe she'd marry one of his aged friends?

"You are dismissed."

Genevieve came to her feet. The click-clack of her father's pen indicated he'd returned his attentions to matters which were of import to him.

And just like that, she was dismissed once more.

CHAPTER 2

"BY GOD, WHERE IS HE?"

Lying on the leather button sofa of the library in his bachelor's residence, Cedric Falcot, the Marquess of St. Albans, turned his head and looked to the entrance. A small grin hovered on his lips as he rescued the bottle of brandy from the foot of his seat. Turning on his side, he filled his empty snifter and then set the crystal decanter back on the floor.

"Y-Your Grace, His Lordship is otherwise busy." The thick walls muffled the stammering of his inexplicably loyal butler. He really deserved an increase in wages.

"...busy." The Duke of Ravenscourt's snort penetrated the wood.

The door flew open, with such force it bounced off the back wall. His father stuck his leg out to keep it from slamming in his face. The Duke of Ravenscourt took in the jacket hung haphazardly over the back of the sofa, the nearly empty bottle, the full glass, and then he settled his icy blue stare on Cedric. "Get out."

It spoke volumes to Avis' foolish devotion that the hard, unyielding command of the duke did not send him immediately fleeing. Instead, he gulped, looking hopelessly to Cedric.

Taking mercy on the young servant, he swung his legs and settled them on the floor. "That will be all," he assured the man.

Avis dropped a respectful bow and then backed quickly from the room but not before Cedric detected the flash of relief in his eyes.

Yes, that was long the effect the ruthless Duke of Ravenscourt had on all. Reviled, feared, and hated by even his own children, there was not a sliver of warmth in the bastard's hardened heart. Only, over the years, Cedric found that his father was just a man…a man with the same weaknesses and vices as him. That realization had broken down the myth of invincibility around the old duke.

"Father," Cedric drawled. Taking a sip of his brandy, he shoved lazily to his feet. "To what do I owe the honor of—?"

"Shut your goddamn mouth, Cedric." The duke shoved the door hard and it slammed closed with such force it rattled the doorjamb. He stalked over and skimmed his stare over the bottles littering the floor. "I don't give a damn if you drink yourself to death—"

"How heartwarming," Cedric murmured, touching a hand to his chest.

"—but not before you do right by the Falcot line."

Ah, yes, because nothing had ever mattered more than that distinguished title that went back to the time of great conquerors. Not even the man's children, certainly not his bastards, and never the long-dead wife who'd dutifully given him two legitimate issues before conveniently leaving the duke a young widower.

Cedric took a sip of his drink. "Isn't it rather early in the day to have this conversation?"

His father snapped his blond eyebrows into a single line. "It is four o'clock in the goddamn afternoon."

Cedric glanced over to the tightly-pulled curtains. "Is it?" God, how he'd delighted in taunting the old bastard. It was one of the true enjoyments he found in life.

In a not uncommon show of temper, the duke swiped his hand over the long table positioned at the back of the sofa. He sent the bottles and snifters tumbling to the floor in an explosion of glass. "I have been tolerant of your carousing and womanizing. I've indulged your excess wagering." A vein throbbed at the corner of his eye. "But if you think you'll shirk these responsibilities, I'll see you cut off without a goddamn pence."

He grinned wryly and propped his hip on the arm of the sofa. Ah, the cut-you-off-without-a-pence threat. Cedric made a tsk-ing sound. "Come, Father, I've merely sought to live to your esteemed reputation. Everything I learned about being a future duke, I learned from you." Placing his own desires and interests before all else, living for his own pleasures, drinking, wagering. All of it had been learned at the foot of this bastard. The most important lesson inadvertently handed down, however, was the selfishness in saddling oneself with a wife and children—either legitimate or illegitimate. And in that, Cedric would have the ultimate triumph over the driven duke.

"And you'll not have to abandon those pleasures." His father tightened his mouth and moved on to his pragmatic explanation. "I understand your aversion to saddling yourself with one woman, but you can take a proper bride, do right by the line, and still warm every whore's bed you so wish."

Cedric tightened his fingers on his snifter. "How very practical," he drawled, earning another frown. Yes, that was what the miserable bugger had done with Cedric's own mother. He'd wed a flawless English lady, given her two legitimate babes, the requisite heir, and then she'd even done him the service of dying in short order. Why, it was everything a heartless, miserable letch like his father could have hoped for in a ducal union. Unfortunately for the old Duke of Ravenscourt, there was one slight, but very important, difference between them. Cedric didn't give a bloody jot about the ancient title. It could go to the grave with his father and Cedric would quite gleefully kick dirt upon both as they were lowered into the ground.

"I expect you at my goddamn ball." The duke jabbed a finger at him. "The bloody affair is for you." It had never been about Cedric. None of it. It had only and ever been about the dukedom. "Find a sweet, biddable bride, or—"

"You'll cut me off," Cedric put in with a half-grin. "Of course. How can I forget?"

His father sputtered and flared his eyes. After all, no one taunted, baited, or denied this man—except Cedric. Then as quick as the flare of emotion had come, it was gone, and the duke smoothed his unwrinkled features into an un-moveable mask. "You've gone through a good deal of the funds left you by your mother."

He stilled. Yes, with the recklessness of youth, he'd wagered too many of those funds, lavished expensive mistresses with jewels befitting a queen.

A slow, triumphant smile devoid of all amusement turned his

father's hard lips. "I can see every creditor called in. One word, and not a single credit will be extended you. This residence," he waved his hand. "Gone. Then where will you be?"

Forced back into that long-despised townhouse where he'd endured relentless training and schooling on all things pertaining to the dukedom as a boy. To the place where he'd received such caring tutelage under his father. That house of ugliness and learned depravity. "Go to hell," he said at last.

His father stuck a finger out once more. "Be at the ball this evening. My threats aren't idle. Surely you know that, by now?"

…I told you. One mistake, and you'll not see light outside this office…

The old memory slapped at the corners of his mind and he fisted his hands. He'd not let the duke know the influence he'd once yielded and that the memories sometimes crept in. No, Cedric had buried those oldest hurts and pains long ago and shaped himself into a man incapable of feeling anything.

The duke peered at him a long while and then gave a slow, pleased nod. "I see you understand." Without giving Cedric another moment to reply, he spun on his heel and stalked over to the door. He yanked it open. "Be there."

"A pleasure, as always," Cedric called after him.

His only living parent slammed the door behind him.

Cedric stood, unmoving, and stared at the mahogany panel the duke had left through. With tension thrumming inside him, he looked to the broken bottles littering the floor from his father's outburst. He scrubbed a hand over his beard-stubbled face. Glass in hand, he went over to the window. Drawing back the crimson brocade curtain, he peered down into the street.

His father exited the townhouse and paused outside to adjust his elegant Long Eaton top hat. The late morning sun glinted off the blond and silver strands of his hair. With his expensive cloak whipping about his tall, commanding frame, he evinced power and control. Odd, how one could look at a person and see regality and, yet, that was just a fine veneer of a black, ugly soul and depravity that ran in his veins. A depravity he'd passed easily to the son he'd taken under his wing as a boy of five and schooled on everything from future ducal responsibilities to the immoral pleasures granted men of their stations.

As the duke climbed into his carriage, Cedric released the fabric and let it flutter into place. He carried his drink over to a leather winged back chair and sank onto the edge. He stared over the rim to the mess left in his father's violent fit.

For years, he'd thrilled at taunting his father. He'd lived for his own pleasures, and with the debauched clubs he attended, and parties he hosted, had earned a reputation of rake. When other respectable noblemen would disapprove of those ignoble escapades, Cedric's had been accepted, even applauded, by his father. His lips pulled in an involuntary sneer. Then, would one expect anything else from the man who'd sent a whore to the schoolrooms to administer Cedric's *lessons* when he'd been a boy of thirteen?

Regardless of fatherly approval or disapproval, he'd lived for himself. All the while he found a secret relish in knowing that the one task his bastard father expected of him was one he'd never grant. For the control he'd exerted over Cedric through the years, this had been the secret, but ultimate, show of power and triumph. Yet, ironically, as a young man out of university and now nearly in his thirtieth year, in his base living, he'd run through funds that had once seemed limitless. A gift given him by the mother who'd correctly seen little worth in her only son.

Now, his father dangled a not unfamiliar threat over Cedric's proverbial head. He swirled the contents of his glass and stared into the burgundy depths. The rub of it was…he'd no doubt his father would ultimately make good on his promise and cut him off if he were to fail the Falcot line.

His lips hardened into a tight line. Yet, Cedric would sooner lob off his right arm and left hand than enter into a union for the purpose of propagating the world with legitimate issue bearing his tainted blood. For all the ways in which he had been a selfish bastard through the years, he was not the complete one Society believed him to be. He'd not destroy a wife and ruin a child the way he had been at his parents' hands. For ultimately, blood let, and blood will tell, and every other cliché statement made about the power of blood.

Cedric, however, did not require those cleverly written words to indicate what he'd learned long, long ago. He was his father's son. And as such, he would never fill the world with miserable bastards like himself.

A knock sounded and he looked up blankly. Thrusting aside the memories of long ago, he called out, "Enter."

Avis opened the door and the introduction died on his lips as he took in the crystal mess littering the floor. "The Earl of Montfort to see you, my lord."

Daniel Winterbourne, the Earl of Montfort, his only friend, another miserable blighter who possessed a dark soul, scowled. From the hard glint in his brown eyes to the notoriously shocking reputation, the earl matched Cedric in his world of wariness and cynicism. "Montfort," he greeted as the other man entered the room.

Montfort stalked over to the sideboard and then paused. He eyed Cedric's jacket and gaping shirt, and then the mess left in the duke's wake. "I see you've had company." A sardonic smile formed on the man's lips. "Next time you're with an inventive whore, tell the lady to spare the brandy. Not even a whore should come between a man and his good spirits." With a chuckle, the earl swiped a bottle of whiskey. He poured two glasses and then with one outstretched, made his way over to the seat opposite Cedric.

Cedric waved off the offering and set down his still full drink. The lure of spirits had, of late, lost their potent dulling of thought and emotion.

His friend waggled his eyebrows. "More for me then," he lifted both in salute and with a grip on both glasses, proceeded to drink.

"Well?" Cedric drawled, sitting back in his seat.

Montfort froze, the glass midway to his mouth. "Well?"

Cedric lifted an eyebrow. "So what is the reason for your visit?" After all, life and time had long proven that no one did anything without specific reason or personal benefit; and that included those one considered friends.

The earl flashed him a hurt stare. "I am offended, chap. Can't a friend simply pay a visit to..." At the pointed look shot his way, a chuckle rumbled past the other man's lips. "There is wagering going on at Forbidden Pleasures."

The more scandalous of the gaming hells, it was a place frequented by lechers, scoundrels, and rakes. All were men bent on their personal gratifications in a place devoid of even the façade of politeness or decency. As such, it had proven the perfect place for a man of Cedric's ilk.

When he remained silent, a sound of annoyance escaped Montfort and he put one snifter down. "Bloody hell, man, would you have me say it? The wagering is about you and your intentions for this evening."

"Oh?" Cedric hooked his ankle across the opposite knee. Having known the other man since they'd been boys at Eton, he well knew Montfort was not beyond coming here to influence the wagering he no doubt had steep funds in. The earl was also desperate. He'd inherited a mountainous debt from the previous earl. His circumstances had not been improved by Montfort's own excessive wagering and, even more, excessive losing.

"Your clubs or the duke's ball." The earl took a long swallow of his drink. "I, of course, wagered on the former."

They'd be wrong on both scores. Cedric didn't have a bloody intention of attending either this evening. "I haven't decided," he said noncommittally.

The other man choked on his drink. "Yes, no doubt," he said with droll humor after he'd finished his sip. "I am certain the first place you'll care to be is at that miserable bastard's polite affair." He spoke as one who knew Cedric; who knew the lifelong loathing he'd carried for his sire. He knew the only places Cedric had ever truly been comfortable were those dens of sin, where he felt less alone in the evil in his blood.

Finishing off his first whiskey, Montfort promptly consumed the other in a long, slow swallow. He grimaced and then set his empty glass aside. "Shall we?" he asked, climbing to his feet.

Neither was the earl above trying to influence the wager, it would seem. Then, Cedric had long ago ceased being shocked by a person's depravity and weakness. "Perhaps, I will join you later," he said.

Despite the low he'd sunk to in life, he'd not enter the living looking like he'd been roused from the streets of London.

A grin formed on the other man's lips, which Cedric wagered had not a jot to do with his actual promise of company. "Splendid," Montfort said and thumped him on the back as he passed.

After he'd gone and Cedric was, at last, alone, he gathered his black jacket and shrugged into it. When had joining his clubs bore the same appeal as spending an evening amidst polite Society? Forbidden Pleasures and the other hells he'd frequented over the years had been the few places he'd felt he belonged, with other like people—equally emotionless and jaded. He'd studiously avoided those polite balls and soirees. Somewhere along the way, there'd become a tedium to both.

Attending tonight would serve to, no doubt, silence his father's pressuring—even if temporarily. However, he'd never lived to placate the Duke of Ravenscourt. Nor would he ever live for that man. His father could go to the devil and someday when Cedric drew his last breath, he'd, no doubt, join his miserable sire in those fiery depths.

With a hard grin, he started from the room.

CHAPTER 3

ꙌHE HATED GRAY.

It was a horrid color that conjured overcast skies and dreary rain. It was miserable and depressing. And it was the color her parents would insist she don. She stared at her reflection in the bevel mirror. Her pale skin, devoid of even the hint of rouges her mother had once insisted on. The painfully tight chignon at the base of her skull accentuated her cheeks in an unflatteringly gaunt way. The high-necked, modest, gray gown concealed all hint of feminine curve.

Odd, she'd spent so many years missing this place and now what she wouldn't give to return to her grandfather's property in Kent.

From within the glass panel, her maid's sad visage reflected back. "You look lovely, miss."

"You are a dreadful liar, Delores." She gentled that with a wan smile. "But thank you."

Perhaps had they been any other maid and lady, there would have been further protestations. The close relationship formed by them through the years, however, kept Delores silent and Genevieve appreciated that. She did. For she didn't need lies and platitudes to tell her anything different than what she felt in her heart and saw in this very mirror. She was bloody miserable.

It had been a fortnight since she'd returned and, in that time, she'd gone through the motions of proper daughter. She'd gone to dreadful fitting after fitting for equally dreadful gowns. She'd been schooled on the lords she might speak to during dinner parties.

The Earl of Primly. Polite, proper, and safe.

The Marquess of Guilford. Respectable, loyal brother and son, and also safe.

The Earl of Montfort. Rake, nearly impoverished, and dangerous.

And she'd been instructed to not dance.

Her toes curled reflexively within the soles of her too-tight slippers. Of everything she'd missed of London, the strains of the orchestra and exuberantly moving through the intricate steps of the waltz and quadrille had been some of them. But then, that thrill had come from a long ago time when she'd carried a foolish girl's dream of a love that conquered all.

The door opened and she looked to the front of the room.

Her sister, Gillian, hovered in the entrance. With her pale lavender satin and artfully arranged whitish blonde curls, she could rival the angels in one of da Vinci's murals. Then Gillian gave her a hesitant smile that transformed her from magnificent to otherworldly in her beauty. "May I come in?" she asked tentatively. But that was just Gillian's beauty; it transcended mere physical looks and delved deep to a purity and goodness that Genevieve had forgotten existed.

"Of course." Genevieve motioned her forward and, with a curtsy, Delores ducked out of the room, closing the door behind her.

Her sister glided over and her satin skirts swirled about her satin slipper-clad feet. She stopped before Genevieve and shifted on her feet.

Strangers. That was what time had turned them into. Two girls who'd once giggled under the covers after Genevieve had returned from balls and put on pretend performances where they'd taken on the role of their proper marquess and marchioness.

Gillian cleared her throat. "You look…" Her expression grew strained. The youngest Farendale sibling had always been incapable of artifice.

"Horrid?" Genevieve supplied, in a bid to break the stilted awkwardness that had existed since she'd returned.

"Never." Her sister gave her head an emphatic shake. "It does not matter what color skirts you wear or your hairstyle, it is who *you* are," she said with the most meaningful of words to pass between them in two weeks. Gillian captured her hands and gave them a slight squeeze. "And I've missed you so, so much."

Her throat worked. This had been the one person who had missed her. Just as Genevieve, tending the gardens in Kent with the sun as her daytime companion and her gruff grandfather in the evening, had missed the friendship of her sister. A sister who now, for Genevieve's shameless flirting and subsequent scandal, found herself uncourted and unwanted. "I am sorry," she managed on a soft whisper.

Her sister made a sound of protest. "Oh, do not do that." She squeezed Genevieve's hands again. "Do not. I would never, ever want a gentleman who'd so judge you and, through you, me." Gillian gave her a wider smile. "I will find a gentleman who loves me regardless of anything and everything. And you will, too."

Find love? The best she could hope for in this old world she'd been dragged back into was a quiet existence devoid of whispers and gossip. There would be no champions or heroes because… they didn't exist. She shook her head sadly. "Oh, Gillian." Had she ever been so hopelessly optimistic in love and the belief in a good, honorable gentleman?

Her sister's smile dipped. "You don't believe," she observed.

Not anymore and not because she'd been in love with the Duke of Aumere. She hadn't. She'd been charmed, and in love with their forbidden flirtation and, even just a little bit, the promise of pleasing her parents and securing that *coveted* title. She was saved from replying and offering any darkly realistic truths to her still-innocent sister by a soft rapping at the door.

They looked as one.

"The Marquess and Marchioness have asked you join them in the foyer."

It was time. The inevitable reentry. Withdrawing her hand from Gillian's, Genevieve smoothed her damp palms over her muslin skirts.

As they walked, her loquacious sister filled the tense silence. "The Duke of Ravenscourt will be our host. Mama believes that means he is trying to arrange a match for his son, the Marquess of St. Albans."

Ahh, the wicked, dangerous one to avoid. Neither was the irony lost on her; another future duke, those gentlemen who believed the world was their due and were forgiven for jilting their betrotheds at the altar.

Her sister dropped her voice to a conspiratorial whisper, stealing a peek about as they walked. "I heard Mother and Lady Erroll say he is something of a rake."

Of course he was.

"But even rakes can be reformed," Gillian said with a girlish innocence that caused Genevieve to miss a step. She stumbled, and quickly righted herself.

With her beauty, and because of Genevieve's scandalous roots, a naïve miss like Gillian would be easy prey for those treacherous gentlemen. "No," she said, the denial ripped harshly from her lungs. "I don't believe they can."

A flash of pity danced in her sister's green eyes.

Tension knotted Genevieve's belly. God, how she despised those sympathetic stares. They were even worse than the sneering, disgusted ones.

Her sister proved the tenacious spirit she'd always possessed as a small child. "My friend, Phoebe is recently married to Lord Rutland. He was rumored to be the darkest of all the scoundrels and, yet, they are hopelessly in love."

They arrived at the foyer and Genevieve promptly closed her mouth. The last debates she cared to have in the presence of their parents were matters pertaining to the heart and rakes.

The marquess consulted his timepiece.

In an unspoken cue that came from years of devoted service, footmen rushed forward with the ladies' cloaks. Meanwhile, Dunwithy pulled the door open. Genevieve followed silently behind her parents with her usually talkative sister, quieted.

How had her spirits not been completely crushed living in this place? As miserable as Genevieve's banishment had been for what it represented, she'd spent her days in the gardens with the sun on her face; a *crime* her mother had lambasted her for since her return with tanned cheeks. The family filed into the carriage.

Moments later, a servant closed the door, shutting the Farendale family away in the large, opulent carriage.

Clasping her hands on her lap, Genevieve stared out the window at the passing darkened London streets. "I do not expect one misstep from you this night," her father's rumbling voice filled the confines of the black barouche.

She stiffened.

"You're to—"

"Sit with the matrons and wallflowers," she delivered emotionlessly. "I know." And there was no dancing or smiling or conversing with gentleman.

He grunted.

Her sister shot her another look—the pitying kind.

And while her father launched into another lecture before the evening's festivities, she stared out the window and dreamed of being any place but where she was.

GENEVIEVE'S FEET ACHED.

She had stood alongside the proper matrons and mamas for the past three hours, nodding at the proper moments and primly holding her hands clasped at her waist. That had wrought havoc on her miserable feet.

To be specific, her biggest toe and the one next to it throbbed with a pounding intensity to match the steady pressure building at the back of her head. A pounding that was a product of the noisy whispers and laughter filling the Duke of Ravenscourt's ballroom. Though at this moment, she was particularly grateful for the distraction as it afforded the opportunity to rub those miserable digits. She discreetly drew her foot up and—

"Genevieve, do put your foot down," her mother, the Marchioness of Ellsworth, said from the corner of her mouth, not taking her eyes off the crowded ballroom.

With a sigh, Genevieve lowered her heel to the floor and winced. Blasted slippers.

Did her mother truly think anyone was giving Genevieve any attention—a young lady long in the tooth in dull gray skirts, deemed unmarriageable because of a scandal from long ago? If she did, well, then she'd a good deal less sense than Genevieve had credited over the years. She trailed her bored gaze over the ballroom and she'd not given her much.

The perverse fascination upon the first event Genevieve attended had dimmed when it became rather clear that the whore from long ago wouldn't don crimson skirts. Nor would she flutter her lashes at wed and unwed gentleman—something she'd never been guilty of, but the myth had been created all those years ago.

Absently, she did a search for *him*. Surely, it was inevitable their paths would cross and when they did, how could she bury the long-burning hatred she carried for the lying cad? She'd been so very enamored of the Duke of Aumere and his effusive charm, she'd failed to note the lies in his eyes and heart. Her gaze collided with a garish fop in yellow satin pants.

The gentleman studied her under hot lids and, cheeks burning, she quickly looked away. Perhaps they'd not forgotten, after all. Her father was a bloody, witless fool. The only stares that would ever be fixed on her were by gentlemen with dishonorable intentions. Something deep inside, something that felt very much like…*regret*, pulled at her. Regret for the dream that had never been, nor would ever be.

Restless, she leaned up on tiptoes and ignoring the pain presented by her too-tight slippers, she searched for her sister. Gillian remained ensconced in conversation with her friend, a Miss Honoria Fairfax. From the sidelines, Genevieve felt very much the younger sister; uncertain, while the cheerful Gillian spoke easily to her friend. Another pang of sadness struck as she looked about her own bright-eyed excitement of years ago. There had once been a magical thrill at these lavish, glittering affairs. How odd to return to these ballrooms years later, at such a very different place in life, while her sister evinced that long-ago excitement.

Her mother shoved her elbow into Genevieve's side and brought her back down hard on her heels. "Do stop frowning," her mother hissed. "Pretty faces…"

Catch pretty titles.

Yes, that had long been mother's silly words for her daughters. And yet, there'd been no more beautiful face than that of Gillian, and what had that gotten her? Not even a single offer or suitor because of a sin committed in her elder sister's past.

Did her mother truly believe she would find a husband? Nor would Genevieve bother to correct her mother of the erroneous assumption that she would one, do something as foolish as to wed a rake who studiously avoided polite affairs, or two, that she'd wed a gentleman who saw nothing more than a pretty face in her. The only gentleman worth wedding was the good and honorable and hopelessly in love one. In short, a man who did not exist.

A tall figure appeared at the front of the room, momentarily distracting the guests, but alas, the sought-after host remained elusive. Genevieve yawned into her glove, earning another sharp glower from her mother. "The marquess might see," she whispered.

"The marquess would have to attend," she returned.

Another tall figure appeared at the threshold of the ballroom and the guests, her mother included, leaned forward. Alas, given the collective groan, the dark-haired gentleman at the front of the room was, in fact, not the future duke.

She cringed at the crowd's tangible desire for that missing gentleman. What bad form. "Why throw a blasted ball?" she muttered. Why, if one had no plans on attending, and worse, forcing others to endure the tediousness of the affair?

"What was that, Genevieve?" her mother asked, returning her attention to her daughter, which was the last thing she cared for—attention from her mother, a mother who'd not given up hope of her only daughter of marriageable age making a match.

"I said, what a splendid ball," she replied, with a smile.

The narrowing of her mother's eyes indicated she knew the lie there and Genevieve gave thanks as her mother's friend, the Countess of Erroll, approached.

The two women greeted each other eagerly as young ladies might. Their friendship went back to their days at Mrs. Belden's Finishing School and, as such, when together, they tended to forget everyone else around. Genevieve cast a special thanks skyward for that blessed diversion.

"…Why else would he host a formal ball, and make an appearance except to find a wife…" the other woman said excitedly.

Genevieve rolled her eyes. She had to tamp down the pointed reminder that the rake's father was responsible for hosting said event, and that the Marquess of St. Albans still couldn't be bothered to attend. Those were hardly indications of a marriage-minded lord. Nor would any sensible person ever mistake that elusive lord as marriage minded. The man had earned a reputation as one of Society's most scandalous rakes and took care to avoid polite affairs.

"Well, I heard from Lady Delenworth who heard from Lady Fitzhugh, that he's going to at last see to his responsibilities and wed." Mother concluded that admission with a decisive nod, as though it declared her words fact.

Every scandalous widow and marriage-minded miss, however, seemed to be of like opinion to Mother. They all eyed the door with a breathless anticipation for the rakish Marquess of St. Albans to make his appearance—to his own ball.

Except, Genevieve. She wanted nothing to do with those rakish sorts. Especially one who couldn't bother with punctuality. She didn't care if the person was a prince or a pauper. In being late, it signified another's belief in their own self-importance and devalued those individuals kept waiting.

She sighed. Yes, she'd be quite contented with a perfectly charming, romantic fellow who read her sonnets and snipped tresses of her hair to hold close. Forcibly thrusting back the painful musings, she looked about the room for a glimpse of a friendly, familiar face. Alas, she knew but one. Gillian, now otherwise occupied with her friend, chatted at the opposite end of the room. Envy pulled at her and she hated the niggling green monster that needled at her for Gillian having friends when Genevieve remained—alone.

"Mother," she said, taking advantage of the other woman's diversion. Genevieve shifted and then swallowed down a curse at the throbbing of her toes. "I am going to see Gillian," she lied, crossing her fingers behind her back. "She is speaking with Miss Fairfax."

"Very well," her mother said, momentarily turning her attention from the next guest to arrive, who was decidedly not a future duke. Fortunately, Lady Erroll otherwise occupied the marchioness.

Genevieve slipped off and promptly winced. Well, *slipped* off, as much as one was able with too-tight slippers and throbbing toes. She limped along the ballroom floor. Couples twirled in a kaleidoscope of colorful satin fabrics that created a whir of movement and distraction, which she welcomed.

Smiling past her pain, Genevieve sneaked from the ballroom and closed her eyes a moment. She relished the dull hum of quiet that melded with the distant strands of the orchestra's waltz. Then, as quickly as her miserable slippers would allow, she rushed down the hall and paused beside a paneled door. She cast a quick glance about. Alas, everyone was no doubt too enrapt with the possibility of first glimpsing the future duke to escape.

She pressed the door handle and stepped inside the darkened

room. Closing the door behind her, she quickly turned the lock and paused, giving her eyes a moment to adjust to the darkened space. Then, the tension left her shoulders.

Alone.

She was blessedly alone. Not that she was one of those solitary creatures who hated company. She didn't. She did, however, have miserably sore toes. Lifting her right leg at an awkward angle, she yanked off the offending article. Of their own volition, her eyes slid closed and she wiggled her toes, driving blood back to the digits. Genevieve settled her foot on the floor and bent down, reaching for her other slipper.

A little sigh escaped her lips. *Bliss. Utter bliss.* At her too-tight slippers being off. And being free of her mother's determined matchmaking. How she envied gentlemen. They were all spared from watchful eyes and free to pursue their own amusements without recrimination or scrutiny.

Shoes in hand, Genevieve looked about the expansive library. With the floor-length shelves lined with leather volumes and the sweeping ceilings, the room contained more tomes than the whole of the collection at The Temple of the Muses. "So this is what a duke's library looks like," she murmured to herself, wandering over to the wall. Odd, she'd very nearly been married to a duke and had entered nothing more than his ballroom and dining room for their betrothal ball. With her spare hand, she trailed her fingertips along the gold-emblazoned spines and did a slow walk down the length of the room.

Absently, Genevieve rested her slippers on a nearby mahogany side table and propping her hands on her hips. She did a small circle fully evaluating the duke's library. She creased her brow. Yes, there were entirely too many tomes. How could one truly know which books one had? One should have far more discriminating taste in literature: the romantic poets, gothic novels. Not… She paused and skimmed her fingertips along one title. "*Elements Of Agricultural Chemistry In A Course Of Lectures*" she mouthed, as she tugged it free. Genevieve fanned the pages and then froze.

Her gaze collided with a tall figure, comfortably seated on the duke's leather winged back chair. With a bottle of brandy at his feet and a crystal snifter in his hand, he sat with the ease of one who may as well have owned the space. Her stomach flipped over.

Mayhap it was her eyes playing tricks of the light. After all, it was dark. Genevieve blinked several times in rapid succession and closed her eyes. Yes, it was rather dark, with the moon casting ominous shadows about the room. Mayhap she'd merely imagined him. Except, a shadow that drank brandy and held snifters? She popped one eye open and found the silent gentleman's cerulean blue eyes fixed on her.

"Hullo."

She sighed. For shadows assuredly did not speak in that low, husky baritone. Nor did they possess broad shoulders and powerfully muscled arms that for propriety's sake really required the benefit of the black jacket now haphazardly swung over the back of his chair. Of all the blasted rooms she could have selected, she'd chosen one occupied by this man. The cold floor penetrating the silk fabric of her stockings, Genevieve shifted on her feet and then froze. She jerked her gaze downward to her very bare feet, where the stranger's attention also rested. Well, not *entirely* bare as she did have stockings.

Exile for life. If her parents discovered this scandalous exchange, she'd be banished forever. At the stranger's continued scrutiny of her nearly naked toes, Genevieve gasped and slipped behind a side table, borrowing some shelter from the Chippendale piece. *Ruined. I will be utterly ruined and sent off again.*

The ghost of a smile played on the stranger's firm lips. He then lifted blue eyes that glinted with curiosity.

Her breath caught. *The sky.* His eyes harkened to the soft blue of the pure Kent countryside skies, when the sun beat on her neck, and the breeze—

At her silence, he winged a golden eyebrow upward.

"Uh, I suppose I might say hullo," she said quickly. It wouldn't do to be rude to the gentleman. After all, she'd invaded *his* sanctuary. Nor would it do to be discovered with him, given her circumstances. "Not that I should say more," she said when he opened his mouth to speak. "It wouldn't do to be discovered alone in the duke's library." Had she imagined his earlier greeting? Now, he gave not even a hint of movement. A sigh escaped her. "Though you were fortunate to find the library first," she said when he continued to stare at her in that piercing manner. She looked about the room. Her gaze caught the massive painting in an ornate gold frame.

The lush woman in dishabille reclining on her stomach would have scandalized most proper ladies. Drawn over to the Francois Boucher erotic work, she admired the manner in which the curves and creases of the bedding molded to the voluptuous woman's rounded form. "It is beautiful," she murmured to herself.

"Lovely room, isn't it?"

Engrossed in the duke's scandalous piece, Genevieve whipped her attention back to the stranger. *I should leave. I should grab my slippers and run tearing from this room.* But what was there to return to? A sea of unfriendly faces, and forever-disappointed parents. "I do favor libraries," she confessed, wandering away from the painting. Particularly those stocked with volumes about art and artistry. That intimate detail she'd keep close. For it belied the logic and reason she'd prided herself on building these past years.

"This is rumored to be the largest in all of London."

"Oh, I have no doubt," she murmured and drifted over to the bookshelf. The Duke of Ravenscourt was in possession of one of the oldest titles in the realm. She ran her palm along the spines. "This, however, is too much; don't you agree?" Genevieve looked over her shoulder.

He did a quick survey of the space, as though seeing it for the first time.

"I would prefer something smaller, more intimate," she supplied when he remained silent. Which only conjured the bucolic dream she'd long carried of curling up at the side of her husband while they read and laughed and did whatever it was hopelessly in love couples did. Given her parents' own aloof union, she was remarkably short of what those things might be.

Instead, her family would see her wed off to anyone willing to overlook her shameful past. She curled her hands tight. God, how she wished to remain shut away here. She cast a regretful look back at the door, dreading reentering polite Society and her mother's angry stares, and the rakish gentlemen with their lust-filled, improper eyes. *I should go…*

"Yet you stay."

She'd spoken aloud? Genevieve whipped her head forward. "Yet I stay," she said softly. For in this moment, there was a safeness that seemed so elusive among the lords who ogled and whispered about her. There were all manner of things indecorous in being here; things which would only fuel the whispers about her virtue, or rather, lack of. Being in this moment, however, with the world carrying on behind that door, where no one knew where she was or whom she was with, was heady stuff, indeed.

The gentleman took a long swallow of his drink and the muscles of his throat moved.

Alas, there was nothing truly safe in being here, alone with this man. Most assuredly not her reputation. Genevieve fiddled with her gray skirts. "I've intruded enough on your company." How very fortunate gentlemen were, not bound to the same constraints and conventions. "Have a good evening, sir." She turned to go.

"You will probably require your slippers before you return," he called out, staying her retreat.

Genevieve wheeled back. "Er, yes." So why did she not rush over and collect the satin pair? Why did she, instead, stand rooted to the hardwood floor, staring—at him?

He swirled the contents of his drink and then took a sip. "Are they uncomfortable?"

"Dreadfully so," she said automatically. She cast a hateful look over at the shoes. With another sigh, she hurried over to the side table and collected them. Except, she chewed her lower lip. The gentleman still studied her intently; unrepentantly bold in his regard. There was still the matter of putting her slippers on, an act she'd completed thousands upon thousands of time in the course of her life. How had she failed to realize how terribly intimate it was until now? "You should look away," she said with a quiet insistence, as she slid into a nearby shell-back chair.

"Yes, I should," he agreed, but he only took another drink from his pilfered spirits and continued to watch.

Her fingers trembled and she turned her attention to the gray satin slippers. She must lift her gown ever so slightly if she were to put them on. Or she could simply leave. Yes, that was, by far, the wisest course. On the heel of that was an image of her exiting the room barefoot and being discovered. A shudder wracked her frame. No, that wouldn't do. That was the manner of scandal that would result in a return carriage ride to the countryside. She chewed her lip. Which in thinking, wouldn't be altogether bad. Quite the opp—

The floorboards groaned and she lifted her head. A gasp exploded from her lips as the stranger sank to a knee. How could a gentleman of his magnificent size and power move with such a stealthy grace? "Wh-what...?"

"Here," he murmured, easily seizing one slipper from her trembling hand. She stared at his bent head. Her fingers twitched with the urge to run her fingers through the unfashionably long blond hair with its faint curl. She wanted to determine if the strands were as lusciously thick as they looked. In a fluid movement, he lifted her skirts, ever so slightly, and captured her heel in his palm. The touch of his hand burned through the fabric of her stockings and roused a wild fluttering in her belly. Her mouth went dry and she struggled with a coherent thought as he slid the shoe on. "There," he said quietly and then slipped the other shoe from her weak fingers.

It was the singularly most erotic, most romantic, moment in her life. Far greater than anything she'd ever experienced with her former betrothed. And it was here in the duke's library, in the midst of the ball, with a man whose name she did not even know. Perhaps that merely added to the forbidden allure of this exchange.

The gentleman sank back on his heels, his meaning clear. She was free to leave. He'd not stop her. And yet, she lingered, not wanting this moment to end. For when it did, she'd be unsought-after-for-anything-but-scandal Genevieve with her throbbing toes and her miserable mother. Then, she couldn't really leave, not without first knowing the name of the gentleman who'd helped her into her slippers. "I am Genevieve," she said, opting to omit the most distinguishing part of her name which would reveal her past.

"Cedric."

There was no effusive, overdone greeting. No title. Nothing but his Christian name that only deepened the intimacy between them. "Cedric," she repeated, testing it. It was strong, harshly beautiful, powerful. A perfect name for the tall, thickly muscled stranger.

"You are reluctant to return." His husky inquiry washed over her. "Why?"

I am reluctant to leave. Two very different matters, altogether. When she left, she'd be thrust back into the ballroom, with the side looks, whispers, and aching toes. In this moment, there was just her and this man who knew nothing of her, and did not treat her with disdain. "I am no doubt here for the same reason you are," she ventured, instead.

"Oh?"

And as she did not know what to make of that vague, noncommittal utterance she stole a look about. "All rather tedious, isn't it?"

He furrowed his brow.

"The ball," she said with a wave of her hand.

"Ah." The gentleman said so little and yet so much with that telling concurrence. "Yes, there is something tedious about the whole affair," he said, his tone gruff.

She nodded. "Precisely. A sea of guests collected on the possibility that a future duke is ready to take a wife." The last thing she desired was another would-be duke in her life.

Another smile pulled at his lips, highlighting the faint dimple in his right cheek. She tipped her head. Odd, that such a harshly angular face should be gentled in that way. Fearing she'd drown herself in the study of him, Genevieve forced her gaze away. Faces of chiseled perfection posed nothing but danger. Time and her own folly had proven that.

Even so, as Cedric shoved to his feet, she mourned that parting. He wandered back to his stolen snifter, rescued his glass, and then with a panther-like grace, stalked over to her. "Never tell me you are one of the ladies in attendance not desiring that coveted title." He took another sip of his drink.

Climbing to her feet, Genevieve studied her fingers. She'd never wanted the title duchess. She'd simply craved the romanticism that came with being in love. "I have no interest at all in the title of marchioness, duchess, or anything else," she said with quiet honesty. Never again.

With those long, sleek steps, he continued coming and she really should be afraid. She was alone with a gentleman, in her host's library, behind a locked door. It was the height of folly and possible danger, and yet there was this inexplicable ease around him. An inherent knowledge that no harm would come to her at his hands. Not a man who could have so gently slid her slippers on her feet. A delicious shiver ran through her and her mouth went dry at the memory. *I am the wicked, wanton they all accused me of being.*

"Not even the Marquess of St. Albans?"

Was there a wry humor to that query? She could not make

source of his peculiar tone past the rapid whirring of her thoughts. She struggled to force out a coherent reply. She recalled her sister's earlier words about the man. "Particularly the marquess." She'd little desire for the notoriety that came with such a gentleman. Rakes, rogues, and scoundrels, they were to be avoided, all of them.

"Here I was believing every lady coveted the role of future duchess," he said dryly. A cynical glint lit his eye and she frowned, preferring him as he'd been a moment prior—affable and slightly mysterious.

"I do not," she persisted, taking a step toward him. She never had. Genevieve looked beyond his shoulder. Her parents had craved nothing less than a duke for their daughter who'd been the toast of the London Season. She'd been so caught up with the glittering opulence and excitement of London, she'd been too naïve to realize…she would have been quite contented with a second son of a lord, in a modest cottage, as long as she knew love. "One would be under constant study and scrutiny," she said at last. Having been so examined after The Scandal, she'd do quite well without the grandiose attention that would come with a title that was very nearly royalty. "That, I could do without," she said softly. Pinpricks of awareness dotted her skin and she looked at Cedric. Her breath caught hard at the hot intensity of his stare.

What was he thinking, this stranger she'd only just met?

CHAPTER 4

C EDRIC, *the* M ARQUESS OF S T. Albans, hadn't had a single intention of attending the lavish ball thrown by his father. Through the years, his sire had commanded and Cedric had quite delighted in turning a proverbial finger up at those orders.

He would have been very contented sipping his brandy while the event carried on in the ballroom. He would revel in the duke's fury and then seek out his clubs when the last of the guests had departed.

Now, staring at the spirited woman casting aspersions upon his future title, there was no place he'd rather be than this very library. His lips twitched. His too-large library.

Over the years, he'd grown accustomed to the false friendships and respect granted him for nothing more than his birthright. He'd come to believe that future title was the single most import-ant thing to every last lord and lady in London. It would appear he'd found the single lady in the whole of the kingdom who didn't give a jot. Curiously, he wanted to know just what else Miss Genevieve With-No-Surname thought of his worthless self.

Cedric studied her from over the rim of his glass. With her hair pulled back with such severity and her dreary, modest skirts, she had the look of a companion and would never be the manner of woman to command his notice. The ladies who'd earned his favor through the years had been the improper ones with plunging décolletages and dampened satin skirts. What was it about this one, then, that earned his note? "You are candid," he said with a small grin. Nothing else explained it.

She lifted her shoulders in a shrug. "I've come to appreciate honesty."

How intriguing. She hinted at lessons learned and he, who didn't give a jot about anyone, wondered about the story there...

It still begged the question as to whether the lady would be so forthright if she discovered the man whose future title she disparaged stood even now before her. He gave a casual swirl of his glass. "I take it you know the marquess, then?" It really was in bad form to wheedle information from the lady in such a manner. Especially as he already knew the answer. A lady with strawberry blonde tresses and full lips made for more than kissing, he'd well remember her. But then, Cedric had never been accused of anything gentlemanly or honorable. Including attending any polite events where this one might have been.

Pity.

"I know enough," she murmured, more to herself as she skimmed her palm over a nearby rose-inlaid table.

"Oh?" he drawled.

The lady froze mid-movement, glanced about, and then dropped her voice to a conspiratorial whisper. "He's something of a rake, you know."

He'd spent years reveling in that very role. If this lady knew the extent of the wickedness he'd been rightfully accused of through the years, she'd have torn out of the room, sore feet be damned. "Actually I do know," he said dryly.

"Not that I know personally," she spoke quickly, a red blush staining her enchanting, heart-shaped face.

"Ah," he said stretching out that single syllable. "The gossip columns." His name had been quite bandied about those rubbish pages. Where most information contained on those sheets was, no doubt, at worst, lies, and, at best, exaggerations, every scandalous tidbit printed about him had been shockingly accurate.

Genevieve With-No-Surname picked up a nearby porcelain shepherdess. She turned the piece over in her hands, eying it contemplatively. "I have it on the words of someone I trust greatly." She set the piece down and quickly lifted her head. "Not that I would form judgments on a person based on another's opinions."

She should. To not do so would be folly that saw her prey to an even more caddish lord than himself. If such a man existed. Although he'd made it a habit of avoiding those pinch-mouthed, proper companions over the years, something about this rigid lady in her gray muslin skirts and her tendency to ramble held him enthralled. Cedric inclined his head. "What else do you know of our distinguished host?" He was suddenly eager to know just what this innocent slip had uncovered.

She opened her mouth and then closed it. She opened it again. "It is in bad form to speak ill of one's host."

Speak ill of? "Now you have me intrigued." He favored her with a wink and dropped his voice in a like whisper. "Then, it is his father who is the host."

A frown tipped her lips down in the corners. That subtle movement plumped the flesh of her lower lip. He narrowed his eyes. Well, for her rigid, unassuming appearance, there was nothing proper about that pouty mouth. A surge of lust ran through him as he imagined the wicked delights and pleasures to be found with—

"It is in bad form to speak ill of anyone," she said chidingly, dousing his ardor with the solemnity there.

He blinked. "Oh, I am sure the marquess is not a man who'd much care."

The lady drifted closer and stopped before him. "I'm sure, despite the rumors, even he cares, Cedric. Even those that Society believes incapable of feeling anything, care."

He studied her, momentarily sucked in a spell cast by the light quality of her whispered words. When they at last registered, he gave his head a shake. The lady in her innocent-spoken words revealed her naïveté and also revealed why he'd avoided those naïve ladies. Despite her whimsical belief, he *didn't* care. He'd spent the better part of his nearly thirty years not caring: about Society's opinion, about his father's ducal expectations and disdain, about the mother who'd forsaken him even before her death. None of it. He'd come to live for his own pleasures and take material and physical gratification as he would.

She again captured that porcelain shepherdess and ran her fingertip over the frilled porcelain skirt. "Regardless, I do not pass judgment on the marquess on mere gossip alone," she added. *Why did he suspect it was important that he knew she was not one of those ladies to judge a person by those words printed on a page?*

He perched his hip on the back of a leather button sofa. "What else have you formed your judgment on?" What, if not the gossip that she spoke of with such disdain? Did that mean the lady herself had been the victim of those scandal sheets? He scoffed. The *ton* would never cut their teeth on an innocent such as her.

"Well, as you're probably aware by your attendance this evening, the gentleman cannot be bothered to be timely to his own ball."

He finished his drink and lowered the empty glass to the floor at his feet. "That is an unforgiveable crime?" If that was the manner of offenses this one would take exception to, then what would she say of the outrageous parties he'd delighted in throwing over the years at his bachelor's townhouse? Except that only conjured an image of her in a silk, dampened gold gown, as the feast at those forbidden parties, while he very deliberately removed every inch of that stiff, ugly dress, revealing her flushed, naked skin to the candle's glow. Cedric groaned.

"Are you all right?" she asked, concern lacing that question.

"Fine," he managed, his voice garbled. "You were speaking of our distinguished host."

"Well, not our host," she reminded him of his earlier correction. "Rather, his son."

"The gentleman who can't be bothered with punctuality." Another thing he'd never given a jot about through the years. He arrived when he wished and departed on his own terms, and not really given a thought as to how others might feel about it.

Genevieve turned her palms up. "It indicates much about his character, does it not?" No, he rather thought it said nothing of importance.

He swung his leg back and forth in a lazy manner. "Explain it to me in a way I might understand, love."

Her mouth parted, even as her eyes formed round, moss green saucers that conjured country fields and summers days. He stilled. God, how he'd always loved the long, summer days in Leeds. He'd been so immersed in the debauchery in London that all those memories had faded to the distant chambers of his mind. Only to be brought forward by the green of her eyes. He choked again. What manner of madness was this, lusting after a barely pretty companion who'd snuck off to remove her slippers?

"You were saying?" he managed, his words garbled.

She shook her head. "Yes," she said matter-of-factly. "Well, if the marquess cannot bother to honor the time of others, it merely means he sees his time as more important."

There was merit to her unwitting accusations. He'd been schooled from the cradle to expect the world was his due and to move as he pleased, when he pleased.

Genevieve flared her eyes, horror filling their expressive depths. "You are not friends with the marquess, are you?"

A wry grin twisted his lips. "I am not."

She breathed an audible sigh. "Oh, thank goodness. What a disaster that would be." The lady might have muttered something under her breath about disapproving parents…

Cedric stared at her with the long-case clock ticking away the moments. There was nothing disastrous about this meeting. Rather, this frank Genevieve With-No-Surname made joining an infernal affair he'd had no intention of visiting something he was suddenly eager to attend. And yet, not the festivities of the ball but rather this prolonged exchange with her here, now, away from prying eyes.

Genevieve wetted her lips and his gaze fell to her mouth. He swallowed a groan. No woman had a right to a mouth like that. It was a walking temptation that no man could resist. The kind of seductive offering that had led Adam down the path of ruin and men to wage wars. "Now, I really must go," she said softly. "Before my absence is noted."

He did not know the guest responsible for this woman's presence this evening from Eve, but loved the bloody woman for her negligence. "Yes," he whispered.

Except neither of them moved. They both remained locked in this charged moment that not even the earth being knocked off its axis could break. Cedric lifted his free hand and cupped the back of her neck. Soft as satin.

The muscles of her throat bobbed as he lowered his head with a deliberate slowness, allowing her to pull away and retreat. "I should not." Her voice emerged on a hoarse croak that spoke to her inner battle.

For all the crimes he was guilty of as a rake, never had he bedded a virgin and never had he forced himself on an unwilling woman. He'd not begin now. The quick rise and fall of her chest and the little whispery spurts of air escaping her lips sent a thrill of masculine triumph through him. He touched his lips to hers and the intoxicating taste of strawberry and mint washed over him. "You taste of summer berries," he breathed as he dragged his mouth down the length of her neck to the place where her pulse beat madly.

"Th-the duke had trays o-of strawberries," she panted with an innocent sincerity that raised a soft smile. Her lashes fluttered as he molded his mouth to hers, exploring the contours of her lips.

"Your lips are made for kissing," he said, between kisses.

"They a-are too big." From any other woman those would have been words to elicit pretty compliments. Yet, with this young lady who spoke her mind freely, she was lacking in all artifice and there was something so potent in that honesty.

"They are perfection." He slanted his lips over hers, first gently and then more incessantly. A little moan escaped her and Cedric slipped his tongue inside to stroke hers in a possessive manner that sent her arms twining about his neck. She pressed her chest against his and he cupped the generous curve of her buttocks dragging her against his throbbing shaft.

They knocked into the table and a porcelain urn tumbled over the edge. It exploded into a spray of splintered glass.

Genevieve cried out and stumbled out of his arms. She blinked and the haze of desire clouding her green irises lifted, leaving in its place a slow-growing horror. They stood unmoving, their chests rising in a matched rapid movement. As she pressed her fingertips against her swollen lips, he braced for her virginal protestations. "W-We've destroyed the duke's piece."

Through the pain of unfulfilled desire, he managed to speak. "I'm sure he won't even notice." And he wouldn't indicate just how he knew that. The duke didn't care about anything; his own children, included.

OH, GOD. STANDING HERE WITH her lips still burning from this stranger's kiss, her body ached to know more of his touch.

Genevieve acknowledged the truth she'd not known, the accusation leveled against her by the *ton* for five years now—she was a wanton. How else to explain this powerful energy thrumming inside her and desire for more of this man's tender ministrations. Nay, of a stranger.

If an imagined act had found her banished, what fate awaited her for this hungering to turn herself over to the power of his embrace? She dug deep for the proper shame and horror. She was the wanton Society believed her to be, for nothing other than her scandal. All she knew, however, was feeling. A desire to be close to him once more, in ways she didn't fully understand. "I must go," she whispered.

"Good evening," he murmured.

Good evening. She wrinkled her brow, hating herself for being a contrary creature. She'd wanted him to protest her going. Alas, he'd offer nothing more than a parting greeting? How could he be so wholly unaffected when this had been the most magical, earth-shattering moment of her three and twenty years? Well, except for the moment he'd slipped her shoes back on her feet. That had been the second most singularly magic moment. Genevieve worried her lower lip and inadvertently drew his gaze back to that flesh. She stopped abruptly. "Cedric," she said and then reluctantly turned to go.

"Wait," he murmured and her heart leapt at his quiet command.

Genevieve looked questioningly up at him.

He stalked over and then stopped beside her. "Here," he spoke in that husky baritone that washed over her. With swift, purposeful movements, he tucked several loose strands into the artful arrangement her maid had worked. She stood breathless, as he quickly put her hair to rights and then smoothed the fabric of her slight puffed sleeves.

She should be appalled; with him, with herself. The sureness of his actions bespoke a man far too familiar with these stolen trysts behind strange doors; the dishonorable, disloyal sorts. So why did she crave more of his embrace? She paused with her fingers on the handle and cast a look over her shoulder. Cedric remained fixed to the spot where she'd received the most passionate kiss of her life. She sought to commit him to memory as he was just then. For in the stilted misery she'd dwelled these two weeks in London, this man had reminded her that she was very, very much alive. And oh, how she loved being alive. "Will I see you again?" Even as the question slipped out, she recognized the foolishness in wanting to see him again.

Another half-grin tipped the left corner of his mouth. "Oh, I suspect you shall."

With fingers that trembled, Genevieve, unlocked the door and hurried from the room. All along, she'd dreaded the Duke of Ravenscourt's ball. Only to find herself looking forward to the remainder of the night. Excitement danced inside her belly and added a jaunt to her step as she fled down the halls. The din of the ballroom increased with each footfall that brought her closer and she forced herself to stop.

Sore toes forgotten, she closed her eyes, and drew in a steadying breath. She should be shamed by the wantonness of that stolen exchange with Cedric, who, with his chiseled perfection, could rival any one of da Vinci's carved masterpieces. He was a man whose full name she still did not know, but whose kiss she'd shamelessly returned, and desperately craved even now. Genevieve touched tremulous fingers to her lips. The handful of words he'd murmured as she'd left, more promise than anything, danced around her mind. *Oh, I suspect you shall...*

And suddenly, she, who'd longed for a frisson of romance and wonder, knew it with a stranger, in the Duke of Ravenscourt's home, no less.

"What are you doing?"

The shocked question brought Genevieve's eyes flying open. Her heart dipped at the unexpected appearance of her sister. Concern radiated from her sister's emerald green eyes. She mustered a smile. Mayhap if she feigned nonchalance her sister would abandon any questions she might have. "I just required a moment." Drat for that slight tremor.

Her sister came to an abrupt stop before her. Gillian peered at her beneath appropriately suspicious eyes. "You required a *moment?*" Heavy skepticism underscored that question.

Genevieve's mind raced. "My slippers." She tugged up her skirts and revealed the miserable satin pair. Her sister looked down. "My toes ached and you do know how Mother is about properness, and I wanted to remove the slippers because they ached. Terribly," she added.

Gillian continued to scrutinize her with regard better reserved for a Bow Street Runner. "Why were you leaning against the wall in that manner?"

Oh, blast, she'd always been relentless. "My toes," she said with another forced smile. "They're still deuced awful."

Her sister said nothing for a long moment and then she nodded. "Mother is looking for you."

Genevieve silently cursed. If Mother had seen Gillian, she'd well know there had never been a meeting between friends, and the last thing Genevieve cared to answer or could answer without thinking of Cedric, was where she'd been. She looped her arm through her sister's and made their way to the ballroom. As they reached the end of the corridor, she cast one lingering glance back.

Was he waiting in the shadows even now? Would he seek her out and request a dance?

"What are you staring at?" Gillian asked, furrowing her brow.

Her cheeks warmed. "Nothing, I am merely reluctant to return to the ball." Which was not altogether untrue. She'd greatly prefer the company of Cedric, alone in the duke's too-large library.

"Well, I am of like opinion on that," Gillian muttered as they stepped out into the crowded hall. Together, they skimmed their gaze over the crowd. "There is Mother." She motioned to Mother's position alongside Lady Erroll.

She sighed. She'd rather walk through burning coals on a hot summer's day than spend any time with her always-miserable mother. By Papa's absence at the same affairs, he was of like opinion. Alas, Genevieve was left alone to endure her mother's machinations to wed her off to…well, anyone with a respective title. Given her betrayal, one would think Mother would seek out an honorable gentleman for her marriageable daughter. Alas…

Her mother looked to her and frowned.

No doubt, she wondered where her shameful daughter had been off to. With reluctant footsteps, she made her way through the throng of guests over to her mother.

"At last," her mother said to Gillian through tight lips, ignoring Genevieve altogether. "You might have missed the marquess' arrival." Mother's relentless dedication to see Gillian wed spoke volumes of her desperation. A loud buzz went up around the ballroom. "He is here," Mother said with an uncharacteristic excitement in her usually bored tones.

As one, ladies throughout the ballroom looked to the entrance of the hall.

Genevieve gave her head a wry shake. How silly they all were, seeking a title and wealth, and not having the sense to crave so much more. *And I had a very brief taste of it and now that will never be enough.* A tiny fluttering danced in her belly as, unbidden, she sought Cedric amongst the crowd.

"…Oh, my goodness. The marquess is looking directly at you, Gillian."

"No, he is not, Mother," Gillian said with a roll of her eyes.

And then their mother blinked. "Why…why…no he's not! He is looking at… *Genevieve.*" That furious whisper pulled her attention to her flighty parent.

Was it a wonder a woman with such flawed logic should imagine glances and interest from the rakish marquess? "He is not looking at me," she said under her breath, resuming her search of the crowd for another. What if she did not see him again? Then, what good could come from seeing him again?

"No. I believe he is." Her mother's angry words interrupted her musings.

An exasperated sigh slipped from her lips. Could she not even just have the pleasure of her thoughts? "Why would the marquess be staring at…?" She followed her mother's none-too-subtle point to the six-foot four-inch, very familiar gentleman at the top of the stairs, standing alongside the Duke of Ravenscourt. Over the heads of the other guests, their gazes locked, and the ghost of a smile hovered on his lips.

Her heart sank. *That* is why he would stare. And from across the ballroom, Cedric winked.

Well, drat.

CHAPTER 5

"IT IS ABOUT BLOODY TIME you arrived." The Duke of Ravenscourt glared at his son. "You missed the entire bloody receiving line."

Cedric rescued a flute of champagne from a passing servant's tray. He downed it in one long swallow to let his father know precisely what he thought of his grousing. "Splendid," he said with a cheerful smile that deepened his miserable sire's frown.

On any other day and at any other event, he would have taken a perverse pleasure in altogether missing the duke's ball. As such, these proper balls were the last place he cared to be.

Except…

He stared boldly at the pale, tolerably pretty Genevieve With-a-Surname-He-Still-Did-Not-Know, relishing the way her lips parted and the round moons formed by her eyes. He would have expected with his deliberate wink she would have looked away and yet she continued to hold his gaze with a directness he admired—and he didn't admire anyone. Largely because no one had given him reason to. How singularly odd that this slender slip of a lady should have earned his appreciation…for matters that had nothing to do with the weight of her breasts or the taste of her lips.

The lady closed her luscious mouth and he grinned. Well, perhaps it did have a bit to do with the taste of her.

"…You can have your pick of any lady here, Cedric." His father waved a ruthless hand over the ballroom, momentarily commanding his attention.

Cedric did a quick sweep of the distinguished guests arranged. Eager, marriage-minded misses in their white satin gowns and scandalous widows eyed him with equal appreciation. His gaze wandered back to the companion in hideous gray skirts, pressed against the Doric column while other more colorfully clad guests chatted about her. Did the lady seek to blend with that towering pillar? Given the pale hue of her skin, and the fabric of her skirts, it would have been an easy feat. If he hadn't already tasted her lips. Then he glanced down.

The lady tapped the tip of her slipper to the staccato beat of the orchestra's song. There was so much revealing about that slight, but telling, tap. The discreet, though eager, movement belied a woman who'd don boring gray skirts and, instead, spoke to the spirited creature who'd steal off to her host's library in the midst of the festivities.

Just then, the Earl of Hargrove stepped between Cedric and his unobstructed view of the companion in her horrid dress, who'd invaded his library.

Bloody Hargrove…

"…Are you listening to me, Cedric?" his father snapped.

Cedric motioned a servant over and deposited his empty glass on the man's silver tray. The servant rushed off. "No," he said and with his father sputtering, he stormed off, cutting a deliberate path through the ballroom.

Familiar widows eyed him with a lascivious suggestion in their eyes and he ignored the heated offers there. Never before had he passed up the forbidden delights those women promised. On too many scores to remember, he'd taken several of them simultaneously up on their offers, behind parlor doors of their hosts' homes. Now, an altogether different quarry called his notice.

A tall figure stepped into his path and with a curse, Cedric ground his feet to a sudden stop. "Goddamn it, St. Albans, what the hell are you doing here?"

"Montfort," he greeted, looking over the other man's shoulder.

From where she hovered on the fringe of the festivities Genevieve With-No-Surname shifted back and forth, eying the twirling dancers. He dipped his gaze to the floor. Between the kaleidoscopes of waltzing couples, he caught the rhythmic tap of her feet.

A proper companion who longed to dance.

Montfort withdrew a silver flask from his front pocket and to the open-eyed censure of nearby matrons, uncorked it and took a long swallow. "I'd wagered you'd fail to appear at your father's ball. Lost a goddamn fortune because of you." The tight lines at the corner of his hard lips bespoke his frustration.

Friend or no, the man's ill fortune was largely his own doing. As such, Cedric had no remorse for Montfort. Or really, anyone for that matter. He'd long ago ceased to care about anyone but himself. It was safer that way. ...*Everyone cares in some way...* The lady's words echoed around his mind.

It was a sure one; Montfort would have won at any other time.

"Well, then, which delicious widow has captured your attention?"

He blinked and shifted his attention to the earl. "What?"

"Nothing else would have you here but the promise of some inventive widow's charms." His friend laughed uproariously as though he'd uttered a hilarious jest.

The orchestra concluded the country reel and the ballroom erupted into polite applause. "I hope she was worth the amount I lost on you."

He narrowed his eyes as the lady occupying Cedric's attention caught his eye. "Who is the matron?" Cedric asked, gesturing vaguely to the woman between Montfort and his library nymph.

The gentleman, who'd long known everyone and everything about Society, followed his stare. "The matron?" he puzzled his brow. "The Marchioness of Ellsworth." Then he widened his eyes. "Ah, I see."

No, Cedric really didn't think he did, as he didn't see himself. Genevieve flared her eyes wide like a hare caught in the hunter's snare and darted her gaze about. As one who'd made plenty of hasty escapes, he recognized one about to flee. "If you'll excuse me," he murmured and quickly stepped around Montfort. He ignored Montfort's sputtering and lengthened his stride. With each step, Cedric kept his gaze trained on his tempting quarry.

And for the first time in the course of his corrupt life, a fleshy, proper matron proved his savior. The plump, expensively attired lady in burgundy skirts stepped into Genevieve's path, effectively staying her retreat.

As the older woman spoke, Genevieve's delicate shoulders went taut and she nodded periodically. He narrowed his eyes. Was his candid lady in the library a poor relation? His intrigue redoubled. She elongated her neck, drawing his gaze and remembrances to her erratic heartbeat a short while ago. She did a small search and then their stares connected once more. Panic flared in the lady's eyes and she made another bid to escape. Cedric reached the trio.

"Lady Ellsworth, a pleasure," he said smoothly, not taking his gaze from Genevieve. The young woman gave him a faintly pleading look. As much as he particularly enjoyed his ladies pleading, this was not the kind he happened to favor. Mixed with that silent entreaty was an unspoken recrimination from within her eyes.

The marchioness squeaked. "M-My lord." She dropped a curtsy. "Wh-what an honor." She tittered behind her hand. "Have you come to meet my Gillian?"

He slid his gaze over to the breathtaking beauty with her purple skirts beside the woman. He expected this lovely lady was, in fact, her Gillian. With her beauty, she befit the usual beauties he took to his bed. However, another had earned his attention.

"Mother," Lady Gillian scolded, a blush on her cheeks.

He looked expectantly at the marchioness. The rotund marchioness emitted a squeak. "F-forgive me. May I introduce my daughter, Lady Gillian Farendale?"

Cedric made the appropriate greetings and looked expectantly to the pale Genevieve.

The marchioness opened and closed her mouth several times, sputtering as she followed his attention.

When no introduction was forthcoming, he lifted an eyebrow.

"And this is my other d-daughter," she choked out. "Lady Genevieve."

He lifted his eyebrows. The lady was a marchioness' daughter? Attired in garments better suited a servant and on the fringe of the festivities, there was little hint of belonging to this family.

Her mother forced an elbow into her side and Genevieve grunted. "My lord," she said with a grudging hesitancy. She offered a belated and, by his way of thinking, insolent curtsy.

Was the enticing pink of her neck and cheeks a product of embarrassment or desire from their earlier embrace? "A pleasure," Cedric murmured, reaching for her hand. The lady hesitated and then placed her fingertips in his. He folded his hand about hers reflexively and marveled at the length of her fingers. He cursed her gloves, and cursed himself for having neglected that flesh when he'd had the opportunity presented to him. He pressed a kiss to her knuckles, relishing in the slight tremble of those long digits.

She made to draw them back, but he retained his grip. The orchestra struck up the strains of the waltz. With a fiery show of spirit, Genevieve gave another tug.

"May I have the honor of partnering you in the next set, my lady?"

Fire flashed in her expressive eyes. "I do n-not dance." A woman who moved with such graceful elegance possessed a body made for dance, and far more.

"I insist," he shot back with a practiced grin. God, with her fire and spirit, she could set the room ablaze.

"You insist," she mouthed. Angling her jaw up, she gave an emphatic shake. "And I insist. I do not dance."

And because he'd long proven himself a selfish bastard who claimed what he wanted, Cedric turned his assault on the marchioness.

The woman fluttered a hand about her neck and looked frantically around. "I…" She appeared one more word away from tears. "I-I am certain Genevieve might partner you in the one set," the marchioness cut in, favoring her daughter with a glare. Mother and daughter locked in a silent, unspoken battle of the wills which was ultimately resolved by Cedric.

Elbow extended, he stepped aside and allowed her a path to the dance floor. The spirited young lady dug her heels in and, for an instant, he believed, in a world where lords and ladies sought to appease him for nothing more than his future title alone, that this slip of a woman would publically refuse his offer. Then she gave a slight nod and allowed him to escort her to the sea of already assembled dancers. "I thought you were going to refuse me," he said, favoring her with one of his long-practiced smiles.

"I should have," she bit out as he settled his hand at her waist. "You do not know what you've done." The faint thread of panic underscored her words. With a deliberate slowness, he caressed his fingers over the soft satin fabric. A shuddery gasp escaped her plump lips and she quickly placed a hand on his shoulder. "That was poorly done of you."

"My touch?"

"Forcing my hand," she said between tight lips.

Who was Lady Genevieve Farendale? This woman who spoke of honor and integrity and sought the anonymity of the sidelines? Or a lady who would steal away to her host's library? The people Cedric kept company with were with men who'd bed another chap's wife on a bet or out of boredom and women who'd take both the winner and loser of that wager to bed. In the course of his nearly thirty years, it had never been about honor.

To counter the unsettled sentiments swirling inside him, he made a tsking noise. "Never tell me you looked forward to part-nering another." His fingers tightened reflexively at her waist.

"It is not a matter of whether or not I looked forward to another gentleman. I politely refused your request, my lord, and you super-seded my wishes because of your desire."

If he wished to truly scandalize her, he'd speak to her about what he truly desired. "Come, Genevieve. Given our *meeting* we've moved beyond those stiff forms of address."

The lady's cheeks blazed such a crimson red, it could have set her face afire but then she surprised him once more. "Yes, there is truth to that." The lady directed her words at his cravat and he brushed his fingertips in a fleeting caress over her lower back until she picked her head up. "However, it was not well done of you."

"What? Discussing the flaws in the duke's home and the inher-ent wickedness of his son?" He lowered his head close and her breath caught. "Or do you refer to our kiss?"

Genevieve missed a step and the color seeped from her cheeks. He effortlessly righted her. "Someone might hear, my lord." She stole a furtive look about.

"Cedric," he pressed. He'd long been accustomed to having his wishes met. He wanted his name on her lips not simply because he desired her, but also because, for some inexplicable reason, he was drawn by the sincerity of her responses around him. She did not fawn or seek to earn his favor. Instead, she was candid in her every emotion; from the passion in their embrace, to her annoyance, and blushing embarrassment.

"I cannot call you Cedric," she choked out so quietly he strug-gled to make out her words.

"Because I am a rake?" He waggled his eyebrows.

"Yes," she hissed. Hurt outrage flashed in her eyes and an unexpected pang that felt very much like guilt needled at his conscience. A conscience he'd not known he'd possessed until this innocent minx trained hurt, accusatory eyes on him. "Furthermore, you knew I mistook your identity. I asked—"

"If I was a friend of the marquess' which I assured you I was not," he put in smoothly. "Because I am not." He placed his lips close to her ear. "I *am* the marquess. Two entirely different things." Cedric twirled her to the edge of the ballroom, away from the center of the activity. "Furthermore, if I had confided the truth, you would have run as far and as fast as your bare feet could have carried you." Which begged the unanswerable question—why had it mattered if she had left?

Because I wanted to taste her lips. Because I wanted to ruck her gown up and lay between her legs...

Only, it hadn't been just about this hungering for her.

"That isn't altogether true." She leaned close. "I would have collected my slippers."

He laughed. Not the practiced, restrained chuckles he called forth at bawdy tales and boring jests, but rather one of sincerity and mirth that emerged rusty from deep in his chest.

"I was not speaking in jest."

His laughter died. Good God, she was enchanting. The manner of interesting that made a man brave boring balls and soirees just for the unexpectedness of whatever words she'd utter next.

CHAPTER 6

WHY, WITH THAT HANDFUL OF words, did Cedric, the mystery gentleman she'd met in the library, have to be correct?

For in the course of their exchange, she'd never pointedly asked if he was, in fact, the marquess. Which in retrospect, with her mistakes laid out clearly before her, she knew would have been an obvious assumption. He'd sat elegant in repose, as though he owned the massive room because…well, because he did own it. Or he would.

Yet, there was something *dishonest* in that lie of omission, a lie that muddied that magical first kiss he'd given her and the beauty of their exchange. A pang struck her heart, which was foolish that she would feel…anything. But it did. He was a whispered about rake and given that ignoble titling, a man who could only compound the gossip surrounding her name. Even now, her skin pricked with the crowd's awareness trained on them.

Genevieve ran her gaze over his harshly beautiful face. With the room doused in candlelight, it illuminated the sharp angles in a way the shadows could have never done true justice to. She lingered on the tight lines drawn at the corners of his mouth. Things that had previously escaped her, now glared strong. For the cynical set to his lips hinted at a man who'd become an expert at manipulating words and people in a way that suited his desires and interests. And she hated the truth of that. Hated that his smile was false and his earlier words, even falser. Hated it because it only confirmed everything she'd come to expect of those lords who lived for their pleasures.

"You have gone silent now, Genevieve?" There was a silken thread underlining those words that sent a mad fluttering to her belly, even as logic lightened this man's hold on her senses.

"You are one who is accustomed to ladies fawning and falling down for you," she said quietly to herself. "You turn forth a grin and a laugh to ease the truth of your coldness." His face froze in an unmoving mask. "Mayhap the world does not see past that. They see what you ask them to see." Just as she naively had allowed herself to see in the library. Yet, that was not his fault. It was hers for wanting to see diamonds in the dust. "They see your smile. They hear your teasing words. They are so focused on those smiles that they do not realize..." At his narrowing eyes, she blinked and let her words die. She'd said too much, to a man who truly was nothing but a stranger.

A stranger whose kiss still burns on my lips.

"They see what?" he bit out. Gone was that smooth edge to his words.

"The façade." She knew because she was a woman who'd donned the same, stifling mask these five years.

A harsh light glinted in his eyes. "You do not know anything of it."

"Oh, I suspect I know more than you'd care to think." Hot emotion flashed in the cerulean blue of his eyes. With his easy charm and the cynical smile that didn't quite reach his gaze, she saw enough to know this man was one to avoid at all costs.

The orchestra concluded the waltz and they came to a stop. Other partners clapped politely and filed from the floor while Genevieve and Cedric remained stationary, locked in a silent battle. His chest moved forcibly like he'd run a great distance.

Belatedly, she curtsied. "My lord."

Where any proper gentleman would have escorted her from the floor, Cedric, future Duke of Ravenscourt, sketched a bow and stalked off, master of this ballroom. Genevieve stood rooted to her spot, agonizingly exposed to the stares and whispers of his distinguished guests and, in that moment, she hated Cedric. Hated him for so effortlessly thrusting her back into Society's focus. *It was inevitable.* Her feet twitched with the urge to flee. *Move. Pick up one foot and place it before the other.* Her breath came hard and fast and then a small arm slid into hers and she started, blinking wildly.

Her sister gave her a reassuring smile. "Come," she said softly and Genevieve's throat worked.

How many times as children had she come to Gillian's aid during her madcap schemes? In an utter role reversal, rescue should now be conferred by her younger sister. "Thank you," she managed.

"If you smile and hold your chin up, they stare less," Gillian said, widening her smile. "And if you laugh, then it really confounds them." With that, she tossed back her head and laughed.

A wave of gratitude filled her and a smile split her lips; real and wonderful for it. That not a single gentleman had seen Gillian's worth and beauty proved them all a lot of fools.

"Mother is not happy," her younger sister said from the corner of her mouth.

Genevieve easily found the scowling marchioness and did a quick search for her father.

"Father is in the gaming rooms."

Some of the tension eased from her shoulders. Of course, he'd eventually emerge. When he did, there would be the discovery that Genevieve had done something as scandalous as publicly waltzing. She nibbled her lower lip. Then, it wasn't so much the dance, but rather the gentleman who'd commandeered that set in a public way…and then in an equally public way had left her standing alone at the center of the dance floor. Which really was quite a cut-direct for any lady, even more damning for one whispered to be a whore who made scandalous offers and propositions to gentlemen.

They reached their mother's side. "Mo—"

"Not a word," the marchioness said, with a patently false smile plastered on her lips. "You are to sit with the other companions." Is that what she was, then? A companion? A giggle bubbled up at the preposterousness of such an idea and she forcibly swallowed her amusement. "I do not want you near Gillian."

Of course, her faithless parents had never seen anyone else to blame where she was concerned. They didn't see or credit the treacherous acts of strangers, but rather condemned the daughter whose blood they shared. Head held high, she turned to go, when Gillian shot a staying hand about her arm. "Mother," she scolded.

Genevieve delicately removed her arm from Gillian's gentle grip. "I will be all right," she reassured. After her public humiliation five years ago, she could certainly manage to hover for another handful of hours on the fringe of the duke's ballroom. In fact, she far preferred it. *Liar. You love dancing. You loved it even more in the marquess' strong, powerful arms.*

With a roomful of observers staring on, Genevieve made her way to the shell-backed chairs along the back wall. She slid into a seat between two other equally miserably dressed ladies. The lady at her right yanked her skirts out of the way and quickly came to her feet. Casting a scathing glance back, she rushed off.

Genevieve trained her gaze forward on the dancers, fisting her hands on her lap. It mattered not what the whispers were, or what people believed. She knew the truth. She knew the ugliest of rumors were, in fact, lies perpetuated by a cad and that knowing was power. Granted a weak, ineffectual power, but a power over her thoughts and sense of her own self-worth. Still, there was something so very lonely in having been cut from the fold of the family. She looked to where her wildly gesticulating sister now chatted with her friend, Honoria Fairfax.

As much as she loved Gillian and had no doubt she was genuinely happy to have her back with the family, so many years had passed that it was oftentimes as though they were old friends trying to return to the way it had once been…when they could never, ever truly go back.

"Thank you."

She froze and looked about. Her gaze collided with the plump woman with a glass of punch in one hand who occupied the opposite chair. With pale, heavily freckled cheeks and too-tight ringlets, the young woman must be near an age of her own. Did the lady remember Genevieve's scandal from long ago? Or mayhap she didn't know it at all and was why she even now spoke to her. "Uh…"

"For sending that one rushing off," she said on a less than discreet whisper. The woman leaned close. "Miserable creature. Hasn't smiled once all night." She stuck her gloved palm out. "My name is Miss Francesca Cornworthy." She grimaced. "Horrid name. You might call me Francesca, which is equally horrid, but only slightly less than Franny, which is what my father calls me."

Her mind spun under the happy chattering and, yet, at the unexpected kindness, emotion filled her throat. Though she caught the flesh on the inside of her cheek hard, it was hardly fair to drag this kind creature down the gossip trail with her. At the stretch of silence and inaction, the woman's smiled dipped and her hand quavered. Lest she misunderstand the reason for her hesitation, Genevieve swiftly placed her fingers in Miss Francesca Cornworthy's and shook. "I am Lady Genevieve Farendale."

A look of relief flashed in her startling violet eyes. "I know who you are." Her stomach dipped. "We made our Come Out the same year," the lady explained.

She knew. Of course, she knew. Everyone knew. "Oh," she said lamely and quickly withdrew her hand.

Francesca raised the glass in her opposite hand to her lips and took a sip of her drink. "Nasty stuff. Nasty stuff."

Genevieve glanced about to the sea of lords and ladies, many of whom well-remembered the jilted-at-the-altar Farendale daughter. "Yes, it was."

"I referred to the punch," Francesca interrupted her maudlin thoughts. "Not your scandal."

And after five years of being a morose, maudlin figure lamenting her past, a very real…lightness went through her. The woman spoke with more honesty and candid sincerity than anyone, including her own family. Everyone, including Genevieve herself, tiptoed around talk of that long ago day, as though that would make it all go away. But it wouldn't. It would always and forever be… The Scandal. There was something freeing in that.

Perhaps the woman was lonely and long in need of a friend, but she carried on her one-sided conversation. "I never did understand how a gentleman was so pardoned for the whole affair, while you were scuttled off. Uh…" She blushed. "You were scuttled off, I gather?"

Genevieve smiled. "I was." Scuttled off. Like the refuse on a shopkeeper's stoop.

"Well, I am glad you've returned."

She was glad she returned. Those words, so sincerely spoken, when no one, not even Genevieve's own parents, had uttered them. "You do not even know me." The words slipped out before she could call them back.

The smile widened on Francesca's face, rather transforming her from pretty into a lovely, glowing woman. "I know enough that it is the height of wrongness to have you hide away from the world." She shook her head. "Not a nice way to live, at all. But you danced tonight, which I imagine was very exciting." She gave her an envious look. "Not that I know anything really about dancing."

With Francesca's kindness and wonderful spirit, and her relegation to the back hall of the ballroom, proved once more— gentleman were bloody fools. All of them. "It was exciting," she conceded, so very happy to be able to confide that in someone. Particularly when she well-knew the carriage ride home would contain a stinging diatribe of Genevieve's wickedness.

It will be worth it...Unbidden, she did a sweep of the ballroom and several inches taller than even the tallest of guests, she easily found him. Cedric stood, with his back angled to her. He leaned an elbow against the Doric column and sipped from a champagne flute while speaking to a handsome, dark-haired gentleman. However, Cedric commanded her attention. How coolly elegant he was. Her heart skittered a dangerous beat.

"They are not all bad," Francesca said and Genevieve looked over quickly. The woman nudged her chin slightly in the Marquess of St. Albans' direction.

Her skin burned at the memory of his touch and kiss. No, the marquess was not bad. He was something far more dangerous—he was wicked.

"After all, he danced with you, which says a good deal about him."

"Does it?" she drawled. It spoke to him being a rake who'd tease a woman in private and attempt to charm her in the midst of the ballroom floor.

"It means he doesn't give a jot about gossip." Francesca wrinkled her brow. "Which I don't care about, either. And," she added, as an afterthought, "he likely saw you tapping your feet."

Genevieve started and glanced down at her miserably sore toes. She'd noticed her feet?

"There really isn't much else to do but look," she said, matter-of-factly.

She gave the woman a wry smile. "I expect sparing me from certain boredom was not at all the marquess' intentions." No doubt, he saw the same wanton everyone did. It was a belief she'd proven true earlier in his library and sought to coordinate an improper meeting. Or rather another improper meeting. Her skin warmed at the memory and, more, the craving to know his kiss, again.

"Why?" Francesca asked, jolting her back from those outrageous musings. "Because he's a rake?" She furrowed her brow. "It hardly seems fair to condemn the gentleman for gossip attached to *his* name." The young woman took another sip and grimaced. "Awful stuff, indeed."

At that telling emphasis, Genevieve stilled and looked out at Cedric once more. With Francesca's innocent and, no doubt, unwitting accusation, she stirred guilt. The gossips reported him to be a rake, but those same scandal sheets reported her to be a wanton.

Then, a black-haired, willowy beauty in gold sidled up to the gentleman. The lady ran her fingertips down his sleeve and he shifted, presenting the couple in profile. With his golden good looks and her dark coloring, they struck quite the pair. That slight, practiced grin turned his lips and Genevieve looked away. There was no imagining a rake or rogue there. The worthless title fairly seeped from his well-muscled frame.

Awful stuff, indeed. From across the room, her mother caught her gaze and motioned to her. Like a blasted hound. "I am afraid I must go," she said with a sigh.

Francesca's face fell. "Oh, drat. Well, I did enjoy your company, Genevieve," she said, easily dispensing with formalities. "Perhaps we will meet again?" she asked hopefully.

Genevieve smiled. "I would like that very much." Reluctantly, she came to her feet and started the march back to her mother, feeling not unlike that fabled queen being marched before the gallows.

"AH, SO THAT IS THE way the wind blows, then?" From his position at the edge of the ballroom, Cedric stiffened and turned as Montfort sauntered up. "That makes sense and is vastly relieving."

"What the hell are you on about?" he drawled, sipping his champagne.

Montfort stuck a leg out. "At first," he shuddered. "Why, at first, I had an ugly worry that a respectable lady attracted your attention." He tapped his chin. "But I quickly rid myself of such mad worries." Yes, there were never any worries about anything respectable where Cedric was concerned. Even his only loyal friend knew as much. "Then, I suspected it was an eager widow, but I haven't seen a single one to command your attention this evening." Montfort grinned and then, as though he'd solved the riddle of life, he said, "It was the Farendale chit. Wanton little piece, isn't she?"

Cedric froze, glass midway to his mouth. Of course, the guests present would note the single dance he'd indulged in this evening. He did not, nor had he ever, however, given a jot about Society's whispers and speculations where he was concerned. So why did he want to slam his fist into Montfort's mouth for speaking about her?

"You've never been one to pursue a respectable miss and you aren't one to start now."

It took a moment for the earl's words to register and as the other man's insinuation became clear, an inexplicable fury went through him. Aware of Montfort's mocking gaze on him, he schooled his lips into an easy grin. "I think a lady in those modest skirts and her hair arranged so can hardly be called a wanton," he said dryly. Even with that hideous chignon, the lady was more tempting than Eve in all her naked splendor.

A flare of amusement glinted in the earl's jaded eyes. "Bah," he scoffed. "I never thought I'd see the day when you dallied with her as she is now."

As she is now.

Which implied… Montfort knew her…when? Montfort and Cedric had passed countless women between each other; from widows to actresses to skilled whores at their clubs and yet… An ugly, resentment twisted around his belly. "And how was she, then?" The lethal edged whisper slipped out.

Montfort downed his drink and motioned a servant over to claim the empty glass. "Ah, you were never one to gossip. How could I forget?"

And for reasons Cedric had never understood, the earl had long been a lover of Society's juicy on-dits.

"Three, mayhap four years ago she was jilted at the altar."

He frowned. "That hardly sounds like the manner of scandal to hold Society's interest." And certainly not for four years. Cedric took another sip of his champagne.

"It is when the groom's brother bandies it about that she was warming his bed, as well as the groom's closest friends. Some believe she was with child and sent away to birth the babe."

Cedric choked on his swallow and his gaze flew to Genevieve. Like hell. The pinch-mouthed lady sat primly amongst the wall-flowers and companions. Her sharp, pale cheeks and the tightness at the corner of her mouth hinted at the strain of emotion. He hooded his eyes and maintained his scrutiny. The lady was no whore. Her kiss, though eager, hinted at her inexperience. He'd not reveal as much to Montfort. For all his crimes, bandying the details about his lovers had never been one of them. "So she's returned," he said, pulling his gaze away. Where had the lady been all these years? "For what purpose?"

"Why I expect the same reasons all ladies come to London." Montfort lifted his shoulders in a shrug. "The whispers are she's here to find some unsuspecting or desperate nobleman. Others think it's merely her parents' attempt to prove she knows how to behave like a lady." The smirk on the earl's lips indicated just what he believed about that latter point and Cedric tightened his grip on his glass to keep from leveling the other man a facer.

…*You do not know what you've done*…

As his friend ran through the other gossip of the evening that Cedric didn't give a damn about, he once more took Genevieve in. The drab skirts, the unwillingness to dance, even as her feet had tapped away at the marble floor. And then he recalled her standing there, as he'd stalked off like a petulant child and all because she'd seen too much. Spoken of him and about him in a way that had been not at all false, and all the more terrifying for it.

And for the first time, Cedric Falcot, the Marquess of St. Albans, who never felt anything, felt something, something he'd believed himself too jaded to feel or know—shame.

No doubt, Genevieve believed the deliberate omission of his name in the library and his maneuverings in the ballroom, nothing more than a product of who he was and more—who *she* was. What the lady could never realize is that Cedric did not bother to judge or condemn because, frankly, there wasn't a more dissolute person than himself.

How ironic that she should be judged so. Even all these years later, when he had been a consummate rake, hosting outrageously wicked parties and partaking in dishonorable wagers. How ironic and... unfair. It was bloody unfair. Reprehensible behaviors were tolerated in those powerful lords, while even the hint of a rumor saw a lady ruined.

He looked at her, seated on the fringe talking to a plump wall-flower and felt like the cad he'd relished in being these years. If the lady's intentions had been to escape notice, then he'd quite robbed her of any potential anonymity with his dance and then abandonment at the end of the set. But it was, for reasons he could not understand and reasons he did not care to examine, important that she know he'd not been making light of her.

The earl tipped his chin. "Ah, now here comes an enticing creature."

Drawn back, Cedric followed Montfort's stare to Baroness Shelley. The midnight beauty was willowy and perfectly curved in the places he enjoyed his women curved. The hard, but enticing, smile on her lips promised endless delights and, yet, as she layered her palm to his forearm, he was...unmoved.

"Lord St. Albans, how," she traced the tip of her tongue over her thin lips, "splendid you should at last arrive."

...*They are too big*... Genevieve's breathlessly innocent gasp rasped around his mind.

Montfort gave him a pointed frown and Cedric immediately thrust aside more pleasurable musings and attended the baroness.

CHAPTER 7

GENEVIEVE'S LUCK HAD NEVER BEEN good and that ill-luck went back long before being jilted at the altar.

But this time, it seemed she'd had a remarkable showing of good luck. They'd taken their leave of the duke's ballroom last evening, without a single word, grumble, or grunt from Father about Genevieve's scandalous dance with Cedric.

"You danced with St. Albans last night."

Alas, she'd foolishly proven herself a remarkable optimist again.

The three ladies seated about the breakfast table froze under the rumble of the Marquess of Ellsworth's words.

Genevieve picked her gaze up from the contents of her dish and looked to her balding, oft-scowling father. She finished her bite and then dabbed at her lips with her napkin. "Father?" Mayhap Gillian had also danced with that respective gentleman? She stole a sideways glance at her sister, who resumed her rapt study of the kippers on her plate.

The marquess narrowed his eyes and strode over to the head of the table. He motioned to a servant who rushed forward with his usual morning fare.

"St. Albans," he repeated, his tone harsh. If he was livid about her waltz with Cedric, what would he say about their chance meeting and talks of friendship, no less? "You were instructed not to dance."

"I had no choice," she said through tight lips.

"She really didn't, Father," Gillian piped in. She gave her an encouraging smile. "He was quite adamant that she partner him."

At her sister's attempt at a helpful response, Genevieve winced. She knew Gillian meant to be helpful. She really did and she loved her for that…

"Of course he did," he boomed.

Fury melded with shame and set her cheeks ablaze. "I could not very well say no," she bit out. "What a scandal that would be." Genevieve looked to her mother; her cheeks waxen, the marchioness wetted her lips. The woman, with her seeming inability to smile and her tendency to scowl at members she'd deemed beneath her notice, was undaunted by all—except her husband.

"S-St. Albans is in the market for a wife," the marchioness put in.

A memory entered of Cedric kneeling at her feet while he slid on her slippers. Her toes curled at the still erotic moment. No, a man such as St. Albans would marry no time soon. Nor did a gentleman who spoke candidly of friendship demonstrate any real husband material.

"Quite a catch, quite a catch," her mother rambled on. "He will be a future duke, you know." Goodness, the things she'd said to the man last evening about his title, his library. Gillian cringed. "Wouldn't that be wonderful to have a duke for our girl, Lord Ellsworth?"

Lord Ellsworth. At that stiff formality, the two sisters exchanged a look and Gillian gave a quick, discreet roll of her eyes. Even as Genevieve knew with her hope for love from a good, honorable gentleman that her requirements in a husband were going to be as difficult as finding the end of a proverbial rainbow, she'd at the very least hope for more than a union where one was so restricted by politeness that they couldn't bear to use one another's Christian names.

"I know St. Albans will be a duke." Father leaned forward and thumped his hand on the table, rattling the glass of water at his side. A servant gulped audibly and set the marquess' plate down before him. "But surely you do not believe he'd make *her* an honorable offer." That slight emphasis sent her shoulders back. "The man is a rake."

Mother cleared her throat and then with a surprising courage, she met her husband's gaze. "I know you *said* the marquess was to be avoided, Lord Ellsworth… but even rakes must wed."

Would a man such as Cedric take a wife and a respectable one at that? From their brief meeting and one waltz she took him as one who would do exactly as he pleased, societal expectations be damned. She curled her fingers hard around her fork.

Blatantly ignoring his wife's opinion, the marquess looked to the servants and, interpreting that silent cue, they filed quickly out of the room.

Genevieve would *never* bind herself to the manner of gentleman who stripped her of her voice. Ever.

"You had strict orders to attract no attention," he barked, snapping that shaking digit at her. "Yet again you've proven your harlotry."

Her gasp blended with Gillian's.

"Lord Ellsworth," their mother scolded, in an uncharacteristic show of defiance.

"It was merely one dance," Genevieve bit out. Why would he force her back to this place? Why, if he could not accept her past was just that…her past? *Because he doesn't believe it. He thinks I'm irredeemable and a blight on the family.* "You are making more of it than it is."

Father flared his nostrils. "I do not want another scandal attached to this family," he boomed and the three ladies again jumped.

No, he'd tolerate not a misstep. Not after Genevieve's scandal. She gritted her teeth at what Cedric had wrought with his careless waltz. "There will be no scandal," she said in more even tones. Not even as she craved more excitement from life than the staid, stilted existence.

A wide smile quivered in her mother's fleshy cheeks. "See, my lord? There is nothing to worry after. Genevieve will be a good girl." She whipped her head around so quickly, her jowls jiggled. "Isn't that right, Genevieve?" Without allowing for a reply, the wife leaned over and patted her still scowling husband. "She'll not encourage any gentleman."

Nauseated by the mollifying exchange, Genevieve looked away. Unable to stomach any more, she shoved back her seat. It scraped noisily on the floor. "I am going to Hyde Park," she seethed.

"You are to bring your maid," her father thundered.

"Of course," she said, pasting on a patently false smile. "I am nothing if not proper." With that, she proceeded from the room with a decorum and grace both of her parents would have been hard-pressed to fault. When she'd put the breakfast room behind her, Genevieve lengthened her strides until she'd disappeared around the corridor where she broke into a sprint, wanting to keep running. Away from this place. Away from the weight of her parents' unending fury. Her skirts snapped about her ankles as she took the stairs and made her way to her chambers. Within the sanctuary of her rooms, she closed the door and leaned against the panel. Her breath came hard and fast from her exertion. Panting, Genevieve slumped against the door.

She stared blankly about the room; a room that may as well have belonged to a stranger. Was this what her life was to be then? Was she to be relegated to the role of distantly removed member of the family, constantly being reminded of the mistakes of her past and never free to move beyond them? Her gaze snagged on the cheerful blue of the sky peeking through the gaping fabric of her curtains. Where was the joy in a life such as this? She wanted... more. Because to remain here, would crush her, destroying her in ways that her exile never could.

Shoving away from the door, Genevieve wandered over to the escritoire. The sketchpads, so precious these years, now forgotten in this fortnight. She pulled out the velvet-upholstered chair and slid into the seat. With numb fingers, she flipped the pages. She paused to steal a glance at the doorway. Should her father see...

Her grandfather's visage. Delores. The maids and servants who'd been more family than her own parents. She turned to a blank sheet. Of their own volition, her fingers, long denied the pleasure she'd found these years at the encouragement of her grandfather, moved. She picked up the pastels and set her fingers to work upon the pages. She sat hunched over the book, chewing her lower lip, as she let her fingers fly frantically over the blank sheet. A strand broke free from the painfully tight chignon worked by her maid that morn and she blew at the errant curl. With each stroke of the pastel, an exhilarating calm stole through her. The beautiful peace that came in this wholly freeing experience was relaxing.

Minutes? Hours later she set the pastel down. Her chest heaved as she stared at the visage reflected back; the dangerously alluring half-grin, the chiseled cheeks befitting an expertly carved stone masterpiece.

A knock sounded at the door and she jumped. Heart pounding, Genevieve slammed the book closed and then cast a quick glance over her shoulder. "E-Enter," she called and coming to her feet, she placed herself between that intimate part of her and the interloper.

The door opened and Gillian stuck her head inside. "You did not go to Hyde Park."

Genevieve cocked her head.

Her sister pushed the door open and took a tentative step forward. "You said you were to Hyde Park and you've not gone."

Her mind stalled. Yes, yes she had. Because ultimately, all she'd sought was escape. "I became distracted," she admitted, fisting the fabric of her skirts.

Sisters stood there, forever friends and, yet, strangers all at the same time. "I am to go to the museum with Honoria and Phoebe. I thought you might join us?"

Except, Genevieve had been too long removed from the woman she'd been; easy to converse, eager for grand adventures alongside Gillian. "Go along without me," she said. She'd become so accustomed to her solitary presence during the days, she no longer knew how to be the garrulous, effervescent young girl she'd been. "I am to Hyde Park." Nor did she want to be that girl, ever again. "Thank you," she added softly when Gillian made to leave.

Her sister opened her mouth and then with a slight nod, left.

When Gillian had gone, leaving Genevieve alone, she turned back to her collection of books. Gathering up the leather folio and her container of pastels, she started from the room.

RapRapRap

The incessant knocking penetrated Cedric's slumber. Through the thick haze of sleep, he forced his eyes open and turned to the window. The thick, gold brocade curtains blotted out all light, but a slight gap in the fabric revealed a crack of sunlight. With a low groan, he rolled onto his back and flung his arm across his eyes. By God, was his man, Avis, asking to be sacked? After ten years in his employ, the bugger surely knew Cedric did not wake before twelve o'clock.

"My lord?"

"Get the hell away," he called to his valet and drifted between sleep and wake, drawing forth the dreams of his slumber—a bare-foot lady and her kiss-swollen lips. His shaft stirred at the welcome remembrance and he burrowed deeper into the smooth satin sheets.

RapRapRap

Bloody hell. "You had better have a bloody good reason to—"

"I have the information you requested, my lord."

Cedric lowered his arm to his side and stared up at the wicked mural painted above his bed. He furrowed his brow. "The information," he mouthed trying to muddle through the fog of last night's overindulgence in brandy and champagne, the haze of desire, and the godawful early hour.

The servant cleared his throat. "You indicated I bring you the information about a certain—"

With a curse, Cedric flung his legs over the side of the bed and stood. Naked, he stalked across the room and yanked the door open. His servant spilled into the room. He slammed the door behind them. "I said discreetly. I don't need the whole of London knowing." Following his exit from his father's ball, Cedric had tasked his loyal servant with the charge of finding out where he might expect to see Lady Genevieve. It was not the first time he'd given Avis such an assignment. It was, however, of reasons different than all the other ones before it. Regardless, the last thing he needed were his servants bandying about gossip about the lady.

When had he ever cared about that, though?

"Uh, right. Yes, my lord." The balding butler held out a folded sheet.

"Nor did I believe you'd bring the information at this ungodly hour." No sane person who valued the need and benefit of a good sleep would rise before the noon hour.

"Forgive me, my lord. It seemed the kind of…er information you would care to be in possession of."

Cedric accepted the page, unfolded it, and skimmed. "Indeed," he said and a slow grin turned his lips up. Yes. His servant's inquiries of a certain Lady Genevieve proved just the manner of information a man of Cedric's reputation would want in his hands. Immediately.

Even if it was at this sinful hour. He looked to the ormolu clock atop his fireplace mantel.

The tall, lanky man shifted on his feet. "I took the liberty of having your mount readied."

By God, Avis was deserving of a raise. "Good work, man," he said and with his spare hand, he slapped his servant on the back.

His face was always an unreadable mask devoid of emotion. Avis dropped a bow and proceeded over to the mahogany armoire to gather Cedric's garments. A short while later, having completed his morning ablutions and with a small, but manageable, throb in his head from his overindulgence last evening, Cedric made his way from his townhouse. He accepted the reins of his mount from a waiting servant.

Adjusting his black hat, he climbed astride and nudged Wicked onward to Hyde Park. In the late morning quiet of the London streets, just before the rest of polite Society ventured into the world, he considered the information uncovered by his servant. What manner of lady paid daily visits to the mazes of Kensington Gardens before the fashionable hour? Montfort's charges about the lady's character slipped in, but he quickly thrust them aside. Genevieve. Her guarded eyes and innocent kiss were not belonging to the wanton described by the earl. Forcing the tension from his body, Cedric patted his horse on the withers and urged him onward, past haggard shopkeepers shoving their carts into position for a day of hawking their wares.

He guided Wicked through the entrance of Hyde Park and drew on the reins, slowing his mount. He did a small sweep of the grounds and then clicked his tongue, pushing the eager horse to stretch his legs along the riding trail. The gates of Kensington Gardens pulled into focus and he, again, drew on the reins, stopping Wicked.

Cedric dismounted, kicking gravel and dust about him as his boots settled on the earth. He searched the quiet, empty area, and frowned. If his bloody butler had proven wrong in his blasted information... As he tied Wicked under a nearby oak, he continued to search the grounds. From across the distance, he located a young maid, conversing with a strapping liveried servant. A wry smile formed on Cedric's lips. Ah, how many ladies had been attended by lax servants, who'd turn their proverbial cheek while her mistress went about her scandalous pursuits so she might know pleasures of her own?

He captured his chin between his thumb and forefinger, surveying the lush, green gardens. The archway to the Rose Garden. Having partaken in too many trysts to count, where would he himself go for a late morning rendezvous? He paused, his gaze lingering upon the tall hedge maze. Of course. Cedric stole another look at the slipshod maid. The young woman remained engrossed in her conversation with her sweetheart.

Never one to neglect a useful distraction or silent footfall, Cedric swiftly made his way into the hedge maze. As he entered the gardens, he continued his search for his quarry while taking in the manicured grounds. The meticulously tended shrubs and bushes presented a woodland setting in the midst of the dirt and filth of London which created a falsified purity. The lush, emerald grass that blanketed the side of the graveled walking path was called to be a natural bedding between a man and woman bent on wicked deeds. Of all the inventive places he'd taken his lovers, how had he failed to appreciate the possibilities that existed in this private Eden?

A faint morning breeze stirred the brush and the crisp boxwoods crunched noisily. Tugging off his gloves, Cedric stuffed them inside his coat and continued his search. Another soft rustle split the morning quiet and he walked deliberately toward that sound. When reaching the back of the hedge maze, he abruptly stopped.

Comfortably settled on a wrought iron bench with her knees drawn to her chest, Genevieve may as well have been in any parlor or library. With her attention devoted to a small leather volume in her hands, the lady lingered over the words on the page. With the benefit of her distraction, Cedric studied her contemplatively. The women he favored did not enjoy books. That was, except those naughty volumes that harkened to sexual gratification. He didn't know what to make of this young lady who stole into a hedge maze better for trysting, all to *read*.

He'd never known a woman to care about a tome before the garments or jewels he could shower her with. Or rather, he'd never taken a moment to learn of past lovers' interests and this discovery, quite by chance, made Genevieve Farendale all the more real. This connection to her was intimate in ways that defied the sexual. He frowned. Another breeze rustled through the gardens and a strand popped free of that miserable chignon, softening her sharp features. The lock tumbled over her brow and she absently brushed the strand behind her ear. His chest tightened. How singularly odd that a single tress could so alter a person's entire visage.

It promptly fell back. He ached with a physical need to yank free the combs holding those strawberry tresses in place and release them so they could cascade about her shoulders in a shimmery waterfall, as they were meant to. He'd wager those strands fell down the length of her back and, God, he would gladly trade his future dukedom to have them fanned out upon his pillow.

Like a doe that had caught scent of impending danger, Genevieve looked up and their gazes locked. Quickly, the lady swung her legs over the edge of her seat, giving a momentary flash of those trim, delicate ankles he'd had in his hands not even twelve hours earlier. The book tumbled to the ground, where it lay, forgotten. He briefly attended that volume, narrowing his gaze in a bid to make order of that image.

She was the first to break the quiet. "You," she blurted. That shocked admission carried in the quiet of the gardens.

He inclined his head. "Me." Had she been expecting another?

Drawn the way one of those hopeless sailors were to those sirens at sea, Cedric wandered closer. First the library, and now her stolen morning in Hyde Park. "You enjoy books, Genevieve." His words were more statement than question.

"That is a bit broad." A becoming crimson color blazed on her cheeks. "I enjoy some of them."

He closed the distance between them and then dropped to a knee beside her. She followed his movements as he gathered her book.

"What are you doing here?" she asked, faintly breathless, as she all but tugged the leather volume from his hands. She drew it close to her chest, almost protectively, and that slight movement only plumped her already generous breasts so that they pressed hard against the fabric of her cloak.

Well, that was hardly the welcoming greeting he was accustomed to from ladies. Somehow that only further strengthened the peculiarity of this woman; set her apart from others. "I always come here in the morn." The lie slipped out easily. Cedric came to his feet. "I enjoy riding with nothing but the privacy of my own thoughts." Which was not altogether untrue. It was the whole matter of time he took liberties with. Then, time meant different things to different people. All relative.

The lady eyed him with a wary skepticism he'd come to expect of her. Montfort had spoken of her being jilted at the altar. Who had been the bloody fool to turn this woman over and put that guarded caution in her eyes? "You come here? I've come here nearly a fortnight now and not seen you once."

"I am not usually this late in my morning ride," he put in smoothly. He offered her a lopsided grin. "Alas, after an eventful evening in the library with delightful company, I'd found myself unable to sleep."

She slapped her fingers to her gaping mouth. "My lord, I think even you would have the decency not to speak of your scandalous pursuits with another lady," she said on a furious whisper.

Even him?

He blinked several times. Then his lips pulled at the corners. The lady thought he spoke of another. Though he was rightfully accused of all manner of black-hearted acts through the years, he'd not bandied about those intimate acts. "I was speaking of *our* meeting."

High color flooded her cheeks, giving her an innocent look he'd long despised in a woman and, yet, on this one...it perfectly suited her and only added to her allure. "You were?"

Cedric nodded once. "I was."

She cleared her throat. "I thought you spoke of another."

"Oh?" he asked softly closing the remaining distance between them. He brushed his fingers down the smooth expanse of her cheek. "Which lady did you suspect?" His gentle caress brought her lashes fluttering closed.

"Th-the woman in the golden gown," her faintly whispered admission earned a grin.

Did the lady realize how much she revealed with that? Despite her studious attempts at avoiding him last evening, she'd noted him. He couldn't even recall a lady in gold or any other gown for that matter. He dipped his head lower, so close their lips nearly brushed. "Was there another?" he whispered. "I saw no one but you last evening." Any other time those words would have been carefully crafted with the sole purpose of luring a coy lady to his bed. Now, they were words uttered in truth. Unease rolled inside him and he thrust it aside. This unwitting fascination came from the newness in dallying with an innocent and nothing more. For he'd no doubt, even with Montfort's allegations, that the lady was, in fact, innocent. For the passion in her kiss, there had been an unbridled, unrestrained enthusiasm that spoke to her virtuousness.

Her breath hitched and any other woman would have tipped her head back to receive his kiss. "You should not be here." This lady again proved herself remarkably unlike any other before. She stepped back, retreating until her knees knocked against the wrought iron bench and peered at him through endless, golden lashes. "Nor do I believe you ride," she challenged, a faintly accusatory thread to that charge.

He rocked on his heels. How easy it would be to feed her a distracting lie that would drive back her suspicions and arouse her desires, but something about this young woman drew him—her honesty, her directness. They were sentiments he'd thought fabrications on the pages of whimsical books he'd never bothered to read. "No," he acknowledged at last. "Rather, I *do* ride daily but not at this hour."

Her lips twitched. "It is just past ten o'clock, my lord."

He grimaced. "Ungodly hour, you know."

Her mouth parted. "I find it beautiful," she countered. "It is even *more* beautiful, when the orange and crimson horizon shove back the night sky." She motioned to the distant sky. "It is like God has taken a paintbrush to a blank canvas and filled it with light. You should wake to see it before you so condemn it." With those words, she spoke more volumes than all the works assembled in his father's library. Yet, he stood transfixed by the wistful look on her face. Had he truly believed her ordinary? No splendorous work of art could dare compete with her plain-stated beauty. "And do you know the best part of it, my lord?"

Incapable of words, he managed to shake his head.

"There is no one here to intrude on the quiet splendor."

Her gaze still fixed on the distance, he continued to worship her with his stare. Mayhap there was something to be said of this early time, after all. Mayhap the lady had the right of it. "I came to apologize," he said quietly. It was hard to determine who was more stunned by that admission.

That snapped her attention back to him. Other ladies of his acquaintance would have tittered and offered veiled, and some not-so veiled, promises. "You came to see me in order to apologize?" She merely looked at him askance. "Why?"

Why? Why, indeed? Cedric tapped his hand against his thigh. What need or use had he of a desperately seeking proper miss, who snuck off to sketch in the gardens of Hyde Park? He could have, and frequently did have, naughty women who expected nothing and certainly didn't ask questions. And yet, the only reason he could bloody well find was, "I like you," he said honestly. She puzzled her brow. "And I don't like anybody." *Most times not even myself.* He thrust aside the maudlin thought. Rising early did nothing for his rational thinking. That thought, in and of itself, was proof enough.

"You *like* me?" A healthy degree of skepticism coated those three words.

"Would you know the truth?" He continued before she could speak. "I know you despise my title." They were of like opinions in that regard. "I know you're refreshingly frank when everyone else stinks of lies and falsity." He held her gaze squarely. "And I would not have you believe that my intentions last night were of the dishonorable sort." He grimaced. When had his intentions ever been of the honorable kind? "There you have it," he finished, lamely.

A sad smile curved her lips. "You did not know last evening that you waltzed with the Farendale doxy? This is the only reason you are here, now?" she asked softly, drifting closer.

Ah, so for the lady's innocence she was not so naïve that she'd be wholly truthful of his motives. What gentleman was responsible for that cautiousness? Tension snapped through his frame. "I'll not lie and say I don't desire you, Genevieve, if that is what you're expecting. For I do. Want you." Her mouth parted on a moue of scandalized shock. He scoffed. *A doxy.* This one was as innocent as a debutante in white skirts with a shy eye. And even with that, he wanted to lay her down on the dew-covered earth, haul her gown about her waist, and bury himself in her honeyed warmth. "But I also like you." How bloody *peculiar.* An inexplicable need to drive back that sad glint in her eyes filled him and he took a step forward, closing the distance between them. "Furthermore, you're no more a doxy than I am a respectable, noble hero."

And what terrified the bloody hell out of him, was that he craved the company of this only faintly pretty, most suspicious, young lady.

CHAPTER 8

By HIS VERY ADMISSION, CEDRIC, the Marquess of St. Albans, was a dishonorable sort whose motives in being here even now should be questioned. He was the manner of man who shamefully took what he wished and who kissed nameless strangers in his father's library.

And yet, in this instance, with those self-deprecating words, his admission nobly raised Genevieve from the mire and gossip that had swirled around her for five years. Her heart caught in a way that belied the wary walls she'd constructed about her after Terrance's betrayal.

On the heel of that, Genevieve thrust aside that foolish weakening. As he continued his forward approach, she held her book up staying him. "By your own accounts, being not at all respectable, you are here, anyway." She hooded her lashes. "All to apologize?" Heavy skepticism coated her words. "Why would you do that?" Why, when the men of his lofty rank had proven themselves self-serving enough to destroy a lady's reputation on nothing more than a whim and fancy? A morning breeze pulled at the fabric of their cloaks and the garments tangled in a noisy dance.

A muscle jumped at the corner of his eye. "You are, indeed, correct," he said stiffly. "I should not be here. I came to make my apologies, which I have since done. Because, even as I don't give a bloody damn on Sunday about anyone, I'd have you know that my intentions last evening were not to embarrass or draw attention to you." Yet, that is what he'd done, whether inadvertent or intentional. The angular planes of his cheek went flush and he sketched a hasty bow. Neither reactions of a man who'd deliberately sought to make light of the Farendale lady. "If you'll excuse me," he said, his tone coolly detached. "I'll allow you to return to your…" His gaze fell to the book gripped tight in her hands.

Following his stare, Genevieve furrowed her brow.

Wordlessly, he took a step forward and as though he'd forgotten her presence, slipped the book from her fingers and rustled through it. He paused on a page creased at the top. "You are an admirer of Turner's work, madam?" he asked not picking his gaze up from the painting she'd previously studied.

Her heart stuttered. Gentlemen did not speak of art or artists and if they did, well, they certainly did not draw from memory J.M.W. Turner's work. That this man did unsettled her already rather faulty, where he was concerned, world. He looked up questioningly and she quickly cleared her throat. "Yes. Are you familiar with his work?" she asked, turning his question on him, not knowing what to do with that discovery about this whispered about rake. Of course, he could have merely read the inscription at the top. Wasn't that the way of rakes? To learn a lady's interests and manipulate them to suit their desires.

"I am." Returning his focus to that page, Cedric trailed a long finger over the dark clouds of night on the page. "I would take you for an admirer of Friedrich's *The Watzmann* and not the darkness of Turner."

A thrill of a connectedness drove back all better reason in being alone with him still. "Do you believe because I am a woman, I should favor pastel, peaceful landscapes?" she countered. How long had she been alone, when these artists' glorious masterpieces had been her company, and now there was another who knew those same wonders?

Another breeze pulled at his cloak. Lowering the book to his side, he briefly cupped her cheek. "No, because I can imagine you alone on those steep, lonely hills. You are a solitary creature, on the side of ballrooms, and hidden in libraries, and in hedge mazes, and yet there is a brightness to you that commands notice." Rakes and rogues were clever with their words and charm. They employed whispered endearments designed to break down a lady's defenses and she was wise to not fall prey to such senseless drivel. Cedric's words, however, had a weight and wealth and meaning to them that sucked at her breath.

Oh, God. As she leaned into his gentle caress, she tried to make sense of the warmth seeping into her heart. Men such as he did not see more than was there. They saw surface beauty and did not delve to the hidden, most important parts that made a person, them. That had been the case with her betrothed and even her parents. But this man saw…and it roused equal parts terror and wonder in her.

"There is beauty in it," she managed, as his hand fell to his side. Her skin pricking with the heated intensity of his gaze, Genevieve slipped the book from his grasp.

Standing so close their shoulders brushed, she flicked through the pages of collected oil paintings and sketches. At the intimacy of this stolen exchange, her fingers trembled and she sought the specifically folded page. She stopped abruptly and ran her palm down the *Fishermen at Sea* masterpiece that she'd studied well into the morning hours on countless lonely evenings in her exile.

"There seems such a loneliness to it," she murmured, more to herself. "As you said, a darkness." In those earliest days following the Duke of Aumere's betrayal, she'd stared bleary eyed at that darkly ominous image, lost in the impending doom hinted at. "Until I came to realize the fisherman was not alone. For the threatening waves that loom, there is the calm of the moon's presence and it lights the sky, showing that there are others there." As much as she'd mourned being cut off from her family, she'd found a soothing balm in the quiet countryside; in the star-studded night skies and the snowy winters days. Through it, she'd let herself believe that there would one day be another. Aware of Cedric's attention trained not on the page but on the top of her head, Genevieve stumbled back a step and knocked into the bench with such force she tumbled into a seated position.

"You were right to order me gone." His cerulean gaze threatened to bore through her. "You are suitably wary, Genevieve." Was his a warning? She'd be a fool to not heed it.

"I have reason to be," she whispered. Not many had given her reason to trust.

"Ah," he stretched out that syllable. "The former betrothed."

Genevieve jolted as his words hit her like a jab to the solar plexus. People did not freely speak of the Duke of Aumere's defection. Their whispers had somehow conveniently omitted that man's identity, while heaping all senseless blame on her. She tried to dredge up a suitable reply, should again send Cedric on his way, but there was…an ease around him. A falseness and sincerity all at the same time. Having spent the better part of five years insulating herself from hurt, she recognized Cedric's own artful attempts. With his effortless grin and guarded eyes, the Marquess of St. Albans may as well construct an entire fortress about him.

Another breeze filtered the air between them. It rustled his too-long, thick golden tresses, sending one tumbling over his brow, softening him, making him real—approachable, and not the sculpted model of masculine perfection able to command with a single look. He motioned to the wrought iron bench. "May I?"

She curled her fingers tight, hating this desire to run her hands through his tresses to explore their texture. "If I said no, would you leave?"

"Yes," he said automatically. "But I'd attempt to convince you otherwise."

Perhaps her soul *was* as wicked and wanton as she'd been accused, for she wanted to know what that convincing would entail. He stared at her pointedly and with a hesitant nod, she slid over onto the corner of the bench.

The marquess settled his tall, heavily muscled frame beside her, shrinking the space between them so that their legs touched. His cloak gaped slightly open. She swallowed hard. Unbidden, she stole a sideways look at the muscles of his thighs straining the fawn fabric of his front-flap breeches. Cheeks afire, she swiftly lifted her gaze, praying he'd not noted her scrutiny, and promptly stilled.

Head tipped back, with his eyes closed, the morning's rays bathed Cedric's face in sunlight. "Who was he?" he asked, unmoving from his repose so much that she blinked several times believing she'd imagined his question.

"My lord?" she asked tentatively.

"The gentleman to account for your wariness."

She drew her book closer. "It would hardly be appropriate to speak of such intimate matters."

"Bah, mine is hardly an intimate question." Opening his eyes, the marquess picked his head up and favored her with a slow, seductive grin. "Were I to ask you the scent of oil you place in your bathwater or the fragrance you dab behind your ears, now that, I would allow would be intimate...*for some.*"

Despite a suitable wariness where this man was concerned, a smile pulled at her lips. With his charm, he was a rogue who could coax the queen out of her chemise. "Tell me, my lord, do you work at shocking a lady?"

"Hardly." He winked. "I assure you, it comes quite naturally."

A laugh bubbled from her lips and it felt so wholly wonderful to be the laughing, bright-eyed young woman she'd been. *That saw you nothing but ruin...* She promptly slapped her hand over her mouth and stole a look about, as with that unexpected amusement logic was restored. He was a rake, a rogue, and all things forbidden. She'd not be so lax in her judgment again—not any more than she'd already been with this man. "You should not be here," she said again. "You came to apologize." When gentlemen made apologies for nothing. Not her father. Not the Duke of Aumere and his dastard brother. "Though I appreciate that gesture." Even as it roused skepticism in her breast. "But for you to remain, only raises further risk of..." Additional censure. She'd already been ruined.

"Who was he?" he asked instead.

She trembled. How easily he followed her unspoken thoughts. What game did this rake play? "Why would you have me speak of it?" Genevieve braced for a charming smile and a lie.

Instead, he held his palms up. "I do not know." They were words spoken with a quiet truth.

She narrowed her eyes suspiciously. Either she was the very greatest of fools or she'd been alone for so very long that she'd see friends in rakes. "Then you'll leave?"

He inclined his head.

Eying him warily, Genevieve wetted her lips.

Cedric unflinchingly met her stare.

A long sigh escaped her. She'd no doubt he'd wait until the sun set for the night before leaving this spot without a name. "The Duke of Aumere."

An inscrutable look flashed in his eyes and she wanted to know the meaning of it. Wanted to know what he thought about her being tossed over by a duke, on her wedding day no less. Instead of leaving, however, he stretched out and looped his ankles.

An exasperated sigh escaped her. "You promised to leave."

"Ah, but I did no such thing, Genevieve." He tugged the errant curl hanging over her brow. "I merely lifted my head in acknowledgement."

How free he was with his movements and words without worry of recrimination. It was she, however, who would bear the lash of Society's censure. Frustration stirred at a lot where women should be so judged, while men were free with their every movement and with that, reality intruded on this stolen interlude. "This is not a game, my lord," she bit out. Her father's earlier warnings that morning came rushing back, effectively dousing the haze cast by talks of artists and paintings.

He winged an eyebrow up. "Do you *want* me gone?"

No. She leapt to her feet and retreated several steps, placing much needed distance between them. "It is improper for you to be here."

Undeterred, he shoved lazily to his feet. "But do *you* want me gone?" he pressed with a dogged tenacity.

She should. She should want him on the opposite side of the world for the danger he presented and with the desire he roused. As his long-legged strides ate away the distance between them, her mouth went dry.

"Do you?" he prodded on a silken whisper that ran over her warmer than any summer sun.

With her pulse pounding madly, Genevieve forced words out. "Have I not said as much?"

"No," he brushed his thumb over her lower lip. "In fact, I've asked you three times with no real answer." The book tumbled once more to the earth, falling between them and her heart skipped a beat, then promptly tripled its rhythm. "You have spoken about propriety and decorum, but what do you want?"

I want your kiss. I want your kiss even as it goes against all judgment and fuels the sinful opinions about me...

He toyed with her lower lip. "What do you want?" he urged in seductive tones Satan himself would envy.

You...

Cedric claimed her mouth in a hard, hungry kiss. This was not the hesitant, gentle questing of the evening prior but rather an explosion of want and desire. He folded his hand about her nape, angling her to receive him, and with a breathless moan, she returned his kiss. Genevieve twined her hands through his hair reveling in the silken thickness of those loose curls. He parted her lips and slid his tongue inside, and the hint of coffee and cinnamon invaded her senses like a potent aphrodisiac. Their tongues tangled in a wild dance as old as time and he drew back.

She bit her lip at the loss of him, but he merely dragged his mouth down her neck, where he nipped at the place where her pulse beat for him.

"Genevieve," he whispered, nothing but her name, and her knees buckled.

He easily caught her and pulled her against the hard, muscled wall of his chest, anchoring her close. At the contact, her nipples pebbled hard against the fabric of her gown and desire; wicked and wanton, and all things wonderful flooded her senses, as she strained close, desperate for...she knew not what, only that she'd never known this explosive passion from any of her former betrothed's chaste kisses.

She sought his lips again and he raised his obligingly, returning her kiss. With every slant of his mouth, he ran his hands searchingly over her; the curve of her hip, her lower back, her buttocks, and heat exploded inside her and threatened to consume her in a fiery conflagration of desire.

"Lady Genevieve?" The distant call of her maid brought them apart.

Genevieve stood cloaked in a thick haze of desire and a slow-dawning horror. She frantically searched about.

"Here," he murmured, as with the same methodical precision of last evening, he put her hair to rights and then swiftly retrieved her book. His remarkable calm bespoke a gentleman accustomed to far too many close calls.

Her belly tightened as a green, vicious envy twisted inside.

"Lady Genevieve?" her maid's voice grew stronger as she drew closer.

Genevieve snatched the volume from his hands. "I am h-here, Delores." She flinched at the tremor to her words. Frantically, she whipped her head back. "Please," she whispered. "Surely you understand, as my every action is under scrutiny, I cannot see you again."

He put his lips close to her ear, and his breath fanned her skin, sending delicious shivers radiating out. "Do you truly want that?"

No. "It matters not what I want," she said on a pleading whisper.

Cedric placed a hard, quick kiss on her lips. "What you want should always matter." He took her by the shoulders and gave her a gentle nudge toward her maid's approaching footsteps. "And Genevieve?" he said in hushed tones, as she turned to go. She looked questioningly back. "Primrose." Her heart jumped. "By the scent upon your skin, I would wager it is primrose you place in your water."

CHAPTER 9

THE EMPTY SKETCHPAD LAY OPEN, the blank pages both mocking and tempting. Cedric sat staring at them, as he had for the better part of the hour. How many pages had he secretly filled before his bastard of a sire had ultimately discovered, and ended, all such trivial pursuits?

…my heir will not do something as foolish as to waste his time with frivolous pastimes. Find yourself a whore, not a bloody sketchpad…

The fury of that diatribe rang around the chambers of his mind, all these years later.

He'd loved sketching. Loved it when he'd really loved nothing. On the pages of those books, he'd found a peace and calm, and a sense of freeness from the constrained world where he was nothing more than a future duke. More, he'd forgotten how much he loved it until a too-brief conversation in Kensington Gardens that morning with a lady who both knew art and was unashamed and unapologetic in discussing it. Where he'd buried that desire to create, tossed his charcoals into the rubbish bin, and yet…he'd retained this old book.

Of their own volition, his fingers found the pen and, dipping it into the inkwell, he proceeded to mark the page. With each slash and slant of the pen, an amorphous image took shape. His hand flew frantically over the previously blank sheet and a long forgotten exultation fanned out dulling the ennui he'd known of late; an ennui which had not been solved by gaming or whoring or spirits.

The door bounced open with such force it slammed against the wall. "By God, I said find a respectable wife. I should expect you'd show up at my bloody ball and dance only once and with the Farendale doxy."

Cedric jerked his gaze up and cursed. His father stood framed in the doorway. The only hint of his barely concealed fury was the vein throbbing at the corner of his left eye. Quickly closing the book, Cedric dropped his pen. "Father." He forced an indolent grin and propped his feet on the edge of his desk. "To what do I owe the honor of this visit?" There had never been any father–son warmth between them. Theirs had been a relationship built on nothing but the unfortunate circumstance of blood and the obligations that went with that same blood.

His father kicked the door closed with the heel of his boot. "Goddamn it, you know what has brought me here." Yanking off his gloves the duke stomped across the room. He stopped at the edge of Cedric's desk and slapped his gloves together. "Put your bloody feet on the floor," he snapped, as though speaking to a recalcitrant child.

Alas, Cedric hadn't been a boy for a long time now. Rather, he'd been shaped into a cold, unyielding figure, masterfully crafted in his father's image. Lounging in his leather chair, Cedric folded his arms at his chest.

With a grunt, the duke slid into the opposite chair. "I could not have been clearer during my last visit."

Visit. Is that what the old bastard would call these meetings? This man had never been driven by familial devotion or regard, but rather for discussions on wealth and power. "Ah, yes," Cedric said, reveling in the way his father's eyebrow dipped. "The very important business of my securing a wife." Important business his father could hold his breath, all the way to hell, and wait for.

"I'll see you in hell before I'll see you wed the Farendale chit." If anything *could* entice him, well, it would be that small triumph over the duke's wishes.

With the depravity of his existence, he'd see him in hell, regardless.

Regardless, his father's worries over Cedric's dance with Genevieve Farendale were irrelevant. Although strangely enchanted by the guarded lady's peculiar interests, Cedric had as much intention of marrying as joining the bloody clergy. That truth, however, did not prevent him from some very deliberate needling "Come, Father, she is a marquess' daughter. Even you cannot fault the lady's birthright."

"She is a whore," his father said bluntly and all amusement left Cedric, replaced with a red haze of fury that sent his hands curling reflexively on the arms of his chair. What he wouldn't give to bloody the old bastard's face.

He swung his legs to the floor refusing to allow the duke to needle him. All the while, a seething fury ran through him. "Other than your dictatorial efforts for the selection of my future bride, is there anything else that has brought you here?" he asked, maintaining a thin grasp on his wavering control. When was the last time he'd been roused to this unholy rage at anything his father said or did? And because of Lady Genevieve Farendale. How in blazes could he account for that?

"A fortnight." The duke's terse utterance cut across his confounded thoughts.

A fortnight…?

"To select a bride," his father said with a triumphant smile on his hard lips. "If you fail to do so, I'll see you cut off from your creditors and funds, until you do decide to cooperate."

When Cedric had been a young man, he'd journeyed by ship to the Continent. Two days into his travels, a violent storm had ravaged the sea. In his fine quarters, Cedric had clung to the high-quality mattress, while his stomach in revolt, dipped and lurched. How very much this moment was to that long ago day.

"Nothing to say now?" his father waggled his eyebrows. "Where is the mocking grin and stinging wit?"

Cedric curled his hands reflexively upon the arms of his chair, his nails leaving crescent marks in the Italian leather. "You will not cut me off," he said at last. The only thing the duke cared about more than his title, was the way in which the world saw that title. Any hint of weakness or shame to that beloved status would shatter the bastard in ways that no emotion or feeling could.

The tightening of his father's mouth hinted at the truth to Cedric's supposition. "Perhaps," he said. "Perhaps not. But is that something you care to wager your security on?"

Yes, Cedric rather believed it was. He'd no interest in spreading the poisonous Falcot seed to some innocent miss, even if that innocent miss was desiring of nothing more than the title of duchess.

...I have no interest at all in the title of marchioness, duchess, or anything else...

"Get out," he said curtly.

And surprisingly, his father stood. "You do not wish to wed, Cedric, and I understand that more than most. The last thing I wanted was to marry your fool romantic of a mother." At the detached emotionality of that admission, a chill iced his spine. How very cold and callous the man was about the wife who'd given him his *precious* heir. "But we are not unalike," his father said pragmatically.

A thousand denials sprung to his lips and he wanted to snap and hiss at the other man for seeing any part of Cedric in him. Instead, he remained motionless, immobilized by the long-known truth. He *was* his father's son. He'd never put anyone's interests or pleasures before his own, and lived for his own physical gratification. The same ugly running through the duke's veins ran hot through his own. After all, in his mother turning Cedric fully over to her husband's control when he'd been a mere boy, she had seen that truth herself. And that had been his mother, who'd dedicated her last days on earth to her other child, Clarisse. What did that say when one's own mother saw her child as irredeemable at just eight?

His father tugged on his gloves. "I am pleased that you see logic," the duke said, misinterpreting the reason for Cedric's quiet. Without any hint of even false pleasantries, he left, closing the door with a decisive click behind him.

Cedric clenched and unclenched his hands as he fought for the restoration of his ordered thoughts and calm, and then with a furious string of curses, he surged to his feet so quickly, the legs of his leather chair scraped noisily along the floor.

He began to pace, a seething tension thrumming inside; a restless energy that threatened to consume him. He'd never been viewed as a person by either of his parents. His father had seen him as a ducal extension and, well, his mother had seen Cedric as an easy thread to snip off and turn over to her husband's care. Now, his father would seek to control him in this way. Never, more had he hated himself than he did in this instance. Hated himself for having lived an indolent life, dependent on all that came from the title he was born to.

His gaze locked on the closed leather book on his desk. With a black curse, Cedric came to a jerky stop. He swiped it off the otherwise smooth mahogany surface and opened it. The smudged rendering in ink, marred from when he'd hastily hid his work from his father's eyes, did little to conceal the sharp features and expressively sad eyes of the very woman his father had warned him away from.

Unnerved by the directness of her silent stare, Cedric yanked open his desk drawer and tossed the book inside. He needed to get bloody soused, find a whore; a hot, eager body who'd serve as a receptacle for his lust and frustration. Not necessarily in that order.

And so taking leave of his office, a short while later, seated at his private table at the back of Forbidden Pleasures, Cedric sipped from his glass of brandy. He passed a bored gaze over the unsavory club. The clink of coins hitting coins on gaming tables blended with the boisterous laughter of gentlemen and the whores who courted their favors.

Only the most dissolute lords and notorious scoundrels frequented the club and, as such, Cedric was far more comfortable with the company here than the polite, dull members of the peerage.

A sensuous woman with red curls caught his eye from across the club. In her frothy crimson gown that displayed her generous curves, she was a veritable feast he would have taken on any occasion. Perhaps on this very table. *Take her. She is what you've come for.* But her hair was a crimson shade and not the strawberry blonde of another. Christ. For some inexplicable reason, however, on this night, there was an ennui; as though he sat on the outside looking in at the wicked deeds being happily carried out by the base lords.

Powerful noblemen with experienced courtesans on their laps, and their hands buried up the skirts of those women. Whores who moved from one lord to the next, without a hint of compunction in their jaded faces. Restlessness surged through him and he took another long swallow.

For the first time in the course of his life, it had happened. He who'd fashioned himself as a rake and thrilled in the debauched life he lived in London, was…bored. And all because he'd met a lady who didn't give a jot about his title or his reputation as an expert lover.

He gave his head a frustrated shake. Of course it made sense. His life moved in a monotonous rhythm. Day in and day out he would visit his clubs. He would lose himself in the arms of widow after widow. He would place obscene wagers; wagers which he more often than not, won. Every day folded over into a remarkably similar day. That was the logical explanation for this bothersome fascination with Lady Genevieve and her moss green eyes filled with rebuke.

"Now you visit your clubs," the droll voice of Montfort brought his head quickly up. Without seeking permission, his friend yanked a wide backed chair out and plunked himself into it.

"Montfort." Cedric shoved his half-empty bottle across the table and the other man easily grabbed it.

"You know with your attendance at that goddamn ball last evening, I lost a bloody fortune." He motioned over the red-haired buxom beauty who'd been previously making eyes at Cedric. She sauntered over with a glass, poured a snifter full, and then promptly climbed onto the earl's lap.

"Yes, you said as much. You should wager less." The wry note to his words earned a snort from Montfort.

"First attending your father's dull affairs, then waltzing at the bloody event, and now talking of giving up wagering?" A chuckle spilled past the other man's lips. "What is next? Attending Lady Erroll's dull dining affair this evening and selecting a bride from those assembled chits?" he asked. Running a hand up the woman's skirt he rubbed the expanse of her cream white thigh. He paused and wagged his eyebrows. "Mayhap the Farendale, chit? Hmm?"

With the memory of his father's threat resonating in his mind, a dull flush heated Cedric's neck. His fingers twitched with the need to yank at his suddenly too-tight cravat. He'd rather dance through the fires of hell than bind himself to a single woman. "There are no worries there," he said with a forced grin. Having been friends since Eton, Montfort well knew the vow Cedric had taken to never wed and propagate the bloody Falcot line. He cared even less for that ducal title than he did for his bastard of a father.

While Montfort busied himself with the whore on his lap, Cedric took another swallow of his drink. Another wave of restiveness ran through him. He'd vowed to never wed. He'd vowed to never spill his seed inside a woman and litter the world with children, legitimate or illegitimate, the way his father had. He had ensured that never occurred by always using French letters when in the throes of passion. The corrupt blood in his veins was a mark the world was assuredly better without, and it would bring Cedric the ultimate triumph to steal that power from his father. No, he took his pleasures with guarded caution and lived for his own physical gratification. But when the thrill of that sinful living dulled and left nothing but numbness in its place, what was there?

"You are quiet," his friend put in casually, as he released the woman's breasts from the low décolletage. The mounds tumbled forth on lewd display and Montfort swiftly palmed the magnificent orbs, earning a small moan for his attentions.

Cedric squirmed. Once he wouldn't have blinked at the other man's casual display with a luscious courtesan. He was growing stodgy in his older years. There was no other explaining his distaste. "Am I?" He knew he was. Montfort knew it. But they did not probe on matters that moved beyond whores, wagers, and spirits.

The earl planted a kiss atop each of the whore's breasts and then shoved her from his lap. A small moue of displeasure formed on her lips, as she landed on her feet. "Perhaps later, sweet." Softening his rejection, he swatted her on the backside, and gave a wink.

With a promise in her eyes, the woman adjusted the bodice of her gown and sauntered off, leaving Cedric and Montfort alone.

Finishing his drink, Cedric reached for the bottle.

"Never tell me this *is* about the Farendale chit."

His hand jerked and he knocked the bottle over. He shot a hand out to steady the decanter but it tumbled over the edge of the table and shattered. He ignored the faintly curious looks cast his way. And because his friend was shockingly, uncomfortably too close to the mark, he said in hushed tones, "My father would see me wed. I've a fortnight to select a bride." The way a man might settle on a broodmare.

The usual mocking glint in Montfort's eyes receded, as the veneer he'd long adopted now cracked revealing a flash of the man under the cold sheen of ice. "He would not dare." For even Montfort knew the Duke of Ravenscourt cared for the appearances about the title above all else.

He shrugged and looked out at the gaming hell, once more. "Mayhap." But mayhap not. There was no saying what the duke would dare or not dare in the name of his title. After all, how many bastards had he denied to protect the wealth of the Ravenscourt fortune?

The earl drummed his fingertips in a grating rhythm and Cedric favored him with a frown. "What?" he asked curtly.

Montfort continued that infuriating tapping. "Mayhap the Farendale chit could prove useful to you, after all."

Shooting a frantic glance about at the lords seated nearby, he bit out on a furious whisper. "What are you on about?"

His friend took a long swallow of his drink. "Why, I merely mean no one will dare wed that one," he said, as he set his glass down. "She doesn't have a hope of asking for more than an ancient lord in need of an heir. Why, in wedding you, it would be the perfect marriage of convenience." As soon as the words left Montfort, he erupted into a bellowing laugh.

Through the man's loud mirth that attracted curious looks, Cedric sat frozen. What the earl proposed was madness. The lady certainly desired, undoubtedly deserved, more than London's most infamous rake, who'd give her a name and nothing more. But a thought trickled in of her hidden away in the hedge maze and in the library.

"Forgive me," the earl said wiping tears of hilarity from his cheeks. "It was not my intention to make light of your situation. A little levity was called for."

He jolted. "Of course." Of course it had been a jest. But as they sat sipping their brandy, the niggling seed planted by Montfort rooted around Cedric's mind. Bloody mad thought. The height of preposterous. He downed his drink and came to his feet. "If you'll excuse me."

The earl looked at him with surprise. "Where are you off to, man?"

"I've remembered I've a previous engagement for the evening." Not allowing Montfort to pose any questions, Cedric turned on his heel and stalked out of the club.

Mayhap he was more than a bit mad.

CHAPTER 10

GENEVIEVE SAT STIFFLY ON THE carriage bench beside Gillian; her body taut with tension over of the Countess of Erroll's impending formal dinner party.

"This will be good," Father boomed. "The sooner the *ton* sees you and the duke are civil and there is no resentment, then the sooner this can be past us."

Us. When had it ever been us? Not when she'd been scuttled away to her grandfather's estate, while the rest of her loyal family remained in London and in their country seat during the summers.

She tightened her mouth. "Oh, yes," she said dryly. "This will be splendid." What good could there come in being in the same room as her former betrothed other than putting her on display like a circus oddity? Nor were hers the sentiments of a broken-hearted woman. Her feelings for that cad had died a quick death following his treachery. On the days she did not hate herself for having foolishly believed herself in love with the Duke of Aumere, she hated him and his lying tongue that had seen her ruined.

Gillian laid her hand over Genevieve's and gave a slight squeeze. She took comfort in that unspoken reassurance. For she was no longer alone. There was Gillian. And for two brief, but meaningful exchanges, there had been Cedric.

Bah, you foolish woman, building castles out of clouds. Her romantic whimsy had led to her ruin the first time, and yet…in just a hand-ful of exchanges with the Marquess of St. Albans she'd shared far more meaningful discourse than anything she'd uttered with and to the Duke of Aumere, all those years ago.

"Yes, yes, Lord Ellsworth is indeed correct," Mother said pull-ing her to the moment. "And of course there is the Duchess of Aumere. Why, everyone is, no doubt, anticipating that exchange, as well."

Her sister shot her a sideways look and Genevieve gave her a reassuring smile. Given her relationship with the duke, of course most would expect there to be resentment for the woman who'd secured that gentleman's hand. Genevieve leaned close and whis-pered into her sister's ear. "I consider myself fortunate that it was her, and not me, forever bound to that man."

"Oh, undoubtedly," Gillian returned on an equally hushed whisper. "She saved you from marrying where your heart is not engaged and now you are free to find your true love."

At the hopeful naïveté, Genevieve's chest tightened. How romantic Gillian was; believing in good, honorable gentleman and forever loves. And though those might, indeed, be realities for un-whispered about fey beauties like her sister, no good, honor-able gentleman cared to have a wife whose name was muddied more than the London streets.

"What are you two whispering about?" their father barked.

Forever incapable of artifice, Gillian flushed, opening and clos-ing her mouth several times.

"We are speaking about how lovely tonight will be," Genevieve easily put in for them. "You are, indeed, correct. It will be wonder-ful to have this meeting concluded."

She was saved from answering any further questions as the car-riage rolled up to the Countess of Erroll's white stucco townhouse, awash in candlelight. A driver pulled the door open and Father angled his sizeable frame through the entrance. The liveried driver handed the marchioness down and then held his gloved palm out to Gillian.

Her younger sister paused. "I would have you know that you are not alone," she said fervently. "You have me tonight."

Emotion wadded in her throat. "Thank you."

Gillian looked affronted. "Why, do not thank me. We are sisters *and* friends." She waggled her eyebrows. "And if you need me to quite accidentally drop my white soup on him, then I am happy to oblige."

A laugh spilled past Genevieve's lips and the servant stuck his head inside the carriage. With a cheerful thanks, her younger sister accepted the young man's assistance.

Drawing in a deep breath, with a fortitude that came from her sister's pledge of support, Genevieve followed suit. As her gray skirts settled about her ankles, she looked up at the impressive Mayfair townhouse. Focusing on the soft tread of her footsteps, she fixed her gaze forward, thinking of Kent in the summer, thinking of Turner's sailors at sea, thinking of Cedric and their talk at Hyde Park.

Would he be here? As a powerful future duke, even with his reputation as rake, his attendance would surely be sought at any event. As she stepped inside and turned her cloak over to a waiting footman, a breathless anticipation filled her. Not for the impending meeting with her former betrothed, but another; a stranger she'd freely spoken to on intimate matters she'd not shared with anyone before.

Following after the butler, they were led through the halls of the impressive labyrinth of a home belonging to her mother's closest friend. As they approached the parlor, the noisy chatter of assembled guests filtered through the open door.

Her ears attuned for a low, smooth baritone of one, and that blessed distraction kept her from thinking of the fact that the moment she entered the room, she would be the center of scrutiny and discussion. Her palms grew moist, as her earlier resolve faltered. *Coward.*

"You are no coward," Gillian said softly.

She started. Had she spoken aloud? It really was a bothersome tendency she'd adopted alone in the country, painting and gardening most of her days.

A twinkle lit her sister's pretty green eyes. "You said nothing. But remember, I'm your sister. I've always known what you were thinking."

As they made to enter the room, their mother looked back. *Pretty faces,* she mouthed. When she'd returned her attention forward, Genevieve touched the tip of her tongue to her nose, earning a laugh from her sister.

And a prompt scowl from their mother.

"The Marquess and Marchioness of Ellsworth, and Ladies Farendale."

And even as she'd been expecting it, the jarring halt to the earlier revelry sent heat up her neck and burned her face. The moment ticked on with infinite slowness and angling her shoulders slightly, she kept her gaze at the tops of the guests who filled Lady Erroll's parlor. A person needn't be looking at people to feel their states and, in this case, the approximately twenty or so stares.

Genevieve's skin pricked under their focus and she concentrated on drawing steady, even breaths. Her toes twitched with the urge to flee. To run from this room and continue running away from London to a place where happiness existed for those whispered about ladies, condemned by Society for crimes they'd not committed.

Then time resumed, in the form of whisperings and the intermittent laugh.

Her sister smiled brightly. "See, that was not so awful," she said with her patent cheer. She slid her arm through Genevieve's and patted her hand.

"Hardly," she said with a wry grin. From across the room, her gaze caught Francesca Cornworthy. Seated on the pink upholstered sofa, the young woman peered around the room with bored eyes when their stares collided. Her face lit up and she gave an eager wave.

"Gillian?"

The sisters looked as one to their mother who stood a short distance away, conversing with Lady Erroll's dandified son. Not Gillian and Genevieve. Rather, just Gillian. The only daughter their parents had hopes of making a respectable match.

Decision warred on her sister's face. Genevieve had no doubt of her sister's loyalty and friendship that Gillian would, in fact, do something as outrageous as ignore their mother's public request. She, however, could not let Gillian brave the wrath of their parents' for her. "Go," Genevieve urged. "I see a friend."

Her sister started. "A friend, you say?" Then she captured Genevieve's hands. "Oh, truly?" She spoke with the same excited awe as if she'd declared she had a formal suitor.

"Miss Francesca Cornworthy," she said, motioning faintly to the forgotten woman in the corner.

"I must meet her," Gillian said excitedly.

"Gillian," their mother said, her tone more insistent.

"Go," Genevieve said again. "Mother has a suitor."

Her sister followed her stare to the young Earl of Erroll. The candlelight shone on the thick wax in his Byronic curls. His interested and just a slightly inappropriate gaze remained on Gillian.

Her sister sighed. "Very well." With slow steps, that only earned a deeper frown from their parents, Gillian made her way to the earl.

And as utterly miserable as it was being cast out by Society, there was an unexpected freeness that came in being spared from their parents' scheming machinations to see her wed. They'd quite happily and eagerly orchestrated her meeting with the Duke of Aumere all those years ago and, as such, she could do without another carefully selected gentleman. She cast a quick look back to where her innocent sister now conversed with the leering gentleman. A frown turned Genevieve's lips. Her parents would see their youngest daughter with another heartless, dishonorable cad, all to secure a title and respectability for her. Nay, it was about more than respectability for Gillian. It was about a restored sense of honor to the marquess and marchioness.

If she ever had children, which she assuredly would not because of the whole lack of suitor and husband business, then she would put that child first. She'd never impose her will or Society's expectations, but rather love and nurture in ways her own parents had remarkably failed.

Genevieve came to a stop before Francesca, who hopped up from her seat.

"Oh, I am so happy to see you," the woman exclaimed before she could say anything.

"And I you." That warm greeting was really the greatest kindness Genevieve had known since she'd entered Lady Erroll's.

An older, reed thin gentleman with a shock of white hair, climbed more slowly up, and Genevieve went still. The hazel eyes marked him as the Viscount Dailey. "Lady Genevieve," he greeted, his voice booming. "A pleasure, indeed. Francesca has told me so very much about you." He patted his daughter's hand. "I will allow you ladies to speak. No need to have a bothersome papa underfoot."

"You are never a bother," Francesca said adamantly and leaning up on tiptoe, kissed his cheek in an affectionate display that only earned censorious stares.

She took in the kindness sparkling in his eyes and the sincere smile on his lips. How was it possible there was this warmth between a parent and child? Envy tugged at her heart, witnessing the devotion of a gentleman who'd indulge even a scandalous friendship for his daughter, if she so wished.

A young woman seated on the chair across from Francesca promptly stood and sailed off in a huff. At that cut-direct, Genevieve's neck went hot. "I am so happy," and relieved, "you are here," she confided. For as miserable as London had been these now sixteen days, there had been kindness from the lovely woman…

And Cedric. There had also been an apology and a meaningful talk of art from that unlikeliest of figures.

Francesca slipped her arm through Genevieve's. "Come, let us walk. You must tell me about that skill you possess." Less than discreetly, she motioned to the departing wallflower. "For five years I've endured so much miserable company and, yet, you have this ease of just," she snapped her fingers once, "ridding yourself of them."

A startled laugh escaped Genevieve, earning reproachful stares from the surrounding guests.

A companionable silence fell between them, as they walked slowly along the perimeter of the room. Unbidden, she sought a taller, golden-haired gentleman who knew of Friedrich and Turner out amidst the guests.

"He does not come to these affairs."

She cast a startled glance at her partner in misery.

Francesca leaned close and dropped her voice to a faint whisper. "Your waltzing partner."

Genevieve shot her gaze about to determine whether anyone had overheard. Alas, who would have attention for two wallflowers; even the scandalous Farendale one. "I don't—"

The young woman snorted. "I saw tapping toes, Genevieve," she reminded her.

Promptly closing her mouth, Genevieve let her false protest wither.

They looked to the front of the room as a servant came to announce dinner. "I do hope you at least have a pleasant guest who doesn't slurp his soup and chat about his hounds," Francesca whispered. She sighed. With the station difference between them, she'd never be graced with the young woman as a dining partner. Which begged the question—

"Lady Genevieve, I have learned I have the honor of partnering you for dinner."

A chill ran along her spine as that smooth, polished voice sounded beyond her shoulder. No. Surely her mother's friend would at the very least spare her this humiliation and not use her as an oddity on display. Then what was the basis of those two matrons' friendship? She stiffened and on numb legs, turned.

He was softer around the middle, with slightly fuller cheeks, but the chestnut hair that hung to his shoulders marked him the same. The same man who'd betrayed her and ruined her, and who even now stood smiling before her. As though they were friends. As though he'd not shattered her world with the lies on his lips.

Aware of Francesca staring between them and the flash of concern that lit her eyes, Genevieve's fingers curled into reflexive balls. For an instant, she thought to flee. This was a world she wanted no part of, so why subject herself to this public humiliation? But she would be damned if she slunk off like a coward in the night for his treachery. "Y-Your Grace," she greeted and sank into a curtsy. God, how she despised the faint tremor to that word.

"May I present my wife, Her Grace, Duchess of Aumere?"

Was he mad?

An icy revulsion seeped from the flawless golden beauty's blue eyes. "How do you do, Lady Genevieve?" By the loathing that coated her words, she'd gladly see Genevieve in hell.

Francesca gave her a slight nudge, startling her into movement. She dropped a curtsy. "Your Grace, the pleasure is mine," she lied.

The duke proffered his arm and, for a sliver of a moment, Genevieve considered leaving him as he was and curtly rejecting that offering. The *ton*, however, would erroneously view that as testament for resentment and envy. She slid her fingertips onto his elbow and allowed him to escort her to the dining room, in absolute stoic silence.

Her sister on the arm of Lord Erroll, shot a quick, concerned look over her shoulder.

"You look as beautiful as you always did, Genevieve," His Grace said, the words so faintly spoken, she strained to hear.

She flexed her jaw. Did the man truly speak of her beauty with all of London's most respectable guests watching on?

"Nothing to say, sweetheart?"

"I am not your sweetheart," she bit out tightly.

They filed into the dining room and as they found their respective seats, their chairs were pulled out. With thanks to the young servant, Genevieve slid into the chair and promptly ignored the duke. Society, her parents, the duke, they could all go hang. She'd not be baited and taunted by this man.

The first course of the customary white soup was set before the assembled guests. Even as her stomach churned from being thrust beside the duke, as long as she was eating, she'd be spared from speaking. Picking up her spoon, Genevieve raised a spoonful to her mouth.

"I never believed you would be so ruined, Genevieve. You must believe that."

She choked on her bite and setting the silverware down with a noisy clatter, she grabbed her water and took a swallow. "Are you mad?" she seethed. With those words, he revealed himself to be either a demmed fool or a bloody arrogant bastard. Then, he was no doubt both. "Did you think I would just be a little ruined?" All ruin was the same. In a Society where a lady's virtue and familial connections mattered above all else, there was no recovering from a blight upon, either.

From across the table, her sister caught her eye and gave her a look of support, and pleading which served to ground her.

"This is hardly the place to discuss such a matter, Your Grace," she said, priding herself on the smooth, even deliverance of those words, when she wanted nothing more than to hurl the contents of her glass in his arrogant face.

"Then where can we speak?" he asked with an urgency in his question.

"In hell on a Sunday," she said with a forced smile, grateful when the gentleman on her opposite side paid her an obligatory remark that required answering.

As she sat through the infernal affair, she counted the passing seconds, as they rolled into minutes. Each moment signaled a point closer to the end of this display and through it, resentment built inside. Not for this heartless cad beside her, but for the parents who'd subject her to this gross humiliation. All to what end? To appease the gossips?

A slight clamor at the front of the room provided a brief diversion and she looked absently as the butler appeared with an unpunctual guest, who no doubt thought the world was his…

Her breath caught. Attired in immaculate black breeches and an equally midnight coat, the snowy white cravat, loosely folded, hinted at a gentleman who didn't give a jot about time or whether that measurement stopped altogether. Cedric did a quick sweep of the room, before his gaze ultimately landed on her. The heat of his eyes threatened to bore through her. Why was he here? Why, when by Francesca's own admission he was a man to studiously avoid polite affairs?

"Lord St. Albans," Lady Erroll called out eagerly. "You are late, my boy."

"Forgive me, madam," he returned with his usual charming half-grin. "I was recently given a valuable lesson on punctuality, so you must forgive me." He directed those words to Genevieve.

"It seems you might benefit from another," she said, chortling at her own jest, while the other guests laughed about her.

"Indeed, madam." He slid his gaze briefly to Genevieve once more. "It is a lesson I'd very much welcome, too."

Her skin burned hot and not at his slight teasing but rather the remembered feel of his hands on her person, the masculine scent of him.

Their hostess thumped the table. "Prepare a spot at the head for Lord St. Albans," she instructed a footman. "Not every day I have a duke *and* a future duke at my table." She chortled. Within moments, a setting had been laid, and a servant showed him to his respective seat, on a slight diagonal from where Genevieve sat… beside, Gillian and an unfamiliar lady.

Ever charming as only a rake could be, he politely engaged the young woman beside him. An unwelcome, unwanted, and decidedly unpleasant sentiment ripped through Genevieve. Something that felt very nearly like jealousy, and…an unfair anger that he should be so casual and calm while she'd been plopped alongside her bloody former betrothed.

Cedric looked her way and her cheeks warmed at being caught studying him. As indecent as it was to hold his eyes from across the table, his powerful stare locked with hers. Did he remember their kiss even now? Was he thinking of their talks of art and…? He inclined his head in a polite, perfunctory manner and then with an infuriating calm, turned his attention to the guest at his opposite side. Gillian.

An ugly jealousy unfurled within her. It tightened the muscles of her stomach and curled her toes until her feet ached, as the pair so easily conversed. For gentlemen like the Marquess of St. Albans assuredly did not wed…until they had to and when they did, they invariably married those bright-eyed, optimistic ladies like her ethereal sister and not said lady's long in the tooth, too pale sister with a fiery scandal to match her strawberry tresses.

Genevieve had convinced herself all these years that she was content with the practical life devoid of emotional connections. She'd convinced herself that she'd become a practical, logical, sensible woman; a woman well past the bloom of her first blush, content to sketch and pour over her books of art. Only to be proven a liar before the same Society who'd cast her out.

She wanted so much more.

Things she would never have. A family, an art room of her own, a garden with which to tend…

"I want you still."

A dull humming filled her ears and she slowly turned her head. "I beg your pardon." Surely she'd imagined the duke's words. Surely he was not so very brazen, so bloody arrogant that he'd—

"My circumstances were dire and your finances were not enough." The duke spoke with the same boredom he might in discussing the weather. She sat numb. That is why he'd jilted her? For a fatter purse? Not for anything beyond the material. He'd ruined her life because of his craving and *need* for wealth. She curled her fingers tight about her spoon to still their tremble, all the while wanting to rake her nails over his face.

"I never stopped wanting you, Genevieve." He spoke the way he might praise a worthy mount and she gritted her teeth. The duke leaned close. "And there is no reason we cannot still be together," he whispered and slid his hand under the table.

She froze as with his large, gloved hand he squeezed her thigh ringing an outraged gasp from her lips. The spoon slipped from her fingers, clattering noisily upon the rim of the porcelain bowl. At the peculiar looks thrown her way, she swiftly smoothed her features. It wouldn't do to be discovered with the venerable Duke of Aumere with his hand caressing her leg. Of course, she'd be the one to blame for encouraging him so. Fighting to quell the fury sucking at her rational thoughts, she discreetly placed her hand on her lap and made to move His Grace's fingers, but he retained his hold.

"It could be so wonderful between us, sweetheart." His stale, wine-scented breath slapped her cheek.

"I've instructed you once. Do not call me sweetheart" With unsteady fingers, she grabbed her glass. Water droplets splashed over the crystal rim. "Remove your hand, Your Grace," she said using her goblet to shield her lips.

He responded by moving his hand higher, sliding his fingers between the juncture of her thighs, bunching the fabric in a noisy manner. She froze as a thick curtain of rage descended over her vision, momentary blinding. How dare he disparage her name with his lies and now sully her with his indecent touch? Suddenly, the hatred she'd carried for him and the cold world in which they dwelled snapped. With a hiss, Genevieve hurled the contents of her glass in his face, gleefully relishing the way he choked and sputtered.

Gasps went up about the table. The sound faintly dulled by the rasp of her own frantic breathing.

Those loose chestnut strands, hung limp over the duke's brow, as His Grace sat immobile, water dripping from his face.

Oh, God.

Reality pulled back the earlier rage and hatred, leaving in its place, a slow-building horror. The collection of guests, Genevieve included, watched in stupefied shock as the duke dabbed at his face with the crisp fabric of his dining napkin and then as one, the entire table looked to her.

Francesca with pride and encouragement.

Gillian with her usual gentle concern.

Her gaze collided briefly with Cedric's thickly hooded lashes and unable to meet his stare, she fixed on but two pairs of enraged eyes. A mottled flush marred her parents' equally fleshy cheeks. Wordlessly, she shoved back her chair, rose to her feet, and then walked from the room with her head held high.

Her father's warning to "Attract No Notice" blared in her mind as she made her undignified march away.

CHAPTER 11

NOT FOR THE FIRST TIME, in the course of the same week Cedric found himself remarkably...awake before the noon hour. And more remarkably—alert.

Seated at the breakfast table with his steaming black coffee at hand and his plate untouched, Cedric scanned the front of *The Times*.

In another shameful scandal, Lady G.F., the elder amidst Lady Erroll's esteemed guests gathered to dine, dumped her bowl of white soup on the Duke of A's lap. The lady's actions speak to her fury at having been denied the distinguished title of Duchess.

It is also said...

Cedric tossed the paper down beside him, where it landed with a fluttery thump. The whole of the *ton* had even less sense than he'd credited them over the years, which was saying a good deal. The closest to truth that had existed on the page was that white soup had, in fact, been served. Beyond that, however, the sheets contained nothing more than fabricated truths, manipulated by the lords and ladies who'd been in attendance, and churned out by a paper to spread through respectable households.

He grabbed his coffee and blew on the steaming brew. Though, in his estimation, the lady's magnificent show with her glass of water had been too splendid for the papers to fail to properly report the detail. Before humiliation had burned her cheeks, there had been fire. It had lit her eyes ablaze and spoke of the passion he'd already tasted in her kiss.

What had precipitated that display? Did Genevieve, in fact, harbor sentiments for that fop, Aumere? He frowned over the top of his glass. Surely the thoughtful, spirited creature he'd met in the park had more sense to have any affection for one such as Aumere?

His mouth tightened reflexively and he forced his lips to relax. It hardly mattered whether the lady wanted to tup Aumere or Prinny himself, or *any* gentleman. What *did,* however, matter was that very public display and her rushed departure…and his own father's recent threats.

For with the sole reason he'd accepted an invitation to Erroll's deucedly dull affair gone, and a scandal left in her wake, Cedric had sat, grinning at the appropriate moments and adding a charming repartee as needed. All the while, his mind had worked through the implications of Genevieve's actions…and what that could, nay, would mean for him. After years of swearing to never wed and propagate the Falcot line, his hand had been suitably forced. Really, forced through his own recklessness these years with funds left him by his mother. Where the prospect of wedding a proper, demure lady caused his palms to dampen and his gut to churn, following Genevieve's breathtaking display, the earlier seed planted by Montfort had grown. And following his departure of that infernal–after–she'd–left affair, the seed had continued to grow.

He required a wife. However, he'd little interest in a proper miss who was expecting babes and a bucolic tableau of marital affection and pretend bliss. What Cedric required was…a wife. Nothing more. Nothing less. What woman, however, would give up the dream of a family and be content with a rake for a husband, living a life where they each carried on their own, very separate existences. Until just this week, he'd have said such a paragon did not exist.

Then Lady Genevieve had stolen into his father's library.

Now he knew that paragon was, indeed, real. A slow grin formed on his lips and he took a long swallow of his drink. Setting his glass down hard beside him, he grabbed the scandal sheet once more. Working his gaze over the page, he quickly found her name; bold and dark and so very damning.

With two scandals now tied to the lady's name, not a single, respectable gentleman would offer Genevieve Farendale his name.

Fortunately for the lady, the last thing he wanted, desired, or needed was respectability.

But what about what Genevieve desires?

A frown drove away his smile. Beyond the physical gratification he was sure each woman who warmed his bed knew in his arms, he'd never been one to think of a lady's desires beyond that. Those creatures had all been the same. They craved wealth and title and expensive baubles.

His gaze remained trained on Genevieve's name. For in just a handful of meetings, the lady had proven herself remarkably unlike all others. From the skirts she wore, to her loathing for those lofty titles, and her desire for solitary time in the garden of Hyde Park, she did not fit with what he knew of ladies of the *ton*. Yet, everyone wanted something. What did she want? And more, how difficult would it be to convince the lady who'd been shunned and shamed by Society that she could find freedom from all that censure?

Loathe the title as she might for the perceived attention it would bring, as a future duchess, she could move freely, just for the rank afforded her.

Footsteps sounded in the hall and he looked up expectantly at his butler in the entrance.

"Your mount has been readied, my lord."

He inclined his head in acknowledgement and as the other man turned on his heel, Cedric remained rooted to his chair. For despite his efforts to convince himself of the logic in offering for a lady who had very few options in the marriage market, and his own need of a bride, his insides twisted in vicious knots at the prospect of forever binding himself to a single person. His parents' union had been a publically miserable one and, given his own similarities to his sire, he could never be a devoted, respectable husband.

But mayhap, given Genevieve's circumstances, that would not matter to the lady. Mayhap, if they both entered into the match with reason and logic, recognizing it as a business arrangement and nothing more, then the misery he'd witnessed in his own mother before she'd left him to her husband's efforts would be avoided altogether.

Cedric tapped the rim of his nearly empty glass, distractedly. If he went into the union with the terms clearly laid out, spelled in such a way that the match was mutually beneficial to the both of them, then there would be no worry over entangled hearts or future babes or…well, anything that surely mattered to most women. All matters he wanted no part of. His lips pulled in a grimace.

Except, laying it out in a cold, perfunctory manner, he was forced to recognize that what he would offer to Genevieve Farendale was hardly the romantic match craved by whimsical chits. And make no doubt, for the lady's clearheaded words and logic in his presence, one who stole into the gardens of Hyde Park and sketched in the privacy of her own company was possessed of a whimsical fancy.

Even with that, she was still the logical choice. They got on well in one another's company; like friends, if there was ever such a thing as a gentleman forming a friendship with a young lady. She had her heart broken before and no doubt wished to avoid that likelihood again, at all costs. And, of course, the very obvious fact being they both required a spouse.

Fueled by that, Cedric finished his nearly cool coffee and set the glass down hard. He shoved back his chair and before he proceeded to create a list of all the folly in his intentions for the day, he started for the door. As he strode through the crimson-carpeted halls, he took in the scandalous portraits hanging on the walls and the dark, heavy furniture best suiting a bachelor's residence. The possibility of sharing these rooms with a young lady sent terror churning in his belly.

It will be nothing more than a business arrangement…a convenient arrangement made only sweeter by the desire raging between them.

And that was, of course, assuming the lady said yes. Given Genevieve's wariness around him and her own past, she was wiser than most women and knew better than to wed a rake. Of course, the lady surely knew by now he could show her more pleasure than she'd ever known her body capable of.

Cedric reached the foyer and accepted the cloak from his waiting butler and then his hat. As Avis hurried over and pulled the door open, Cedric stalled. The moment he stepped through that front door and inside the Marquess of Ellsworth's townhouse, he'd be abandoning a lifelong pledge he'd taken to thwart his father's wishes for him. *Not truly*, a voice reassured at the back of his head. There would still never be that coveted heir and a spare to secure the line. Instead, it would carry on through a distant relative his father disapproved of. Fueled by that assurance, Cedric jammed his black Oxonian on his head, and before his courage deserted him, strode over to the front door and stepped outside.

Having convinced himself of this madness, all that remained was bringing Genevieve Farendale around to his way of thinking.

CHAPTER 12

$\mathcal{S}$EATED ON THE FLOOR OF the nursery room with her sketch-pad on her lap Genevieve let her fingers fly over the page. With each slash and stroke of the charcoal, the frustration and rage and restlessness rose to the surface.

Bloody bastards.

Her frantic movements sent a curl tumbling over her brow and she blew it back, not pausing to brush it back. All of them. Her loathsome, former betrothed, who'd so disrespect her. Her father who would hold her to blame. Her mother who would let him hold her to blame. Every last one of them, along with Lady Erroll and her guests could go to the devil.

The charcoal scratched noisily upon the page, as the half-grinning gentleman's face materialized upon the sheet, revealing the charming, roguish, and, importantly, distracting Cedric Falcot, Marquess of St. Albans.

She bent her head, concentrating on the thick strands of his tousled hair. She had always loved charcoal and, in this moment, hated it for its failure to capture the thickened golden hue of sunshine and barley fields. At last, Genevieve paused and assessed the partially completed sketch of the gentleman as he'd been last evening. Seated beside her sister. He'd been the only guest at Lady Erroll's who'd not had horror or glee stamped on his face. Instead, there had been that inscrutable expression; an almost nonchalant air of a person so thoroughly bored by it all. Society. The gossip. The falsities. And there was something so very riveting, so captivating, in that. For in a moment of another public shame, there had been someone who'd not looked at her with pity or scorn.

A faint click cut into her musings and she glanced up suddenly.

Gillian closed the door. Unlike all the previous times since Genevieve's return when she hovered uncertainly, this time she closed the door without request. "I thought I might find you here."

Yes, because even for the four years of age separation between them, they'd once been the best of friends. Hadn't her younger sister found her here before all others on the night of her wedding? With an absolute want for words, she said, "Hello, Gillian." For what else was there to talk about?

Her sister strolled forward and in one effortless move, sank to the floor in a flurry of white skirts. They settled about her, as she dragged her legs close to her chest in a way that would have sent their mother into a fit of vapors. "Father has…" Her words trailed off and, belatedly, Genevieve followed her gaze downward.

Heat streaked across her cheeks as she quickly snapped the damning sketchpad closed. As much as she loved Gillian and had only called her friend, there was something too intimate, too personal, in sharing her unwitting fascination with the Marquess of St. Albans.

Thankfully, her sister continued and let the matter go unsaid. "Father sent your maid looking for you."

She sighed. "Of course he did." Just as she'd been unable to hide forever all those years ago, now was no exception. Ultimately she was located, summoned, and brought before her father—the arbiter and executioner of her fate.

Gillian rubbed her chin back and forth over her ruffled skirts. "Do you care to talk about it?" she asked tentatively.

Genevieve stilled, horribly motionless. Exposed by her sister's discovery and then…

"I've no doubt he deserved it," her sister continued. "You'd never have thrown your water in his face unless he'd gravely insulted you."

As the meaning of her words sank in, she blinked. Of course with the flurry of whispers following her ignominious departure and her family's slightly delayed retreat from Lady Erroll's, the real

matter that *should* command Genevieve's attention were the implications of her behavior last evening. And yet, it wasn't. Instead, she
was distracted by a rake who'd witnessed that humiliation. What
had Cedric, a man so coolly elegant and in possession of his every
emotion, thought of such a display? She gave her head a disgusted
shake.

"Did he?" her sister asked, pulling her back to the moment.
"Deserve it, that is."

She tightened her mouth. "He most assuredly did." Genevieve
curled her fingers hard about the leather book in her hands. Her
nails left crescent marks on the soft leather. "Father will never see
it that way." She was unable to keep the bitterness from tingeing
her words. Her parents had as much faith in her virtue and honor
as the rest of Society.

"No he won't," her sister said quietly. "He wants us to make a
match."

Both their parents did. Perhaps with an equal intensity.

She furrowed her brow, staring with concern at Gillian. Would
her younger sister, with her desire to please all, compromise her
own happiness? Surely with her romantic spirit, she'd not allow
their father to so influence her. "*You* will make a match," Genevieve said and claiming her sister's hand, she gave her fingers
a slight squeeze. She, on the other hand, would not. Ever. One
scandal could mayhap be forgiven by an old reprobate in desperate
need of a bride…such as Father's friend, Lord Tremaine, but never
two scandals. She steeled her jaw. She'd see her father in hell before
she allowed him to bind her to that ancient lord.

Her sister's face pulled. "I do not want just any gentleman." Which
their parents had, by the few events Genevieve attended the past
fortnight, diligently thrust in their youngest daughter's way. "Nor
am I concerned about my marital state." A slight, reproachful frown
formed on Gillian's usually smiling lips. "I am here because…" She
darted her gaze about and then scooted closer. "I overheard Father
whispering to Mother."

Genevieve's heart skipped a beat. "They are sending me away,"
she breathed. Where that thought had once roused terror and
agony, now a giddy lightness filled her chest; a desperate hungering to put this place behind her and carve out a quiet, albeit lonely,
existence for herself in the country. There would be no caring

husband and no loving, chubby-cheeked babes. A vise squeezed about her heart.

"Sending you away?" Her sister cocked her head as though that very thing hadn't been done five years earlier. "No. They are talking about you marrying."

She fanned the pages of her sketchpad. "Do you mean they are talking about me not ever marrying?" What gentleman would want a perfectly scandalous lady, nearly on the shelf, for his wife? Feeling Gillian's gaze trained on her face, she made herself go still. And her uncooperative heart again faltered. "What is it?"

"Father wishes you to wed Lord Tremaine."

Some of the tension eased from Genevieve's shoulders and she leaned over to pat her sister's fingers. "I know."

The other-worldly, beautiful young woman opposite her shot her eyebrows to her hairline. "You know?" Incredulity underscored those two words. "And you are not horrified."

"Father shared his intentions when I arrived in London." She'd allowed herself to forget the old widower would be coming to town to size her up; had allowed herself to be distracted from the possibility of even seeing him. Now it all mattered not. For the horror to dog her since she'd fled Lady Erroll's, a little thrill of triumph increased her heart's beating.

Gillian searched Genevieve's face. "And you did not tell me?"

At the wounded glimmer in Gillian's expressive eyes, guilt swiftly doused all that previous, unholy enjoyment. "Oh, Gillian," she said softly.

"I am your sister and you act as though I am a stranger," she said faintly, accusatory. "And I know it is wrong and petty of me to speak of our relationship even now, but I wish to be your friend. I hate seeing you alone and you are so determined to be alone."

She started. Since her return, she'd mourned the loss of her friendship with Gillian and lamented the loss of her brighter, more cheerful, self. Was her solitary state something she'd imposed upon herself as a means of protection? "You are right," she said quietly and surprise lit her sister's face. She hugged her sketchpad close, finding comfort in its solid, reassuring presence. It had been there when not even her family had. "I have spent so many years alone, Gillian," she said, needing her sister to understand. "Grandfather—"

"Was cold and miserable?"

"No," she said with an automaticity born of truth. That was how Society saw the old Earl of Hawkridge. That was how even Genevieve herself had. Those opinions had been fabricated by a girl's fears of the austere, stately earl. "Grandfather has a clever wit and a dry humor," she said, defending the man because it was important Gillian knew that, of their miserable family, Grandfather never was, nor ever had been, the problem member. "He is old, though." She could not keep the sadness from creeping in. "He spends much of his days resting or sleeping. But when I was there, he was more a friend to me." Unable to meet the other woman's probing stare, Genevieve dropped her gaze to her knees. "But I no longer know how to be around company."

"Bah, you were always cheerful and witty."

Her sister's unintended slight, earned a sharp bark of laughter. Goodness how she'd missed her raw honesty and innocent sincerity. But then her mirth died. "I will try to be more a friend to you." To go back to the way they'd been when they were sisters, crafting ways to drive their parents mad.

Gillian narrowed her eyes. "And you'll not keep secrets from me?"

She opened her mouth, but then followed the pointed stare to the book clenched in her fingers. Cedric. "There are no secrets." *I am a liar. There was a kiss that seared my soul and burns on my mouth even still.* But there would never be anything more. Rakes did not rush to take brides and certainly not ruined ones. Not that Genevieve wished to be his bride. Except…what would it be like wed to a man such as Cedric? Her parents' union had been coolly formal, with barely a smile between the couple and certainly never laughter. Marriage to Cedric would, no doubt, be thrilling and filled with passion. Butterflies danced wildly in her belly at the forbidden prospect.

"I daresay I would rather see you wed to a charming gentleman like the Marquess of St. Albans than Lord Tremaine," her sister said jerking her back from such fanciful and, more, dangerous musings.

If Genevieve was of the marrying sort, she would most assuredly choose Cedric over an old widower, trying to beget heirs on her like a broodmare. With a man such as Cedric as her husband, there would at least exist laughter and desire in a marriage. A thrill fluttered in her belly. "Yes, well, neither is truly an option." There were none.

A knock sounded at the door and, as one, they looked to the front.

Delores peeked her head inside. Light streamed into the nursery. "Lady Genny?" Her gaze landed on the sisters stuck in the corner. "Oh, there you are, miss." A look of pity flashed on her face.

The time had come.

"His Lordship has requested your presence in his office."

Even as she'd been expecting it, her stomach dipped. Mustering a smile for her sister's benefit, she shoved to her feet. "Delores," she said as she walked over and gave her sketchpad to the young maid. "Will you deliver this to my rooms?" The young maid nodded and then rushed off.

Genevieve stared after her a moment. It had been inevitable. Of course, all great shows of disobedience were met with a stern lecture. This, however, was no mere disobedience. This was another great scandal when she'd been so thoroughly warned. The floorboards groaned, indicating her sister had moved, and she cast a look sideways to Gillian.

"Perhaps if you speak to him," Gillian said hopefully, with every word demonstrating the extent of her innocence. "If you explain how His Grace offended you, then he'll be understanding."

Many words had been leveled at the Marquess of Ellsworth: pompous, arrogant, respectable. Among them, however, understanding had never been one of them.

"I will speak to him," she promised.

Her younger sister held out her elbow. "Would you like me to accompany you?"

"No," she said, gentling that refusal with another smile. "I'll visit after my meeting. I promise," she added, when Gillian still hesitated. The last place she'd have the innocent, still-hopeful young woman was outside Father's office while he delivered a dressing down like she was a recalcitrant child. She sank her teeth into her lower lip…or worse, a harlot who'd visited shame upon the family once more.

Without the benefit of her sister's unwavering support, Genevieve made her way through the corridors. This moment was remarkably like another. And mayhap, if she were fortunate, like that long ago night, she'd be sent away.

But then what? a silent voice needled. Did she truly wish to be a relative forever dependent upon the charity of her family?

A short while later, she found herself seated at the foot of her father's desk while he scribbled away at those very important ledgers that commanded more attention than his daughter ever had. *Scratch. Scratch. Scratch.* No, the only notice he'd paid her had been when she'd brought shame to his name and title. *Scratch. Scratch. Scratch.* And who she might wed. Why, when the then recent Duke of Aumere had set his cap upon her for that too-brief a time, she'd brought pride. That fleeting emotion had been quickly replaced with his furious disdain. All the old annoyances boiled to the surface and threatened to spill over. She fisted her hands on her lap. "You wished to see me," she said tightly.

His hand slid and left a sloppy, inky trail from the jerkiness of that movement. She took a perverse delight in unsettling him. Prepared for his blustery show of disapproval, she was taken aback as he dropped his pen and reclined in his seat. He wiped a tired hand over his face; defeated, when he was usually only condemning. "My hopes for you were great, Genevieve," he said quietly, as though he spoke to himself. "Your entry into Society was a wondrous one." He shook his head sadly.

Perhaps she should feel *something* at that parental disappointment, but how could she feel anything but this frustration running through her at the blame forever heaped on her shoulders? Filled with a restive energy, Genevieve leaned forward. "What Aumere did five years ago, the lies he spread, marks him as a cad. And you, as my *father*, should see that," she said quietly.

The marquess wrinkled his nose. Was it the sincerity of the words on her lips that earned his distaste? Or her blatant challenging of him? When he still said nothing, she settled her palms on his desk. "Just as what happened last evening was not my fault," she said calmly. Surely he saw that?

He held her gaze. "It is never your fault," he said tiredly.

In her defense, it hadn't been. Either time, where Aumere was concerned. He was a gentleman who'd seen her as less than a person; a material object there to suit his whims and fancies. For the shock and scandal she'd caused, she would never make apologies for last night. Not to that man.

"Tremaine will marry you."

Lost in her own musings, it took a moment for Father's words to penetrate. She frowned. "Father?" she asked, incredulity lacing her question. What gentleman would marry a notoriously whispered about lady? *A desperate one.* An ancient one without heirs. Disgust scraped along her spine. At her father for dare suggesting it and the old lord willing to do it.

Her father gestured to the pages in front of him and, wordlessly, she followed his motioning to those pages he'd been so enrapt in. "Following our return last evening, I met with the earl." His lips pulled. "He was not at all pleased about another scandal being attached to your name, but for our friendship, he will overlook it."

So *that* was why Father had not summoned her posthaste for his verbal dressing down. He'd had matters of business to attend with his ancient friend. "Are you mad?" The question tumbled from her lips, before she could call it back.

Not that she wished to. For even with the narrowing of her father's eyes and the rage flashing in their depths, an unholy fury licked away at her senses. "He is seventy if he is a day, and you'd marry me off to mitigate a scandal?" She continued, not allowing him the opportunity to speak. "I am no longer the scared child you sent away, blindly obedient." She jutted her chin. "I did nothing wrong and will not rush off and marry an old lord to appease you." Or anyone. The decisions she made would be strictly with her own happiness and future in mind. No one else's.

The leather groaned in protest as her father leaned forward. "You would reject his offer?" Shock coated his words. "When I've already assured him you would be agreeable to the match?" His mottled cheeks and furious eyes hinted at the thin thread of control he possessed.

Genevieve drew in a steadying breath and swallowed down a string of curses. Neither of her parents had appreciated or welcomed shows of spirit or temper. It was one of the reasons they'd so favored Gillian. Mayhap her father could be reasoned with. "I am…" Nauseous. "*Grateful* for the earl's offer, however, we would not suit." The least reason of which had to do with the fact that he was the same age as her own father and more to do with the domineering tendencies he'd exhibited with his daughters at their family's picnics over the years. Those young women, nearly her age, were shadows of people and that is what she would become if she bound herself to that old lord.

"You would not suit?" Her father slashed the air with his hand. "You'll have a title and respectability. What more do you require than that?"

There was a finality there that fanned her annoyance. Happiness be damned, he'd base his assurances on nothing more than his expectations that his daughters were both broodmares there to be auctioned off to the most respectable and highest bidder. She narrowed her eyes. "You did not even speak to me about what I wished—?"

His patience snapped in the form of a furious fist pounding the surface. "What you wish?" The papers leapt with the force of his movements and she jumped in time to them. "What you wish was forfeited five years ago, Genevieve."

She continued, tenacious. "Allow me the funds you've settled on me when I reach my majority. I will leave you and Mother and you'll not have to be constantly reminded of me." And more, she could be free of him.

"The whispers will remain," he shot back. "Nor would I be so imprudent as to give a young chit who has demonstrated such ill-judgment time and time again access to a single farthing." The finality in his words reached up to his eyes and spoke of a man who'd run out of patience. Whether she was truly to blame or not, mattered not at all. It only mattered how it affected his name.

She set her jaw. "I am not marrying him."

Her quiet pronouncement echoed around the office with the same force as if she'd screamed it from her lungs.

"Very well," her father said, sitting back in his chair. He picked up his pen and proceeded to scribble onto the pages of his ledger.

Befuddlement creased her brow. "Very well?" Surely he'd not capitulate so easily? As long as she remembered, the Marquess of Ellsworth had been wholly unyielding and certainly never one to show weakness before his daughters.

"I cannot allow two of my daughters to remain without a single prospect." Her father didn't deign to pick his head up, but devoted his attention to the book before him. "I expect Tremaine will prefer your sister, anyway."

A loud buzzing filled her ears. "What?" her question came as though down a long hall. Surely he'd not said… Surely she'd imagined…?

The marquess briefly glanced up. "The truth is, Tremaine never truly wanted you," he said, raking an icy stare over her. Did he believe to hurt her with that admission? "He asked for your sister, but I expected she could make an advantageous match of her own. Where you…?" He gave his head a shake and diverted his attention to that page.

She shot to her feet. "No," she gasped and again planted her hands on his desk. "What manner of father are you?" She'd sooner see her father dead than allow him to marry off her sister to that doddering lord.

He scoffed and at last looked up. "I'm not in a mood for your displays of emotion. One of you will marry."

Moments ago, she'd lied to herself. There was someone whose happiness she'd put before her own—Gillian. His threat hung on the air between them. And she wanted to lash out at him. To spit in his face, and then send him and his prospective match to the devil where he could burn for being a faithless sire.

I cannot do this… Except, meeting her father's ruthless stare confirmed his resolve—he'd see one of his daughters married. "Please do not do this." She curled her toes into the soles of her slippers. "Send me back to Grandfather," she beseeched, hating that she'd been reduced to a desperate, pleading girl, as much as she hated the world in which women's happiness mattered not at all amidst their cruel, contrived Society. "Gillian will find a proper husband. A man worthy of her."

Her father stared at her for a long while, saying nothing, and hope stirred in her breast; hope that he'd let her go and she could carry on sketching and gardening without fear of recrimination or worry over what anyone said. But then, he sank back in his seat once more. "You'll not be able to remain hidden with your miserable grandfather forever." Miserable. The earl, even with his gruff edge, was warmer and more of a father than this man had ever been.

"But—"

"Tremaine will arrive later today to formally request your hand. Do I have your acceptance?"

Tell him no. Tell him he can go to the devil… She pressed her eyes closed. Ultimately, would Gillian have the same strength to reject their father's efforts? A slow, painful acceptance settled around her belly.

When she'd been a small girl, she'd been tiptoeing back and forth over a fallen branch that extended out into her father's lake. In one faulty misstep, she'd tumbled into the frigid water. Pulled down by her skirts, the water had muted her cries so all she heard was the panicky hum of silence and her own muffled screams. She'd fought her skirts, to scrabble her way back to the surface, choking and gasping until she'd grabbed that rough trunk and pulled herself back to safety. Her chest heaved in the same desperate rhythm of that long ago day.

"You may go," Father said and dragged his ledgers forward.

There was a finality to his dismissal that numbed her. For if she wed Lord Tremaine, her spirit would die. She would become a lady to breed him babes and adorn his arm as a proper societal matron and the light would go out until all that remained was a shadow of a person…like her mother.

With stiff movements, Genevieve stood. "You may go to hell," she seethed and took an unholy glee in the way he sputtered.

When she'd stepped out into the hall and had the safety of a closed door panel between them, Genevieve tore down the corridor. She raced so quickly through the halls, her lungs strained from the pace she'd set. Distance between herself and the future had laid before her, she collapsed against the wall. Her chest rose and fell and she borrowed support.

In all her reservations of returning to London, she'd been riddled with anxiety about being the focus of Society's attentions. Never, had she anticipated…this. This absolute and total disregard for her wishes, and hopes, and dreams harkened to feudal times where daughters were chattel. A bitter-sounding laugh bubbled past her lips. But then, isn't that what women ultimately were? Their interests and desires mattered not, but rather the wealth attached to their name. Gentlemen wanted docile, biddable wives to give them babes while they carried on as they pleased.

She pressed her eyes closed as her breathing settled into a calm, even rhythm. Given her father's determination, nothing short of a miracle would prevent him from going forward with binding her to Lord Tremaine and Genevieve had long ago given up on—

"There you are, my lady." The faintly out-of-breath tones of her father's normally unflappable butler brought her eyes flying open. "You've a visitor." She cocked her head. At this hour? No fashionable visits were made at this time. "Your maid has been searching for you. I've asked the gentleman to await you in the Blue Parlor—"

Her heart sank to her toes. "A visitor," she repeated, her voice blank. As the butler spoke, her thoughts rolled together. The earl would come and put his formal offer to her and her father would expect nothing but her acceptance. *I cannot do this. I cannot…*

"My lady?"

She blinked slowly. With the butler staring perplexedly at her, she turned and marched onward to the Blue Parlor. She reached the edge of the doorway and nausea roiled in her belly. To steady her trembling fingers, she smoothed them down the front of her gray skirts. Yes, nothing short of a miracle would save her now. Schooling her features, Genevieve stepped inside. "Lord Tr…" Her greeting trailed off, as her gaze landed on a tall, broadly powerful, well-muscled gentleman who was most assuredly *not* the aging earl. "You," she blurted.

Standing at the empty hearth, with his hands clasped at his back, Cedric, the Marquess of St. Albans, turned slowly. The patently rakish, and more than slightly charming, grin on his lips kick-started her heart. "Me." He winged up a golden eyebrow. "Were you expecting another?" All the trepidation and horror at her father's goals for her momentarily lifted. And for whatever reason that Cedric found his way in her home now, she would be eternally grateful in ways he'd never know or understand for the distraction he presented from the hellish situation her father would impose.

Avoiding his question, she slipped further into the room. "I am sorry," she murmured. "I did not expect…" She bit off those additionally revealing words. She'd been closeted away in the country for so long she'd ceased to be the young lady to masterfully handle exchanges. Drawing in a deep breath, she shoved aside apologies for who she was. "I am surprised to see you here," she admitted with an honesty that deepened his grin and set off a dangerously familiar fluttering in her belly, momentarily obliterating the horrifying intentions her father had for her.

He took another step closer and waggled his eyebrows. "A good surprised, Genevieve?"

She'd wager there was no other kind where this dangerously skillful rake was concerned. "Indeed," she conceded with a smile of her own.

For, when Cedric, the Marquess of St. Albans, was around, she ceased to be the sorrowful, lonely creature she'd been all these years. She recalled how to smile, laugh, and talk again. Genevieve knew not why or how he elicited those carefree feelings inside her, better suiting the naïve girl she'd once been.

She only knew—she enjoyed it.

CHAPTER 13

CEDRIC REALLY SHOULD BE FOCUSED on the business that had forced him out of bed and into a respectable home at this ungodly hour. Yet, Genevieve Farendale had a smile to rival the song of a siren at sea, and as she settled her willowy frame into the King Louis XIV chair beside him, he froze, fixed on the sharp angles of her face, accentuated by the tightly drawn back strawberry blonde tresses. Desire ran through him. For with the passionate embraces they'd shared, he'd had a glimpse of those strands loose about her shoulders and was riveted with the possibility of seeing them fanned upon his pillow.

He took the seat nearest hers. And all of a sudden, a marriage of convenience presented more enticing for altogether different possibilities; ones that had nothing to do with the properties he'd acquire and freedom from his father's machinations.

At his scrutiny, a pretty blush stained her cheeks. "What is it?" She patted that hideous chignon.

How very honest she was. That reminder drew him back to the reason for his visit. A woman who did not skirt or dance about words and inquiries was a perfectly practical creature who'd see the benefit of his offer.

Cedric stretched his legs out before him and hooked them at the ankles. "You were expecting another," he observed, studying her through hooded lashes.

A sea of emotions paraded across her face; none of which he could sort out. She cast a hopeful look to the door. Alas, her maid, God love the woman, remained perfectly absent. When Genevieve returned her attention to him, she spoke hesitantly. "Yes." She paused. "No." Four endearing creases marred her brow. "Does it matter?" she turned a question, instead.

Carefully, Cedric tugged off one glove and then the other. He beat them together. "Yes, I rather believe it does." It mattered for the plans he had for them together and not because of the pebble in his belly at the prospect of a suitor come to call. "Who is he?" he drawled, infusing a deliberate boredom into that inquiry, even as tension gripped him.

The lady's smile slipped. Did she take umbrage with his bold questioning or that affected boredom? "I would rather not discuss him," she said softly, glancing down at her folded hands.

The ladies he associated with, really no ladies at all, but bold, wicked creatures, would have, no doubt, taken his question as one borne of jealousy and delighted in goading him for it. With her truthful response, Genevieve was a manner of woman he did not have any experience in dealing with, and searching through his years of experience in enticing a lady, came up…empty.

Cedric dropped his half-grin, and uncrossed his ankles and sat upright. "Very well, then. Shall we discuss Aumere?" He asked the question that had dogged his thoughts from the moment she'd fled the countess' dining table, until now.

Her lips twisted in a smile that was more a grimace than anything. "And I'd rather discuss him even less."

This pressing need to know redoubled at her vague non-response. He folded his arms at his chest and continued to stare. "Did the gentleman offend you in some way?" Tension thrummed through his veins.

With a total lack of artifice, she dropped her chin into her hand. "Why should it matter to you?" she asked instead with a soft curiosity in her tone.

He shrugged. "It shouldn't," he said honestly and the lady stiffened. "Yet, it does."

She met his gaze squarely. Then, she gave her head a befuddled shake. "I do not know what to make of you, my lord."

"Cedric," he gruffly insisted. He'd have his Christian name on her lips and his title, both present and future ones, could go hang. He lifted his shoulders again. "Nor is there anything to make of me." He was, exactly as he was seen by Society. Unrepentant rake. Carefree rogue. Charmer.

An inelegant snort escaped her. "Come," she scoffed. "Of course there is. You arrive here, unexpectedly and," she waved a hand in his direction, "you wear that false grin." He furrowed his brow. How did she see that? How, when no one else had ever delved underneath the surface of what he presented?

"Do you have a problem with my smile?" he asked, wholly unnerved by the depth of her awareness.

"Yes. No." She threw her hands up and an exasperated sound escaped her. "I do not know. All I know, my… *Cedric*," she amended when he gave her a pointed look. "Is I do not know what to make of you," a rake, "showing up." A panicky light lit her eyes as she darted her gaze to the door. When she returned her attention to him, she dropped her voice to a hushed whisper. "Showing up in places where I happen to be and asking questions about me." With the rapidity of her gesticulating, the lady was going to do herself injury. "What should I matter to you that you'd wonder about my former betrothed or the gentleman I'm expecting to call?"

He started. For people did not matter to him. Did they? He'd seen to it that he needed no one—not his mother, his bastard of a father, even his sister. Yet…

…*the gentleman I'm expecting to call*…

Which indicated there was, indeed, a suitor coming by and it mattered very much. Surely it only mattered because of Cedric's own intentions for the lady?

Unnerved by that staggering revelation he couldn't sort through, he reached inside his jacket and removed a small silver flask. "It matters," he said at last and his revelation brought her lips faintly apart in a slight moue of surprise. As she proved remarkably unforthcoming, he altered his questioning. The lady's eyes followed his every moment. "What happened with Aumere last evening?" He removed the top and took a quick swallow.

She opened her mouth and closed it. Then tried again. "Are you drinking at this hour?" The delicate shock there froze his hand halfway to his mouth.

He followed her disappointed stare to the drink in his hand.

"Er…" He'd never mingled with polite Society. Of the people he kept company with, the least offense of which they were guilty was indulging in a spot of brandy in the morning hour.

"Would you drink in front of any lady, no less?" she asked tartly.

Offending the lady one intended to offer for, hardly proved favorable for said woman's respective capitulation. As such, he put the stopper on and returned the flask to the front of his jacket. "I generally avoid ladies all together." As soon as the words slipped out, he cursed himself. How was he, a practiced rake with a smooth tongue, bungling this so badly?

She narrowed her eyes but not before he detected a glimmer of outrage.

Fortunately for Cedric, Genevieve's maid appeared at the entrance of the room.

"Delores, will you have tea readied for His Lordship and me," she said, not taking her gaze from his.

Unfortunately for him, her obedient maid looked between them, spun on her heel and quickly darted off.

He told himself it truly only mattered for his intentions toward her. He told himself, as much…even as it felt like a lie. With her maid gone and not allowing Genevieve an opportunity to order him gone as well, he spoke. "You wonder about my motives," he said with more solemnity than any topic he'd ever spoken of in the past. "You wonder why I should come here and put questions to you." He leaned close, shrinking the space between them. "Given my reputation, you are, of course, wise to question anything where I am concerned. I've told you before, Genevieve, I like you." And friendship between them was convenient for the marriage he intended for them.

She trailed her tongue over the seam of her lips and he swallowed a groan as lust slammed into him. Mayhap, a good deal more than friends, then. "I daresay you could have found all manner of details on my exchange with the duke in any of the gossip sheets," she said and he clung to what had brought him 'round this morning and not on his body's maddening response to her.

"Bah, scandal sheets," he said slashing the air with his hand. "Rubbish that is best burned for kindling." Her eyes softened. He'd not mention that he'd thoroughly read each scandal sheet for information about the lady that morning. Having been present and witness to her magnificent showing last evening, he recognized the rot printed on those pages.

She glanced to the open door and then looked to him. "The gentleman…" Crimson fired her cheeks, stirring his intrigue, all the more, "was indecent with his words and actions." And now he had his answer, which was really no answer at all. Instead of being satisfied with at last a vague knowing what had resulted in her magnificent display, it fueled a thousand questions and wonderings. He gritted his teeth so tightly, pain shot along his jaw. As she continued speaking, he struggled to attend her, while his thoughts meandered down a path that entailed him bloodying Aumere senseless.

"Who were you expecting a moment ago?" he asked, neatly returning them to the question she'd sidestepped.

The earlier glimmer in her green eyes dimmed and left in its place a stark emptiness that chilled.

Desperate to drive back that melancholy, he stuffed his gloves inside his jacket. "A game of short answers then? Single syllable word responses with no limit to the number of words in your sentence, as long as they are single syllable words."

His words rang a startled laugh from her. "Surely you jest," she said as her shoulders shook with mirth.

"Why must I be?" he countered, shifting forward in his seat.

She pointed her eyes to the ceiling. "Because rakes do not simply show up unexpectedly at a lady's home and ask her to take part in parlor games."

It was hardly in his favor if the lady saw him as nothing more than a rake. "Do you eagerly await a suitor?"

She snorted. "Hardly."

He made a tsking noise. "That is two syllables, love."

For a long moment, the lady said nothing and he expected her to abandon the game as foolhardy. Then, she wetted her lips. "No. Not at all."

A lightness filled his chest as she, with her words confirmed that there was no eager suitor in the wings. He clapped his hands slowly. "Brava. A splendid four points." Cedric captured his chin between his thumb and forefinger and rubbed. "For my next question, then." Dropping his palms onto his legs, he leaned closer. "Who is the person you're waiting for?"

Her mouth tightened so that the blood drained from the corners of her lips, but a spirited glimmer sparkled in her eyes. "He's an old peer who wants a wife. A friend of my…" She paused, chewing at her lower lip as she searched for her next response. Then her eyes lit and she jabbed the air with her finger. "Da." As soon as the word escaped her, it was as though reality sucked her back, draining the sparkle in her eyes.

Cedric ran his gaze over her face as his mind turned over her words. Then the slow, horrifying truth trickled in—the reason for the lady's upset. "Your father intends to wed you to one of his friends." No doubt, a faulty bid to bury the gossip and be rid of his daughter. Given his own grasping, emotionally deadened father, her words did not shock. He gripped the arms of the chair. Nay, rather they stirred fury inside.

Genevieve glanced down at the tips of her slippers. "Thank you for the diversion," she said softly and then coughed into her hand. "Now, I would truly wish to speak of something else."

Ignoring the lady's faint pleading underscoring that request, he shoved to his feet and knelt at the foot of her chair. Her little shuddery gasp filtered the air between them. "Wh-what—?"

Uncaring if her maid or mother happened by, he brushed his bare knuckles over her cheek, savoring the satiny softness of her skin. "Who is he?" he asked quietly.

She pursed her lips and, for a moment, he expected she'd ignore this question, too. "The Earl of Tremaine."

He choked. "Tremaine?" Cedric sank back on his haunches. The man was sixty-five if he was a day. It would be a sin before God if this vibrant, spirited woman was bound forever to that old, fat bastard. Furthermore, he'd little intention of losing his match of convenience with Genevieve to that lackwit.

"Those were my sentiments exactly," she muttered, with a remarkable calm for a woman whose father sought to sell her on the Marriage Mart to a man old enough to be her grandfather.

Yes, the lady was remarkably low of options. With a furious father determined to marry her off to an ancient lord, her prospects were limited. The lady's desperation worked only in his favor and, yet, even as he would have a marriage of convenience between them, he wanted her to come to the union not because he was her only choice.

He gave his head a hard shake. Bloody hell, why should he care if desperation fueled her acceptance? All that mattered was that she said yes and agreed to the terms he'd lay out before her. In a contract that would see him forever bound to one woman; a woman whose happiness he would be responsible for seeing to. His palms moistened and he brushed them on the sides of his breeches. What did he truly know of another person's happiness?

Genevieve tipped her head. "Why are you staring at me like that?"

He furrowed his brow.

"Like you've swallowed a plate of rancid kippers."

"Is there any good kipper, though?" he put in with an effortful grin that raised another laugh from Genevieve.

"Yes, well, there is truth to that."

Absently, Cedric took her hand in his and worshipped the soft skin with his gaze and touch. He pressed his thumb against the inset where her hand met her wrist; to the spot where her pulse pounded wildly. "What do you enjoy, Genevieve?"

She moistened her lips once more. "Enjoy?" That one-word utterance emerged breathless.

He stroked his finger in a small circle over and over. Her skin was softer than the finest satins and silks. Gloriously smooth and perfect. "Ah, but that was two-syllables."

Genevieve gulped and her lashes fluttered. "Art," she whispered. "I love art."

"What else?" he pressed, raising her wrist to his mouth and brushing his lips over the delicate skin.

Her thick, strawberry blonde lashes swept down, but did little to conceal the desire radiating from within her expressive eyes. "B-blooms and buds."

Ah, the lady tended gardens. A wholly feminine pursuit, encouraged by the *ton* and, yet, those three words uttered in that breathy whisper conjured tempting images of the two of them in that famed Garden of Eden, together, tasting all that was forbidden.

"I've just one more question?"

She stared at him through heavy eyes. "What is that, my…Cedric?" *My Cedric.* Yes, he rather thought he preferred those two words together on her full, luscious lips.

"Marry me?"

CHAPTER 14

CEDRIC FALCOT, THE MARQUESS OF St. Albans, was a sorcerer. With his wicked touch and his teasing eyes and charming words, he could tempt a nun to forsake her vows or, at the very least, muddle a lady's thoughts.

In Genevieve's case, that was precisely what he'd done. His words brought her eyes open as she blinked away the thick haze he'd cast with his seductive touch. He stared at her with such casualness, he may as well have commented on the weather or a cup of tea. Surely she'd heard him wrong? Surely…?

"Marry me, Genevieve," he repeated and reclaimed her hands.

No, she'd not heard him wrong. Her heart tripled its beat, pounding an eager rhythm. But for a handful of exchanges, she knew this man hardly at all and, yet, he'd come here and offer for her? She searched his face for some hint of teasing, an indication that he made light of her. Rakes did not wed and they decidedly did not wed ladies they'd met only a handful of times. *No matter how passionate the kisses were between us.*

She held her palms up. "I do not understand," she spoke haltingly, trying to make sense of his request. "You do not know me."

"I know you enjoy art." And given his knowledge of the artists in her book, the gentleman shared that love. "I know you enjoy gardening."

"Only because I just mentioned it," she pointed out.

He leaned forward and her breath caught. *He is going to kiss me. He is going to kiss me and my maid will arrive any moment, or my family might happen by, and I do not care.* She leaned close to take his kiss. "I know there is passion between us." His breath, a blend of coffee and brandy, tickled her lips and she fought back a tide of regret when he drew slightly back, ending the possibility of his kiss. "And I require a wife," he said matter-of-factly, no hint of passion or desire in his husky baritone.

A slight frown marred her lips. How effortlessly he moved from seductive rake to coolly unaffected gentleman. Then his words registered. Her heart dipped. He required a wife. By his words, his offer was made for no other reason than necessity. Battling back irrational disappointment, she found her voice. "You require a—?"

"Wife," he easily supplied. "I've need of a wife."

Hearing him state that admission so plainly once more, tugged at the romantic hopes she'd thought dead and long buried. For the reality of being jilted at the altar and hidden away in the country, a part of her had hoped for…more. Mayhap not love, but…well, more. He stared patiently at her and she furrowed her brow. "And you believe I, a woman you've only really just met, will do?"

Cedric nodded automatically. "I do," he spoke so matter-of-factly about their being joined together, forever, bound by vows, name.

Footsteps sounded in the hall and, dazed, she looked to the doorway as Delores reappeared with the tray of tea, thankfully interrupting her muddled thoughts. The maid's gaze landed on an unrepentant Cedric kneeling at her mistress' feet and then she quickly averted her stare. Of course, a rake such as he would have no compunctions about the whispers that could ensue if they were discovered so. Genevieve murmured her thanks as the young woman set refreshments down on the mahogany long table. "Will you fetch my sketchpad, Delores?" she asked as the maid started for the corner of the room. Then, the gentleman had offered marriage.

Delores hesitated and then dropped a curtsy, leaving them alone once more.

With the young woman gone, silence fell, punctuated by the ticking clock atop the mantel. "I…I…" Did not know what to say. Unnerved by Cedric's cool in the face of his offer, Genevieve pushed to her feet and hurried over to the tray. Her gaze caught the couple painted upon the porcelain teapot. The suitor in knee breeches knelt beside his lady in ruffled skirts. She trailed her fingertip over the pair. Was that moment one where the couple had spoken of necessity and needs, or were there whispered words of love?

Cedric settled his hands on her shoulders and she started, shooting a startled glance back at him. How did one of his magnificent size and power move with such a stealthy grace? When he spoke, he revealed an unerringly accurate take on her silent musings. "What I propose is surely not the romantic hopes you once carried." Once carried. He, too, erroneously assumed that the scandalous Farendale girl had safely buried her hope of love. He angled her around to face him. "You will have whatever your heart desires." Everything, except love. "You may garden and sketch and paint until your fingers are no longer capable of movement," he promised.

Unable to meet his piercing blue stare, she looked past his shoulder to the mantel. "Why do you require a wife?" She cocked her head. "Are you a fortune-hunter?" If so, with her modest dowry, there was any number of more suitable brides for him.

A bark of laughter burst from his firm lips. "God, no." His broad shoulders shook with amusement, but then he grimaced. "Not necessarily."

"So you *are* in need of a fortune?" she asked slowly, trying to untangle his conflicting words.

"May I be blunt?"

She inclined her head. "Please." Given his offer, she rather thought there was only ground for bluntness.

"I am a rake." *Am*. Not was. Genevieve curled her toes into the soles of her slippers so tightly, her arches ached. Of course she well knew his reputation, by the whispers and warnings from her sister and mother, and even from the gentleman's admission, himself. Still, hearing it, she hated the truth, anyway, even more now. "I was…" He paused and tapped his fingertips along his thigh in an endearing way she'd come to know after their handful of meetings that bespoke his hesitancy. "Unwise with the funds left me by my mother," he said at last.

Hearing him lay that particular piece before her, made him

flawed in ways she did not wish him to be. A man who ran through his inheritance and carried a flask of brandy to drink at the early morning hour was not who she wanted Cedric Falcot, the Marquess of St. Albans, to be. She preferred the gentleman who spoke of art and drove back her sadness with his smile. "And are you still unwise with your funds?"

Cedric rested his hip on the edge of the sofa. "I still wager, but I am not the same reckless man I was in my youth who'd gamble away a fortune."

In his youth. She studied the chiseled planes of his rugged cheeks. There was no hint of boy in the Marquess of St. Albans and, yet, with that statement, he just reminded her of how little she knew of him. "I do not even know your age." And yet, he'd have her marry him. Then, would their auspicious beginning be really all that different than the formal arrangements entered into every day between other lords and ladies?

"I'm nearly thirty." He smiled wryly. "What say you? Thirty years younger than Tremaine?"

She snorted. "At the very least."

Silence fell between them once more. As the quiet stretched on, she reflected on Cedric's glib way with words. He had an innate ability to muddle a lady's senses so that she focused on his charming jests and not the reservations blaring around her mind. Then, wasn't that the power of a rake?

Which only left her with the question…did she want to spend her days married to a man who, by his own admissions and actions, was one who wagered and drank spirits, and—

"You are quiet," he observed, drumming those long digits still.

Genevieve turned her palms up. "I…do not know what to say," she conceded, letting her hands fall to her side.

He flashed one of those wicked half-grins that wrought havoc on her senses. "Then say yes," he encouraged, in a satiny smooth voice that so enticed, Satan himself would have envied the skill.

"In marrying, I will be turning my funds, my children, my very happiness over to a man." Having witnessed the miserable state of her parents' own union certainly gave one a suitable caution in entering into an equally failed match. Particularly after herself bearing the scars of a faithless bounder's influence. Women were powerless. Wasn't her father's earlier threats proof of that? "How could I trust—?"

"I obtain unentailed lands left me with my mother's passing. The estates are lucrative and come to me when I marry." Ah, so the need for a wife. "Your dowry is yours," he cut in, his earlier grin now gone, replaced by a solemnity she'd seen but on a handful of instances from him. "I've no need of your funds and will cede all of it over to you."

Her mouth fell open. "What?" Gentlemen did not give control of any property or possessions to their wives. At least, that had been the worthless example set by her own father.

"Nor will you have to worry after children," he pledged. "Or hosting balls or throwing soirees or dinner parties. Your life will be yours." How very tempting the gift he dangled—freedom, control in a world where women were wholly lacking of such things.

Yet, she'd learned long ago to be wary of any gentleman's intentions. "And what benefit would you gain in marrying me?" she asked, putting a question to him. A gentleman, who would one day possess the most distinguished, respected titles in the realm could have his choice of bride. Why should he choose a lady riddled with scandal, whispered about by all?

"I—"

"Like me?" she interjected, lifting an eyebrow.

"Yes, well there is that," he said with a wink.

Was this veneer of charm a means for him to keeping anyone from delving deep under the surface to see who he truly was? She'd wager for his reputation as rake, with his disdain for Society's whispers and lies, that there was more good than he'd ever have the world know of, inside him.

He palmed her cheek and she leaned into his strong, powerful hand. Warmth radiated from the point of his touch and sent heat spiraling through her. "You require a husband," he said softly and she stiffened, as the blunt fact of those words doused her with the reality of what his offer truly was. "But that is not why I'd have you marry me."

Her heart thumped hard. *He desires more than the marriage of convenience he presented...*

"I would have you marry me because you should not be subjected to censure or stares." A rush of disappointment killed that fleeting, foolish, romantic thought. "As my wife, you'll wear whatever color gowns you wish and I'd wager it isn't gray." Seafoam green. "I'd wager you'd don satins in a seafoam." She gasped. How did he know that? He continued over her shocked exclamation. "As my marchioness, you'll be permitted to take your slippers off in the midst of Almack's if you so wish it." She wanted no part of that distinguished hall where ladies were subjected to the nasty sneers and whispers. "You should paint and garden and do whatever it is that brings you happiness."

You bring me happiness. Since her miserable return to London, the only joy she'd found had been in his presence. The truth of that held her frozen, unmoving, with his words enticing her with the dream he presented. He would offer her all that. "Ours will be a marriage of convenience?" Disappointment tugged at her and she held her breath praying he did not hear the regret steeped in her words.

"Exactly," he said with a nod, dislodging that errant, loose curl that she ached to brush back.

What did she expect of an offer that came after just a week knowing a gentleman? "There will be no… no…" A blush burned its way from her toes up to her hair.

He folded his arms. "No…?"

"We will not be intimate, then?" And if it was possible to blush to death, by the heat burning her skin, she was moments away from going up in a fiery conflagration.

Understanding glinted in his eyes. In one smooth movement, he lowered his hands to the table at her back, framing her in his arms. "You misunderstand," he whispered, brushing his lips to her temple and then her closed eyes and finally her lips, in a too-fleeting kiss that had her swallowing back a cry, demanding more. "I will make you my wife in name and in body," he pledged. "It will be a true marriage."

She wanted to grasp on to what he held out and not solely because, in wedding him, she'd be free of her father's hold and spared a match with Lord Tremaine, or any other desperate lord who wanted a broodmare and not a wife. Cedric spoke as one who knew her interests and celebrated them. An unrepentant rogue, he'd never stifle her spirit or crush that which brought her joy. Genevieve nodded slowly. "Yes," she said softly.

His broad shoulders went taut and the muscles rippled the black fabric of his immaculately cut jacket. "Yes?" Surprise stamped his features.

How endearing to find one so unwavering in his confidence should know indecision because of her. "Should I say no?" she teased.

"Oh, undoubtedly." A smile formed on his lips. This smile was not the mocking, rogue's grin, but rather an endearingly warm one that glinted in his eyes. "I am, however, happy you have not." He released her with an alacrity that left a void at the loss of his touch. "I will speak to your father." Of course, as a future duke he'd command a meeting with nothing more than a single word uttered.

She called out, halting his retreat. "Lord Tremaine is to arrive today." All the panic that had weighted her chest, the cloying desperation at having no choice lifted. For Cedric had presented her one. It was full of so much more promise and joy than anything her father would have insisted she agree to.

He wheeled around and stalked back toward her like a sleek panther, setting off the butterflies that only he'd ever stirred within her. "Then I shall speak to your father right now," he pledged and lowered his brow to hers.

Tremaine and Father had been friends since Eton and an unofficial arrangement had been reached…even as neither gentleman had inquired about what Genevieve wanted. "My father might deny your request," she warned.

"He will not deny me." Cedric spoke with a confidence borne of a man who'd not been denied anything in the course of his life. What must it be like to have complete command of your life? Envy pulled at her. Then, with his pledge, he'd offered her that.

So why did she selfishly want so much more? "And if he does?"

Their breath danced and melded. "Then I'll marry you anyway," he pledged. The resolve in his tone spoke of a man who wouldn't be denied. Surely that came of more than a marriage of convenience.

"But what if—"

Cedric took her lips under his. Heat spiraled, as it invariably did, from his embrace. She wound her arms about his neck, anchoring him close as she met his kiss, accepting his tongue as he plunged it in her mouth and stroked hers in a primitive dance that she returned.

A shocked gasp at the front of the room brought them apart.

Her maid stood, blushing like a beet caught in the summer sun. Mortification curled Genevieve's toes and she studiously avoided the girl's eyes. With the maid's devotion, Genevieve had no doubt she could rely on the girl's silence. And there was still the truth that Cedric would speak to her father.

With the ease that could only come from a gentleman who'd been discovered so scandalously too many times before, an unrepentant Cedric sketched a bow. "My lady. I bid you farewell." Without another word he stalked over to the door and paused at the entrance to toss an all-knowing look over his shoulder. "For now," he promised and winked.

Genevieve touched a hand to her racing heart and stared after him. He would marry her. He would offer her everything. Everything, that was, *except* love.

And though there was no love, there would be friendship and passion. Which was a good deal more than existed within most marriages. So how, staring at the empty doorway, could she account for this knot of disappointment that pebbled in her belly?

CHAPTER 15

"BY GOD, NEVER TELL ME the rumors are true and congratulations are in order?"

The next morning, seated at his table at the back of White's, Cedric glanced up from his half-empty glass of brandy.

Montfort grinned and without awaiting permission, hooked his ankle around the chair opposite Cedric and pulled it out. He motioned over a servant and relieved the liveried footman of a glass. The earl cast a look about the famed, but respectable, club and grimaced. "Imagine my surprise when I received your note last evening to meet here, of all places." He waggled his eyebrows. "Given the news on the front of *The Times* regarding your foray into respectability, however, it does make sense."

Cedric made a crude gesture that raised a laugh from the other man. "Go to hell, Montfort." His being at White's had nothing to do with his amusements once married. To visit one of his scandalous gaming hells or brothels when he'd only just become betrothed would earn unwanted and unneeded gossip. And though he didn't give a jot about what Society said of him, it clearly mattered to the lady who'd agreed to marry him. The least he could give Genevieve was freedom from gossip—for now, at least.

"I never thought I'd see the day you'd abandon your gaming hells for this bloody oppressive place," Montfort muttered as he poured himself a glass from Cedric's bottle. He glanced up from his task. "What is next? Attending Sunday sermons with the soon to be Marchioness of St. Albans?"

Cedric offered a wry smile. "Hardly." He swirled the contents of his glass. "The lady was quite practical in seeing our arrangement as nothing more than a matter of convenience for the both of us. As such, I've little intention of changing how I live." After more than seventeen years of debauched existence, he didn't know any other way and given his own father was really rather incapable of anything but sinning.

His friend choked on his swallow. "If you believe *that* then you know a good deal less about ladies than has been credited. No lady happily tolerates her husband's carousing."

"The lady has little interest in my faithfulness or how I spend my days," he argued with a frown. Didn't she? *"...In marrying, I will be turning my funds, my children, my very happiness over to a man. How could I trust...?"* A frisson of unease ran through him. He'd been quite clear that they'd carry on their own existences. He shrugged, thrusting aside the doubt his friend had raised. "I was quite clear in my requirements and she was equally clear."

Montfort kicked his chair back on the hind two legs. "Oh?" he drawled. "And just what requirements would a lady have to agree to marry one such as you?"

The insult easily rolled off Cedric. With their lifelong friendship, no one knew better than Montfort the dissolute bastard that Cedric was. "It matters not why she agreed." Just that she had. She'd be taken care of and through that, they'd both be spared the wills their own sires would have imposed on them.

At the memory of meeting with her coldhearted bastard of a father, he gripped the crystal snifter. Cold. Condescending where his daughter was concerned, her father had proven himself remarkably like Cedric's own ruthless parent.

"Yes, I suppose it doesn't," Montfort agreed, righting his chair. He took a swallow of his drink. "Then I suppose you'd meet little resistance from the desperate Farendale doxy." With that dismissive statement, Montfort looked about the club. "Few options for that one."

An unholy fury rolled through Cedric and the crystal snifter cracked under the pressure of his grip. "She is to be my wife," he bit out.

His friend returned his attention to Cedric. "Beg pardon?" he blinked several times.

With a growl of annoyance Cedric swiped his free hand through his hair. "Nothing," he snapped. He was not one of those respectable gents who was offended or bothered on anyone's behalf—not even his own. So what accounted for this urge to drag his friend across the table and bury his fist in said friend's nose?

Montfort swirled his drink. "Why the reason for meeting at this ungodly hour?" he asked, thankfully diverting Cedric's attention from his confounding thoughts.

"Is it early?" His gaze found the long-case clock at the opposite wall. Ten o'clock. Yes, certainly not an hour he'd generally be awake, after late night carousing. Except he'd not partaken in those scandalous revelries into the early morn hours…for nearly a week. Peculiar stuff.

"Oh, undoubtedly." Montfort followed that with a loud yawn.

"I had business to attend to." An early morn visit to secure a special license from the archbishop. Said paper now burned inside the front of his jacket for what it portended. He waved over a servant and put in a request for an unbroken glass, which Cedric promptly filled.

A sharp bark of laughter split Montfort's lips. "You had business to attend to that wasn't wagering or whoring?"

"I'm to marry this morning. Eleven o'clock," he added. In short time, he would break every silent vow he'd taken to thwart his father's wishes and forever bind himself in marriage to one woman. Anxiety roiled in his gut. That ultimate sense of failure he'd bring to a woman, just as his father had brought countless women. *Genevieve is different. She requires a husband. I require a wife. This is practical…* Thrusting aside the whispering of misgivings churning in his mind, he spoke quietly. "I would ask you to stand up with me this morning." Ultimately, he'd deny the bastard that which he desired above all else—that beloved heir and spare to carry out his polluted line. For what his father had never expected was for Cedric to find a bride content to settle for a practical arrangement where both benefited.

"Of course, I will be there," Montfort spoke with a seriousness that Cedric had thought him incapable of. The earl's amusement faded and his eyes reflected back the same horror and regret

Cedric had felt one week earlier over the expectations his father would have thrust on him. He propped his elbows on the table. "I am sorry," he spoke the way one would at the passing of a loved one. "I know you'd rather dance in the fires of hell than shackle yourself to one woman."

Cedric remained silent. Yes, his friend was, indeed, correct. Yet, there were certainly worse things than wedding a lady unafraid to challenge him, one who kissed with a wild abandon that promised a spirited wife who delighted in the marital bed. Lest his friend note that grin and make more of it than was there, he took a long swallow to conceal it.

"No need to be so glum, old friend," Montfort said misinterpreting the reason for his silence. "There is some good to come in marrying the lady," he continued, following Cedric's own thoughts. "The duke is no doubt enraged by your selection in a bride?"

"Undoubtedly," he confirmed, lifting his nearly empty glass in salute. As elated as Genevieve's own miserable father had been after they'd worked through the formal arrangements, was as livid as Cedric's own father had been when he'd visited him yesterday afternoon. His mind still resonated with the furious bellowing his pronouncement had met. A surge of triumph gripped him.

"Which, in itself, makes her the perfect bride," Montfort added.

Yes, at one point that would certainly have been true. And even as his friend's words were steeped in logic…there was…more that made Genevieve perfect.

"…*Do you believe because I am a woman, I should favor pastel, peaceful landscapes…?*"

Unsettled by the irrational sentiment, he cleared his throat. "My family is assembling at eleven o'clock in Kensington Gardens." That particular detail had not come only because of his father's insistence that the hasty affair be conducted in his ducal office, but for the significance of that location for the meeting place it represented.

Montfort erupted into another bevy of laughter. "Kensington Gardens." He leaned forward and slapped Cedric on the arm. "If you believe a romantic lady who insists on getting married outside in a garden is the logical sort who'll allow you to carry on as you've done these years, then you'd be wise to turn tail and run as quick as Aumere did, years earlier."

His jaw tightened reflexively with such intensity his teeth ground together at the mention of Aumere. The bloody fool. Regardless, Genevieve was better off without that one. *And do I believe she is better off with me?* "The place where the wedding takes place is neither here nor there," he grumbled under his breath. He'd certainly not point out that he'd decided on said location.

His friend inclined his head. "Given the hour, we should be along, then? Wouldn't do to be late to your own wedding."

Cedric swung his attention to that clock once more, and squinted at the numbers. Fifty minutes past ten. He'd but ten minutes to find his way to Hyde Park.

Bloody hell. With a curse he shoved back his chair and sprinted through his club.

NEVER MORE HAD GENEVIEVE BEEN so grateful for the shelter afforded by the high hedge maze of Kensington Gardens.

Looking past the vicar, she trained her gaze on the green boxwood. Anything but the cold, unspeaking Duke of Ravenscourt, or on the concern radiating from her sister's eyes, or her flushed and furious father. Or Cedric's sister and brother-in-law, the Marquess and Marchioness of Grafton.

Especially that united pair.

Except... From the corner of her eye, she took in the flawlessly perfect golden-haired lady, and the chestnut haired stranger at her side, their hands twined together. She swallowed hard and redirected her attention forward. *I did not even know he had a sister.* He was a stranger in every sense of the word, this man she'd so quickly agreed to wed. *I know nothing more than his love of art and the liquefying power of his kiss.* Genevieve pressed her eyes closed a moment. And she knew his own self-profession of being a rake.

"He is not coming," her father spat a third time.

Mother patted his hand and murmured placating words. "I am certain the marquess is just detained." She looked to the duke as though hoping, expecting, he'd concur.

Genevieve's stomach dipped. This moment was so eerily similar to another that a dull buzzing filled her ears, muffling her parents' exchange. Not again. Surely, Cedric would not so humiliate her in this way. Surely, he'd not leave her standing at this altar of flowers and greenery. *But what do I really know of the gentleman?* He was a rake and risky and all things to be avoided and, yet, she'd been swayed by the promise he'd dangled before her. Freedom. Control. What happened to a lady twice jilted? A nervous laugh escaped her, capturing the attention of Cedric's sister.

"He will come," Gillian interrupted her fast careening thoughts.

Blankly, she looked as her sister wove her fingers through Genevieve's. "I—" She struggled to drag forth suitable words, with her own self-assurance, but then her gaze landed on the duke as he yanked out his watch fob and consulted his timepiece. The austere lord gave his head a disgusted shake and stuffed the gold piece back inside his jacket.

Genevieve swallowed past a tight throat. "I know." That faint whisper barely reached her own ears. Only, she knew nothing of the sort. She scanned the area for a hint of his tall, powerful frame. *He is not coming.*

"It is nearly thirty minutes past the hour," her father snapped at the duke. "Your son is late. I expect him t-to…" The graying Duke of Ravenscourt leveled him with an icy stare and the remainder of those words went unspoken.

A pall of silence fell over the collection of gathered guests. The muffled whispers of Cedric's sister and brother-in-law reached Genevieve's ears and her gaze went to the young couple. The gentleman leaned down and whispered something close to the lady. Then, with a white-gloved finger, he tucked a pale, blonde strand behind his wife's ear.

The tenderness of that act slammed into her like a gut-punch and she folded her arms at her waist. That beautiful display of warmth and love, all gifts she'd given up on… Or had she? Seeing that couple now, she realized the dream was just as alive and strong as it had ever been. For even with Aumere's betrayal all those years ago and her subsequent exile, she'd lived with the secret hope that there would be a life of joy and laughter with another. The secret she'd kept so well, even from herself, that she'd not truly considered the implications of a marriage of convenience to Cedric. Genevieve's belly churned with unease.

As though feeling her gaze, the young marchioness looked to Genevieve and she hastily averted her eyes, retraining them on the empty entrance of the gardens.

The vicar cleared his throat. "Perhaps the marquess is not coming?" he ventured, the first to vocalize the thoughts everyone had surely been thinking that morning.

The duke tapped his fingertips on the side of his leg; that movement so very much Cedric's that emotion went rolling through her.

"He will be here." She stilled, startled by the sound of her own voice.

"If you humiliate this family again, Genevieve Grace..." Her father let that threat trail off.

If I humiliate this family? A healthy dose of fury drove back the pained dread of waiting for one's absent groom in the middle of Hyde Park. After all, what threat could her father make now? He'd already cut her out of the fold of the family five years earlier? What did one do with a daughter a second time?

"Mayhap he is lost?" Gillian put in helpfully.

She smiled at her sweetly innocent, hopelessly optimistic, sister. "Perhaps," she agreed, unable to muster any real conviction. Genevieve looked to the wrought iron bench they'd occupied two days earlier.

...I'll not lie and say I don't desire you, Genevieve, if that is what you're expecting. For I do—want you...

Was desire enough to bring Cedric 'round to do the honorable thing? Yes, by his admission, he stood to benefit from the funds and properties that came when he married, but as a marquess and future duke, he was in possession of some wealth. A confirmed rake who had no interest in marriage, he'd no doubt had compunctions about tying himself to one woman. And she was certainly not the manner of beauty to hold a gentleman such as him in thrall.

As though in agreement, the late spring breeze stirred the fabric of her very gray skirts. The one loose curl she'd insisted her maid drape over her shoulder played in the wind; that one fragile, but important, control on this, her wedding day. *And now, just as before, I am powerless.* Subject to the whim of a—

The heavy tread of footsteps drew her eyes to the front of the gardens. A sheen of perspiration on his olive-hued skin and his gloriously long, blond hair disheveled as though he'd run a distance and he'd never looked more magnificent. His gaze caught hers and at the small, repentant half-grin on his lips, emotion swelled in her throat. No man had a right to such golden perfection. Cedric bowed his head and then started forward.

Ignoring her family's collectively relieved sighs and her father's muttering thanking the gods above, Genevieve walked off and met him halfway. They stopped a hands-breadth apart. She opened her mouth, when a tall, dark-haired gentleman, far less rumpled and slightly bored, entered the gardens. She recognized him from the duke's ball as the man who'd been conversing with Cedric. The more than slightly handsome gentleman sketched a bow. "Never mind me, love," he said, and walked promptly past her. Bemused, Genevieve stared after him a moment as she was reminded once more of just how much she did not know about Cedric and, more, this desire to know everything of him.

"You look surprised to see me," Cedric said quietly, bringing her focus back to him. He brushed his knuckles briefly along her jaw. "Did you believe I'd not come?"

"I-I thought it was possible you might not." Uncaring of the witnesses at their back, she closed her eyes and leaned into his touch. "You *are* late," she whispered. "And I thought you realized you'd made a mistake."

He made a tsking sound. "I'm not so great a fool that I'd dare let you go, Genevieve." Her heart beat an erratic rhythm, robbing her of words. How easily Terrance had let her go and in the most public, horrendous way, and for nothing more than a fatter purse. And this man before her spoke of her as though she was a cherished gift to be held close. "Though, I confess, I would certainly benefit from additional lessons on punctuality." He lowered his lips close to her ear. "That is, if you would be willing to provide them." Unrepentant rakes such as Cedric could never, would never, be schooled. They would march to the proverbial beat of their own drum.

A smile quivered on her lips. "Given your less than punctual arrival at Lady Erroll's and your own wedding, I'd make you a rubbish instructor."

Cedric tossed his head back and laughed and her breath hitched. With the early afternoon sun glinting off his honey-blond hair, he had the look of a fallen angel, banished forever for tempting the mere mortals around him. He proffered his elbow. "Shall we?"

Without hesitation, Genevieve placed her fingertips on his sleeve and, while they made their way over to the small collection of familial guests gathered for their hastily thrown together ceremony, a sense of absolute rightness filled her and, with it, went all the doubts about his suitability or the risks that went in wedding a rumored rake. For any gentleman who coordinated their wedding in this special spot, offered more than just a formal arrangement. She was going to be all right.

Nay, they were going to be all right.

They took their place before the vicar and the man of indiscriminate years opened his book. "Shall we begin?" The wind pulled at the pages of his leather tome. "Dearly beloved, we are gathered together here in the sight of God…"

CHAPTER 16

BETWEEN THE DUKE OF RAVENSCOURT'S scowl and Genevieve's own parents' tendency for stilted, always proper discourse, the wedding feast would have been a dismal affair. That is, if it weren't for Gillian and Cedric's friend, Lord Montfort.

Through the cheer of her ever joyous sister and the Earl of Montfort, the table was filled with chatter, laughter, and discourse, easily supplied by her garrulous sister.

She listened as Lord Montfort regaled the table with a tale of Cedric's antics at Eton. At her side, Cedric's unrestrained, unapologetic laughter filtered about her. How easy he was in all Social situations. At one time, she, too, had been that way. She'd delighted in *ton* events and been a hopeless flirt, which hadn't worked in her favor when the gossip came to light years earlier. Instead, it had only fueled the whispers circulated. As such, and through the exile imposed by her parents, Genevieve had learned to say little. Instead, she'd become something of an observer. It was why she was now more comfortable observing her husband.

She fiddled with the handle of her fork.

Her husband.

Her husband.

Her husband.

Her *husband.*

She rolled those words through her mind, in very many variations; words she'd thought would never be linked with her name, for the scandal that had belonged to her. In the dreams she'd allowed herself of having a family, she'd not ever contemplated wedding a notorious rake. Though, in fairness, she'd never really considered marrying *anyone* after Terrance's betrayal. Now, she would have so much of what she'd thought beyond her reach.

She'd just not have everything she'd always dreamed of.

Unbidden, her gaze went to Cedric's brother-in-law seated across from his wife. As another silent, special exchange passed between that pair, Genevieve hated herself for envying them that unadulterated love. Using the tip of her fork, she shoved her largely untouched eggs about her plate and stole another look at her husband.

What would their marriage be like? He'd spoken to her of living a life of her pleasures; a life that included artwork and gardening, and no infernal balls or soirees, but she'd been so enrapt in his knowledge of her interests and the freedom he'd presented, that she'd not allowed her mind to consider what *they* would look like—together.

Mayhap I did not consider it because I didn't truly wish to know…

Her throat constricted under the weighted truth—she wanted to matter to him. Surely, with his romantic gesture in selecting Kensington Gardens, surely there was more there. Even as he'd given no indication that he anything more than *liked* her. With trembling fingers, Genevieve set her fork down as terror stuck in her chest.

Cedric settled his larger hand over hers. She started. "You've not touched a bite," he whispered close to her ear and delicious shivers fanned out at the point of contact. "Lady St. Albans."

She started. Lady St. Albans. There was something foreign and at the same time…terrifyingly *right* in being linked to this man. "I find I am not hungry," she conceded.

He tipped his head to where the duke sat, frowning at the head of the table. "Mayhap you'd care for the kippers, then?" he asked, just as the icy lord placed one of those oiled fish in his mouth.

Cedric rang a laugh from her lips and there was something so very freeing in being permitted that unrestrained expression without recrimination or chiding from her strait-laced parents.

From his seat opposite her, Lord Montfort called out, interrupting her teasing exchange with Cedric. "I confess," he said loudly, as all the other guests fell quiet. "I am intrigued by the woman who has brought the notorious St. Albans up to scratch."

Necessity. With the collection of stares trained on her, she could hardly provide that unromantic, if very true, reality. She gave him a wry smile. "There is hardly anything intriguing left about me, my lord. I daresay I'm well known by most."

Her mother's horrified gasp echoed from the room.

Cedric captured Genevieve's fingers and twining them with his, he raised their joined hands to his mouth. "My wife is being modest." Actually her words had been anything but modest. It was, however, nigh impossible to point out such a fact when he caressed the inseam of her wrist with his lips in that heady, distracting way. "It was our mutual love of grand libraries," he said, directing his words at her.

Her throat worked as he took her down a not-too-distant path of his hand on her foot in the duke's library.

The earl erupted into a fit of hilarity. His shoulders shook with the force of his laughter. "St. Albans and books," he said during his bout of amusement. "Next, you'll tell me the gentleman prefers art and poetry."

How was it possible for a man who'd known Cedric since he'd been a boy to know even less than she did about the gentleman? She frowned and opened her mouth to disabuse him of his erroneous assumption about her husband, but Cedric lightly squeezed her fingers. Genevieve looked up questioningly, but he gave a slight shake. She frowned. "Do you find a problem with artwork and literature, my lord?" she put to the earl, refusing to let the matter rest.

The gentleman settled his elbows on the table and leaned forward. "Not *all* artwork and literature," he said on a whisper infused with a wicked edge.

"Ah." She continued, not missing a proverbial beat. "Then you must surely be a devotee of *I Modi* by Raimondi?"

The rakish earl closed his mouth and opened it, and then promptly closed it. A slow, approving smile turned his lips.

"I do not understand," her mother looked from her daughter to Lord Montfort. "What is *I Modi*?"

And apparently, even a sinner was capable of embarrassment for the earl flushed. "I am unfamiliar with that artist." The roguish glimmer in his eyes bespoke the lie there as he promptly redirected the discourse. "I must know Lady St. Albans, what was it that had you select Kensington Gardens for your nuptials."

Her selection? She furrowed her brow. "My lord, I don't—?"

Cedric grabbed his glass of wine and held it aloft. "A toast," he called out quickly. "To my wife, the devotee of art who, with her beauty, can rival any masterpiece." His words were meant to distract. That much was clear by his hasty interruption and the mottled flush marring his cheeks. Yet, his toast combined with the heated look he trained on her, momentarily obliterated the confusion stirred by Lord Montfort's incorrect assumption.

A brief moment later, he was drawn into a discussion with the earl. Genevieve sat there, studying her husband as he spoke: his practiced grin, his effortless words, and the ease with which he charmed a smile from even her mother. Compliments from him slid off his tongue with an ease a bard would have been hard-pressed to not admire. She picked up her drink and took a sip of water. But what was real where Cedric was concerned? Rather, what was real where *she* was concerned with her husband?

"I have not properly welcomed you to the family." The blonde beauty at her side jerked her attention sideways. With the delicate planes of her face and piercing eyes, she possessed a regal beauty that painters would vie to capture on canvas. For that beauty, however, there was a wide smile that reached her eyes. "So please, allow me to rectify that." She held out her fingers. "Welcome."

Genevieve quickly took her hand. "Thank you, my lady."

The marchioness gave her a gentle look. "Please, we are sisters, you must call me Cara."

Sisters. Yet, she knew nothing of this woman who shared Cedric's blood. Were they close? Had he been the protective sort of brother? With each piece she discovered about him, there was a need to know more about who he truly was. Unbidden, she again slid her gaze over to her husband who now conversed with Gillian. Whatever he'd said roused a snorting laugh that earned a frown from her mother; raising the gentleman a notch in Genevieve's estimation.

"What was he like?" she asked quietly, looking to her new sister-in-law.

The young woman froze with her fork halfway to her mouth. She hesitated and then lowered the silver utensil to her plate. "What was he like?" she murmured. Except, the way she worried her lower lip and skirted Genevieve's question spoke more than any word could.

"As a boy?" she prodded.

"I..." Lady Cara briefly settled her gaze on her brother. "I do not know. Cedric was taken under my father's wing early on and schooled in the ways of a future duke." The faintest smile; a sad smile hovered on her lips. "A duke does not have much need of a daughter."

Genevieve cast a pointed look in her own father's direction. "Neither does a marquess," she said gently.

They shared a slight smile borne of understanding; a kindred connection that came from two women who'd really served no worthy purpose beyond the match they might make. As she took in the hard, emotionless set to the duke's face, Genevieve's heart tugged. Where her father's disinterest had afforded her a world of make believe, pretend, and the friendship of her sister, what must it have been like for Cedric? What must it have been like for a boy to grow up under that coldness?

"There are...*no* stories you might share of him?" she asked tentatively, hating that she craved those pieces like cherished treasures.

"We are not close," Lady Cara said with a directness she appreciated but that brought a frown to Genevieve's lips.

Are. Not were. Having been best friends with Gillian until that relationship had been severed with her removal, it was anathema to all she knew about siblings to expect Lady Cara didn't know something of her brother.

"You see, my brother has long lived for h-h..." she stumbled over her words and paused, appearing to search for appropriate words. "Himself," she settled for.

The muscles of her belly clenched. Even as the charming rogue with an ever-present grin, the gentleman who'd met her in the gardens and spoken of art, or chased away her sadness with a game of short-answers, that was not a man who cared only for himself.

Lady Cara searched her face. "But," she put forward tentatively. "I saw him in the gardens this morn and beside you even now," she cast her gaze briefly in her brother's direction. "And the way he is with you is not how he is or has been ever with anyone."

Emotion swelled in her heart. The romantic Lady Cara who wore her love for the gentleman she was married to would see stars amidst dust. "Oh," she said softly. "There is nothing there." Not on Cedric's part. At least nothing that moved beyond the practical. Genevieve fiddled with the stem of her crystal glass.

"You do not care for him, then?" Lady Cara asked, surprise flaring in her eyes.

Stealing a quick look to be sure Cedric remained engrossed in discussion with Gillian and Lord Montfort, Genevieve spoke in hushed tones. "You misunderstand me." She cared for him. More than was practical or sensible and more than could ever make sense for their brief acquaintance. "I do care for him. He, however." Her lips pulled involuntarily. It would be unfair to allow his sister to believe Cedric had given her anything different than what he'd pledged.

"However?" Lady Cara gently encouraged.

"Ours is a marriage of convenience," she settled for lamely. Even as the words slipped from her, she winced. How mercenary that admission painted her.

The other young lady said nothing for a long moment. "Perhaps," she said, a pensive glimmer in her cautious eyes. "But there is more. I see it in you and I see it in my brother." She leaned close. "When I've never seen *any* emotion from him, ever."

The Marquess of Grafton called his wife's attention and Genevieve was left with her thoughts and Lady Cara's fanciful words.

GOOD GOD, HE WOULD HAVE traded all the property coming to him with his marriage this day to be done with the infernal wedding feast.

And it was not because the polite event was hardly his usual pleasures or pursuits, because if he was being just a bit truthful with himself, even with his miserable father at the head of the table, there had been something…rather pleasant in the laughter of his wife and the handful of other assembled guests. And in Genevieve's subtle challenge of Montfort's words. Except with her mention of *I Modi*, she'd only served to conjure all manner of wicked acts and positions marked in those wooden engravings and captured on forbidden pages.

Now he sat beside his very casual wife, conjuring an image of looking through that notoriously scandalous book and putting all sixteen deeds into practice with her. Ultimately, however, he wished to spirit his wife from this oppressive townhouse he'd called home for nearly twenty years, reserve her smile for himself this day, and make love to her at last.

As it was, she remained engrossed in a conversation with his sister.

His skin pricked with the sense of being watched and he pulled his gaze away from Genevieve. His father stared back, his ageless face a familiar, expressionless mask, but then he turned his lips up in a slight, mockingly triumphant grin that glinted in his hard eyes. Wordlessly, he lifted his glass in Cedric and Genevieve's direction.

Cedric narrowed his eyes and tension rolled through him. But for the handful of curt words and furious eyes, the bastard had given little indication of his thoughts yesterday when Cedric expressed his intentions of wedding Genevieve. Sitting beside his bride, there was a perverse satisfaction in being married to one his father so disapproved of.

"Are you all right?"

His new wife's quiet inquiry pulled his attention, jerking him back from thoughts of his coldhearted sire. Cedric transferred his glass to his other hand and claimed Genevieve's fingers, raising them to his lips once more. "How can I not be all right when I'm wed to a minx who knows Raimondi's work?"

A becoming blush stained her pale cheeks. "You are a shameless flirt who is a master at diverting questions, Cedric Andrew Josiah James."

He grimaced. Did the lady miss nothing? "And you recalled that mouthful?"

She smiled. "Yes, well, it is a lot of name for any man. I'd imagine even more so for a boy." Then, Genevieve favored him with a slow wink. "I daresay we must be more judicious for the sake of a child when selecting names for our own."

Her words roused another flurry of wicked musings that involved guiding her naked form upon his massive four-poster bed, and laying between her legs… Until the reality of what she'd said trickled in. He yanked at his cravat. "Er…yes…" Because really, what did a gentleman who'd been clear that they'd never need worry after a child say to that?

Little silver sparkles danced in her expressive green eyes. "I am merely teasing, Cedric," she assured patting his hand and his shoulders sagged with relief. "Your name is a splendid one, too."

This was familiar. Pretty words and compliments he could handle. Not the serious talks of babes and anything that grounded them in the permanency he'd spent the better part of his life avoiding. "Thank you Genevieve Grace Falcot." Their names went perfectly together; melded as though they'd been meant to be united. Inwardly cringing, he shoved aside such blasted romantic musings. What had she done to him that he didn't even recognize himself in a mere week of knowing her?

She waggled her eyebrows. "Well, I do say my mastery of your list is more commendable than the mere two you had to recall."

"You could have hundreds of them and I'd have recalled them all," he said quietly, the words coming from a place of truth and sincerity that terrified the hell out of him.

Her lips parted as all her amusement faded, replaced with a shocked solemnity that only ratcheted up his level of panic. Then she quickly closed her mouth and gave him a slight smile that didn't quite reach her eyes. "As I said, Cedric, you are a rake who possesses a skill with words The Bard himself would have envied you for."

She believed his words spoken as nothing more than flirtatious repartee. She was right to that opinion and he'd not bother to correct her with the truth.

Sipping from his glass of wine, unnerved by his wife's potent hold over him, Cedric fixed on the passing minutes, until the last bloody course was at last cleared away.

In short order, the assembled guests filed from the breakfast room. At his side, his wife stole intermittent glances up at him. Why could he not dredge forth the practiced charm? They reached the foyer and servants rushed over with their cloaks. A young footman helped Genevieve into her gray muslin garment and Cedric frowned at the gentle smile she favored the strapping man with that raised a blush on his cheeks. When had he ever cared about whom a lady reserved any or all of her attention for? Yet, the sight of his newly-minted bride charming a damned servant sent a spiral of red fury rolling inside.

"All the same, aren't they," his father bit out in hushed tones for Cedric's ears. "Get me my heir before that one goes tupping your servants."

Cedric jerked and, reflexively, he curled his hands into tight fists to keep from bloodying his sire senseless. He'd not show the bastard a hint of emotion. "Go to hell, Father," he said cheerfully.

Genevieve threw her arms around her sister. Folding her in a tight embrace, she whispered something against the young woman's temple. Tipping his head, he took in that exchange. The young ladies spoke in hushed whispers, exchanging the occasional, periodic nod. There was a familial affection he'd thought impossible. For the first five years of his life, he'd known that warmth from his mother, but those moments had been so very fleeting they may as well have been imagined. He looked to his own sister, smiling alongside his equally smiling brother-in-law, the Marquess of Grafton; two people who, even given their connection, may as well have been strangers.

He'd attended their own wedding as more a formal guest, who just by a matter of chance happened to share the blood of the bride. And he'd not imagined it could be any other way among family.

Catching his gaze, the Marquess of Grafton came forward with a hand outstretched. "St. Albans." Gone was all hint of the earlier warmth the man had shown Clarisse. In its place was a frosty reserve.

Ah, so the man had, at some point, gleaned his wife's brother was, in fact, a shameful rotter. "Grafton," he returned, accepting the congratulatory handshake and then he let his arm fall to his side. Suddenly even more eager to be rid of the lot of them and the niggling of caring about their ill-opinion of him, he held his elbow out to Genevieve making her goodbyes to Clarisse. "My lady. Shall we?"

His wife said one more thing to Cedric's sister and then came over, took his arm, and let him usher her outside the walls of the oppressive townhouse he'd spent the better part of his life trying to be free of.

He sucked in a clearing breath of the spring air.

"It is awful, is it not?" Genevieve murmured, as they made their way to his waiting carriage.

Cedric raised his brow. "Awful?"

"The air," she said by way of explanation.

Motioning away the waiting servant, Cedric easily handed his wife inside the black barouche. "I rather fancy breathing. The whole allowing a person to live, business."

She laughed. "Oh, hush." His wife settled her lithe frame in the red upholstered squabs. "I referred to the staleness of it."

He paused. "Is it stale?" Cedric cast a glance back out the open door at the hazy blue skies. He spent so little time in the country, but a handful of weeks each year in the hunting season, that he'd never really given it a note. His recent winnings last year of the country manor and properties had been in such rubbish shape, he'd been more fixed on the challenge of attempting to resurrect the basic heap of stone. The steward he'd selected oversaw the growing prosperity of that, allowing Cedric to return to London. He claimed the seat opposite his wife.

Genevieve widened her eyes to large green pools. "Never tell me you've never noticed the difference between country air and London air?" Shock underscored her words. "Cedric Andrew," she said, when he remained silent.

The servant closed the door behind them. "Then I shan't tell you."

"It is impossible to not note it," she said sounding both befuddled and beleaguered that her husband hadn't noted the same drastic difference. "It smells…" She wrinkled her mouth in a preciously endearing manner. "Cleaner and pure. And the stars…"

His wife, the gardener and artist, preferred the country. That truth was reflected in the faraway distance of her gaze. Cedric reached over and scooped her up, startling a squeak from her as he settled her on his lap. "I will just have to teach you how splendid London is," he whispered against her lips and then he took her mouth under his in a hard kiss.

A breathless sigh escaped her and he slipped his tongue inside swallowing that sound of her desire. She angled her neck, allowing him greater access to her mouth. The carriage lurched forward, jolting them apart. Her cheeks flushed and her chest rising and falling with the evidence of her breathless desire, Genevieve captured his face between her delicate palms. "And I intend to show you all you've missed these years, Cedric Andrew."

And because he did not know what to do with the depth of emotion in her eyes and promise that belied the marriage of convenience they'd both agreed to, Cedric took her lips once more in a kiss, so that all he could focus on was this desperate hunger for Genevieve Grace and not the sea of meaningful questions he did not care to explore.

CHAPTER 17

$\mathcal{S}$HE'D NOT SEEN HER HUSBAND since they'd entered his townhouse, nay, *their* townhouse. Genevieve found the gilt clock atop
the fireplace mantel where a small fire burned, six hours ago.

It had been six hours since they'd arrived, greeted by the line of
assembled servants.

The housekeeper Mrs. Fennyworth, had shown her abovestairs…
where she had been waiting ever since. Surely, her husband had
not left her on her wedding night. Surely, he'd not sought out his
clubs or…a dark, ugly, niggling thought slid in…visited someone
else.

…I am a rake…

"Are you sure you are not hungry, my lady?" Delores asked.

Looking up quickly from the sketchpad on her lap, Genevieve
shook her head. "No, I am quite well. You may leave the tray." With
the knots churning her belly, the last thing she cared for was food.
"That is all, Delores," she said softly. "You may go."

The young lady nodded and then quickly hurried across the
room. She pulled the door open and gasped. "Oh, excuse me, my
lord."

Genevieve whipped her gaze to the entrance and her fingers
curled tight on the book in her hands as Cedric stepped aside,
allowing the maid to make a hasty retreat. Her heart tripped a beat
at the sight of him. Absent of his jacket and attired in nothing but

his white shirtsleeves, breeches and boots, he closed the door and leaned against it. With a cool elegance, he propped the sole of his boot against the wood panel. Her mouth went dry. No gentleman had a right to such sophisticated ease. She hopped up from the Louis XV red, giltwood Duchesse and her sketchpad tumbled forgotten to the floor.

By the ghost of a smile hovering about his lips, he'd noted her scrutiny. "Genevieve," he greeted on a satiny whisper.

Nervousness tripped inside her belly. "C-Cedric," she fiddled with the charcoal in her fingers, belatedly realizing the dark mess she'd made of her already slightly stained fingers.

"You did not take an evening meal," he observed, his gaze going to the untouched silver tray that had arrived several hours ago.

She'd spent so much time worrying he'd not come, that she'd not given due attention to nervousness of what it would mean when he *did* arrive. "No," she conceded, unable to the keep the disappointment from her words. No bride cared to take her first meal as a wedded woman in her chambers, alone.

Cedric pushed away from the door and stalked over with long, sleek steps, then came to a stop. His gaze fell downward and she appreciated the thick luxuriance of his golden hair. Her fingers twitched. Surely a wife was permitted the luxury of running her fingers through those strands when she wished? And…

She registered his still otherwise diverted attention and she belatedly followed his stare. *Drat.* His partially completed likeness stared back at her. Embarrassment curled her toes into the thin Aubusson carpet.

Wordlessly, he sank to his haunches and scooped up the book. She dug her fingernails into her palm to keep from ripping that book from his hand. That book which had served as a window into her thoughts, dreams, and actions, for the past four, nearly five years. He remained crouched at her feet and she braced for that gentle teasing and mischievous smile on his perfect lips. Instead, he flipped through the pages. The crackle of the thick sheets turning loud as a shot in the quiet room. He lingered on the gardens she'd tended in her grandfather's Kent property.

"They are my grandfather's," she said into the silence, needing to fill that thick void.

Cedric glanced up a moment. "You miss it." There was faint

surprise in those words which were more statement than anything else.

"I do," she replied, anyway. She reclaimed her spot on the chaise. "I cried as though I might break when my parents sent me to him. I loved London." Not unlike Cedric himself still did. "And I hated Kent from the moment I arrived at his country property." The memory trickled in of those earliest days. The fear and anxiousness around the heavily wrinkled, gruff, ancient earl who growled more than he spoke. Until he'd ordered her outside and so desperate to be free of those growls, she'd looked at the world anew. "What I wouldn't give to be back in the country," she said softly. "While I was there," she motioned to the butterflies etched in black. "I noticed all those things I previously missed in my family's brief trips to Father's country seat."

Cedric stared questioningly back.

"The beauty of night's song; the birds and crickets chirping in harmony. The sky is bluer and when you lay on the grass and stare up at the sky you see nothing but an endless blue, so that you think you can stretch your fingers up and touch the heavens."

He hooded his thick, blond lashes. She balled her hands into fists and braced for his witty repartee but, instead, he resumed his study of her book. "You are quite good," he said, with the same matter-of-factness of an instructor speaking to a favored apprentice.

"Thank you," she murmured. There was something so raw and exposing in having one's work examined so.

He flipped to another page that contained his partially completed and abandoned likeness, and paused.

"I've not completed sketches of people," she explained, when still he said nothing. Perhaps it had been all the years she'd spent away from people, at a time when art had been her companion. "The angles, the shadows," she continued motioning to his image. "My proportions are disastrous."

In one fluid movement, he shoved to his feet and claimed the spot beside her. His broad, powerful form swallowed the space of the lounge. "Here," he murmured, rescuing the charcoal still hopelessly staining her fingers.

Her breath caught at the electrifying thrill of that too-brief contact.

Cedric flipped to an empty page in the sketchpad. He swung his

muscular leg over the opposite side of the chaise, straddling it, and
then he guided her between his legs.

"Wh-What are you doing?" the tremulous whisper slipped from
her lips as his breath, scented with brandy and mint, filled her
heady senses.

"Providing you an art lesson," he said, his tone so calm, so very
matter-of-fact, it slightly steadied her rapidly beating heart.

"Y-you are an artist?" she asked with some surprise. Pleasure
blossomed in her chest; at this deeper connection shared between
them. "What else do I not know about you?" And how she longed
to learn every detail.

"Shh," he whispered against her ear. "Questions later." Bracing
the open leather book in their left hands, he brought his other arm
about her, enveloping her in his embrace.

Her lashes fluttered wildly. How had she failed to note, until
this instant, how very erotic creating art was? Because she'd not
received a lesson from Cedric Falcot, the Marquess of St. Albans,
was why.

"When you sketch a person's likeness," he said softly against her
ear. "You must use the negative space to check the shapes between
the features."

His quietly spoken instructions momentarily pulled her out of
the eddy of desire she'd been swirling in. Genevieve cast a look
over her shoulder. "I don't—"

"You must imagine a straight line down the model's face,
directly through the pupil. From that line, you must think, where
are the eyes placed in relation to it? Where is the lip set?" Placing
the charcoal in her fingers, he proceeded to guide them over the
page. "When you are sketching people, Genevieve, it is the details
about a person that makes the portrait unique," he murmured.
"Are the lips properly full? And the lower lip slightly narrow?"
The scratch of the charcoal on the page blended with her slightly
rasping breaths.

How was he so unaffected? How was he able to think of art
when their bodies were flush as, together, they created the work
upon the page, as one?

"You do not need to overaccentuate the features, but on some
subjects, this one," he clarified, "you can slightly overemphasize
the curve of a hip, the fullness of the lips…but then…some sub-

jects are perfection and to overemphasize is a travesty."

Through the thin slip of fabric of her nightshift, her body tingled. To keep from dissolving into a puddle of desire in his arms, she concentrated on their fingers as they danced about the page. They went on that way until their purposeful strokes transformed the empty page into… Her fingers trembled at the familiarity of her visage as it stared back.

Cedric immediately righted the charcoal in her grip and proceeded to finish the sketch. "You are perfection."

Perfection.

Of course, his were the words of a rake or rogue but, in this moment, with their love of art shared between them, it felt like something more and another thrill went through her at this bond. Cedric continued his mastery over the page until a familiar room materialized; lined with books and a scandalous piece of artwork, and seated at the edge of that room in her bare feet was her. From her slightly parted lips, to the glimmer of passion in her eyes, he'd expertly captured the maelstrom of emotion she'd known that day in his presence and every day since.

Their first meeting.

She registered the silence and, blinking, she looked down at his suddenly still fingers and the completed sketch he lay down in front of her.

"And that is how you create the human form, Genevieve." He brought his mouth close to her ear and worshipped the sensitive shell with the softest kiss. Then, folding his arm about her waist, he drew her closer to him so her back was pressed against the hard wall of his chest. "*You* are perfection." His smooth baritone washed over her as he trailed his mouth lower to the sensitive skin just behind her lobe.

Genevieve's pulse jumped and she angled her head to better open herself to his ministrations. "I expect you have said that to any number of women," she whispered and closed her eyes, savoring the delicious explosion of sensation buffeting her senses.

"Yes," he confessed softly. With his large hands, he palmed her breasts through the modest fabric of her nightshift. "But this is the only time I've ever meant it." Her nipples puckered at his skilled touch and she proved herself the shameless wanton she'd been accused of all these years, for she leaned into his expert caress.

Not allowing her anymore words, Cedric angled her around and devoured her mouth with his.

His was the unbridled, unapologetic kiss of a man fueled by desire and there was something heady in knowing she'd moved *this* gentleman in this way. He guided her leg over the chaise so they each straddled the upholstered seat. The wickedness of her positioning rucked her nightshift high above her thighs, but Cedric would not allow her the deserved modesty. Instead, he wrapped his hands about her hips and dragged her closer to the vee of his legs. Her womanhood throbbed with a tender awareness, only heightened by the drag of the upholstered fabric against that forbidden flesh.

Delicious shivers fanned out and she leaned into him, meeting his kiss, tangling her tongue with his in an erotic dance. She moaned into his mouth and raising her hands, twined her fingers in the long, luxuriant strands of his golden-blond hair.

He growled his approval and that primitive sound rumbled up from his chest as he deepened their embrace and she boldly turned herself over to him.

CEDRIC HAD HAD SCORES OF women in his life. Inventive whores, clever courtesans with wicked mouths, eager widows. Wanton women. Women whose depravity had only been matched by his own. Not a single one of those women had raised his blood to this feverish pitch, as did his wife. With her blend of bold and innocence, there was a sincerity to Genevieve's every movement that only fueled this fierce hungering for her.

He ran his palms down the small of her back and slid his fingers under the generous swell of her buttocks, holding her close. A low, keening moan escaped Genevieve who melted even further into his touch. Fueled by that breathless sound of her desire, Cedric clasped her white nightshift at the hem and tugged it over her head, exposing her as he'd ached to since their first chance meeting a week earlier.

He studied her with a hungry gaze. He'd always favored women with generous breasts and, yet, Genevieve's small mounds with engorged pink buds, caused desire to blaze inside. His bride followed his gaze and her skin pinked with his focus. She made to hug her arms close to her chest. "Don't," he commanded gruffly.

Genevieve hesitated and then lowered her arms to her side.

Incapable of words, he explored her. Palming her right breast, he weighed it in his hand. "Softer than satin," he murmured. He captured her nipple between his thumb and forefinger, rolling the peaked bud.

A throaty moan spilled past her plump lips. "A proper, respectable lady should not feel this way." Her head fell back, accentuating the length of her neck.

"A proper *woman* should feel this way," he said, his voice roughened with his need for her. He lowered his head and claimed the neglected tip of her left breast in his mouth.

Genevieve cried out and curled her fingers in his hair, anchoring him close. A hungering for her rolled through him, threatening to draw him under. Buffeting his senses and reveling in the reflexive undulation of her hips, he continued to suckle her, laving the swollen bud, teasing it, tasting it until the room reverberated with the echo of his wife's breathless pleas.

Suddenly, he stopped and she cried out a protest but Cedric only shoved to his feet and, in one swift moment, swung her into his arms and carried her to the four-poster bed at the center of the room. Passion glazed her green eyes as he laid her carefully down.

Not taking his gaze from hers, he stepped back and proceeded to disrobe. She widened her eyes as he pulled his shirt over his head and revealed his naked chest to her innocent stare. The blush on her cheeks deepened, but she did not look away. Until he tugged free his boots and breeches. His brave bride stole a quick peek at his jutting erection and then whispered something that might have been a prayer. "A-are you certain you'd not care to continue with our art lesson?" Her breathless stammer raised a small grin.

And he, who'd long abhorred all hint of innocence, was enthralled by this woman's artlessness. "Quite certain, love," he whispered.

Genevieve looked up at the ceiling, past his shoulder, over at the hearth, anywhere that was not him. "It really was an invaluable lesson," she rambled. "I am quite eager to put all your lessons to use." As though she'd registered the suggestiveness of his words, she shot her gaze to his. "That is, your art lessons."

With a gentle smile, he came down over her, bracing his elbows on either side of her so she was folded in his embrace. He touched his lips to her closed eyes; first one and then the other, and then he trailed his mouth down her cheek, before ultimately finding her lips. Some of her hesitancy melted away. Genevieve reached for his kiss, but he hovered with their breaths dancing and melding. "I have wanted you from the first moment I saw you in the library, Genevieve. I wanted to lay you down and waken your body to the passion within you."

Emotion leapt in her eyes and, later, he'd allow himself the panicky fear of the truth behind those words. For now, all he could focus on was spreading her cream white thighs and burying himself deep in her honeyed warmth. "And I have wanted you." Her husky contralto sent a bolt of lust through him. Then, his spirited wife closed the faint space between them, twined her arms about his neck, and kissed him.

A groan of approval rumbled from Cedric's chest. They continued to mate with their tongues in an age-old rhythm that matched his rapidly beating heart.

Needing to taste all of her, Cedric dragged his mouth in a deliberate trail, lower, to her neck, downward to her small breasts, and then he slid a hand between them and found her hot center with his fingers.

A little hiss exploded from Genevieve and she shot her hips off the bed, arching into his caress. "Cedric," she moaned as he parted her folds and toyed with her center. Her wet warmth coated his fingers and slicked his entry as he slipped a finger inside her.

"That is it, love," he encouraged as she lifted into his caress. She bit her lip and worked herself against his palm. He continued his deliberate ministrations until her movements grew frantic, hinting at her rapidly receding control, and then he withdrew his fingers.

She cried out a protest, but he slid his body over hers and positioned himself at her well-readied, hot entry. He slid his shaft slowly inside her tight walls and an agonized groan lodged in his chest. Cedric stilled and welcomed her heat as it enveloped him. In all the women he'd taken, he'd never made love to a virgin. He'd made it a point to avoid those mewling women. Rather, he'd preferred the women who graced his bed to be as skilled as the most practiced courtesan. Staring into Genevieve's flushed face, there was an overwhelming emotion; one that he could not explain, a gratefulness that no other had ever known her in this way.

Her lashes fluttered open and she looked up with a thick haze of passion clouding her eyes. "What is it?" she whispered. She cupped her hand to his cheek. "Are you all right?"

At her gentle concern, a surge of tenderness mixed with an incontrollable yearning to know Genevieve in this way. In an act he'd taken part in so many times, the intimacy of that joining had ceased to matter. Until now. Until her. Terror licked at the edge of his lust. "I am fine," he whispered, even as his tumultuous thoughts proved anything but that. To keep from thinking about the implications of his body's need for her and to silence any questions he didn't have an answer to, Cedric claimed her lips in a long, deep kiss, so that all she was capable of was more of her breathless whimpers and moans.

At the evidence of her longing, blood surged to his shaft and he continued to push deeper into her, slower. He pressed his eyes closed and relished the sensation of their bodies joining as one. What was it about this woman that was so different from all others before? He withdrew and she cried out, scrabbling at his back. Moisture beaded on his forehead as he again found her with his fingers. He delved his fingers inside her slick passageway, preparing her further for his entry until her movements grew jerky and then he slid inside her once more, inch by agonizing inch.

A broken groan spilled from his lips as a hungering unlike any he'd ever known gripped him, to possess her as no one ever had. Blood pounding loudly in his ears, Cedric layered his brow to hers. "Forgive me," he groaned and then he pushed past the thin barrier of her virginity.

The room echoed with her cry and he stilled, giving her time to accustom herself to his length filling her. A lone crystalline tear slipped down her cheek and the sight of it ravaged him, momentarily dulling his desire. But he found her again with his fingers and caressed her center again until she slowly undulated into his touch, once more. Shifting his weight forward on his elbow, Cedric claimed her lips under his and then began to move. He drew his shaft out and then pushed forward, repeating the motion with slow, determined strokes until a little keening moan was bubbling from Genevieve's lips.

"Cedric," she gasped. Folding her arms about him, she lightly raked her fingers over his back. At that unrestrained hint of her need, he increased his rhythm. A strand fell over his sweaty brow as he continued to thrust. With tremulous fingers, she brushed it back and met his expert strokes as their bodies became lost in a dance that only they two knew.

Her movements grew frantic, even as her body went taut. He plunged deeper and then bent his head to draw the tip of her breast in his mouth, once more. It sent her careening over the precipice. Her hungry wail filtered throughout the room and it pulled him forward as he went hurtling with her. He stiffened and with a low groan, poured himself deep inside. The walls of her womanhood clenched and unclenched about him, draining all of him, until he collapsed atop her, replete.

Their breaths came hard and fast. As reality intruded, Cedric rolled off his wife's sated, limp form. Heart pounding out of control, he laid there and stared with panicked eyes up at the mural at the center of the room. Never had he spent himself inside a woman. French letters had been his constant companion when with a woman. It had been the one masterful control he'd exhibited over his life; the assurance that for all the ways he was like his father, he would never be like the current Duke of Ravenscourt in that one essential and very important way. And even as this woman was his wife and certainly getting a child with her was expected, it was something he'd vowed never to do: to spread his blood, to give his father that coveted future duke, to allow that intimacy with any woman. In desperate need of some distance, he swung his legs over the edge of his bed and fetched a kerchief to gently wipe the stains of their lovemaking.

Her cheeks awash with color, Genevieve lay silent through his ministrations and then, when he'd finished, she flipped onto her side.

Cedric cleaned himself and then made to stand. His new bride looked over her shoulder, a tender invitation in her eyes. *Leave… there is no reason for you to stay…*

Except, ignoring that voice in his head, he reluctantly claimed the spot beside her.

Genevieve swiftly turned in his arms and curled her warm, slender frame against him. He stiffened, as she snuggled against him like a contented cat that had just supped on the cream. She layered her palm to his chest and his rapidly beating heart kicked up another frantic pattern. He did not sleep with women. After finding his release, he'd always taken his leave or his partner had gone back to the miserable blighter she'd been unfaithful to. Sex was just a meaningless exchange, with two people taking their base pleasures and nothing more. Genevieve at his side challenged that long-held belief. Her breath fell into a smooth, settled, even cadence.

Cedric waited several moments to make sure she slumbered and then when a little snore escaped her lips, he made to ease away from her. Except... Another snore filled the quiet. He angled onto his side to study her in sleep.

With her mouth slightly parted, there was a peace to her. It was the same one that followed her in her waking days. In her sleep, the ghost of a smile played on her lips so that he ached to know what thoughts slipped in and out of her dream. Cedric went still and then blinked several times in rapid succession. What madness plagued him that he would...moon over his own wife? He gave his head a disgusted shake. He'd never been, nor would he ever be, one of those romantic, lovesick fools. Yet here he sat, appreciating his new wife's smile, of all things. No, theirs was strictly a formal arrangement between two strangers, with the additional benefit of mutual passion. He grimaced and swung his legs over the side of the bed.

A little bleating snore filled the quiet and he whipped his head back around.

She...snored and then in her sleep, she shifted about. Did she search for him in her slumber? Tenderness unfurled inside him and Cedric swiped a hand over his face. He was tired, was all. It was the only reason he even now stared at the place she occupied on the feather mattress. And it was the only reason he reclaimed a place beside her.

And with the ticking clock atop the mantel and the wispy puffs of air escaping her lips, it was the only reason Cedric closed his eyes. Except, as sleep pulled at him, he couldn't help but feel he lied to himself.

CHAPTER 18

THE SUN SHONE HIGH IN the early afternoon sky, beating down on Genevieve's neck. Seated on the ground of the overrun, ill-tended gardens of her husband's townhouse, she picked her head up toward the sky and let the warm rays caress her face.

Open sketchpad forgotten on her lap, she closed her eyes and a smile played on her lips. She had a husband. And a garden. And a husband who sketched and enjoyed artwork, and… Her skin went ten shades hotter in an act that had nothing to do with the warm spring day and everything to do with the pleasures Cedric had awakened in her body.

Abandoning her sketchpad, she drew her knees close to her chest and assessed the overgrown space. Thick ivy climbed up the high brick walls. Weeds choked the tangled rose bushes and forsythia. In its neglect, this sheltered, artificial homage to the country spoke to Cedric's disinterest and disdain for the countryside. By his own admission and everything she knew of him, he was a man most comfortable in the world beyond these walls. He'd not take the time to see spaces of nature cared for. Unease churned inside her.

It really should not matter. They needn't have everything in common as a husband and wife. In fact, given their hasty marriage of convenience, they needn't have anything in common. It should be enough that he had his funds and she had her freedom, and then anything else shared between them was a bonus she'd no right to expect or demand.

The wind stirred overhead and pulled at the loosened strands of her bonnet. So why did it feel like a lie? Why did it feel like she wanted so much more from the man who even now still slumbered? Chewing at her lower lip, she cast a quick glance over her shoulder. Or she expected he still slept. When she'd left him several hours ago to take her breakfast and set about exploring her home, he'd been silently slumbering in her new chambers. A smile played about her lips as she recalled him as he'd been. Sprawled on his back, with his hand flung over his eyes, it was as though, even in slumber, he'd sought to keep the day at bay.

He was a man who slept late. And yet that same man had also sought her out in the gardens of Hyde Park a week ago…to apologize. Returning her attention to her sketchpad, Genevieve picked up her book and charcoal. Cedric's art lesson still resonating around her head, her body thrilled with the heated memory of his touch. She proceeded to sketch his devilish visage. Scrunching her brow, she muted all sounds and concentrated on her efforts.

Everything melted away—time, questions about just what she was to Cedric, the Marquess of St. Albans, if anything, what tomorrow meant for them. She fixed her gaze on bringing his tall, powerful form to life on a page, when all attempts before had proven futile.

Of their own volition, her fingers flew over the sheet as his form materialized before her. Her bonnet dipped over her forehead and she hastily shoved it back, before returning to her task.

No gentleman had a right to be so beautiful.

Or outrageously charming.

Or…

"You are a determined young woman, aren't you, my lady?" Cedric's amused voice sounded from beyond her shoulder.

She screeched and her finger slid across the page, scratching a black mark along the outside form of her husband. Heart pounding, she hurriedly climbed to her feet. She wheeled around and found him at the entrance of the gardens. Arms folded at his broad chest, he lounged negligently against the ivy-covered wall. How long had he been there? And more…had she uttered anything aloud while he'd been secretly observing? "You are awake," she blurted and snapped the book closed. It dangled at her side. Her entire body blazed as last night came rushing forth. The feel of his touch. Her own wanton moans, blended with his gruff words of encouragement.

"I am," he said, his grin widening as he shoved away from the frame and took slow, languid steps closer.

She pulled her sketchpad close to her chest. "That is, of course, you are awake." *Stop talking.* "It was just I did not expect you'd be here." He continued coming. "Not that I really gave a thought as to where you would be at this hour." She lied. She *had* wondered. Wondered if even now he was at his wicked clubs and doing… whatever it is wicked gentlemen did at those halls. Amusement flickered to life in his eyes as he came to a stop before her. Genevieve sighed. "What I meant to say is, good morning."

Why could she not be the same artful flirt she'd been all those years ago? Not that she wanted to be a flirt with other gentlemen. It would, however, prove valuable to have equally witty and clever words for her endlessly charming husband.

"You've been awake long?" he asked.

Five hours now. She nodded slightly. "I am an early riser." A pit formed in her belly as she was reminded once more of how little they truly knew of each other.

"Ah, yes," he murmured. Capturing a loose curl, he tucked it behind her ear. "The masterful skies; that canvas of purples and pinks." Yet for her reservations, Cedric so easily spouted words she'd shared with him from one of their first meetings. What was she to make of that?

"There is that," she admitted. "There is also the quiet of the day." Before the world intruded, it was just her with her thoughts and Society with its judgmental opinions abed.

"And what do you have planned on your first day as marchioness and master of your freedom?"

Master of her freedom. An excited little thrill gripped her; it blotted out all earlier, whimsical musings. For in a world where she'd had so little, with the name he'd conferred to her, she was no longer under the oppressive thumb of her parents or polite Society. "I thought to go to the museum. But today, after seeing the gardens, I thought I might have gardening equipment found by the servants so I might set to work clearing this space." She gestured animatedly as she spoke.

Cedric scanned the grounds and grimaced. "Rather a mess, aren't they?"

She nodded eagerly. "Oh, yes," she agreed. Then, one who didn't garden couldn't truly understand. "But not unlike a blank canvas, in a way." Genevieve motioned to the space. "There is so much to craft and so much character to this space."

He returned his gaze to hers and her heart skittered a beat under the intensity of his scrutiny. "You are a true artist," he said more to himself. He slipped her book from her fingers and proceeded to skim through those pages, until he reached the recent likeness she'd completed of him.

She shuffled on her feet. "I do believe I've done—"

"A magnificent job," he said quietly. "You've done a magnificent job."

And looking at it beside him, she could admit with an honesty to herself that she'd expertly captured his half-grin as he stood at the entrance of Kensington Gardens; his jacket rumpled, his hair haphazard.

Suddenly uneasy with this window into her world, a window that showed his influence on her life, Genevieve cleared her throat. She held out her fingers and he returned to the book, but then swiftly captured her other wrist in his hand.

A breathless gasp slipped from her as he drew her close. "You are well today, Genevieve?" he whispered his question against her ear.

His gentle kiss brought her lashes fluttering and the book tumbled forgotten to the ground. "I a-am," she managed, not pretending to know what he referenced.

Cedric swiftly loosened the strings of her bonnet and tossed the article aside. It caught a gentle breeze and sailed several feet away. He found her lips with his and devoured her mouth as though he sought to burn the taste of her upon his tongue. She twined her arms about his neck and leaned into his embrace. Her husband swiftly moved his questing lips lower, to her neck, downward to her modest décolletage.

She automatically clenched her fingers in the luxuriant strands of his hair. "I expect I should have a modicum of properness and point out that it is daylight," she panted and tipped her head to the side to allow him better access to her neck.

Cedric guided them down so they knelt before one another.

"Properness is wasted on your lips," he rasped, taking her mouth under his, once more. She moaned as the heady taste of coffee and honey filled her senses. "This should be celebrated between us." He dragged his lips over her neck, nipping at the flesh, and ringing a cry from her lips.

As he laid her upon the earth, her heart picked up its rhythm and she lifted her arms in invitation. The press of the door handle shattered the quiet, like a shot in the night, bringing them apart. Cedric jumped up and helped her to her feet in one fluid motion, so that as his butler stepped into the sun-filled gardens, his employer knelt with her sketchpad proffered in his extended hands.

He cast a bored look over his shoulder. "Avis," he said in lazy tones.

How many times had he been discovered so, with other women, that he'd become such a master in prevarication? She hated that he had and hated even more that it should matter. In marrying him, she'd been so fixed on the idea of a formal match between them, that she hadn't given true thought of what it meant being married to a rake; not truly. Those questions now whispered strong around her mind; where did he find his pleasures and how…? Her stomach muscles tightened involuntarily.

The young servant averted his eyes. Alas, too many times, if his flushed butler's cheeks were any indication. "Lord Montfort has arrived, my lord. He said you were expecting him."

Lord Montfort? The earl. Genevieve stared blankly past her husband's shoulder.

"Tell him I'll join him momentarily," he assured the man.

For all the knowledge that hers was nothing more than an arranged marriage, there was a tug of disappointment in her breast that Cedric did not turn away his friend. *What did you expect? That you'd sit in his gardens and sketch artwork together, discussing your hopes and dreams?* Avis sketched a bow and as her husband returned his attention to her, Genevieve pasted a smile on her lips until her cheeks ached. Her arms tightened hard about her book.

He worked an uncharacteristically solemn gaze over her face and then called out. "Avis?" The servant stopped with his hand on the door handle. "Tell Montfort, I am unable to join him today," he said, not taking his eyes from her.

Her heart quickened. "Very well, my lord." Avis sketched another bow to his employer's back.

"Oh, and Avis, one more thing? Lady St. Albans requires gardening equipment. Will you see the footmen have it brought posthaste?"

Even with the space between them, Genevieve detected the flicker of surprise in the servant's eyes. "Of course." The young butler hurried off, leaving them alone, once more.

She searched her husband's face, trying to make sense of this man and his deviation from his daily plans. Cedric Falcot was a man rumored to place his pleasure above all else. He was certainly not a man to enter into an arranged marriage and renege on plans he'd made with his equally rakish friends, all to be with his new, unwanted, but necessary wife. "…I have never seen him look at another person so…" His sister's softly-spoken words trickled around her mind. A blackbird sang overhead and another gentle breeze tugged at Genevieve's skirts.

Cedric loosened the buttons of his jacket and shrugged out of the sapphire blue garment. Her mouth went dry as he tossed it to a nearby rusted, metal bench. "What are you doing?" Her words emerged a faint squeak.

He flashed a grin. "I thought you said we were gardening, my lady?"

We. This man was no rake. This man was more than an even charming rogue. With his abandoning his previous bachelor's plans and joining her today, he was very much a devoted husband. And even as this moment was nothing more than the fantasy of what could be between them. It felt so very real and she did not want to let the moment go—ever.

Genevieve smiled. "Then let us begin."

THE SUN BEAT DOWN ON Cedric's neck and perspiration beaded on his brow. If anyone had told him one week and one day ago that he'd be not comfortably closeted away in his clubs but on his knees in his neglected gardens, tearing out weeds alongside a respectable lady, he'd have laughed in the humorous bastard's face.

He paused and dusted the back of his hand over his brow, using the brief break to study his fully engrossed in her task wife. Digging a small hole, she replanted a small, twig-like scrap. A strawberry strand fell across her brow and she blew it back, but continued working.

The sight of her in her modest gray skirts, working away, momentarily froze him and a dull humming filled his ears. He was not a gentleman who found pleasure in the close company of others. Montfort was a friend, but their relationship had been forged as two miserable buggers who'd delighted in thumbing their noses up at polite Society.

This—a wife, a person, who desired his company—he did not know what to make of. He didn't want a person to be dependent upon him as his mother had been dependent upon his father. For ultimately, he'd fail Genevieve in the same way his father had failed his mother...and selfish bastard that he was, Cedric still loathed the idea of destroying her unfettered smile. He didn't want to be responsible for her happiness, because if she let him, ultimately he'd be the one to destroy it. A name he could give. Her freedom. Those were safe matters of practicality. But to join her in the gardens and sketch alongside her only built this false, fragile world between them, which was destined for failure.

He scrambled to his feet and Genevieve pulled her attention from her task. "Cedric?" There was concern underscoring her soft inquiry that only roused the terror in his chest all the more.

"I have business I must see to."

Her expression fell. "Of course." Yet so much emotion bled from the depths of her eyes, that his mouth went dry; emotion he didn't know what to do with. He turned to go. "What manner of business do you oversee?"

Her words froze him. Had they been uttered by any other woman, they'd have been accusatory in nature. Genevieve's, however, conveyed a curiosity to know more about him. Cedric momentarily eyed the door, contemplating a swift answer and a swifter retreat. Instead, he lazily collected his jacket. "I won property in a wager and have been working to see it restored to its former greatness."

Her lips tipped down in the corners. "You won it?"

He frowned, hearing the slight reproach there. "You disapprove?" he asked, instead. If she disapproved of wagering, what would she say to the truly dissolute lifestyle he'd lived these years? It would shock her into regretting the very marriage she'd entered into yesterday.

Genevieve stretched her back, momentarily diverting his attention to that languorous sight, which conjured all delicious memories of making love to her last evening. "It is hard to approve of wagering," she said quietly, pulling him back from his desirous musings. "Particular wagering that sees a man divested of his properties."

He fastened the buttons of his jacket. "If it weren't me, it would have been another," he pointed out, not knowing why her ill-opinion should matter. When was the last time he'd ever cared about what anyone thought of him?

"Yes, well, two wrongs infer one right."

In one fluid motion, Cedric swept her to her feet and brought her to his chest. "Have you always been this proper, Genevieve?" he asked, brushing his lips to the sensitive skin behind the lobe of her ear, ringing a breathless laugh from her.

"Are you trying to distract me?"

He moved his lips lower, to the spot where her pulse pounded in her neck. "Is it working?" he breathed against her satiny soft skin.

"I-Indeed," she rasped.

"I will delight in teaching you the joys of wickedness."

They were the wrong words to say. A solemn look replaced the earlier lightness etched in the delicate planes of her face. "You've been so immersed in wickedness that you've lost sight of the joys of life around you."

Her words, devoid of teasing, spoken more to herself, penetrated the indifferent attitude he'd adopted these years. He loosened his hold on her, but did not relinquish her from his arms. "What do you find joy in? Sketching? Gardening?"

Her skin pinked under the faintly mocking emphasis he infused in those words. "You would condemn my pursuits without knowing them?"

"Touché."

Genevieve settled her teeth in her lower lip. "We know so little about one another," she said more to herself.

Yes, and he quite preferred it that way. All of this was entirely too much. Too much probing, and…talking, when he didn't speak to anyone. *Ever.* Not about anything that mattered, anyway. "Come," he whispered, lowering his lips to hers. "Shall we continue where we were before Montfort's interruption?" Bloody Montfort.

Genevieve turned her head and his lips grazed her cheek. A slight frown marred her lips. "You don't care to speak of yourself, do you?" She peered at him closely. "Rather, you don't truly wish to speak of anything of importance."

Disquiet rolled along his spine. How much she saw, this woman he'd bound himself to. She looked when no one else bothered. In a bid to reclaim control of his tumultuous thoughts, he forced a lazy grin and stepped away from her. "What is there to know about me that you don't already know?" he drawled and gave a roll of his shoulders. "I enjoy my clubs and gaming hells. I like to wager and drink and attend wicked parties." He added that last part in a bid to silence any further questions from the lady.

Genevieve furrowed her brow. "Wicked parties?" Instead of proper shock, there was a healthy dose of curiosity and he silently cursed.

For now that he'd mentioned the whole wicked parties business, distaste burned in his mouth at actually speaking of what those entailed. He gave a tight nod.

Understanding dawned in her eyes. "Ah, as in the masquerade Lord Montfort will host?" He went still. Surely, she didn't know of Montfort's annual masquerade? "Hmm?" she prodded when still he said nothing.

"What do you know of—?"

His feisty bride snorted. "It's hardly a secret when mention of it appears in *The Times*..." She paused. "As well as wonderings as to whether the newly married Marquess of St. A," she gestured to him. "That would be you. Plans to attend."

Regardless of where it appeared, he'd not discuss Montfort's orgies. Not with her. His friend closed out every year with a scandalous affair, attended by only the most jaded souls. "Montfort's... masquerade," a term which could only be loosely applied, "is not until the end of the Season." As such, there really was no need to further discuss—

"What makes them so very wicked?"

They were the manner of event no proper, respectable miss would be in attendance. It would be a den of sin, visited by only the most depraved, scandalous lords and ladies...and suddenly, the idea of her being part of those festivities gave him pause. "They are different than events you are accustomed to."

Her lips twitched. "Well, *that* is hardly enlightening." She waggled her eyebrows. "Rather a disappointing description by a man rumored to be a rake."

Rumored to be? By God, she truly didn't know whom she'd married. What did she take him for, then? On the heel of that, terror slithered a slow, torturous path around inside him. Surely, she didn't see him as anything...*more?* "I am," he gritted out, determined to disabuse her of any potentially romantic sentiments.

She tipped her head at that bloody endearing angle so he didn't know if he wished to kiss her into silence or grit his teeth and storm off.

"I am a rake," he said through clenched teeth, lest she forget precisely whom she'd married.

"Do you take me for one of those simpering misses who'd be outrageously shocked?" she shot back, wholly ignoring his statement.

There wasn't a thing simpering about Genevieve.

Then, she dusted her palms together. "Very well."

He cocked his head. "Very well?" What was she on about, now?

"You've joined me in the garden and sketched with me. I'll allow you to take me to one of Montfort's wicked parties when it comes, Cedric, and then I'll form my opinion."

Cedric closed his eyes a moment and, in his first attempt at prayer in the whole of his life, he prayed for patience. Of course, he'd been drawn to a marriage of convenience with Genevieve because of her unwavering spirit...after all, if he was going to be eternally bound to someone it should, at the very least, be someone *interesting.* But this...a spitfire who'd insist on attending Montfort's orgy? This woman he didn't know what to do with.

"Are you praying, Cedric?"

He opened his eyes and found Genevieve staring boldly, more questions in her eyes. "No."

She slowly nodded. "Yes, well, I didn't take you for the praying sort." Did she just insult him? He was still too flummoxed by her earlier question to take proper offense.

Not only had his wife neatly maneuvered her way deeper into his world. She also, by her questioning, *expected* more than a functional, purposeful arrangement that allowed them to live their separate lives and merged their lives in a way he'd not truly considered. And he needed to regain a foothold of his life. "You are not going." It mattered not if Montfort's ball was today, tomorrow, or ten years from now.

She had a tenacity that could have ended Boney's bid for domination better than all the greatest armies combined. "Will you be attending?"

He always did. He had quite enjoyed the carnal sin he'd found with the masked strangers there. "I will." Years prior, that unflinching affirmation would have come because he was wholly immersed in sin and wickedness. His palms moistened. Now, this need to go was a desperate attempt to hold on to a piece of who he was; a part that felt like it was rapidly slipping away.

"He is your friend. You are my husband. I will be there, too," she said calmly and then casually wandered over to her neglected garden tools.

Her words, however, roused images of Genevieve as the carnal feast presented before a room of lascivious, depraved lords all waiting a chance to avail themselves to her luscious body. "You're not going to the bloody party." The words exploded from him.

She stopped, hand on her small garden shovel and looked back. "What did you say?" A faint breezed stirred the air.

He counted to five and when he trusted himself to speak, managed four words; "You are not going." He'd safely insulated himself from all caring and feeling years earlier. He'd not lose any more pieces of who he was.

She held his stare and he looked unflinchingly back, braced for her fight; wanting it. "Very well," she said. With that, she returned her attention to her gardening.

Cedric frowned. He should be pleased with her capitulation. It was what he'd desired, after all. And yet…there was this rush of disappointment. "That is all?" he eyed her warily.

Genevieve paused from her work and lifted another blonde-red eyebrow. "Is there something else for us to discuss?"

He shook his head jerkily. And like the demons of hell were at his heels, Cedric fled.

CHAPTER 19

Later that night, Cedric stood before the bevel mirror in his chambers. His valet helped him ready into his evening attire for a night out in a ritual that was everything predictable and familiar.

And yet, nothing, all at the same time, was familiar. As such, he needed to regain control of his rapidly careening out of control world.

His gaze caught the smooth glass and he took in the tight lines at the corners of his mouth, his furrowed brow. Waving off his servant, Cedric proceeded to knot his own cravat. Wordlessly, he accepted the proffered black jacket and shrugged into it.

"I've had your carriage readied, my lord," Avis murmured.

He nodded slightly and dismissed the servant. With Avis gone, he was left alone with nothing but his own thoughts.

I am married.

He was married, when he'd vowed to never bind himself to any woman in that eternal state. Yet, in a week's time, his father with his threat had flipped Cedric's life upside down. When presented with the prospect of abandoning his comfortable lifestyle, marriage to Genevieve Farendale had really been the only palatable option. A match between them was one of a practical nature that required no emotion…except…

His gut clenched.

After turning away Montfort to tend gardens alongside his wife that morning, he'd detected more in her eyes. She *wanted* more. Expected it. She asked questions that he didn't have answers to. And it scared the bloody hell out of him. Because he wasn't capable of more. He was an island. Very much a tall, impenetrable fortress at the center of a sea.

Squaring his jaw, he strode to the front of the room, yanked the door open, and stepped out into the hall.

A startled shriek rent the quiet, followed by several soft thumps. His wife, clad in her modest nightshift and wrapper stared at him, her lips parted in a soft moue of surprise. Several books lay scattered at her feet. "Cedric," she greeted and her intelligent gaze took in his immaculately clad frame. Disappointment lit her eyes. "You are going out." It would seem they'd picked up where they'd left off in the gardens.

He opened and closed his mouth several times, as they remained frozen, locked in some silent battle of the wills. Then Genevieve schooled her features and dropped to a knee. "Not that you are not permitted to go out," she said, before he could speak. "You are, of course, permitted to do whatever it is you wish. I just wish…" She clamped her lips closed and began to hastily collect the leather books.

She wished what? To accompany him? To have him remain behind with her? What was it? Tamping down the questions, Cedric stared at her as she neatly stacked her pile; warring with himself. He should go.

With a sigh, Cedric strode over and fell to his haunches beside her. She paused and looked questioningly to him as he gathered the leather tomes. "You've quite the collection of reading material," he said with a wry smile.

Genevieve gave her head a little shake and then jumped to her feet. "Yes, well, you do have a marvelous collection of works on art. My father's library was vastly neglected in this area." There was an animated quality to her words that matched the excitement in her eyes, momentarily freezing him. He preferred her like this. Lively and eager for his company, to the disappointed, disheartened woman he'd known since the garden. She cleared her throat and held her arms out.

He followed her gaze to the stack in his grasp. "Where do you wish them?"

"I do not require help, Cedric." A muscle jumped at the corner of his eye. For he wished to help. "I was taking them to my room, and…" Cedric started for her chamber door. He shoved it open and stepped inside. "You may set them down on my nightstand," she said softly. He deposited her collection of books beside her bed.

His wife hovered at the entrance of the room and the soft glow cast by the hearth leant a translucent quality to her nightshift. He took in the dusky brown hue of her nipples, pressed against the front of the garment. A wave of lust slammed into him. "Close the door," he commanded softly.

She cocked her head.

"Close the door," he urged.

Her eyes formed moons and she hurriedly slammed the door. As he stalked over, her chest moved in a frantic rhythm and she laid her back against the wood panel. He came to a stop before her, and then layering his elbows on either side of her slender figure, he framed her within his arms.

"I want you," he said, his voice roughened with desire. When would he tire of his innocent, wide-eyed wife? Mayhap, once he had his fill of her, he could go back to the carefree rake he'd been.

Her lashes fluttered and she turned her face up to receive his kiss. Their mouths met in a passionate, almost ruthless, dance. There was no gentleness, but rather a desperate hunger that came from two people who wanted to meld their bodies in the most primitive of ways. He lowered his hands to her hips and dragged her hard between the vee of his thighs so she could feel his aching shaft pressed against her. She cried out and he reveled in the sound of her desire. He dragged a trail of kisses from the corner of her mouth, downward to her neck, her décolletage, and lower. Then dropping to his knees, he shoved her modest nightshift up, exposing her creamy white thighs to the night air.

Her breath caught. "Wh-what are you…" Her words ended on a hiss as he parted her legs and positioned his face between the apex of her thighs. Then he slid his tongue inside her molten hot folds. "Cedric!" She cried out and her legs buckled. "Surely, this is forbidden."

"Shh," he whispered against her womanhood, until a keening

moan exploded from her lips. "Let yourself feel, Genevieve. There is no shame in wicked. Only splendor. Let your body feel it."

She stiffened and then with a cry, let herself go, undulating into his mouth, taking what he offered. Twining her fingers in his hair, she held him close. All the while he thrust his tongue in and out of her, in the mating ritual that brought a franticness to her thrusting. He sucked on her nub. Then her body went taut and a piercing scream split her lips as she came in his mouth. He continued to wring every last drop of pleasure from her and then he freed himself from the confines of his breeches. Cedric pushed to a stand and parting her legs, he thrust home. The door rattled noisily as he pumped, over and over, until she was moaning once more in his arms. And he reveled in it. Celebrated it. When he had nothing to truly give her, he could give her this pleasure. Sexual gratification he knew. It was safe.

"Cedric," she wailed and the sound of that sent him spiraling over the edge of desire into a world of pure color and light.

A shuddery groan escaped him as he poured himself inside her and then replete, he collapsed against the edge of the door, catching himself at his elbows. His heartbeat pounded loudly in his ears as his wife ran her long fingers up and down his back.

"That was wonderful," she said, a wistful quality in those words coming faintly out of breath, as though she'd run a long distance.

It had been wonderful. It had been the mindless act he'd performed too many times to remember, but her release, in its purity and newness, roused a masculine sense of pride. Except, as Cedric drew back and removed the kerchief from his pocket then proceeded to clean her, an uncharacteristic awkwardness he'd never before known, descended. Why did he not know what to say? Hell, why was there even a need *to* say anything? They'd both had their pleasure and now could go about their own affairs. As he adjusted his garments, his skin pricked with the intensity of Genevieve's eyes on him as she righted her nightshift. She sought words from him. What were they? His feet twitched with the need to flee the unrestrained emotion spilling from her too-honest eyes.

"Will you join me?" she asked, a veritable Eve before him. Genevieve motioned to the books on art resting on her nightstand and he blankly followed her gesture to the stack.

This question she put to him, this intimacy, was far greater than the passionate explosion between them moments ago. He cleared his throat. "I'll not interrupt your plans for the evening."

She snorted. "My plans, Cedric? I'm not going anywhere. I haven't been anywhere since we were married." She arched an eyebrow; her meaning clear. His wife wished to accompany him out.

He straightened his cravat, adjusting the slightly wrinkled knot. Beyond a place in his bed, ladies didn't ask for much from him. That this one did roused a greater terror than facing down the Queen's regiment without a weapon in hand. Cedric started for the door. He'd just grabbed the handle, when Genevieve called out.

"What are you doing?" his wife spoke in clipped tones.

He wheeled slowly around and then sighed. Genevieve stood with her arms folded at her chest. Of course, a lady of her spirit wouldn't take to being summarily dismissed. Through her thick, strawberry lashes, fury sparked in her eyes. When he remained silent, she drummed her fingertips on her arm. "Are you leaving?"

By the fiery glimmer in her direct gaze, he was one erroneous word away from a display he'd rather do without. He tugged at his neck piece. "I pledged to meet Montfort." For years, he'd never accounted for his actions or decisions and he squirmed, discomfited with her show of spirit and the questions she'd put to him.

Silence reigned, punctuated by the ticking of the clock. "Montfort," she said at last, and by the way she managed to stretch those syllables into forever, hinted at her slow-building fury.

"I never presented myself as something other than I am, madam," he said dragging a hand through his hair. He'd not led her into this union with the promise of anything beyond security and freedom. Her words and actions these two days were those of a woman who expected more…nay, desired more. Nor did it truly matter what she did hope for or expect of their union. Or it shouldn't. Perhaps he was not as much a heartless bastard as he'd believed these years. He captured her delicate chin between his thumb and forefinger and tipped her head up. "You do not understand," he said quietly.

"Then make me," she said with a steely insistence.

"This is who I am."

She planted her hands akimbo. "That isn't an answer, Cedric."

Ultimately he'd fail her. His blood was his father's and she would invariably become the same broken figure in the gardens below that his own mother had been. And he'd rather she hate him now and retain her spirit than see her turned into that empty creature at his hands. He tried to make her understand. "I visit my clubs and attend mindless *ton* amusements and—"

"And you come in here, make love to me, and leave." Crimson suffused her cheeks and she jutted her chin up. "You'll give me your body, but that is all, like I am nothing more than the whore Society purported me to be."

A thick curtain of black fury fell over his vision. At the *ton* who'd so condemned her and himself for this vitriolic rage at the word she ascribed to herself. "You are no whore," he bit out. "I'll not continue this discussion," he muttered and made to leave once more.

"No, *you'll* run, instead," she said quietly, those words more powerful than had she roared them from the top of her lungs. "Just as you do every night." She twisted that dull-blade of truth inside, like a dagger that carved away at years of indifference.

His entire body jerked. She'd accuse him of cowardice? *But then, aren't you? Have you ever met anything or anyone more terrifying than Genevieve and her hold over you?*

"A whore is what you'd have me be, Cedric." Her words echoed around the room. "I am nothing more than a mistress who shares your name." She turned her palms up. "I married you, for what? My financial freedom? My own security? How does that not make me a whore?"

He snapped his teeth so hard, pain shot along his jawline. "Do not say that," he said sharply. *We had a bloody goddamn arrangement. This probing had never been part of it...*

He braced for her additional fury, welcomed it. But alas, she proved as unpredictable as she'd been since his father's ball. "Those...amusements where you find your...pleasure," she began unexpectedly. "You have attended them since you were in university, no doubt."

Earlier. He'd had his first whore at thirteen. He'd not taint her ears with that ugly truth.

"Do you enjoy going to them?" Her softly spoken question cut across his silent musings.

He considered her question. *Did he enjoy them?* She nodded.

Cedric started, not realizing he'd spoken aloud. "It is what I know," he said with a frown. Feeling burned, he released his gentle grip on her chin and took a hasty step away from her.

Genevieve wandered over to the nightstand, drawing his gaze to her every slow, deliberate movement. She perched on the edge of the mattress and picked up the top copy of her books. "I used to love London," she said softly. "I thought it was very grand and romantic and exciting."

He curled his hands. Her former betrothed. Why should it matter that she'd thrilled at the gentleman's presence?

"Yes, how very grand it all seemed." She absently fanned the pages of the book. "The orchestras and scandalous waltzes." Genevieve lowered her voice to a conspiratorial whisper. Once more with her unwitting words, she proved the depth of her innocence. "I do love to waltz, you know." Actually he hadn't. What else did he not know about the woman he'd married? "The evenings that seemed unending. The magnificent gowns. I thought how much I loved the thrill of it all." She lifted her gaze from her book. "Until I was sent away to the country and came to find a freedom that existed outside the confines of London. Joy driven by your own interests and not what Society believes your interests should be. Wagering. Waltzing. Shopping. What is the purpose of all that?"

Cedric shifted on his feet as the unabashed honesty of her admission shook him. This world he lived in was one he'd been born to; one that, by the very nature of his blood, had become one that was comfortable to him. "There is something to be said for the comfort to be had in familiarity."

"Yes," she agreed. A small smile hovered on her lips. "But the thrill of the unfamiliar…now *that* is something to revel in." Silence fell, punctuated by the snapping hiss of the fire in the hearth. "Stay," she urged.

His mouth went dry. "I cannot," he said hoarsely.

Before he did something borne of madness like join her in that bed to peruse those books on her nightstand, Cedric spun on his heel and marched from the room like the hounds of hell were nipping at his heels—and left.

CHAPTER 20

ℐN THE FOLLOWING WEEKS ᏀENEVIEVE and Cedric settled into a predictable routine.

She would rise first, and he, much, much later. During the day, they sketched and read and gardened.

And if the days were to stop at four o'clock in the afternoon, one would say they were the model of a devoted, loving couple. Which was, of course, madness. There was no love in a formal arrangement such as theirs. But each evening…for seven weeks three days, two hours, and a handful of minutes, if one wanted to be *truly* precise, Cedric left.

Oh, there was lovemaking. Scandalously during the day and then sometimes when he returned in the dead of night, from wherever it was he went. Then, the papers had proven quite valuable in indicating just where her husband spent the later part of his days and nearly the whole of his nights.

On her haunches, Genevieve glanced up from the small hole she now dug to where her husband now sat. With his eyes closed and his head tilted toward the sun, she used the moment to study him. He had the look of a bronzed Apollo; the manner of beauty that still quickened her heart, these weeks later.

He opened his eyes and not wanting to be caught gaping like a fawning schoolgirl, she quickly devoted her attention to the moist soil. Genevieve reached her fingers into the soft patch to remove a large rock and her fingers collided with a fat, slimy earthworm. She gagged, nausea broiling at the back of her throat, and quickly yanked her hand back.

"Never tell me you're squeamish, love," her husband's gentle teasing brought a smile.

She furrowed her brow. Squeamish? She'd taught her sister to bait hooks as they'd fished on their father's country lake. She'd named spiders she'd found in her schoolroom. No one would ever accuse her of being squeamish. "Oh, hush," she teased. "It is quite easy to make light of one working in a garden while sitting in the sun, soaking up the sun's rays like a fat cat."

"Fat cat, am I?" he waggled his brows.

There wasn't an ounce of fat on his muscle hewn frame. "La, are you searching for compliments, sir?"

"Mayhap a bit." He winked, eliciting a laugh.

Her bonnet tipped over her brow and she brushed it back. Returning her attention to the soil, she withdrew the other pebbles and stones littering the space, taking care to avoid the… She gagged again and swiftly pulled her hand back. Good God, what was wrong with her?

A wave of nausea assailed her, just as Cedric's booming laugh echoed around the gardens. She concentrated on her breathing to keep the nausea at bay. It was on the tip of her tongue to point out that she was very near to casting her accounts up in the blasted hole she'd just dug when he shoved lazily to his feet and strode the small distance between them. But he yanked off his gloves and tossed them aside. "Here," he murmured, sinking to his haunches beside her.

Her breath caught hard in her chest at the sight of him, bent over the slight hole, and she concentrated on her view of him. He'd earned the reputation as a rake. But how many gentlemen would sit beside their wives in this domestic tableau, staining their hands with dirt?

He handed over the thin branch with its exposed roots. Together, they planted the small bush, shoveling dirt back onto the roots. Genevieve dug a slight circle about the base. "My grandfather gardens," she said. "One would never expect it of him." Of any earl, but especially not the Earl of Hawkridge. Just as they'd, no doubt, never expect Cedric Falcot, the Marquess of St. Albans, would spend his early afternoons in the garden with his wife. "He taught me to build the earth up in a small circle about the base of the tree or bush and then it helps bring moisture to the roots when it rains."

"Is that where you went when you were gone from London?"

His question brought her head up. For everything they did speak about since their marriage, the personal stories of their life had remained closed between them. Since she'd challenged him in her bedchambers weeks earlier, they'd discussed and explored the safeness of shared interests…but never the parts of their earlier years. "It was where I was sent," she corrected. Genevieve dusted her palms together and then settled onto the ground. "The Kent countryside." She drew her knees close to her chest and dropped her chin atop the mud-stained apron wrapped about her. "I was so fearful when they first sent me to my grandfather. My memories of him were of a gruff, often scowling, old man." Having gone to live with him, she'd learned in short order that there was so much more to a person than the world saw of the surface. "He taught me that there is more to people than the thin layer Society sees and judges."

Cedric remained squatting, his gaze fixed on that slight circle. "Do you believe that?"

"No," she said automatically, bringing his gaze to hers. "I know that," she said. Genevieve laid her cheek against her skirt. "Society saw in me, nothing more than a shameful wanton."

His mouth tightened. "They are bloody fools, the whole of them."

She winked at him, warmed by his fury on her behalf. "Yes, well that is really the point, isn't it? I believe there is more to everyone."

"Aumere?" he asked, without malice, a challenge there.

She wrinkled her nose. "Well, mayhap not *Aumere*." That man had shown enough ugly in his soul to prove that there was nothing but blackness there.

Cedric pushed to a stand, unfurling to his full six-feet, four-inches. "That is true in some cases, but not all, Genevieve."

She'd have to be deafer than a post to fail to hear the cynical resignation in his protest. He spoke of himself. A frown pulled at her lips. "Do you think there is nothing more to you than the image you've crafted for the world?"

His body stiffened and just like that, for the first time in the nearly eight weeks since they'd been wed, she'd moved their conversation away from the light, gentle teasing and into the solemn realness they danced around. "I haven't crafted any image," he said flexing his jaw. "I've told you before, this is who I am."

"I know that because you make it a point of saying it, frequently." As though in saying it, he'd convince himself of the truth.

He hardened his mouth and gone was all hint of the affable charmer who could tempt and tease. "Do you want to know the manner of youth I was?"

More than anything. "I'd venture you were quite mischievous and grayed the hair of your nursemaids."

"My father brought me a whore when I was thirteen," he said bluntly, startling a gasp from her. "I seduced my last governess soon after, before I went off to Eton. Is that the manner of wicked you'd been thinking?"

Genevieve opened her mouth. And then closed it. She opened her mouth again. She'd been imagining a rapscallion who poured ink in tea and snuck spiders into the family home. Not...this... By the tight lines at the corner of his mouth and the derisive glitter in his eyes, he expected her shock. But...there was more than shock. Pain stabbed at her heart. She'd long believed her father was a monster, but this was the kind of evil and ugly that made her father look like a loving, doting papa. No wonder Cedric had grown into this jaded, cynical rake.

"Nothing to say?" he taunted, a hard edge to his words.

Slowly Genevieve pushed herself to her feet. "I am horrified," she said, giving him the truth. As she came forward, his body went taut. "I am horrified that as a child, your father subjected you to that baseness. Where was your mother?" she asked quietly. If they were ever blessed to have a babe, she'd protect it, keeping it from this vile depravity.

A humorless laugh spilled past his tight lips. "They lived two very separate lives." Unlike the manner of comfortable existence she and Cedric had settled into. Mostly. "After my sister's birth, my mother quite easily handed me over to my father's tutelage. No doubt, she'd quickly gleaned the manner of son she had."

Is that what he believed? That his mother had seen ugly in his soul and left him to his father for it? Genevieve held her palms up. "I do not know the manner of woman your mother was." She chose to believe that she'd defend her own children, fighting even the king himself, if it meant their happiness. "But I cannot believe she saw anything but her son, when she saw you."

With a dismissive noise, her husband scrubbed a hand down his face, leaving an endearing trail of dirt.

Footsteps sounded at the entrance of the garden and she wanted to stamp her foot in annoyance at the interruption. Of all the words they'd exchanged since their marriage, in this she'd learned more about Cedric than she'd ever known before. And now it was not enough. She wanted to know all of the past that had shaped him into the man he'd become. Even the dark, painful parts he, no doubt, had buried these years.

"Miss Cornworthy arrived to see you. I took the liberty of showing her to the parlor and having refreshments brought."

Disappointment filled her. "Thank you," she murmured. As much as she looked forward to her frequent visits with the fun, eccentric Francesca Cornworthy, she'd learned much in this short exchange with Cedric and was reluctant to abandon this moment. "You have plans for this evening?" she asked, after the butler had taken his leave.

"I intended to meet Montfort at our clubs."

She didn't wish to be that wife who frowned on disreputable company for her husband, but just once she wished her husband chose to stay in with her. "Of course," she said quietly and annoyance stirred at the attention he devoted to that blasted timepiece.

"I shall leave you to your company."

Just as you always do…

And she stood in watch as Cedric retreated with the speed of Boney marching through Russia in the dead of winter.

WITH HIS WIFE'S WORDS ECHOING around his mind and that damned optimistic, hopeful glimmer in her eyes, Cedric strode quickly through the corridors. He'd not spoken of his mother in years…

Nay.

Never. He'd never spoken of his mother, or that long ago night in the schoolroom, or his seduction of the governess to anyone. He was not the type of man who *spoke* to another person on things of import. He spoke of spirits and wagering and whores and his own material comforts.

Cedric strode across the opposite corridor and collided with his flushed, slightly out of breath butler…and…

"Montfort." A mottled flush stained his neck at the earl's mocking half-grin as he took in Cedric's gloveless, mud-splattered fingers.

"Never tell me you're…" He lifted an eyebrow. "Gardening?" There was a wealth of mockery in his question.

Quickly yanking out a handkerchief, Cedric dusted his palms. He waved his butler off and started for his office. "You've still not sent 'round your acceptance for my party coming."

No, he hadn't. When the invite had come around more than a fortnight ago, he'd simply ignored the routine invite to the scandalous party. Then, he'd forgotten it. Aware of his friend's stare and the question there, he hedged his words. "And you've come over at this unfashionable hour to determine the status of my invitation?" It wasn't something the other man might have asked him, say, any other evening he'd run into him at their clubs?

"Not that alone," the earl confirmed. His friend easily fell into step beside him. "There are wagers being placed," he said without preamble as Cedric pushed the heavy oak door of his office open and stepped inside.

Ah, so that was what brought Montfort 'round. "Have your finances vastly improved since your losses at the club last evening that you've entered into new wagers?"

Montfort's booming laugh filled the office as he entered behind Cedric. He pushed the door closed and then started over to the sideboard. Cedric splashed several fingerfuls into one glass and then held the bottle aloft.

The earl inclined his head and Cedric finished pouring another. "The wagers are, of course, about you," he said, accepting the glass.

"Oh," Cedric drawled and carried his snifter over to the leather winged back chair beside the cold, empty hearth. He'd ceased to pay attention to the bets that went into the book at White's or anywhere else over the years.

"You know," Montfort said, settling himself in the chair opposite

Cedric. "There was a time you'd ask about the betting and place your own ungodly wager."

He swirled the contents of his drink. Yes, as he'd shared with Genevieve when he'd asked for her hand in marriage, there had been a time he'd been imprudent with the funds belonging to him. Perhaps it was a tedium with the lifestyle he'd lived these many years or perhaps it was the hold he'd allowed his father to have over him with those weaknesses but the gaming tables no longer held the same pull.

"The wager is also about your wife," Montfort said and Cedric froze mid-movement with his glass halfway to his lips.

He gripped his snifter so hard the blood drained from his knuckles. "Oh," he drawled with forced nonchalance. Odd, he'd never given a bloody damn what the gossips said about him, but he wanted to take apart the bastards who'd mention her name in any way. Cedric took a long swallow through tight lips.

The earl leaned forward, shifting his weight over his legs. "There are bets about how long until the ducal heir makes his appearance."

Cedric choked on his swallow and glared as his friend's booming laughter echoed throughout the room.

"Knowing as you do, my wager was firmly in the 'never' column." He leaned back and his humor was immediately gone, replaced with a piercing intensity he didn't believe the other man capable of. "And given what you've shared with me through the years, I trust my wager is the safe one?" His words were more a question than statement.

Cedric rolled his shoulders. "I don't have any intention of discussing my marital affairs with you, Montfort." He forced a grin.

A flash of surprise shone in the other man's eyes and he opened and closed his mouth several times. "You have dirt on your face," he blurted.

Swallowing a curse, Cedric removed the same handkerchief and brushed at his left cheek. He neither wanted, nor needed, his friend's mockery. When had the man's presence begun to grate?

"The other side," Montfort clarified, his lips still twitching with amusement.

"You've come then to angle an answer about me regarding my marital activities?" he asked, with annoyance. Childhood friends or not, somewhere in this stilted exchange, Montfort had crossed a proverbial line. "All to win a wager?"

Even the morals lacking earl had the good grace to flush. "You were never above anything yourself, St. Albans, so do not go acting as though we're cut of entirely different cloths."

No, they weren't. But then, neither had Cedric cheated to win a wager. His skin pricked with the concentrated stare the other man passed over him. Then Montfort whistled long and slow. "What is it?" Cedric bit out.

"By God, you care about her."

He shook his head once.

The earl nodded.

He shook his head again. "I…" *Do not care about anyone.* He'd been a bastard of a brother. A miserable, albeit deliberately miserable, bastard of a son. And…yet…his friend's words knocked the breath from his lungs. He cared about her. His palms grew moist with the horrifying implications of that. He'd only make her miserable. He was his father's son. "Our marriage is a practical one," he said, after a long stretch of silence.

"Is it?"

Yes, it was. "I visit my clubs every evening." And had begun to tire of them, but that was neither here nor there, nor a point he intended to mention to Montfort.

"You were gardening."

He scoffed. "I was hardly gardening." Merely digging a hole. *For my wife.* He grimaced.

"You've still not accepted nor declined the invitation to my ball." The earl lifted an eyebrow. "Is it, perhaps, that your new bride will not allow you to take your amusements where you will?"

God his friend was relentless. He gritted his teeth. "Of course, I'll be there." Because he'd attended every year since Montfort began throwing them ten years earlier.

The earl appraised him in an assessing manner. Did he seek the veracity of a claim Cedric was no longer certain of? Montfort drummed his fingertips along the arm of his chair in a grating, rhythmic pattern. "So there will still be no heir then?"

Of course. Back to the wager. For ultimately, Montfort was the same self-serving bastard he'd always been. It was why they got on so great. "There will be no heirs or spares." Granted he'd not taken precautions prior with Genevieve…but the earl's words served as an all-important reminder. He'd not bring a child into this world, only to subject it to his corrupted influence. He was a bastard. He wasn't a complete bastard.

The earl chuckled and raised his glass in salute. "And you thought your marriage to the Farendale girl would be your ultimate revenge against your bastard of a father? There is no greater revenge than this."

Montfort spoke the truth, and yet…there was a sourness in Cedric's mouth at having his calculated efforts thrown so effortlessly in his face. "Now," he said, shoving to his feet. "If you'll excuse me?" he said, for the first time he could remember, eager to be rid of the other man's presence. Had he always been this…bloody bothersome?

CHAPTER 21

THE FOLLOWING AFTERNOON, PERCHED ON the edge of the blue upholstered sofa with her sketchpad on her lap, Genevieve brushed her charcoal over the page bringing the image of the now cared for garden to life.

Usually, sketching proved a welcome diversion. This morning, however, proved the exception. Unbidden, her gaze went to the scandal sheets open on the table before her.

Two months married and all thoughts of a love match between the Marquess of St. A have undoubtedly been laid to rest.

Undoubtedly.

Nightly visits to Forbidden Pleasures…

A vise squeezed about her heart. A place called Forbidden Pleasures was hardly the respectable White's and Brooke's visited by respectable gentlemen. No doubt there were scandalous women and naughty deeds and… *Oh, God. Why did this truth hurt as much as it did?*

"Will we go out this evening?"

She snapped her attention over to the sole friend she'd made since her return to London. Francesca Cornworthy nibbled at a puff pastry. Since she'd been married, Genevieve had taken to joining the young woman at those dull, polite affairs. It had made facing down the knowing stares of cruel gossips bearable. Her lips twisted. God, how she abhorred the whispers.

Wetting her lips, Genevieve abandoned her artwork. "I had not intended to," she confessed and a guilty twinge pulled at the other woman's crestfallen expression.

"Yes, well, I expect if I had the benefit of marriage, *I* would avoid all the miserable *ton* events, as well."

Alas, expectations were vastly different for young, unmarried women than young, married women. There were freedoms to attend or not attend events. To don colorful skirts. And in Genevieve's case...to stay indoors sketching and reading and gardening while the Season marched painfully on. How tedious and tiresome life in London had become. A yawn escaped her and she looked to the doorway for the next expected visitor for the morning.

"It is rather tiresome, isn't it?" Francesca murmured. "I daresay if a lady had a dance partner and a devoted suitor then it would make all of this," she waved her hand and flakes of powdered sugar fell to the floor, "exponentially better."

Genevieve's gut clenched.

As soon as the words left Francesca's mouth, she softly cursed. "Oh, Genevieve, I did not mean..." She let the partially eaten pastry fall to the delicate porcelain dish before her. "That is..."

"It is fine," Genevieve assured her with a reassuring smile. Her friend only spoke the truth. It was that truth that had brought her 'round to her plans for the evening. Nervousness mixed with excitement and kicked her heart up another beat.

"I'm quite rubbish with words. What I *meant* to say is that I am certain the marquess is most devoted."

Cedric had proven himself devoted...only in the most wicked ways one would expect a rake or rogue to be devoted. Memory of his touch in the early morn hours, sent heat racing from the tips of her toes to the top of her head. Yes, there was no shortage of passion between them. With his artful caress and attentiveness in bed, he'd proven himself a tireless lover...when he wasn't absent in the evening. She firmed her lips. Well, that was no longer enough. She'd tired of carrying on a separate existence with her friends while he went off to whatever club or hell he wished. She wanted all of him...or nothing.

Liar.

Her stomach turned over itself. For was she truly prepared to be entirely closed from his life?

With a frustrated sigh, she set aside her sketchpad and reached for the porcelain teapot. To give her fingers something to do, she proceeded to pour herself a cup of tepid tea. Yes, how very tiresome this London life had become. It was a wonder that her husband so loved this miserable place.

But then…she didn't know the enjoyments that kept him so occupied…

Ignoring another sharp twinge in her breast, she tightened her mouth. She would. Soon she would step inside his world, even as he'd not invited her in. Even as he'd expressly forbade her from entering. Then, her days of blind obedience had ended when she'd been sent away five years earlier.

Footsteps sounded on the hall and she jerked her gaze to the door.

"Lady Gillian Farendale," the butler announced.

At last.

"Gillian," she greeted as the butler backed out of the room.

"Hullo, Genny." A stack of newspapers in her fingers, Gillian stepped inside the room, just as she did every week since Genevieve had been married. This time, however, the slightly forced, more than concerned smile customarily wreathing her lovely face was tipped in a mischievous turn. "Francesca," she greeted. Between bites, Francesca lifted a hand in greeting. She returned her attention to Genevieve. "I have the information you—"

"Shh," she said, looking pointedly past her shoulder.

Shifting the scandal sheets in her arms Gillian, shoved the door closed with the tip of her slipper and then carried her papers over to where the ladies sat. She dropped the stack down on the rose-inlaid table, rattling the tea cups.

Genevieve shot a hand out and steadied the pot. "As you know I asked you both here today…" she repeated.

The young ladies stared expectantly back.

"Gillian, you mentioned you have the information?"

Her younger sister nodded. She reached for the papers on the table and shuffled through them. "This arrived from Honoria just before I came. It arrived during breakfast." Her pulse quickened its tempo and she resisted the urge to grab the page from her sister's fingers. "Mother was staring," Gillian prattled, artless as always. "I tucked it within the scandal sheets and otherwise distracted her."

Her lips twisted wryly. Of course, beyond the gossip rags, there was no reading material their mother approved of. As such, seeing Gillian make off with those pages would hardly be grounds for suspicion or concern.

Of which there should be.

And certainly would be, were their mother to have known.

"What is it?" Francesca asked. She alternated her stare between the sisters.

Genevieve came slowly to her feet. She crossed over to the front of the room, locked the door, and turned slowly around. After all, she couldn't risk Cedric entering and interrupting this particular exchange. "It is about my husband," she whispered.

Worry filled Francesca's expressive eyes. "Are you happy?"

The unexpectedness of that question stalled her thoughts. Was she happy? After years of being hidden in the country, she was now forever free of her parents' influence. She was able to sketch and garden all day without fear of recrimination over her subjects. But was she happy? Her gaze wandered to the door. Sometimes she was happy. In fleeting moments spent with her husband during the day, when she could pretend that they were something more… "Yes," she said, at last. "And also no."

"That is what I thought," Gillian said with a knowing nod. "I see you several times a week and I cannot help but see the desire for more in your eyes."

She firmed her mouth. Yes, and she had the same hope. "This is why I've asked your help." She looked to Gillian. Had she been so very transparent? Did Cedric know, even now, and that was why he went about his pleasures in the evenings? "Gillian, were you able to learn?"

She held her breath, until her younger sister gave a little nod. "Yes. Phoebe and Lord Rutland had been off for the country. As such, it took longer for me to communicate with her."

"Rutland?" Francesca asked, befuddlement in her tone. "The scoundrel?" Her eyes formed round moons.

"Oh, he's no longer a scoundrel," Gillian said reassuringly and patted the other young woman on the knee. "Now, he is quite content and hopelessly in love with Phoebe."

Envy dug its vicious talons inside.

Her sister slapped her fingertips to her mouth. "I am sorry, Genevieve. I didn't mean…"

"It is quite fine," she assured. Except it wasn't. She knew it and her friends also knew it. It was also why she'd required assistance from her sister…and a stranger who'd been a scoundrel, who now loved his wife. Or at least by Gillian's admission, anyway. Mayhap those rakes and rogues were incapable of reform. Genevieve only knew she'd not truly be happy—until she tried.

She drew in a steadying breath and reclaimed her previously vacated seat. "My husband and I are, at best…*friends*." Friends who made passionate love nearly every day and laughed together during the days and who parted ways in the night. But friends, nonetheless, as he'd said to her long ago in the gardens, when they'd but recently met. And for most women, that arrangement would be enough. Not her.

"Friends?" Gillian snorted.

With her faint mockery of that word, Gillian would sully the one thing she *did* share with Cedric.

"There is nothing wrong in having just friendship with your husband," Francesca said, and patted Genevieve on the hand. "But there is also nothing wrong in wanting more." Her friend spoke as one who knew and who wanted more. And one who deserved more.

She looked blankly to the stack of scandal sheets in her sister's package. Just as Genevieve deserved more.

"My husband is attending the Earl of Montfort's…party."

The other young ladies said nothing. After all, what proper, respectable, unmarried lady spoke of those outrageous affairs, only whispered about on the pages and in ballrooms?

"And I intend to go," she said into the quiet. "However, the actual location of the earl's event is only sent to invited guests." Of which she'd never be.

Silence met her announcement. She looked between them. She'd not known what she expected. Perhaps mild shock? Horror? Not this…silence.

Then, two like smiles formed on the other women's lips.

Her sister leaned over and swiped a note from the top. "Here." With a flick of her wrist, she tossed it at Genevieve. It fluttered onto the edge of her lap and she quickly grabbed it to keep the pages from sailing to the floor.

Quickly tearing open the note, Genevieve skimmed the page. Nothing more than an address stared back.

Francesca leaned over her shoulder. "What are you looking at?" Her eyes went to the same place Genevieve's did.

"The location of the earl's wicked party," Gillian explained. "The Marquess of Rutland, I expect, has an easier time obtaining such information than you or I ever would," Gillian explained.

Lifting her head, Genevieve favored her sister with a smile. "Brava, Gillian."

"I do not understand what makes the event so scandalous," Francesca muttered and searched her gaze over the tray of largely eaten pastries.

No, neither did Genevieve. She could only begin to suspect.

Gillian grabbed a scandal sheet and tossed it to Francesca who caught it. "Go on. Read it," her sister said. "Front and center of the top page."

Ah, front page news on this Cedric story. Wanting to be a coward and ignore whatever words were contained on those pages, she kept her stare trained on Gillian while Francesca read aloud.

"*...The Earl of M's scandalous affair, no respectable lord or lady will attend. It is rumored the guest list will include the gentleman's closest friend, the recently wed Marquess of SA. There are no surprises that the gentleman finds his pleasures else—*" Francesca gasped and dropped the page as though burned. "That is horrid."

Genevieve's fingers twitched with the urge to crumple the pages into a neat ball and hurl them into the low-burning hearth.

"Have a pastry, you'll feel better," Francesca said, waving the lemon-filled tart out.

"He gave you his name and owes you his love and loyalty." Gillian's quietly spoken words were more powerful than any roar or shout. They contained truth and expected Genevieve to confront the marriage she'd entered into.

"She is right," Francesca said quietly, echoing her own thoughts.

Her only two friends in the world exchanged a look. Genevieve would have to be blind to fail to see the pity seeping from their revealing eyes. Nausea churned in her belly and she swallowed back the bitter taste. Did they expect she would be one of those miserably sad wives who'd don a sad frown and never attempt to make her life better? No. That had been her of long ago. Not anymore.

She firmed her jaw. "Cedric made me no promises of more… but I want more from him, anyway. I want to be part of his life." There was something freeing in breathing those words into existence. A weight lifted. A lightness in her chest. And for the first time in the nearly eight weeks since she'd been married to Cedric, she smiled. A true, honest, smile devoid of sadness. Genevieve bent down and fished around under the sofa. Her fingers collided with a heavy box and she lifted it up. She dropped the package beside the tray of pastries and it landed with a thump.

The two ladies looked as one to the package.

Filled with a restlessness, Genevieve surged to her feet. "I have tired of it," she said and needing space between herself and the two, sympathetic ladies, she retreated. "Every day he sketches with me."

A whispery sigh escaped Francesca. "How have I not known that? That is hopelessly romantic."

Yes, it was. And it was something only Genevieve and Cedric shared. "And we garden together and that is a good deal more than most couples have. But I am tired of carrying on as a blissful new bride during the day while he goes out on his own, every night." Every. Night. She began to pace. "Though, it is quite a deal better than most unions, certainly our parents'," she said, pausing a moment to give Gillian a look, needing her to know she deserved more, as well. "I want it all. I want his friendship, and his heart, and a life together." She slammed her fist into her palm and continued her frantic movements. "And I'll have it all or noth—" Genevieve spun and at the rapidity of the abrupt movement, the room dipped. She shot a hand out and caught herself against the edge of a nearby side table.

"Genevieve?" her sister asked, concern lacing her words.

She blinked several times, driving back the fog. "I am fine," she said. *Pfft. Now I've become one of those wilting, swooning sorts.* She stiffened her spine. "In every way." Or she would be. She'd convinced herself of it, until Gillian came in here and yanked the world out from under her feet to confront the truth—she wanted more.

A humming filled her ears.

"Genevieve?" Francesca's inquiry came as though down a long hall.

She again blinked. Energized once more, she motioned to the box. "Open it."

With tentative fingers, Gillian removed the cover of the box. Pushing back the tissue paper covering the article contained inside, she withdrew the seafoam satin dress from inside. With gold overlay capped sleeves and a band of gold underneath the bodice, the piece shimmered and shined with a beauty fit for a mermaid. Wordlessly, she stood and let the garment cascade to the floor. The pleated fabric fluttered and danced, highlighting the delicate gold flowers etched through the hem of the gown. It was…

Her two loyal friends spoke in unison.

"Magnificent," Fanny whispered.

"It is my gown for this evening," Genevieve said with a smile. "I am no longer going to sit and wait in the wings while my husband goes about his affairs. I am going to the Earl of Montfort's scandalous party and I am going to bring my husband up to scratch."

THE GOWN GIVEN HER BY her sister, was splendid. Gripping the edge of her vanity, Genevieve grunted and sucked in her tummy as Delores tugged hard at her stays.

As the young woman managed to lace them, she released a labored breath. Her maid, humming a jaunty tune, rushed to the bed and collected the satin garment. "It is a beautiful dress, my lady," she murmured, as she drew it over Genevieve's head and then pulled it down.

It was beautiful. She stared at her reflection. The fabric hugged her frame indecently, with her large bosom straining the fabric in such a way they shamefully threatened to spill out. It just… "It does not fit," she said, blushing as she took in her own outrageously clad frame. Is this the manner of gowns the ladies who attended those scandalous parties donned? Either the gown did not properly fit or she'd added a stone to her weight. She wrinkled her nose. Which really didn't make sense as her appetite had not been as it usually was.

"No, I do not expect it would," Delores said with a smile in the mirror.

Perplexedly, Genevieve stared as her maid began working the

intricate ties down the back of her gown. Whatever did the young woman mean?

"I began letting your stays out nearly a fortnight ago," Delores said, her gaze trained down on her work. Letting her stays out? Then her maid looked up from her task and their stares collided. She blinked several times in rapid succession. "You did not realize," she blurted.

Genevieve gave her head a shake. "Realize what?" Except even as the question left her lips, the truth slammed into her. She gasped and touched a hand to her lips. The frequent bouts of nausea, the fatigue... Her mind raced as she sought to remember the last time she'd had her monthly courses.

"I expect you are nearly seven weeks along, my lady," her maid happily supplied for her and then finished lacing Genevieve's gown.

Seven weeks along. She opened and closed her mouth but no sound came out. *A baby?* The dream of a child she'd abandoned and given up hope on after her banishment to the countryside. And now there was marriage and Cedric... Genevieve touched her still flat belly. There was now a baby. A joyous thrill unfurled; a shocked awe that sent thoughts tumbling through her head.

Grateful for Delores' distraction as she saw to Genevieve's hair, she considered Cedric. All noblemen desired a son, that necessary heir. But would he be equally happy if the child was a girl? Her heart pulled. She imagined he'd be one of those fathers who lifted his babe upon his shoulders and raced about the house to the woes of the nursemaids. He'd never be the cold, emotionless figure her own father had been. Tears misted her eyes.

"Yes, that is quite common, my mum said," Delores said, as she gently pulled her back into an intricate coiffure. "The weepiness and nausea and fatigue. All of it." She angled Genevieve. "Turn this way a bit, my lady." She plucked a hair comb from the vanity.

Genevieve winced as it pressed into her scalp. Continuing her happy whistling, Deloris worked. Genevieve's mind sought to process her recent discovery. She would be a mother. Another sheen of tears filled her eyes. And she would be nothing like her own mother. She would be loving and there would be laughter, and her child would be free to sketch and garden or fence or sculpt, or do whatever it was that brought her joy. Or him. Mayhap it was a boy; a boy who had loose, golden curls and a mischievous smile like his father.

"There you are, my lady." Delores moved and Genevieve's gaze caught on the stranger staring back at her. The strawberry blonde curls artfully arranged half-up, half-down in a clever haphazard manner. Several curls hung over her back, while others dangled over the front of her décolletage, bringing attention to the maid's masterful work.

She'd only seen herself as, at best, passably pretty, and even that passable prettiness had been dulled by the hideous gown and garments her parents insisted she don. Staring at herself, as she was now, there was a freeness that roused a breathless excitement. She was no longer the silent, tucked away daughter of the Marquess of Ellsworth, but rather a woman...who with Cedric's practical offer, had found freedom.

And by the lively glitter in her eyes, there was great joy in freedom. He might not ever love her, or give her affection, but he had given her this important gift. A smile softened her full mouth. And he'd given her another precious gift, too.

"You look beautiful, my lady," her maid said on a reverent whisper.

Genevieve continued to study the bright-eyed stranger before her, and with her visage bathed in candlelight staring back, she acknowledged that she was, if not beautiful, at least...pretty.

"Now for the mask." Delores gathered the seafoam piece adorned in crystal and placed it over her eyes. The mask settled heavily on her face, obscuring much of her cheeks, and she struggled to breathe a moment. Whyever would anyone wish to attend any event so? Uncomfortable. Stifling. Beautiful as the delicate piece was, there was a falsity to the article that she chafed at.

She drew in a steadying breath. Now, came the part of meeting her husband...at an event he'd expressly forbade her from attending. She steeled her jaw. She loved Cedric and she'd no doubt, if not now then in time, he could come to love her. But it most certainly would not come if they carried on their separate lifestyles. "Have you—?"

"The carriage is readied and waiting, my lady."

Genevieve nodded. She should move, but instead she remained fixed to the floor. The scandal sheets and gossip columns spoke in veiled, sparse words, about where her husband went and the activities he took his enjoyment in. Going to the Earl of Montfort's event this evening, uninvited, Genevieve would have her first true glimpse of the world Cedric had immersed himself in all these years. And part of her feared what that glimpse would mean…

With the click of the door resonating in the quiet, she smoothed her palms along the front of her satin skirts, and before her courage deserted her, started for the front of the room.

CHAPTER 22

CEDRIC SIPPED FROM HIS THIRD crystal flute of champagne and, with a detached gaze, skimmed his gaze over the Earl of Montfort's ballroom. Transformed from an elegant hall into this den of sin, a dais had been set up at the front center of the room alongside a small orchestra. Half-clad couples took their pleasures with one another against the Scamozzi columns while others put themselves on lewd display, availing themselves to the other guests' charms at the makeshift stage set up.

The chandeliers cast a shimmery glow off the satiny gowns of scandalously clad ladies in attendance, and an even shinier glow off the perspiring bodies of the women in flagrante dishabille. He'd never favored polite *ton* events. The impolite events…well, these had always been the ones he'd been quite at home, attending. This restlessness in him now was, no doubt, a product of too many of the very same affairs. In all, it was a sight he'd viewed too many times apparently. For there was a tedium this night.

Cedric downed the contents of his glass and motioned over a servant. A young, partially-clad beauty sidled up to him, an invitation in her smoky eyes. Ignoring the offering there, he swapped his empty flute for a full one.

"You've not availed yourself to a single beauty, yet." He stiffened as Montfort, in a blatant absence of a mask, came up to him. An arm wrapped about the young, nubile woman at his side, he toyed with her naked breast. The other man made a tsking noise. "You've become a good deal more selective since your marriage."

"And weren't you just recently speaking of the benefit of finding a wife," Cedric said dryly. "Throwing lavish parties is hardly going to get you out of the mire of your circumstances."

"Indeed." Montfort nibbled at the masked woman's ear, eliciting a breathy giggle. "But this is so vastly preferable to marriage, isn't it?" He skimmed a hand down her body and brought her closer against his frame. "Then, I was a fool pushing the Farendale chit your way, when she could have neatly improved my financial circumstances."

Cedric's body jerked erect, as an insidious thought slithered around his mind like a venomous serpent. Montfort and Genevieve, together. The other man laying her down and... His fingers tightened reflexively upon his flute, until the blood drained from his knuckles. Though she deserved better than Cedric as a husband, she'd deserved a whole lot more than Montfort.

His friend continued with a nonchalance that made him want to slam his fist into his mouth. "A meek-mouthed lady who wanted nothing more than your name and who is quite content to allow you to seek your own pleasures?" His friend sighed. "You have all the luck, chap."

Is that how the world saw Genevieve? There was nothing meek about her. Contemplative. Whimsical. Intelligent. But never meek-mouthed. And for the first time, with the Earl of Montfort's guests looking in his direction and whispering, the implications of being here as a married man spoke volumes to Society about his and Genevieve's marriage.

He took another drink and then steeled his jaw. What did it matter if the *ton* saw exactly what was there? *Because it makes her a target of Society's gossip and whispering...* Just as his being here invariably did.

Where he didn't give two goddamns on a Sunday what they said about him, Genevieve, who snuck away behind high-hedges and hid in libraries, did care. Very much. For the truth of it was, she'd certainly gotten the rotted end of the marital deal in the arrangement they'd made. Yes, the lady had her freedom and ability to move freely about Society. But a lady with her soft and gentle spirit, no doubt craved more; love and sonnets and pretty words

and quiet nights reading and sketching. Not quick, frantic couplings against the doorway like a Covent Garden doxy.

For the first time since his friend had proposed Cedric marry
Genevieve, he considered…her—and all she'd given up in becoming his wife. He'd never much liked himself. He liked himself a
good deal less in this moment.

Then, from across the length of the room, his stare collided with
the tall figure of a graying man, too powerful for a mask; a hated
figure. It may as well have been a glimpse into his own future,
thirty years from now. His father surveyed the spectacle unfolding
at the front of the room. Then, their stares collided.

Of course, with the level of sin and depravity featured in this
room, it was the perfect place for a man such as the duke, but he'd
also learned long ago to be suspicious of his father's movements
and motives. "What in hell is he doing here?" Cedric gritted out.

"Who?" Montfort followed his stare and then yanked at his cravat. "Can hardly say no when the Duke of Ravenscourt requests
something, chap. Surely *you* know that."

Actually he did. All too well.

"Lord St. Albans, I would recognize you anywhere." The husky
purr sounded over his shoulder, yanking his attention from his
father and Cedric stiffened. "Why am I not surprised to see you
newly married and rid of your wife so very quickly?"

The Baroness Shelley, with her lace overlay satin gown of crimson, had the look of a sinful Eve and where one time the sight of
her dampened dress layered to her delicious curves would have
enticed, now he found himself comparing his previous lover to a
respectable woman who now had the benefit of his name.

"Baroness," he drawled. Accepting her fingers, he raised them to
his mouth for the requisite polite greeting. He made to release her,
but she wrapped her clever fingers around his wrist, maintaining
a talon-like grip.

Montfort grinned and lifted his head. "I shall leave you to your
amusements. The evening's entertainments are beginning," he said.
Sketching a bow, he backed away with his companion in tow.

"I miss you in my bed, Saint," the young widow whispered,
ignoring the earl's departure, as other guests hurried to the seats
about the dais.

"I've been otherwise occupied," he said dryly, ignoring her angry pout. He made to pull his hand back but she wouldn't relinquish her hold. Absently, Cedric stared at the young, naked beauty being led to the center of the dais. The crescendo of the orchestra's discordant music filled the ballroom as the woman allowed herself to be tied upon a four-poster bed at the front of the room. Through the years, with their equally wicked proclivities, Cedric and the baroness had been lovers on and off. One time, he would have escorted her to the center of the hall with everyone looking on and availed himself to her body.

"You've neglected me for too long," the baroness persisted, catching his hand once more.

"You've never been one to beg," he softened that rejection with a wink and made to pull back. What was to account for the ennui?

The baroness retained her hold. "I'd believed you were preoccupied with that mealy-mouthed virgin you wed," she said on a sultry purr, skimming her fingertips down the front of his lapel. "But seeing you here," she leaned up and her champagne-scented breath caressed his ear. "Seeing you here, I know you're still the same wicked lord who has warmed my bed. I want you," she whispered. She opened the clever ties at the front of her gown, revealing herself to him and, unbidden, his gaze wandered down to her enormous breasts as he braced for a rush of familiar lust. "That is it. You like what you see." She drew his hand to one of the generous cream white swells. "Take me here, as you did at Montfort's last party, with everyone watching. You know you would like that. You know you want that," she enticed, like the devil with that apple held in hand. "*I* want it."

And he should want her, too. Yet, staring down at her blousy flesh and rouged nipples, he was singularly unmoved. He did not want her. Just as he'd been unaffected by her bold advances in his father's ballroom, now too was he uninterested in her blatant offering. He made to remove his hand, but she layered her spare one over his, anchoring him in place. Annoyed by her cloying attempts, he steeled his jaw. "I…"

A noisy commotion sounded at the front of the hall and he looked to the entrance of the room to the figure who'd attracted the crowd's notice.

The breath stuck in his chest. From her vantage, the splendidly curved woman at the top of the stairway surveyed the room as though she were a queen, assessing her subjects. The glow of candlelight cast by the chandeliers illuminated her pale green satin gown in a soft shimmer while the light danced off the strawberry blonde tresses artfully arranged about her scandalous décolletage. Cedric devoured the sight of the siren. There was something so very familiar about her and, yet, all at the same time, not.

Over the heads of the other guests assembled in Montfort's ballroom, their gazes collided. Then she looked to the forgotten woman at Cedric's side, the woman whose breast he still touched, and the tremulous smile on the satin-clad Athena's generous mouth withered. She spun in a flurry and rushed from the ballroom.

The air left him on a swift whoosh. *Genevieve.* His wife? Surely not. But he'd be blind to fail to note her piercing gaze through that mask, or the shocked hurt he'd seen there. Oh, God, what was she doing here in this sin of decadence? She was the only goddamn goodness in the world and he'd ushered her into the darkest depths of depravity. His stomach revolted.

"Saint?"

Nausea twisted in his belly; the bitter, acrid taste of bile. Ignoring the petulant chiding of the baroness, he disentangled himself from the determined woman's grip and sprinted through the ballroom. Moving between copulating couples and lovers embracing, he set out after her. His pulse came hard and fast in his ears. He'd convinced himself these weeks that their marriage was an empty one. With the horror and pain that had contorted her face, he was forced to recognize the truth—he cared.

He had to find her.

GASPING AND OUT OF BREATH, Genevieve raced through the marble hall, desperate to be free. Of this place. Of the sight of the sins her husband enjoyed. Forbidden deeds no respectable person should ever witness. Acts she could not imagine sharing with anyone other than Cedric.

You fool. You fool. You fool. It was a litany inside her head.

A shuddery sob burst from her lips. This was his world. This was the dark ugly he'd spoken of. And now that she'd seen it, she wished to un-see it and burn the memory where all other hideous thoughts went to die.

But she could not.

Just as she could never cease to remember the sight of his long fingers on another woman's naked skin. That beautiful act they shared every night, now forever sullied by the truth that she'd never truly mattered, nor any of those beautiful joinings she'd believed special. It had all been nothing more than empty, physical couplings he shared with so many other women. Why, he'd no doubt returned many evenings and sought out her bed after worshiping the bodies of other women…

Her stomach pitched and she gagged. Another cry escaped her as she turned the corner and promptly collided with a tall, powerful frame. The air left her on a whoosh as she sailed backward and landed hard on her buttocks.

The gentleman easily pulled Genevieve to her feet and steadied her. Incapable of words, she gave her dazed head a shake. "What an inviting welcome to the evening's festivities," a hated voice drawled.

She stiffened, as the Duke of Aumere's words sent waves of revulsion rolling off her skin. "Release me," she bit out and yanked herself away, but he retained his hard, punishing grip.

The duke flared his eyebrows. "Beautiful, Genevieve," he murmured, as though he'd solved a difficult riddle. Then he tossed his head back and roared with laughter. He'd not even known it was her.

What manner of gentlemen were these? Faithless cads, depraved, heartless bastards. Cedric had spoken about the blackness of his world. Naively, she'd just failed to realize how ugly it was. What an innocent fool he'd, no doubt, taken her for. She wrenched away from the duke's hold once more. "I said release me," she seethed, finding a safe fury in her anger as it dulled the agony of her husband's betrayal and the death of her dreams.

"Do you know, Genevieve," Aumere murmured contemplatively, lowering his face to hers. "I don't think I shall." He crushed his mouth to hers and she struggled against his punishing hold, but he easily gathered her wrists in a ruthless hold that would raise bruises.

He groaned and her alarm and fury grew. *My God, he is aroused by my struggles.* A panicky desperation filled her as she twisted against him. Then he stuck his tongue inside her mouth.

In the end, salvation came in the unlikeliest of forms. She gagged, and Aumere drew back. "I'm going to be ill," she rasped and then promptly threw up at his feet. The duke cried out and she swayed; an inky blackness pulled at the edge of her consciousness. Dimly, she registered a furious growl and looked to the sound of the beast who'd come upon them.

Her husband stalked forward, hands outstretched. The harshly beautiful planes of his face were etched in a black fury. She huddled into herself, hastily backing away. The sight of his tall, powerful form striding forward sent despair spiraling inside her already breaking heart. She wanted to slam her fists into his face over and over until he was empty and broken inside like she herself was. How was it possible to both love a person and hate him all at the same time? Their gazes collided and in his blue depths was a host of regret, pain, and shame.

Odd, she'd expect a soulless man incapable of such emotion. Then it was gone so she expected she'd only imagined it. Of course Cedric Falcot, the Marquess of St. Albans, was incapable of any and all emotion.

"St. Albans," Aumere greeted. "I would suggest we'd enjoy the pleasures of your wife together, but the chit had the bad form to cast up her accounts—"

Cedric felled him with a single blow and came down over his form. As he rained his fists down in an impressive display of fury, Genevieve hurried away. Her chest rose hard and fast, as she escaped him; this man possessed, she did not recognize. Her ragged breath filled her ears as she continued her flight.

Not waiting to see if her husband followed, she shoved past the butler and pushed the door open, sucking in desperately needed breaths as she searched the line of carriages. Her feet were in agony from her race through Lord Montfort's home. Genevieve yanked off her slippers and then raced down the steps, onward to the safety of her carriage.

Her driver jumped down from his perch, concern radiating from his eyes. "My lady?"

"Home," she managed to rasp, accepting his hand as he assisted her inside the carriage.

Then, within the confines of her carriage, she yanked her mask free and hurled it to the floor. As the conveyance lurched forward, she sank back against the squabs of the bench and promptly wept. What a fool she was. She'd donned her gown and mask not truly thinking about the manner of party she'd attend. She'd known the world her husband dwelled in was a wicked one, but not…this. The tableau she'd witnessed of the other guests; lovers wrapped in wicked embraces, while others watched. Her husband enjoying the softness of another's skin. She cried all the harder and huddled against the bench. He'd worshiped that lady's breast the way he'd worshiped hers so many times. *I believed his caress meant something more…*

Her chest ached from the force of her sobs. She'd believed he could care for her. She'd believed so many things. In him. Of them. Of a life together; with their child… She sobbed until her body ached, never more grateful than when her carriage drew to a stop outside her home.

Home. This was no home. She buried her face into her hands and wept until she shook with the force of her despair. This was the cold, empty life he'd offered and she'd foolishly accepted. Only to realize now, in this moment, she wanted more. So much more.

For her.

For her child.

Tears continued to seep down her cheeks. The driver drew the door open and she placed her shaking hand in his and allowed him to help her down. Then, finding her feet, she sprinted the remaining distance up the steps.

And God love Avis, he stood at the entrance with the black wood panel agape. As though he'd been waiting. The man averted his gaze and she sailed past him.

No doubt, he'd had the sense to realize his mistress was mad in attending that sinful affair and wouldn't last amongst his employer's world. She cried all the harder, the tears pouring from the place where despair and agony dwelled, and stumbled up the steps. Uncaring of the scandal she left in her wake, she sprinted down the corridor. She skidded to a stop outside a particular door and then shoved it open. Stumbling inside, she allowed her eyes to adjust, finding a solace in the inky darkness.

The empty schoolroom, and in this closed-in, untouched space, she closed the door behind her and sought out the corner. Sinking to the floor, she drew her knees closer to her chest and dropped her chin atop the smooth satin fabric, her life coming to an ironic, full circle.

CHAPTER 23

CEDRIC'S CARRIAGE ROLLED THROUGH THE crowded streets of London. With the infernally slow pace set, the tension thrumming inside him grew and grew until he thought he would snap under the weight of it. After he'd bloodied Aumere senseless and peeled himself off the man's inert form, he'd had to have his carriage called. By then, Genevieve had been long gone. How many minutes had passed since she'd stepped into the ballroom and then promptly stumbled out?

Only to be accosted by her former betrothed. His stomach revolted and he wanted to return and beat the Duke of Aumere all over again.

Except...

It is really me who's to blame... She was there because of me and was assaulted by that bastard for it... A low, agonized groan rumbled up from his chest. For there had also been what she'd witnessed prior to Aumere's assault. From where she'd stood, and what she'd observed between him and the baroness.

To give his fingers something to do, he yanked the red velvet curtain open and stared blankly out into the dark of the night. He should be thinking about what words he'd string together to ever pardon what had transpired this evening. Instead, he was unable to muddle through anything other than the staggering sight of her in the midst of that depravity. Of her former betrothed's lips on hers. Of the fear, revulsion, and despair in her eyes as she'd looked at Cedric. It was the moment her innocence had died and it had been at his hands.

He'd had the whole of the carriage ride from Montfort's townhouse to determine exactly what he'd say to his wife. But as the black barouche rocked to a halt outside his home, not a single bloody word had come to him.

Cedric bound up the handful of stone stairs. Avis pulled the door open. "My wife," Cedric demanded.

A flash of antipathy lit the loyal man's eyes. Just then he very much despised himself. "She is abovestairs, my lord." Without elaborating and in a telling display of loyalty to his mistress, the man stalked off.

Not bothering to shed his cloak, Cedric climbed the stairs. The fabric whipped noisily about his legs as he raced to her chambers and pressed the handle expecting the door to be locked. "Genevieve," he barked, scanning his gaze over the room lit only by the faintest burning fire in the hearth. His gaze alighted on her maid who stood, turning down the bed. "Have you seen your mistress?"

Loathing glared strong before she lowered her eyes to the floor. "I have not, my lord."

He'd wager what was left of his sanity in this moment that she knew, just as Avis knew, and they all protected the lady from her bastard of a husband. She deserved that loyalty and he their contempt. Spinning on his heel, he stalked off so quickly his cape snapped about his ankles. He strode purposefully down the hall, shoving door after door open, doing an inventory of each room. With each frantic search, the painful vise squeezing his lungs choked off air so that his breath came in hard, angry spurts. He concentrated on that pain to keep from thinking what Genevieve had witnessed this evening.

She, the only unsullied person who'd seen good in him, had entered his world and it was a sight she'd forever remember. "Genevieve," he called, as he reached the end of the hall. He pushed open the last door of the corridor and scanned the darkened nursery.

Cedric turned to go, when his gaze snagged the soft light cast by the moon's glow and he followed it. His heart squeezed painfully. He closed the door softly behind him, but the unoiled hinges squeaked loudly in the silence.

From where she sat in the corner, knees drawn to her chest, Genevieve stiffened, but remained silent. Silent, when she'd always been one to fill voids of quiet as she'd done since their first meeting. Agony lanced his heart. And as she'd done every day in the gardens she tended so diligently, while he lazily lounged like the worthless cad he was. He came forward, loosening the fastenings of his cloak, and removing the garment. He set it aside.

She remained motionless, with her cheek layered against her skirts.

"Genevieve," he said quietly, because really, in this instance, what else was there to say? She'd had no place in Montfort's. A lady of her character and worth did not belong in the underbelly of his world. He'd told her that and, yet, she'd waded in anyway…and now, he wished he had been an altogether different man, worthy of her. He sank to his haunches beside her. Her cheeks shone with the sheen of tears. Her swollen eyes pools of empty despair. His belly contracted with an agonizing pain. *I did this to her. I am my father's son.* "I am sorry." It was the first time in the course of his life he'd uttered those words to anyone.

She picked her head up and eyed him. "Why? Because I interrupted your evening's entertainment? Or because I saw you with your lover?"

"She is not my lover." The denial ripped from his lungs. For it mattered that she knew that. For reasons he could not sort through in this jumbled moment.

The cold emptiness in Genevieve's eyes chilled him from the inside out. "How free you are with your touch then, my lord." The bitter cynicism underscoring her words hit him with all the force of a kick to the gut. It spoke of a newly found jadedness that he was responsible for and he hated himself for it. "Regardless," she said in weary tones. "There is nothing to apologize for. You never promised me more," she said, looking beyond his shoulder. "I am wrong to ask for or expect anything more." Her slight shuddery breath, the only crack in her remarkable composure."

He stiffened. She wanted nothing to do with him and with all deserved reasons, of course. "Are you saying you'll deny me my rights as husband?" he demanded with a harshness that brought her head up. Lying in her arms, he felt a completeness he'd never before known.

She gave him a sad smile. "Come, Cedric. You're not *truly* my husband. Nor do you wish to be. You spend not even a handful of hours with me during the day and visit my bed. But that's not truly special to you." A soft, humorless laugh escaped her that ravaged at his insides. "No, you are the manner of man who engages in those acts with any woman—"

"I *was* that man," he cut in, his tone gravelly with emotion and the lie he'd told her...that she didn't matter, or her ill-opinion didn't matter, proved false, in this moment. "But I've not touched another woman since the day you stepped inside my father's library." From that moment she'd upended his world and he'd never been the same since.

The long, graceful column of her throat moved. "Well, that isn't altogether true, is it?"

The baroness. His skin heated. "I will allow you, it was damning."

With effort, Genevieve pushed to a stand. Panic swelled. By God, did she intend to leave? He shoved to his feet, and positioned himself between her and the doorway.

"Damning?" she asked in clipped tones, advancing toward him. "It was damning? You come to my bed, night after night. Make love to me, and then go and bestow your attentions on another?" With each word, she took a step closer, until they were a mere hairsbreadth apart. A healthy dose of outrage sparked in her previously devastated eyes and he preferred her this way; spitting and hissing to hurt a broken man. She jabbed him with a finger. "You've nothing to say?"

For the first time in his life, he who was never without a clever retort came up—empty.

A sound of disgust escaped his wife. "I have all but begged for your attentions. What a bloody fool you must have taken me for."

"Never." The denial burst from his lungs. With her clever wit and stunning spirit she was unlike any he'd ever known. How could he desire anyone beyond her? And how had he failed to realize it—until now?

"I actually insisted you take me to that party," she continued with another little laugh, as though he hadn't spoken. As though his contradiction was useless and mayhap it was for as little as he'd proven himself to her. "Why should you want me around this evening to interfere with your," her lip peeled back in a sneer, "pleasures."

I am losing her. Panic rattled around his mind. "It was nothing more than an empty touch," he said futilely. "She put my hand there." A goddamn caress he'd not even wanted. As soon as the words left him, he winced.

"Well, you certainly did not move it." The fight went out of his wife as she passed another sad glance over his face. "And her touch would, no doubt, have been a good deal more if not for my poor timing," she said in tired tones that spoke of a woman who'd given up on him.

"It wouldn't have," he insisted. A cloying dread spiraled inside as she took a step around him. He shot a hand out. "Please." Another never before word uttered, spoken for this woman. Only, he didn't know what he pleaded for. Her forgiveness. For joining her to his worthless self. For who he was. For who he could never be.

Genevieve stilled, but said nothing and with an intuitiveness that came from a place of knowing, realized what he said in this instant would determine so much of their future. There was so much to say and yet he had no idea where to even begin. "I am sorry you witnessed that display, tonight," he said quietly. "I am sorry because it is an ugly, shameful world that you do not belong to, and I hate that you became part of it because of me. But I need you to know that I have not been unfaithful to my vows." The irony of this was not lost on him; he, a caddish Falcot, pledging his fidelity.

Genevieve searched her gaze over his face. Did she seek the veracity of his claim? "Mayhap not yet." She sighed, a whispery exhalation of sadness. "But the time will come and I do not want to be the poor, pathetic, whispered about wife whose husband takes a string of lovers."

He swiped a hand over his face. "I do not want any woman other than you," he repeated. She had slipped inside and held him in an unyielding grip...and he did not want to be free of her.

His wife tipped her head at a small angle. "Why?"

"Why?" he repeated dumbly.

"Yes, why?"

Except he could not give her an answer. He raked a hand through his hair.

Genevieve gave him a sad look and turned her palms up. "I do not know what we are, Cedric. For nearly eight weeks, I've existed in this dual universe, convincing myself during the day that there is a tenderness between us, affection."

"There is," he managed to get out past a thick tongue. These words she gave him, they were unfamiliar to him; words never before uttered from the women who'd shared his bed because they knew what he offered—nothing.

"But then you leave and go off to your clubs and your scandalous parties, and we are any other loveless, coldhearted couple," she continued as though he'd not spoken, as though his admissions were throwaway statements he'd made about the weather or some such mundane matter. "I love you, Cedric, and it terrifies me for I am certain I have made the gravest mistake in giving you my heart."

His heart gave a jump, picked up a frantic beat, and then slowed to a stop. "You love me?" he repeated dumbly. When was the last time anyone had uttered those words to him? He struggled to drag forth the words she deserved, to be that man…

"You must think about what you desire in our union. Do you wish to be a family?" With a father and sister still living, Cedric still didn't even know what that meant. "Or do you wish to live our separate lives?" And yet, the idea of a life without her in it ravaged him. "It cannot be both." Which is what it had been. "But I cannot dwell in this suspended world where I'm always wondering what we are or hoping we are more. And you owe it to me to tell me what we, in fact, are." She held his gaze. "And you owe it to yourself."

He curled his fingers into fists. She was…correct. He'd crafted this alternate existence for them, where he was the rake he'd been and the…husband…which he did not know how to be. He'd inevitably muck it up. This evening was proof of it.

Genevieve stared at him as though seeing the battle he waged within himself.

A knock sounded at the door and Cedric cursed. "Get the hell away," he shouted.

Silence fell and then an incessant rapping resumed. "My lord?" Avis called from the other side.

By hell, this bloody townhouse had better be ablaze and death imminent to merit this interruption. "What the hell is it, Avis?" he thundered.

Which apparently constituted an enter. The fearless servant shoved the door open. "The duke is demanding to see you, my lord."

"Tell him to go to the devil," he snapped. His father and his late night visit could go hang, so very irrelevant they were when compared with the stoically silent woman before him.

Except, his butler remained. He cleared his throat. "His Grace indicated you'd no doubt say as much and said he'd tear down every door until he found you if you weren't in your office posthaste."

Posthaste. Like he was a bloody servant. However, the duke had also proven his threats were no idle ones and he was not above following through on those threats. Nonetheless—"I said—"

"Go," Genevieve urged. "It is late. I am tired and there is nothing left for us to say."

She was wrong. There was everything to be said. "This is not finished," he said curtly and then turning on his heel, he marched off. His butler stepped out of the way and Cedric continued his forward march, rage growing inside him with every step. And he clung to that safe emotion. Found strength in it. Let it fuel him. For the building fury with the man who'd sired him was safer than the tumult of emotions his slip of a wife had unleashed inside him. Eager for the impending fight, Cedric reached the room and paused outside. His father stood at the window. Hands clasped behind his back, he stared into the grounds below. To those long neglected gardens, his wife had toiled over. By all intents and purposes, the duke may as well have owned this very townhouse. He curled his fingers into tight balls, as not for the first time in the recent years that he resented not his father, but rather himself, for being the wastrel who'd lost so much and had developed a need for his father's assistance. Yes, it was the way of their extravagant world, but he'd come to hate every part of it.

"What the hell do you want," he said without preamble as he entered, bypassing his father and made for the sideboard.

The duke didn't draw his attention away from moon-filled sky and Cedric clenched his jaw. Of course, his father would not give him the fight he was spoiling for. "Do you know," his sire said at last as he turned slowly around, tapping the ornamental cane at his side. "I've long known you were cut in my image." A hard smile lined the man's cold lips. "In nearly every way," he added, waggling his eyebrows meaningfully.

Cedric tightened his grip on the snifter in his hands. Yes, they were the same manner of lecherous reprobates. Their presence at Montfort's this evening was proof of that. "Is that why you've come, to wax proudly as a father?" he asked, carrying a decanter of whiskey and a crystal snifter over to his desk. Perching a hip on the edge, he proceeded to pour himself a tall drink.

His father snorted. "I said we're alike in nearly every way. Not every way. Not in the ways that matter, Cedric."

The ways that matter. What were those?

Then all false humor faded from the duke's eyes. "Wives always are kept separate from your whores," he snapped. "For the integrity of the line, you do not bring her to those events or share her with others, until you at least beget a few mewling, legitimate brats on her."

Of course. The way that mattered. Cedric's own mother had lived a solitary existence, shut away in the country while her husband lived *his* separate life in London, carousing and whoring. He stilled... "What she said about living separate lives..." He'd cut out his own tongue before he ever admitted to this man that he'd kill a man with his bare hands before willingly sharing Genevieve with another.

"Is that what this is? A late evening ducal lecture on my responsibilities?" he swirled his drink in a slow circle.

With a bemused look, the duke took in his lazy movements. He swung his cane in a slow, deliberate circle. "Do you know, Cedric, I never believed you would marry."

He stilled, his glass halfway to his lips and said nothing. What game did the man play now? Time had taught him every word on the duke's lips, every action, decision, was with purpose. "Your Grace?"

His father strode over to the leather button sofa. Laying his ornamental cane on the edge, he settled into the folds of the seat. "Married," his father repeated, spreading his arms wide. "Until you, I never thought I'd see a man less eager to wed than myself. For all my threats regarding if you did not hurry and beget an heir for the Ravenscourt lineage, you have been inordinately stubborn.

I told you I did not approve of Lady Genevieve Farendale."

Cedric tossed back his drink. He well knew. It was what had made the prospect of wedding palatable. He made to reach for his bottle, when his father's words froze him.

"That sweetened your decision to marry, eh? Especially when the seed was planted by your *friend*…a man you trust."

He narrowed his eyes, that ugly niggling of suspicion grew, and then the true weight of those words slammed into him. Surely not. Surely the one person he'd called friend had not…

His father flicked a cold stare over Cedric's person. "You were clear that you'd no intention to wed. Yours was nothing more than a petty, irrational decision bent on revenge." He flicked an imagined piece of lint from his immaculate coat sleeve. "Alas, I knew you'd never dare wed one of those proper misses whom I approved of. One of those spiritless ladies like your mother who would be the biddable, subservient creature all wives should be." The niggling grew, and with it, a slow dawning horror. "But when presented with the carrot of wealth I dangled and presented that with my disapproval of the whorish Farendale girl…?"

He was going to be ill. The mastery this man had and continued to exercise over his life was unrelenting.

"You see, Montfort is not unlike us, either, Cedric. Only in that one's case, his vice of wagering has made him weak in ways this family will never be." He winged a ducal eyebrow up. "But it has proven useful to obtain information from the man and to enlist his help."

The air left him on a whoosh. Every conversation about Genevieve, every suggestion that Cedric wed her, all the inquiries he'd put to Cedric after he'd wed had been well-placed questions, not of a friend, but rather, just another coldhearted bastard manipulated and used by his father.

"Never going to marry, were you?" his father taunted, twisting his maniacal triumph all the deeper, so that fury rose up potent inside him, cutting off all words and logic. "Did you believe I didn't know of your interest in that lady? The same one who kept you closed away in my library." The duke arced his cane in a slow circle. Back and forth. Back and forth. Until Cedric wanted to grab it, break it, and beat the ruthless bastard with it. "How do I know that, you wonder?" his father looped his ankle across his opposite knee. "Surely you've gleaned by now, I know everything. Including your library visitor in the middle of my ball." Cedric's mind stalled. "You see, my servants are very loyal to me, Cedric. Very loyal." He gave him a meaningful and, more, triumphant look that sent fury skittering along Cedric's inside. "I know you've begun," he said as he peeled his lip back in a sneer, "sketching again, since you met a certain scandalous lady."

By God, how did he know that? Fury melded with embarrassment; it lanced through him. Were there any secrets from this man?

"And now you are gardening?" The duke threw his head back and erupted into a humorless, if exultant, laugh, until Cedric's fingers twitched and he was besieged with the urge to bury his fist into his father's smug face.

Oh, God. How neatly he'd been maneuvered. In Genevieve, he'd believed she was the one choice that he'd had, a decision to wed her that went against the lifelong vow he'd had to never marry. And he'd merely been led into that union by a seed planted by Montfort and fed to him by his father. And through that, Genevieve had been a pawn in his father's machinations; ultimately finding herself with Cedric for her husband when she'd deserved so much more. This emotionally deadened bastard was, once more, proof of the ugly flowing in his veins. This night, from Montfort's party to his exchange with Genevieve in the schoolroom to this farcical drama, was just proof why he'd no right to her or getting any child on her. His tightly held control snapped. Cedric slammed his glass down hard enough to send liquid drops spiraling over the rim of the glass. "Say whatever it is that brought you here," he seethed. "And get out."

"Surely you must see the humor in it from my end?" his father went on as though he'd not spoken. He spread his arms out, that cane dangling from his fingers. "You, who've been so adamant to shirk your responsibilities, now married…and…by accounts, besotted by your wife." His neck heated and he resisted the urge to yank at his cravat. "And the way you ran after her this evening." He chuckled. "Well, she must mean something to you." Those words were spoken as though he could not puzzle through that very real truth.

"What game do you play?" he managed to bite out through the rage consuming him. The air left Cedric on a swift exhale. The bastard…

"How have you, of all people, not yet gleaned that I will not be thwarted?" Another slow, ugly smile split his father's lips. "Besotted by your wife. No doubt, bedding her every night, hmm?" A dull flush heated Cedric's neck. "It is only a matter of time before you get me my next heir." He abruptly stopped swinging his cane. "Checkmate, Cedric."

He started. He'd not taken care the way he had to ensure Genevieve remained childless. Cedric flattened his lips into a hard line. He'd not be so unwise in the future.

For once again, his father, the master manipulator who'd orchestrated his life, had maneuvered him in the most final of ways, into a state he'd pledged to never take part in. Cedric gripped his snifter so hard, the fragile glass cracked under the weight of his palm. But there was one area in which his father was wrong. By God, he thought he'd have the ultimate victory over Cedric? He'd see the old bastard in hell first. Setting aside the glass with a trembling palm, he folded his arms at his chest and gave him an equally cold smile. "Ah, yes, it would seem that way. You're so determined to have a future heir. But there will never be a child."

His father snapped his eyebrows into a single line. "What are you saying?" he barked.

Reveling in the sudden reversal, Cedric widened his smile. "I may be married, but as you know, there are ways to ensure there will never be children, Your Grace." He delighted in the ever-narrowing of his sire's eyes. "Or, given the number of bastards you've littered about England, perhaps you do not know that. But, I repeat, there will never be children." The duke dropped his brow. "Checkmate."

CHAPTER 24

CHECKMATE

She hadn't meant to eavesdrop. Genevieve had long known no good could come from listening at keyholes and, yet, she'd done it anyway. The only reason she'd been in this very corridor was because she'd had to pass her husband's office on her way to her chambers.

And now, coward that she was, she wished she'd never appeared at the doorway, uninvited.

...revenge...

Her stomach turned.

...there will never be a child...

Touching a hand to her belly, a panicky laugh bubbled past Genevieve's lips sounding like cannon fire and she froze, praying they'd not heard her. Praying that she'd not heard what she'd heard. For an instant, she entertained the possibility of running. Running away from this frigid meeting between ruthless father and angry son, and continue running until she forgot all about the ugly that existed on the other side of those walls. Except, for all that had come, she'd never been a coward.

With silence reigning, she schooled her features and stepped into the entrance of the room. Shock marked the harsh, angular planes of her husband's face. Unable to meet his gaze, she slid her stare beyond his shoulder...and collided with the cynical eyes of his sire. The man eyed her with cold, emotionless eyes. Is this what her husband would become? A chill stole through her. Unnerved by the piercing emptiness of that stare, she looked to her husband.

Cedric met her gaze and there was a remarkable crack in his composure that he easily concealed, replaced by an unflappable calm that sent fury roiling through her. How could he be so calm, after being discovered with his whore and now uttering such cold words about their marriage? *Because those words were true… He never promised me anything more than his name.* She'd simply allowed herself to believe from a handful of endearing acts, carried out by a stranger, that there was or, at the very least, could be something there.

Again, sliding her gaze away, she found her father-in-law. "Your Grace," she greeted, again, priding herself on the steadiness of those words. From the corner of her eye, she detected the flash of annoyance in her husband's stare.

"He is leaving," Cedric replied before the duke could respond.

The slightly bored looking gentleman stared at her with an emptiness in his gaze. "I was just leaving," he said, climbing to his feet. Collecting his cane, he strode over to the door.

She stepped inside and allowed her father-in-law to step around her. Without so much as another glance for her or his son, he swept out and left Genevieve with a rather uncertain fate looming before her. Is this what her husband would one day become? A hard, unfeeling man who looked through her and not at her? And for the first time since she'd bound herself to Cedric and this family, the ramifications of that hasty decision rocked her unsteady world.

"I am sorry you heard that." Once again, words he'd uttered in truth that he only regretted her hearing for the implications it would have. "I should have instructed you to stay away," her husband said at last, through tight lips. He shoved himself from the edge of the desk and made his way over to the sideboard.

Annoyance stirred. "Do you mean like a dog, Cedric? Or a dull, biddable wife who stays at home while you bed your whores?" She spoke in clipped tones that caused a momentary falter in his steps. If he thought he'd acquired an acquiescent, biddable bride, he was to be disappointed. She found strength in her fury, for it prevented her from thinking of how, in the span of an evening, he had torn apart her every happiness.

She stared at his retreating back. By God, he meant to carry on as though she'd not been listening at his door and heard all manner of confounding and agonizing words. Entering the room, Genevieve drew the door closed behind her and rested her back against it for support. "Why would you say that?" she asked quietly.

"Why did I say what?" he asked, not picking his gaze up from the drink he now poured. As though that singular task of pouring and consuming spirits was so much more important than her...or, more importantly, their future. All of it. Any of it.

"About never having children," she clarified, quietly.

Cedric settled the decanter down with a firm thunk. "Because there will not be," he said with a damning matter-of-factness as he carried his glass around the opposite side of his desk and claimed a seat. He took a sip and then settled his snifter down. Then in a dismissive manner, he opened the middle drawer, withdrew a sheet, and reached for a quill.

He would simply move on to other matters as though he'd not neatly stated the remainder of their existence together. "What?" she repeated, trying to muddle through the madness of this exchange.

He paused and glanced up. In his eyes was reflected back her own confusion. "We've already discussed the matter of children," he said the way an instructor might tire of doling out the same lesson to a recalcitrant student.

Her mind moved from a stall to a run. They had spoken of children and he'd promised he'd see them cared for. Genevieve pushed away from the door and the wood panel rattled noisily. "Yes, we did." She stopped before his desk and planted her hands upon her hips. "You promised..."

His sound of annoyance cut across her words. "I promised you'd never have to care for children and you won't." Cedric sighed. Who was this cold stranger she did not recognize? Where were his charming grin and his teasing words?

"I do not under..." ...*Nor will you have to worry after children...* "Do you believe yourself unable to sire children?" she ventured.

He cocked his head. "Unable to...?" A hard grin formed on his lips. "Oh, I've no doubt the potency of my seed. The number of bastards my father has littering England is testament of that."

Genevieve pressed her fingertips against her temples and rubbed.

"I don't understand," she said once more, knowing she must sound like the veriest lackwit. "We've made love."

Cedric carried his drink over to his desk and perched his hip on the edge. "I've not taken precautions before. I promise to...rectify that in the future."

Bile burned at her throat and she choked. "Precautions?"

He gave a tight nod. "There are...*ways* to ensure you do not become with child."

Now he'd have this discussion? A hysterical laugh bubbled up past her lips and she stymied it with her fingers. The irony of his timing not at all lost on her. Cedric spoke with such a cool remoteness. She sought glimpses of the gentleman who'd been tending the gardening beside her. "When you said I'd never have to care for child—"

He cut in to her words with a sound of impatience. "I meant because we'll never have to worry after offspring."

Worry after offspring? Is that how he viewed children? Then, should it surprise her when a man who seeks out his own pleasures each night and attends torrid affairs like Montfort's? The earth dipped and she gripped the edge of the nearby sofa. The gentle assurance he'd made before they'd married, a promise given, she'd so horribly misunderstood. "I did not know," she whispered. "I misunderstood." And what a monumental misunderstanding with which to build a union on. Except...none of it made sense. "But, you did not take care." Many times. Many, many times. Her cheeks exploded with heat and her tongue could not move for the scandalous words to speak of what they'd done.

Glass between his hands, her husband shifted his weight. "Mistakes on my part." With every admission, his words confirming the ugliest murmurings she'd heard from the opposite side of the door, ripped a wound inside her heart that could never heal. He looked down into the contents of his drink. "Surely, given what you... witnessed tonight." Montfort's. "You see why it is best that we do not bring a child into this world."

She folded her arms close to where his babe even now rested. Her stomach pitched. Given her failed betrothal with Aumere, she'd abandoned the hope carried by all young ladies—of a loving, doting husband and a passel of babes. In one short night and in one stunningly practical, but beautiful, offer of marriage, Cedric had allowed her to open her heart to all those long-buried dreams. Unable to meet his coolly blank gaze, she dropped her eyes to that untouched page on his desk. "But there…" Is a babe. "Has to be a child. For the succession of your line," she said quickly, lifting her gaze. *Needing* him to want this child.

"I do not give a jot about the Falcot line," he said, drumming his fingertips on his glass in a staccato rhythm that set her jaw on edge. "Long ago I resolved to never have children."

"But why?" She hated the faintly pleading edge to the question there. He was a stranger. In every way.

Her husband shifted. "Children are so important to you?" he asked with a discomfort she'd never before seen from him and one she doubted he ever showed the world, in any way, for anything.

It did not escape her notice that he'd failed to ignore her question. "They are." How little they truly knew one another. He knew she enjoyed art and she knew he was a skilled artist, albeit a silent one. But on the things that mattered in a marriage, what did she truly know of him? Nothing.

"If they are so important, then after this evening you surely see how you are far better off without children from me." Cedric grimaced and took another drink of his brandy. "I am sorry for the confusion on that score," he said as he settled his glass down.

Genevieve shoved away from the chair and swept over in a rustle of noisy skirts. "You are *sorry* for the confusion?" she parroted back, planting her palms on the high-backed leather chair opposite him and leaning across the surface. "You did not purchase me the wrong ice at Gunther's, Cedric. You did not lose the place in my book." Her voice climbed with an increasing urgency. He flexed his jaw, but said nothing for so long that her fingers twitched with the urge to slap him, or shake him, or to rouse some kind of emotion in him. When he remained silent, she pressed him for every last truth. "Did you marry me on a matter of revenge against your father?"

Because even as entering into a union on a matter of convenience had slashed at her still-hopeful, romantic heart, this truth threatened to shatter all those moments she'd built up between them.

Cedric held his palms up.

"Did you?" she rasped.

"I care for you," he said softly. Care not love. Then…she skimmed a bitter gaze over him. Given what she'd seen and heard this evening, the Marquess of St. Albans was incapable of that sentiment. No, he hadn't ever given her reason to believe there would be love or children. Which made this all the worse. It made her folly her own and it was a mistake that could never be undone.

She recoiled. In ignoring her query, he'd answered it with more affirmation than any words. "My God." The words escaped her as a prayer and she again dug her fingers into her temple. She swayed.

"Genevieve," he said, concern lacing that hoarse utterance as he came to his feet.

"Do not," she cried out, stumbling away from him. "Do not come near me."

And a man who chafed at being given any direction from anyone, including his own sire, remained at his desk.

Genevieve began to pace as truth settled in and drove back the girlish whimsy she'd not even realized herself guilty of until this moment. And with each furious step, and her new husband staring on, she accepted with a staggering clarity—this was her fault. Cedric had never made her promises of more. He'd never pledged affection. He'd never spoken of a future with them joined as a loving couple. Those were castles she'd built of sand within her mind and heart…ones she'd not even realized she'd constructed—until this moment. But now, there was a babe and a father who did not want that precious life. Genevieve jerked to a sudden halt. She raised her gaze to his. "I have so desperately wanted to be part of your life and I wanted you in my life."

"Genevieve?" There was a gruff quality to that word, which spoke of a man as uncertain as she herself was; two strangers trying to work through a delicate, uneven balance between them.

She motioned to her gown. "I donned this dress and thought to be the bold, proud woman asserting her presence in her husband's life. Tonight," bile burned her throat and she swallowed it back, "witnessing that party you so enjoy attending and listening to you with your father, I realized something." She lifted her eyes to his. "I do not want to be part of your life, Cedric. I do not wish to be part of any of your world."

His expression grew shuttered but, otherwise, he gave no indication he'd even heard her. Of course, did she truly expect her admission should matter to him? Genevieve gave her head a sad shake. "If you'll excuse me." She walked with steady, even footsteps. But as she stepped out in the hall and found freedom from his stony gaze, she sprinted down the hall. Her breath came hard and fast as she raced away from every vile word her husband had uttered. A shuddery sob tore from her lungs as she reached the shelter of her room. She shoved the door open and slammed it hard behind her.

"My lady?" Delores called, rushing over. "Are you all right?"

She would never be all right again, because she'd done something the height of all foolishness—she'd fallen in love with her husband.

Her maid folded Genevieve in her arms. "Come, my lady, 'tis not good for the baby." Which only caused Genevieve to cry all the harder.

Now what?

CHAPTER 25

THE SOFT SCRATCH OF GENEVIEVE'S charcoal filled the quiet. Sitting so very still for so long as she had, her back ached and through that pain, she shifted but continued working. She found a healing in each line drawn, in each brush of the charcoal over the page.

It prevented her from thinking of him. Faithless rake. Regret and despair twisted her insides in a vicious pain. Her husband had never invited her along last evening, or any evening, because he'd had plans to see another woman. Unable to gaze at the small face upon the page, she looked up and found her friend, Francesca, and sister, Gillian, staring at her.

For their benefit, she gave them a smile. If her smile grew any tauter, she feared her face might shatter. "Forgive me. I'm wool-gathering today." She made for miserable company.

"Oh, Genevieve, your smile is really more of a grimace," Francesca whispered.

"I am so happy you're here," she said softly. If it weren't for the other young ladies' company, Genevieve would be alone in her chambers weeping tears that would never end. God, how she despised all of this. The folly in coming here, entering this world she no longer belonged to, resonated all the more.

"Well, I'm happy *you* are here," Francesca beamed. "London had been so very dreadful until you arrived."

"It is a dreadful place, isn't it?" she said more to herself. How could Cedric wish to live here? There was nothing sincere or real in this place. Then, mayhap that is what he preferred—the artifice and veneer of falsity painted by soulless lords and ladies.

"I heard Mother and Father speaking of what happened last night," Gillian said softly, snapping her attention back to the moment.

Of course they had. She cringed, just imagining what her always disappointed mother and father thought of their daughter attending one of those shameful affairs. Then, it was hard to give a jot about angry parents who'd never truly approved of her.

"I am sorry you are hurting, Genny."

Gillian and Francesca sat side by side on the opposite leather button sofa, shoulders pressed together in a wonderful display of supportive friendship.

Genevieve mustered her first smile since her life had fallen apart last evening. "It is not your fault, Gillian. Who could have known…?" She let those words trail off. For even with these two young women, loyal friends she trusted implicitly, she could not bring herself to utter the shameful, wicked things she'd observed last evening. Her throat worked. Though, the copy of *The Times* had quite delighted in enumerating every last scandalous detail.

About the Marquess of St. Albans…and the woman he'd bestowed his attentions on last evening.

About the poor, pathetic marchioness who'd appeared at the center of that shameful event.

Fury melded with the agony of Cedric's betrayal and with a growl, she picked up her book and resumed her sketching. She embraced the silence of the room as she concluded the sketch. Once done, she eyed the completed figure. Setting the charcoal aside, she blew on the page. The tiny little likeness with cherubic cheeks, with his almond-shaped eyes and crop of slightly curled locks was very much the image of a certain other. A man who didn't even want him. Or her. He never had. Their cold arrangement had been colder than she'd even known. Pain, like a thousand jagged needles, stuck in her chest.

Genevieve rested the book down and picked her attention up. Her sister and Francesca sat patiently, staring. How good they were. How loyal. They certainly deserved more than her morose silence.

And she truly needed their friendship.

"It was horrendous," she said at last. She grimaced. That did nothing to truly capture the pain and humiliation that came in being married to a rake. Genevieve clasped her hands before her. "Needless to say, for Francesca's optimistic opinion, the gossip proved invariably true last evening."

A shocked gasp split her sister's lips. "Surely not." Rage lit her eyes.

Genevieve sighed. "Regardless, last night simply confirmed everything whispered about Cedric. It proved the rumors true." And now she would never be the same. Her heart spasmed. So this was what the death of a dream felt like. Absently, she picked up the sketchpad and studied the babe's form done in Cedric's likeness.

"What will you do now?" Francesca asked haltingly.

What would she do? What did women do who were married and a part of cold, loveless unions? If she stayed in London, she would die. Her spirit would wilt until she became a shadow of the person she'd always been. Her lips twisted. Then, isn't that what she'd become since returning? Her time in London had been like a slow death, with Cedric proving the only brightness in this otherwise dark world. She shook her head. "I don't know." She fiddled with the pages of her book. "Do you know, I believed there was nothing worse than being unwed, always on the fringe of Society, without a promise or hope of marriage. Today," she turned her hands up. "Today, I would say this marriage to Cedric is so much worse." This one-sided relationship where her husband cared for her was not enough. And it was her own fault for convincing herself it could be.

"I have to believe he cares for you," Gillian put in, once more showing her optimism, which Genevieve hadn't been without herself yesterday. "The man you describe who gardens with you and sketches is not the man the papers write of." Her sister spoke with the same naïveté Genevieve had once carried.

Francesca continued her defense of a man who could never be defended. "I do not believe that woman mentioned in the papers is…*more* to him."

On what did Gillian and Francesca base their flawed assumptions? On the morsels of happiness Genevieve had fed them? Morsels she'd allowed herself to believe were so much more. Her throat worked and, hating the sheen of tears that clouded her vision, she trained her gaze on her friend's hand. "Yes, well, it really wouldn't matter if she was," Genevieve said, her voice curiously flat. "Our world is one where ladies and gentlemen carry on as they wish."

Her friend made a sound of protest. "I cannot believe that or accept that. There are some unions that are formed on love. My parents," she said softly. "Until my mother died, were very much in love."

Genevieve lifted her gaze to meet the other young lady's pain-filled eyes. "I'm so sorry."

"She's been gone ten years and it still feels as though I've just lost her sometimes. But the most important lessons she gave me are that love is real and it matters. Above all else."

Those words resonated around the chambers of Genevieve's mind. A pebble knotted her belly. Francesca's very valuable lessons, imparted too late. For Genevieve had allowed herself to believe that stability and freedom were all she was entitled to. Only to find, with her husband only distantly interested in her and in the basest of ways, love was all that mattered. And they could never have that as long as he wished to live the same rakish lifestyle he'd lived all the years before her.

"I have seen the way the marquess looks at you and it is very much the way my father looked at my mother," Francesca said, pulling her to the moment.

Her observation startled a sharp, empty laugh from Genevieve. "You are mistaken." Just as Francesca had seen more in that first waltz, so, too, was she hopelessly wrong in this.

"I don't believe she is," Gillian pressed. "I—"

"He was touching her," Genevieve said with a bluntness that elicited matching gasps from her friends. She tightened her mouth. "Are those the actions of a man who cares for me?"

Gillian pressed her fingers against her mouth. "Surely not?"

She gave a terse nod. "Indeed. I arrived to…see it." The memory of Cedric's long, tanned fingers against that woman's perfect, white flesh assaulted her and Genevieve pressed her eyes momentarily closed to blot it out. "And then I promptly left. That manner of event is not one I wish to be part of. Even to be closer to my husband." She'd not elaborate that her husband had, in fact, been caressing the woman's naked breast. Such details were not fit for any lady's ears; friend or sister. None of what she'd witnessed last evening had been. For his protestations afterward, the fact remained that Cedric had been there. Any of the remorse or regret he'd expressed last evening wouldn't have existed—if he hadn't been discovered by her. Nor was that the greatest pain he'd inflicted last night. She ran a tired hand over her face.

"What happened?" Francesca put in tentatively. At Genevieve's furrowed brow, the other woman clarified. "When you left the… er…party." Her full cheeks bloomed with color. "What did the marquess do?"

She sighed. "He also left." At the look exchanged by her friends, she frowned. "What?"

Francesca cleared her throat. "Well, it just occurs to me, that if he were the manner of lecherous rake and scoundrel whispered about, he'd hardly *care* if you arrived and saw him so. Such a gentleman would, no doubt, continue on with his own…um…pleasures. But by *your* accounts, the marquess left."

"Hmm," Gillian murmured, tapping her chin.

Her frown deepening, Genevieve alternated her stare between the two young ladies. In the haze of shock and despair, she'd not given thought about Cedric's following her. Why had he left his evening's enjoyments if he was the coldhearted rake the world purported him to be? Except, the memory of his exchange with his father trickled in and twisted the blade of agony all the deeper. A sound of frustration escaped her and she leapt to her feet. Needing distance from the babe on that sketchpad, she wandered over to the hearth. "The marquess married me on a matter of revenge." She shot a glance over her shoulder. "Against his father." Hardly an auspicious beginning.

Francesca scratched her brow. "What did you do to the Duke of Ravenscourt?"

A laugh burst from her lips and she managed her first real smile. God love Francesca Cornworthy in her optimism and unaffectedness.

Gillian laid her hand on the other lady's. "I believe she means because His Grace did not approve of her."

"Why—?"

"The scandal," her younger sister supplied.

"Ah, yes. Of course."

Of course. The scandal that had sent her from London and saw her returned as the shamed, whispered about lady. It had also found her married to Cedric for it. Her stomach twisted as a sharp pain stuck at her. God help her for being a fool. Even with everything that had come to pass, she loved her husband still.

"If I may?" Francesca ventured, clearing her throat. "By your own admission, you married the marquess for matters of convenience."

Yes, but it was different.

"Why is it different?" her friend persisted.

She started not realizing she spoke aloud. "It matters because I love him. It matters because, even as I agreed to marry him for a mutually beneficial arrangement, I cared for him then." *And I love him now.*

Gillian pushed to her feet. "Isn't it possible," she began softly, coming over. "Isn't it possible that His Lordship mayhap entered into your marriage feeling much the same way and that he, too, has come to love you?"

...I care about you...

Not love. It had never been about love with Cedric. Not on his end.

Even if they moved on from Lord Montfort's party, it was what had transpired after that made their union impossible. "There are too many insurmountable challenges between us," she said tiredly. The greatest being the child nestled in her womb. Another agonizing pain struck low in her belly. For that was just another detail about her husband she could never share with her sister or Francesca. Somehow, breathing the words about his antipathy for children would make that truth more real in ways that would shatter her. She shifted as another twinge pulled at her back.

"What is it?" her sister asked, concern underscoring those three words.

Genevieve opened her mouth, when a cramping low in her belly robbed her of breath. She shot a hand out, finding the mantel. *What is wrong with me?*

A slight gush between her legs wrung a gasp from her and she swayed, dimly registering her sister's cry as Gillian caught her about the waist. She heard Francesca's frantic calls for help. Another spasm wracked her middle as agony plucked at the corner of her consciousness. Gillian guided her down to the floor.

"Something is wrong," Genevieve managed to rasp. Noting the footsteps of rushing servants and her sister's frantic cries, she remembered nothing more.

CEDRIC HAD DONE ANY NUMBER of rotten, vile things in the course of his life. Never had a word uttered or a deed committed given him so much as a fleeting afterthought.

Seated at the back table of his club, with a half-empty bottle of brandy before him, he found with no little amount of shock that he was capable of—guilt and pain and every other bloody emotion he'd believed himself immune to. A pressure tightened his chest and, in a bid to dissipate it, he took a long swallow of his drink. Alas, the dulling power of the spirits had long ceased to have any effect.

...I do not want to be part of your life, Cedric. I do not wish to be part of any of your world...

She didn't want him in her life. And why should she? He stared into his drink. He'd proven himself unworthy of her time and time again. He'd married her for the worst of reasons and last night, he'd inadvertently pulled her into the ugly world he'd dwelled in; a world she had no part in. She was goodness and purity. And after last night, with the revulsion and horror in her eyes, he'd instantly shattered whatever fragile happiness they'd built between them.

...I love you...

She loved him. His gut clenched. Or she had. That gift he had no right to.

Aside from heartache and pain, what had he to offer her? Nothing. It was why he was his father's son. He was undeserving of love and incapable of giving it. Wasn't last night proof of that? The memory of her trickled in as she'd stood at the center of that ballroom, with an innocent smile on her generous lips. And the moment that innocence had died. At his hands. A groan lodged in his throat and he rubbed at the dull ache in his chest. To no avail. It continued to throb. Just as it had since Genevieve had walked away from him last night.

Following her retreat, he'd sat in the silence of his office contemplating the man he was. He'd been a rake, a rogue, and a shiftless bounder. He'd wagered too many good funds and fleeced other gentlemen out of theirs. Through all those years of inanity, he'd sought to lose himself in a mindless existence that prevented him from accepting the truth before him—his life was an empty one. He ran a tired hand over his face. She deserved more than Cedric Falcot, worthless Marquess of St. Albans. And yet, stuck with him, she was.

God help him for being a selfish, grasping, self-centered bastard. Even with her hating him as she did, he wanted her anyway. Throughout his life, he'd disavowed marriage. So when threatened by his father, Cedric could have easily found an equally ruthless, heartless lady who'd be Cedric's perfect match in every way.

He went still.

Yet, he hadn't. He'd wanted Genevieve. Nay, needed her. Even as he'd convinced himself the offer he made was one born of necessity for the both of them, now, with only his miserable self for company, he at last accepted the lie he'd perpetuated against himself. Against the both of them—he'd wanted her. He wanted her in every way. Not because he required a wife. Not because he wished for an empty marriage where he was free to carry on with countless whores and widows.

He wanted her because she'd reminded him what it meant to smile; not the practiced, false grin she'd easily seen through the day he'd offered her marriage, but rather, a smile borne of happiness. He wanted her because she celebrated his love of art and did not mock him for that interest as his father and friend had. When the world, when his own family, had seen nothing but the self-centered, worthless rake, Genevieve had seen more. Seen more, when he'd never been deserving of her faith.

His throat worked spasmodically. Then, in one faulty, unforgiving misstep on his part, he'd destroyed all of that. Her innocence. Her smile. And more, any hope of happiness between them. A cold emptiness filled him. To drive away the coldness, he tossed back the remaining contents of his glass and glanced across the club.

His gaze automatically narrowed at the familiar figure cutting a path through the club—a man he'd called friend. Odd, he'd known the Earl of Montfort for almost twenty years and Genevieve for less than three months, and she had been more a friend to him than the faithless bastard striding over to him now.

"St. Albans, my good man. How are you?" the earl asked with boisterous cheer as he swiped the bottle of brandy and motioned for a servant.

Cedric studied the other man's lazy movements; the way he poured himself a snifter full and then searched around for an available whore. Montfort caught the eye of one woman and the young beauty sauntered to their table. "How much?" Cedric asked quietly.

The earl blinked several times.

"How many silver pieces does it take to betray one's friend?"

The beauty he'd previously summoned stopped before the table. "Not now, love," Montfort murmured, his gaze still locked with Cedric's.

Fury thrumming through him, Cedric concentrated on the safe, hollow sentiment, for it prevented him from thinking about the only person who truly mattered. The only woman who'd ever meant anything to him. "You bastard," he seethed.

Montfort rolled his shoulders.

Cedric curled his fingers into hard fists to keep from bloodying the other man senseless. How had he ever called him friend? "Nothing to say?" he asked coolly when the other man remained silent.

"I gather you're speaking about my involvement with your father?" With an infuriating calm, Montfort shrugged. "I didn't do anything different than what you yourself would have done had you been in my shoes."

Cedric surged forward, rattling the glasses on the table. "I called you my friend," he bit out. Other gentlemen peered over in curiosity and he lowered his voice to a furious whisper. "I confided in you things I shared with no one. And knowing all of that, about the man I hate, you betrayed me, anyway?"

The earl tightened his mouth. "Oh, how difficult it must be for you," he spat. He swiped his hand in Cedric's direction. "You speak as though your life has been a rotten one. Why? Because you had a nasty father?" He leaned forward shrinking the space between them. "We all have miserable fathers. Children serve but one purpose. To advance our lines. Yet, you," he peeled his lip back in a mocking sneer, "you act as though your father is somehow different. Hate him all you want." He lifted his glass in salute. "But the man has built a fortune you'll one day inherit, whereas men such as me are left in near dun territory because of my sire's recklessness."

Cedric sat unmoving, staring across the table to the man he'd called friend. How had he failed to see the ruthlessness in him? He'd long considered himself cut of the same proverbial cloth as the Montforts of the world and yet… "I do not even know you," he said to himself, puzzling through a twenty-year friendship in the midst of one of the most scandalous clubs in London. "You knew about my fears and the goals I had and it mattered not at all. All you cared about was the coin dangled before you."

"Oh, come," the earl scoffed. "With your indignation and holier than thou attitude, you of all people would take me to task? *You?*" He placed a mocking emphasis that deepened Cedric's frown. "You can hate me all you want and act the offended party for me having placed my own needs before yours." Montfort jerked his chin in Cedric's direction. "But you are the same as me."

"I am nothing like you." The denial sprung easily to his lips. "I would have never put my interests before yours."

"No." Montfort propped his elbows on the smooth surface of the table. "You'd only put yourself and your happiness before that of your wife."

The air left him on a slow hiss and he opened his mouth wanting to refute those mocking words. To lash out with the truth that he was nothing like the Earl of Montfort or the Duke of Ravenscourt. And yet… His throat constricted so that it was painful to draw breath. Genevieve *was* proof that he'd always placed his needs and desires before anyone else's.

"You see that I am correct," Montfort observed. The too-casual earl picked up his glass and reclined in his seat. "You thought about your need for coin and saw the Farendale chit as the easiest way to fill your coffers while maintaining your dissolute lifestyle." With every word uttered in truth, the blade of guilt twisted all the deeper. Montfort flicked his hand. "There is nothing wrong with that decision. Nor is there anything wrong with the lifestyle you live." There had been everything wrong with it. Too many errors to now count. Too many sins he could not undo. Genevieve's once smiling visage flashed to mind and pain wracked his heart. "You merely did what any gentleman would do." Montfort held his gaze. "Just as I did. But allow me to buy you a drink and the comforts of a beautiful whore to make up for the ill-will."

Bile singed the back of his throat. Cedric was everything like this man...and yet, at the same time, nothing. A commotion sounded at the front of the club, momentarily distracting, and he glanced past Montfort's shoulder just as a servant pushed through the two men who stood as sentinels at the front of the club. A liveried servant. He furrowed his brow. *His* liveried servant.

What...?

The man, gasping and out of breath, skidded to a stop before his table with the hulking brutes racing after him. "My lord," he said, panting from his exertions. He held out a note. "It is Her Ladyship."

He cocked his head, not making sense of the words. "Her Ladyship?" he repeated dumbly. Unable to process. Not wanting to process. The world hung suspended in an unending moment of humming silence and then it resumed in a whir of noise. He ripped the sheet from the man's hands and skimmed the words. His heart stopped.

"St. Albans?"

Montfort forgotten, Cedric surged to his feet so quickly his seat toppled over with a loud thwack. He sprinted from his club.

Heart pounding a frantic beat, Cedric raced outside, searching for the youth whom he'd turned his mount over to. Finding the boy, he rushed across the street, dodging past a quick moving phaeton. He concentrated on his every movement or else he'd descend into a level of madness that he'd never be able to climb back from.

Her Ladyship is unwell.

His pulse beat loudly in his ears, muting sound. The handful of lines that said everything and nothing. Throwing a purse at the lad, Cedric swung his leg over his mount and kicked it forward into a breakneck speed that earned him furious stares and shouts.

He nudged Wicked ahead faster.

Why had he gone out?

Because she had no wish to see me. Because I was too much a coward to remain in the same townhouse with her and be reminded of the weight of my sins.

Terror licked at his senses as his ride stretched into forever. At last, his townhouse came into focus and he urged Wicked onward past other lords setting out in their carriages. He jerked on the reins and his mount reared, pawing at the air with his hooves. Cedric swiftly dismounted and a servant waiting outside hurried to collect the reins.

In wait, Avis pulled the door open.

"Her Ladyship," he rasped as this moment unfolded in an eerily similar way of last night's hell.

"Her ch-chambers, my lord." He briefly noted the ashen hue and the tremble to the man's words and it fueled his panic. "I summoned the doctor. He arrived a short while…" Letting those words to go unfinished, Cedric surged up the stairs, taking them three at a time.

He stumbled and then righted himself at the top landing and then tore down the hall. Sucking in ragged breaths from his constricted lungs, he staggered to a halt. Two ladies lie in wait outside his wife's chambers. Tears stained the cheeks of his sister-in-law and terror anew licked at his every sense.

"Oh, Cedric," Gillian whispered as he rushed over. She placed herself between him and the oak panel. "She is not well." His heart lurched and he sought words. "I've summoned my mother."

Incapable of words, he made to step around her just as a maid came out.

His stomach revolted at the bloodied rags she carried. The young woman averted her gaze. "You should not go in there, my lord."

In a daze, Cedric stepped past his sister-in-law and entered the room. He froze in the doorway. A dull buzzing filled his ears and an inky blackness played at the corner of his eyes. Genevieve lay at the center of the bed, moaning. He shot a hand out to steady himself. The old family doctor who'd long served the St. Albans family looked up and said something to a young woman at his side.

"You should not be in here, my lord," Dr. Craven murmured, rushing over. The doctor took him by the arm and steered him away, but not before Cedric's gaze snagged on the crimson towels.

Blood. So much of it. An agonized groan ripped from his throat. "Genevieve," he roared. What had she done? *What did I make her do?*

"Come, my lord. It will not do Her Ladyship well to see you like this," the physician said with the same firmness he'd used when he scolded Cedric as he'd cried over his broken nose as a boy of eight.

"My wife," he managed to rasp as the doctor closed the door behind him. His wife's two loyal sentinels retreated, allowing Cedric his privacy. He dragged a trembling hand through his hair as his world threatened to ratchet down about him. "Will she l—be all right?" There was no life without Genevieve in it; no life that was worth living.

The doctor removed a kerchief and mopped at his damp brow. "Your wife will live."

He slid his eyes closed on a prayer. "And you may rest assured, my lord, there will be others."

Cedric opened his eyes and gave his head a shake. "Other what?" he demanded gruffly.

Surprise stamped the other man's weathered face. "You did not know?"

"Know what?" The entreaty ripped from him.

"Her Ladyship was with child."

CHAPTER 26

GENEVIEVE WAS RESTRICTED TO HER bed, cared for by Dr. Craven, and suffering through the wrenching pain of her loss. An agony that defied the mere physical pain ripping at her insides, Genevieve found herself fixing on the ceiling to keep from going mad.

Except madness was a powerful thing. It licked at the corner of her mind, until all logic and reason disappeared under the cacophony of pain and despair. When insanity nearly dragged her under, she fought to stave it off.

It was then she'd first noticed the twelve cherubs in the mural above her bed. She'd come to notice one peculiar, particular detail each time. That particular number continued to surface.

From the doctor, to the maids, to her only two friends in the world, and even her mother, there were twelve people who'd alternated their presence over the course of the sennight.

It took Dr. Craven twelve steps to reach her bed and another twelve to march the same path out of her chambers.

There were twelve cherubs in the mural overhead.

And twelve letters in the name Cedric Falcot. Twelve more in Lord St. Albans.

And it had been twelve hours.

Twelve hours was all it had taken for her life to come apart.

In the early morn hour, with her maid hurrying about her room tucking her dresses and garments into her trunks, Genevieve lay on her side and stared at the opposite wall. With the brocade curtains tightly drawn, not even a hint of sunlight penetrated her chambers. The porcelain clock atop her mantel ticked the passing moments in a grating rhythm punctuated by Delores' cheery whistling.

"Oh, I will be so sad with you gone," Francesca said on a forlorn whisper.

Genevieve forced herself into a sitting position at the edge of her bed. It had been a fortnight since her world had fallen apart. But it wasn't fair to wear her misery before Gillian and Francesca who'd been loyal, daily visitors.

"I still think it's a rotten idea for you to leave," Gillian grumbled, giving her a disappointed look. "It's cowardly to leave. You should stay and fight for love."

How beautifully innocent Gillian was. A believer in love triumphing over all. She gave her sister a gentle smile. "Sometimes love is not enough."

A sound of impatience escaped her younger sister. "Rubbish. If you love one another then you can conquer all." From where she stood at the vanity, Gillian planted her arms akimbo. "And I saw your husband. That man is in love with you."

Francesca gave a concurring nod. "It is true. He's seated like a stone statue outside your room whenever I come."

Throughout the weeks, Cedric's voice had penetrated the wood panel, but since he'd staggered into the room and then promptly out, she'd heard nothing more than his muffled words as he'd spoken to the doctor.

...will she live...?

...if anything happens to her, I will hold you accountable...

...By God, man, I do not care about a future heir, I care about her...

Her heart convulsed and she pressed her lids tightly closed to blot out the memory of those furious whispers; words that said so very much about Cedric's regard for that now-gone life and also about her.

She'd never doubted Cedric cared for her in some way. Time had proven, however, they were friends and lovers, but never anything more. They'd never be a husband and wife in the truest sense. She'd held that dream ever since she had first arrived in London, bright-eyed and idyllic, seduced by the glittering world of London

Society, all those years ago.

They would never be the bucolic couple upon the porcelain perfume bottle.

They would never be parents. Not because of the loss she'd suffered, but because she'd bound herself to a man who never wanted to be a father. The truth scoured her skin like jagged glass. But she'd not disabuse her friends of their romantic sentiments. "What has come to pass between Cedric and me..." she began softly. "It goes beyond love." The chasm between them was a gulf so wide; of divergent dreams and wishes on every aspect of life.

She made the mistake of looking to the sketchpad on her nightstand. With her friend and sister debating the power of love, Genevieve leaned over and grabbed the book and flipped through the pages. Cedric's visage danced along the fanning sheets. She paused. Her own countenance as she'd been on their wedding night, a lifetime ago, stared back. The clock continued to mark the passing moments and her heart squeezed painfully as she touched her fingertip to the face she'd sketched with Cedric's hand guiding hers. The smile, the grin that reached all the way to her eyes, spoke of the naïve girl she'd been. Even with Aumere's betrayal and her parents' defection, there had been hope and laughter... and a dream for more.

Unable to stare into the reflection of now-dead innocence, Genevieve continued flipping the pages. And stopped.

A tiny little babe; an imagined being with his father's eyes, hair, and mischievous grin that would never be. Agony sucked at her, threatening to pull her under an abyss of despair she'd never climb from. How was it possible to mourn so for a being she'd only just discovered she carried? With trembling fingers, she tugged the page out and brought it closer to her eyes, studying the fictional boy. She dusted her fingertips over the charcoal, faintly smudging the cherubic cheeks.

Because he'd been hers. Even as fleeting as the moment of knowing had been...he'd been real, a piece of her and Cedric combined, that created a miraculous life. Her fingers tightened reflexively on the corners of the sheet. A child that would never crawl or walk, or call her mama or mum or ride a horse or simply be. Despair brought her eyes closed again. With nothing more than an empty numbness inside, she pulled deeper into herself.

"Oh, Genevieve," Gillian said, touching a hand to her shoulder.

Go away, she silently pleaded. She didn't want any more of the pitying stares or the devastated tears or the words of sympathy from anyone. This had happened to *her*. It was an aching loss that had left her empty inside. It was an ache that could never, ever heal. Tears pressed behind her eyelids and leaked their familiar trail down her cheeks. For even as Cedric had never wanted their child and even as it would have been the height of selfishness to bring a child into the world already disdained by his father, she'd wanted the babe anyway. She'd wanted it for her. She'd wanted to cradle him close and sing him songs and she would have had enough love to make up for the parent who'd never care for him.

Genevieve was grateful for the interruption at the front of the room—until her gaze snagged on the plump, oft-frowning figure in the entranceway. Her mother pursed her lips, her gaze taking in Delores' efforts and the darkened space. "If you'll excuse us a moment," Genevieve said to her two friends, hurriedly tucking the page inside the leather book and setting it aside.

In quick order, the two young ladies filed from the room. Gillian paused a moment and shot her a supportive look, before pulling the panel closed behind them.

"Your father sent me." The marchioness spoke as though she needed to justify why she'd visit the daughter who'd left their family so scandalized.

"How touching," she said with a mocking smile. Where most mothers would come to their daughter's side through the loss Genevieve had suffered, her own parent could not be bothered to enter such a gross display...as she'd heard the day she'd come and remained outside the room. It was the first and last time she'd entered this house—until now.

Her mother took in the nearly packed trunks. "You are determined to steep this family in scandal," she snapped. "Do you know the gossip that will come in leaving your husband?"

Probably not as great a scandal that came in visiting naughty parties and running out in tears. Then, she'd rather not discuss that particular scandal.

The older woman slapped her fingers into her opposite palm. "You do not attend the events your husband does. You do not show that gross display of emotion before Society because your husband carries on with another woman." She made a sound of annoyance. "Did you truly expect your husband to be faithful to you?"

"Yes," she said matter-of-factly. "I did." She'd demand nothing less. She was deserving of her husband's fidelity.

"You are a fool." Had there been malice there it would have been easier than that cold delivery. It spoke to a heartless woman who valued nothing more than her status and power.

All the years of resentment and fury at her parents' disdain boiled to the surface and spilled over. She shoved to her feet. "How dare you?"

Her mother widened her eyes. "I beg your pardon?"

"As you should," Genevieve said icily, deliberately misinterpreting the meaning of those words. "You have been nothing but condescending of me. You have shunned me because of the lies put forth by another man." Her voice rose in pitch as she gave in to years of suppressed emotion. "I am your *daughter*. And yet you sent me away for something I'd never been guilty of."

"There was your sister—"

"Bah, do not pretend you care for Gillian any more than you care for me," she cut in and her mother's cheeks blazed red. "And do not come into this house and scold me as though I'm a child. This is my home." Or it had been. "I do not want your lectures and I do not want your disloyalty. Get out."

From over her mother's graying head, she caught the flash of approval gleaming in Delores' eyes. Genevieve found strength in that slight, but meaningful, show of unspoken support from a woman who'd been more of a friend through the years than anything.

"Well," her mother said on a huff and in an uncharacteristically undignified way, all but flew to the front of the room. She yanked the door open and collided with her son-in-law. The marchioness didn't so much as bother with a greeting but continued walking.

Cedric ignored the older woman; his gaze fixed on Genevieve.

Unable to meet his eyes, she quietly excused Delores. The maid dropped the dress in her hands inside the trunk and quickly left.

Cedric closed the door, leaving them alone. "Genevieve," he murmured.

Drained from her exertions, she slid onto the edge of the mattress, presenting him her back. Did he truly think to come in here after a fortnight with a casual greeting? After all they'd lost? After his betrayal and treachery? Emotion broiled in her breast.

The tread of heavy steps penetrated her misery as Cedric came to a stop beside her. Wordlessly, he dragged over a chair, the scratch of wood noisy in the quiet and then he slid into the delicate, upholstered seat.

His jacket discarded, he wore nothing more than his rumpled white shirt, breeches, and stockinged feet. He searched his gaze over her face, lingering his stare on the tracks of misery left by her earlier tears. She stiffened, hating that evidence of her despair.

"Are you…?" he grimaced.

"What do you want?" she asked tiredly, closing her eyes, unable to meet his unreadable gaze.

"Did you know you were with child?" he asked in a hoarse baritone.

At last they'd have this conversation. Of course, it had been inevitable. She managed an awkward, jerky nod.

"And you did not tell me."

A half-laugh, half-sob escaped her and she opened her eyes. "You thought I should share the happy news with the expectant father to be?" She laughed, the sound ugly and sharp. She fixed on the healthy anger so as to not cave under the weight of all she'd lost. "Why should I have told the man who didn't even want the babe, anyway?" A spasm contorted his face and she steeled her heart. "No. Your knowing would have changed nothing, Cedric. You never wanted to be a father and now you need never be one. So your life is the same today as it was yesterday."

"Is that what you believe?" He dragged his chair closer to the edge of her bed. "Do you think me a monster who will casually carry on as though…"

As though they'd not created life together.

The muscles of his throat moved.

"Do you know what I believe, Cedric?" she asked softly.

He shook his head.

"I believe we were two people who met by chance in a library." Tears popped up behind her eyes once more. That night, when he'd taken her bare foot in his hands, may as well have been a lifetime ago for all that had come to pass. "We were two people who felt a spark of passion, a–and who even became friends." She bit her lower lip. "But artwork and gardening are hardly a foundation with which to support a marriage or sustain it."

Cedric narrowed his eyes, his thick, golden lashes swallowing his irises. "What are you saying?" he demanded roughly.

"There was never anything more between us," she whispered, the truth coming from deep inside, from a place where she'd long buried it. Now breathing it to existence cemented the reality she'd long denied. "I thought you were someone different than who you are." She lifted shuttered eyes to his. "That is not your fault. That is mine. I wanted you to be something you can never, ever be." A loving husband. A devoted father. Oh God, she hugged her arms close to dull the blade of agony twisting inside. "Ultimately, we are two very different people. You love London."

"I would give this place up for you," he rasped. "Tell me what you want and I'll get it for you." How could he realize, no material item could fix this? No gift could ever be enough. "Tell me who you want me to be." His imploring words hinted at a desperation she'd never expected of the rakish lord.

"Oh, Cedric." Genevieve pressed her fingers to her quivering mouth. "D–Don't you see? I do not want you to give anything up for me. To force you to leave a place you love or to force you to have something you don't want…" She sucked in a ragged breath and forced the words out. "A child. I don't want you to become someone else for me. To expect you to be someone else or to want something else, simply because I do, will only make you hate me. I cannot tell you who I want you to be. *You* need to figure out the man you wish to be…for *you*."

He dropped to a knee beside her bed and brushed his knuckles back and forth over her cheek as he'd done so many times before. "I want to begin again." There was a faint entreaty in his ragged words. For a sliver of a heartbeat, she wanted to take everything he held out. She wanted to selfishly take for herself the sacrifice he'd make.

But that could never be. Genevieve looked at him and a lone tear slipped down her cheek. He easily caught it with the tip of his thumb. "Do you know there are some moments I wish I'd never stepped into that library, Cedric?" He froze mid–movement. "I wish I'd never entered that room because then you never, ever would have noticed me on the side of that ballroom and I'd never have allowed myself to hope for something that could never be." His hand fell to his side. She looked over to her trunks. "I am leaving."

Her husband jerked. "You are leaving?" he repeated his voice, hollow.

She nodded. "I am going to my grandfather's."

I AM GOING TO LOSE HER.

Panic lapped at the edge of Cedric's senses.

With every word, Genevieve slipped further and further away. There was an anchor weighting his chest. It threatened to drag him under, into a black, empty void.

Nay, I've already lost her. He'd lost her slowly with each day of their marriage when he'd spent those fleeting hours with her and left her at night. For even though there had never been another woman in his bed, there had been a growing divide between him and Genevieve, widened by the statement he made every time he visited his clubs or attended those wicked parties.

If he was capable of any emotion other than despair, he'd have found hilarity in the great irony of discovering that he, the man who'd believed himself incapable of loving and being loved, did, in fact, love. And it was a raw, powerful, piercing emotion that consumed him. How long he'd spent believing the sentiment weakened a person, only to find Genevieve had never made him weak. Rather, she'd made him stronger. She'd helped him see the life he lived as an empty one without purpose. There was no shame in this emotion.

He rose from his seat and perched on the edge of her bed. "Genevieve Grace," he said gruffly. The words in his heart, the words of love she'd been deserving of, had belonged in another moment. In their garden. Over laughter. Or sketches. So many other instances, which had been full of joy and not this gripping agony of despair. It was just one more mistake he'd made that he'd do over…if that gift was, in fact, real. "I have made so many mistakes," he said quietly. "Since I met you. I've faltered and will, no doubt, continue to stumble. But I need you to know, the day you stepped into that library and into my life, you transformed me." She turned her head and he palmed her cheek, forcing her gaze back to his, willing her to see the truth that spilled deep from inside. "I want to try again, because I love you."

Genevieve stilled and her green eyes, which had always been expressive windows into her soul, gave no hint of emotion.

I did this…

She caught her lip between her front teeth and gave a jerky shake of her head. "Sometimes love is not enough." Her words emerged so faint, he strained to hear and when they reached him, it was like a lance had been thrust into his heart. He jerked. "Too much has come to pass. There is an ocean of differences between us that no bridge can close."

"Genevieve," he tried again, imploring her with his eyes.

"I am tired," she whispered. "Please, go."

Cedric searched his gaze over her treasured face. He took in the white drawn line at the corner of her lips, the despair in her eyes. He'd done this to her and the damage he'd wrought to them was not something he could ever repair in a single note; particularly not this one. He flexed his jaw and then gave a brusque nod. "Of course. When do you leave?" How was his voice steady? How, when he was breaking apart from the inside out?

She glanced down at her interlocked fingers. "Within a couple of hours."

Two hours. He had two hours left with her, before she went and stole his every happiness. "Very well," he said quietly as he came to his feet. "Do you require anything?" *If you wish for the stars, I'll climb to the heavens and gather them for you.*

She shook her head. "No."

Sketching a bow, he turned on his heel and started from the bed. He paused, staring at the oak panel and then wheeled slowly around. "I would have you know, it was never my intention to hurt you." He'd rather lob off his limbs with a dull blade than be the root of her pain.

Tears welled in her eyes, glimmering like emerald pools of despair. "I know." Her faint whisper barely reached him.

"I want you to be happy," he said roughly. He'd never, ever worried over anyone's happiness but his own. "I want you to smile again and laugh, even if I am not in your life." For to imagine a world in which she was the broken, anguished creature before him would destroy him.

A tear slid down her cheek. And before he did something foolish and useless, like get down on his knees and beg her to take him back, he pressed the door handle and did the first honorable and selfless thing he'd done in his life—he left.

CHAPTER 27

THREE WEEKS LATER

Cedric sat at the back table of White's. A bottle of barely touched liquor sat beside a completely untouched snifter of brandy. He stared blankly about the club. Gentlemen seated about the club entertained friends, while others wagered with acquaintances. Laughter periodically rose up, filtering about, punctuated by the clink of coins hitting a pile of coins.

How many years he'd spent losing himself in wagering and attending mindless amusements, only to find out now on his thirtieth birthday, how absolutely meaningless it had all been.

There were no true friends. There was not, nor had there ever been, a true purpose to his life beyond his pleasure. What a meaningless existence he'd lived. He'd dwelled in shadows and never realized it, until the sun had shone on him and then left, leaving him in darkness once more.

A pressure weighted his chest. It was a familiar tightening that had neither dulled nor died, in the weeks since Genevieve had left. To give his hands something to do, Cedric swiped his glass and swirled the contents in a small circle.

What an absolute muck he'd made of his life. He'd had happiness laid out before him; a gift that had stepped into his private sanctuary. Never had he truly appreciated the extent of just how Genevieve had filled his life. She'd awakened him to what it meant to live and laugh. And in the span of one careless night, he'd thrown it all away.

"Care for company?"

He stiffened and looked up with a detached surprise. Since discovering the other man's betrayal, he'd not seen a glimpse of him. Nor had he given a jot for seeing him. There was but one person whose absence had left a hole in his heart—and she was gone. In a deliberately dismissive gesture, Cedric returned his gaze to his brandy.

Montfort didn't wait for permission, but slid into the empty seat. "If anyone had said even months ago that I'd be in White's with you seated across from me, I'd say they were cracked in the head," the man muttered. He spoke with the carefree ease of a man whose *friendship* went back to boyhood.

And perhaps it was the misery that came from being alone with torturous thoughts about the one woman who would never belong to him, even with the ultimate irony of their names being irrevocably interlinked. Or perhaps it was the absolute silence he'd lived in since her parting. Or mayhap it was that it was his birthday, a day not a single person gave a jot about, and he spent it alone.

Grudgingly, Cedric shoved his bottle across the table and motioned for a footman. The liveried servant rushed over with a glass and then bowing, he backed away.

In a remarkable show of constraint, Montfort poured himself a glass and remained silent. Once more, Cedric returned to skimming his bored gaze over the guests scattered about the club. Nearly the end of the Season, many of the respectable members had already rushed off for the countryside, leaving only the most dissolute reprobates who dragged their proverbial heels, all to keep the mindless amusements of the London Season alive.

…The sky is bluer and when you lay on the grass and stare up at the sky you see nothing but an endless blue, so that you think you can stretch your fingers up and touch the heavens…

He closed his eyes a moment and when he opened them, Montfort was staring back. "I am leaving for Somerset this weekend. The summer hunt and all." Montfort winged an eyebrow up. "Would you care to join?"

The only thing borrowed of respectability for the earl's hunts was, in fact, the name itself. Members of the *ton* well knew the scandalous affair hosted by Montfort each summer. Just a year ago, there had been no question of whether Cedric would have been in attendance. Where else would he be? Now, regret stuck like a thousand dull blades at the remembrance of the last wicked affair he'd attended. "I am afraid, I'm otherwise occupied." He inclined his head.

Montfort sipped his drink. "You are certain? I am to have some inventive—"

"Quite," he easily interjected.

The earl quirked his lips up in a half-grin and gave his head a slow, wry shake. "By damn, I never thought I would have seen it. It was a wager I'd have staked the rest of my meager coffers on."

Cedric looked quizzically back.

"The day the Marquess of St. Albans fell in love." A mottled flush stained the earl's cheeks and he swiftly yanked at his cravat.

Of course, rakes didn't fall in love and they certainly didn't discuss that sentiment written in sonnets and songs. "Some ladies are worth giving up all for." He fisted his glass hard. Only he hadn't given anything up. He'd continued to live his nights as a bachelor. Yes, there had never been another woman since he'd made Genevieve his wife, but he'd carried on separately. *Because I was a coward.* Ultimately, he'd always known he would hurt her. "You'll find that someday."

The earl choked on his drink. "Yes, well, taking in your state," he motioned to Cedric. "Morose and miserable, old fellow... I'm quite content to carry on with an equally base lady who wants nothing more than pleasure in my arms."

Yes, there had been a time when he had thought that very same thing. He'd craved an emotionless, empty entanglement and offered nothing more than that. He'd offered Genevieve her freedom to carry on as she wished and with whom she wished. Then, in a display of the utmost irony that the devil himself would have found hilarity in, Cedric wanted a life with her—a woman who wanted nothing to do with him. He swirled the contents of his drink.

"Will you retire to the country for the summer?"

He'd not given much thought to where he'd go or what he'd do. He'd given no thought to anything but Genevieve. "I've not decided," he said at last. He thought to a discussion, too long ago.

...It's hard to approve of wagering. Particular wagering that sees a man divested of his properties...

There had never been anything honorable about him. Even his half-hearted attempts to restore that property to rights, were merely an extension of the shiftless life he'd lived.

Montfort finished his drink and set it down on the table.

Cedric motioned to the bottle but the other man waved him off. "I am going to visit Forbidden Pleasures." He stole a glance about. "Being in this place is like being in Sunday sermons."

A wry smile pulled at Cedric's lips. Not long ago, he'd have been of the exact mindset.

"Will you join me?" Montfort offered as he pushed back his seat.

He waved his hand. "You go on without me." His days of disreputable clubs were at an end. The wickedness found in those hells had once provided a diversion from the tedium of an otherwise empty life. No longer.

His friend hesitated. For even with his betrayal, and even as Cedric would forever be wary of his loyalty, desperation made a man do rash things...and they went back years to some of the loneliest of Cedric's life. "Happy Birthday, chap."

He mustered a smile.

The earl stood, but did not leave. He hovered at the edge of the table. "For what it is worth," he said, clearing his throat. "I am sorry for betraying you." He gave a lopsided grin. "But then, mayhap you should thank me if you do love the lady?"

The words hit him like a punch to the belly. Yes, if it hadn't been for his father and Montfort's machinations, even now Genevieve would be wed to the ancient, doddering Tremaine. Or mayhap it would have been another... Mayhap it would have been a gentleman who'd seen past her scandal to her beauty, wit and worth. And God rot his soul for the bastard he was, Cedric was selfish enough to find relief in her belonging to him, instead—if even, just name. "It is fine," he managed to say. He'd spent his life hating his father and in the end, in the greatest twist, the Duke of Ravenscourt with his maneuverings was responsible for the only happiness Cedric had ever truly known.

"Are you certain you don't wish to—"

"I am certain," he cut in. For the unexpected had happened. He'd been tamed, won, and enchanted enough so that all those amusements held no appeal.

Montfort dropped a bow and then wandered off. Cedric stared at his retreat and then resumed his study of the glass in his hands. He existed in this peculiar limbo of life. In the three weeks since Genevieve had left, not a moment of his day was spent not thinking of her. *Is she happy? Is she sketching?* Did she miss him?

He thrust aside the pondering, even now. She'd been quite clear when she'd ordered him away, that anything she'd felt for him, nay, the love she'd carried, had died. So when he readied Wicked to set out after her, he'd promptly climbed down. He'd been a selfish bastard since the moment she'd exploded into his world. In this, he would make the ultimate sacrifice—giving her freedom... from even him. After all, why should she want him? What had he brought her, other than heartache?

Then, he'd never been a very good person to anyone. He'd never put another person before himself. Setting down his drink, he came to his feet and made his way through White's. He absently inclined his head in greetings for the respectable lords who raised their hands.

The servant at the front drew the door open and, with a murmur of thanks, he stepped outside. Collecting the reins of his mount from a waiting street urchin, Cedric turned over a purse with a small fortune in it for the youth and froze. The green of the lad's eyes and the ginger crop of curls tucked under his cap, held him suspended, as he envisioned another child. A child who'd almost been, but would now never be. A child he'd never wanted. Pain cleaved his heart, raw and real, and agonizing for it.

"Guv'nor?"

Cedric gave his head a clearing shake. "Many thanks," he said gruffly and released the purse. The boy peered inside. His eyes made round moons. As though fearing Cedric would change his mind, he sprinted away. Swinging up into his saddle, Cedric nudged his mount onward. What a muck he'd made of his life. Only, he'd bumbled it all since he'd been a boy. He'd been a miserable brother and had proven an even lousier husband and son. He continued riding through the fashionable streets of London he'd long avoided, onward until he came to a pink stucco townhouse on Mayfair.

Two black lacquer carriages sat outside the posh residence. Servants bustled back and forth from the home to the conveyance, loading trunks atop.

Without thinking, he dismounted and motioned over a young boy. A new lad with shades of red in his hair rushed over. Another spasm wracked Cedric's heart. She was everywhere, in every child he'd meet. This was to be his penance for a lifetime of sins; this great, gaping loss and a forever reminder of it in the faces of even small strangers. "I'll be but a short while," he said, reaching for a coin. "There will be more," he promised. As he slowly made his way up the steps, servants stepped around him.

Almost reflexively, he knocked once and stared at the wood panel. *What am I doing here?*

He gave his head a shake and turned to go, just as the door opened. "My lord?" the butler inquired at his back.

Cedric wheeled slowly around. "I..." His neck heated. He'd never stepped foot inside these doors. It spoke volumes of the manner of man he was. He'd been too busy living for his own pleasures.

The servant stared inquiringly at him.

With wooden movements, he reached inside his jacket and withdrew a calling card. "The Marquess of St. Albans to see Her Ladyship."

The butler of middling years accepted it. A flare of surprise widened his eyes, which he quickly concealed. He motioned Cedric forward.

Even in the folds of his gloves, Cedric's palms moistened. He'd no place here. For that matter, why had he even come? Was there a sort of absolution he sought? One he'd never be deserving of? "Forgive me," he said quietly, and pivoted. "I—"

"Cedric?"

He froze, his skin heating as he spun about. His sister stood at the end of the corridor, her head cocked at a small angle. Shock marked the planes of her face. Their mother's face. She was her image, in every way. While he, he was their father. He cleared his throat. "Clarisse. Forgive me. I should not have arrived unannounced." At all. He shouldn't have come at all. There was no accounting for his visit. Furthermore, why should she even want to see him?

She held her arms out. At that subtle movement, the fabric tightened over the front of her gown revealing a slightly rounded belly. And a wave of unexpected agony assaulted his senses, sucking away logic, leaving him standing there in a world of remembered horror. Genevieve's blood. The muffled sound of her weeping as he'd sat outside her chambers and tortured himself with every blasted sound of her misery. "Come," his sister said with a surprising gentleness that brought his eyes open.

He blinked several times. "I have to leave." His voice emerged as a faint whisper.

Clarisse moved over in a flurry of satin skirts. "You can visit for a bit," she said gently, but a steely strength underscored her words.

"I see you are leaving."

"For the country," she said with a nod. "But we are not to depart for several hours. Come," she urged.

His sister fixed a benevolent look on him. Cedric's feet twitched with a panicky urge to flee.

"Come," she repeated.

Wordlessly, he followed at her side as she guided him to an empty parlor. He followed behind her and paused. Several easels had been set up about the room, close to the floor-length windows. Drawn to the colorful paintings, he strode past Clarisse as she claimed a seat on a pink upholstered sofa.

He eyed a painting of a small urn of colorful blooms. It spoke volumes that he'd failed to know all these years that his sister, too, had a love of art. By the work tacked to those easels, she was quite good. He clasped his hands at his back and moved on to the next, riveted by the pale blue, summer sky. Soft, white clouds filled the canvas and he leaned forward, sucked back to another moment.

...The sky is bluer and when you lay on the grass and stare up at the sky you see nothing but an endless blue, so that you think you can stretch your fingers up and touch the heavens...

"Would you care for refreshments?" his sister asked and he spun about.

"Refreshments?" At her nod, he shook his head and returned his study to that summer landscape. He dipped his head once again and then wandered over to another easel. A winter storm raged on the canvas. Tree branches heavy with snow hung low and at the center of it was a couple, cloaked in their winter garments. He peered at the man and woman; their bodies close, but their faces remained concealed. How similar he was to the pair trapped in a storm raging about. Cold in ways that he'd never be properly warmed.

Registering the silence, he abandoned his examination of the painting. "Did you paint these?" he asked, as he strode over to a nearby gilt rimmed arm chair and settled into the seat.

"I did." She eyed his movements.

"You're quite good."

"Thank you." A small smile hovered on her lips, but for that faint expression, she revealed none of what she was thinking. Then, all the Falcots had long proven themselves masters of their emotions.

Cedric layered his palms to the arms of the chair and drummed his fingers while looking about the room. How little time he'd spent learning anything but his own interests these years. A sad day, indeed, when one at last confronted the manner of person he truly had been all these years.

...You need to figure out who you want to be...

Clarisse cleared her throat and he ceased tapping, glancing over to where she sat. "I do not believe you've come today to discuss my artwork," she ventured.

"No." Except he didn't know why he had come this day. He looked over the top of Clarisse's head. He said nothing for a long, long while, searching for words. "I was a rather miserable brother, wasn't I?" he spoke more to himself. It said much about his sister's character that she did not simply concur with his obviously true statement. How much of his life would he gladly redo? Only there was no changing the hands of time. There was no righting past wrongs. There was just this empty acceptance of who he'd been and all that he would never have from life because of it.

"You were certainly not the most devoted," she said softly, jerking his attention to her face. He expected to see disgust, even loathing, in her pale blue eyes. Instead, there was—forgiveness. For him? He scoffed. Surely not.

"That is being generous," he muttered.

A smile twitched on her lips. "Yes, it is."

He flinched. *That* he was deserving of. "I came to apologize." It was harder to say who was more shocked by his pronouncement; his sister or Cedric himself. Her lips parted on a small moue. "I'm not so much a fool that I believe an apology can right the lifetime of wrongs." Genevieve slipped in and agony bore him down, momentarily sucking away his breath.

"You are forgiven."

How quickly she spoke. Surely there had been a lifetime of loathing from her; deserved loathing. He'd not been the devoted brother to protect her from unwanted suitors. Hell, he couldn't even recall her having a Season. She'd been married off so hurriedly... He balled his hands. No doubt, her union had been forced upon her and he'd not even given a thought to her happiness or that she'd be forever bound to a man. He couldn't be bothered over whether she'd be safe and loved and cared for at that man's hands. "Your husband is good to you?" he asked gruffly, more than half-fearing her answer.

Surprise shone in Clarisse's eyes. "William?" Her eyes took on a wistful, far-off quality. "We are quite in love."

A vicious envy ripped at his insides, proving, once more, the selfish bastard he was. He shook his head.

His sister shifted. Was she as uncomfortable with talk of emotion and past mistakes? What strangers they were. Then, he had quite expertly shut everyone out in the ways that mattered. "I read..." She promptly grimaced. "That Genevieve has gone."

Not gone. "Yes," he said in hollow tones. Left. "She left." Three weeks, twelve hours, and...he looked to the long-case clock across the room...twenty-three minutes ago.

"I am sorry," Clarisse said softly.

"Yes, well." He tugged his gloves off and beat them together. For really, what else was there to say? He could hardly admit that every day it felt as though his heart was dying. How he woke up, avoiding any room his wife had been in because the memory of her was so strong that her laughter still echoed around his mind. "No one to blame but myself," he said to himself. He'd been the one to attend Montfort's and... that was really just only the tip of the sins of which Cedric was guilty. His skin pricked with the directness of his sister's stare trained on him. Unnerved by that focus, he managed a lopsided grin. "In the end, I'm very much our father, aren't I?"

His sister frowned. "I do not believe that," she said chidingly.

A rusty, empty laugh escaped him. "No?" He'd celebrated the same base pleasures, broken his wife's heart. He was exactly the man's image.

"If you were like him, you'd not be here even now."

He lifted his shoulders in a casual shrug. "Perhaps."

Clarisse gave an emphatic shake of her head. "No. Not perhaps. You wouldn't. Do you know how often he's visited?" She didn't wait for him to venture a guess. "Never."

"One unannounced visit is hardly a good deal more."

She scooted to the edge of the sofa, closer to him. "It is a very good deal more." She held his gaze. "Because of what it *signifies*, Cedric."

Uncomfortable with the show of emotion, he pulled his gaze away. "Sometimes it is too late to change or be anyone different."

"I don't believe that," she said automatically. "I did," she added. "But not anymore. My husband showed me differently."

At the emotion teeming from Clarisse's words, he looked back at her. Her gaze distant, so much love poured from their depths that another wave of envy assailed him. How very close he'd been to having all of that. But in one careless night, he'd thrown it all away.

Clarisse fiddled with a ruby heart necklace about her throat. He stared at that piece, dimly recollecting it about another woman's neck. "It was Mother's," she said, following his attention.

"I...recall." He'd forgotten—until now. So resentful over her having simply turned him over to his father's tutelage, he'd forgotten much about the woman who'd given him life. "Even she knew what I was," he said, unable to keep the bitterness from seeping in.

His sister flared her eyes. "Is that what you believe?"

It's what he knew. He allowed his silence to serve as his answer.

"Our father had little purpose in either of us, Cedric. You were the heir and I was the chess piece to increase his power...but you were the one who served the most purpose for him." Cedric had known as much. It was what had fueled his motives of revenge against the old bastard. "So many times when we would go outside, Mother would talk about you and how, before I was born, you were her partner in the gardens."

A pressure that was oddly constrictive and freeing all at the same time blossomed in his chest. "Did she?"

Clarisse nodded. "She did. Father put a cease to those visits, she said. Alas, future dukes did not take breaks from their studies to play in their gardens, though, did they?" She spoke with an almost rote quality to her voice, the way one who'd heard words uttered so many times she'd had them memorized.

"Yes," he said tiredly. "Well, it hardly matters now." Knowing did not change who he'd allowed himself to become. It did not replace this aching, empty void left with Genevieve's absence.

The ticking of the clock filled the room as silence otherwise reigned.

"You love Genevieve, don't you?" his sister said without preamble.

His throat worked and he dug deep for a careless, witty rejoinder about being a rake and rakes never needing or wanting love. But he couldn't force the words out. Instead, he gave a disjointed nod.

"Go to her, Cedric. She loves you. I saw that the day you were married."

A sound, half-groan and half-growl, lodged in his throat as a memory slid in: Genevieve walking up to him that day in the hedge maze with so much emotion he'd not known what to do with it. It simply poured from her emerald eyes. "I bumbled it all," he said hoarsely. And there could be no going back.

"I suspect you did." His sister waggled her golden eyebrows, wringing a pained laugh from him. "But you can fix it. Go to her," she repeated.

"It is more complicated than that." There was the babe, lost. A child he'd never wanted because he'd hated the Falcot line, and hated even more the possibility of spreading his vile blood to another being. Those pieces he couldn't share with Clarisse. For he didn't know what would happen to him when he breathed those words into existence. It would force him to confront what he'd almost had and what he'd lost. A gift he'd never *known* he wanted.

"I do not doubt its complexity, Cedric," Clarisse said, pulling him to the moment. "But if you do not go to her, you'll never be happy. You'll be destroyed by loneliness and regret." More than ten years younger, how could she be so very much wiser? "Love has a wonderful power to heal. Trust that." And how could he trust that when he'd spent the whole of his life—alone, resisting love, warmth, *any* emotion?

Heavy footsteps sounded outside the doorway and they looked as one to the entrance as the Marquess of Grafton stepped inside. "Love, are you—?" His words abruptly ended as he took in his wife's visitor. A flash of antipathy shone within the previously warm eyes.

Could he blame the other man for his hatred? He'd been a careless brother to Grafton's now wife. As such, Cedric would not force Clarisse's husband to suffer through his company. "I was just leaving," Cedric murmured, coming to his feet.

His brother-in-law proved once more the nature of his honorable character. He schooled his features and strode over, hand extended. "St. Albans," he greeted, his tone colder than a winter frost.

Cedric returned the hard handshake.

His sister quickly came to her feet. "Isn't it wonderful that Cedric came to call?" From the corner of his eye, he caught the unspoken look pass between husband and wife. There was a wealth of meaning and significance to that private exchange; they were two people who needed no words to know the others thoughts and he felt like the worst sort of interloper on that special bond. Pain scraped at his heart. *I had that. I had it and let it go…*

"It is," the other man said at last.

"You surely have much to do before you leave," Cedric murmured, stuffing his gloves inside his jacket front. "If you'll excuse me?" Except, he lingered. How did a brother, in fact, say goodbye to a sister? He'd not been one, for the course of his life that he didn't know how to be…just as he'd not known how to be everything Genevieve had deserved in a husband. "Yes, well," he said awkwardly with the couple staring expectantly at him and he started for the door.

Focused on the soft tread of his footfalls, he made his way from the room and down the empty corridor.

"Cedric?"

He spun about.

His sister rushed down the hall, her skirts whipping noisily at her ankles. "I want you to have this." She fiddled with the latch at her throat and removed the ruby pendant. "Mother gave it to me in love." She pressed it into his palm and his fingers curled reflexively over the warm metal. "It is for your Genevieve."

He made a sound of protest and made to return it. "I cannot…"

"You can." She closed her hands over his and gave a squeeze.

"Mother would not have wanted—"

"She would have, Cedric," Clarisse cut in and released his hands.

Agonized regret clogged his throat and, unfurling his palm, he stared down at the gleaming ruby heart. "Thank you." He blinked, his eyes stinging. Surely dust. How else to account for the dratted sheen blurring his vision? He stiffened as his sister folded her arms about him, while his hung awkwardly at his sides. Of their own volition, his arms rose up and closed her in a hug. A pressure eased in his chest; freeing and light. He closed his eyes. Perhaps there was such a thing as forgiveness, after all. Cedric let his arms fall. "Thank—"

"Do not thank me." She leaned up on tiptoe and kissed his cheek. "We are siblings. Now go."

Cedric hesitated and then with the cherished gift conferred by his sister in his possession, he left her townhouse and made the short horse ride to his own fashionable, Mayfair townhouse. As he climbed the steps, the doors were opened with a familiar ease by Avis. Cedric didn't break his stride. He continued abovestairs and strode the length of the hall. He did not stop until he reached his wife's chamber. Pressing the handle, he stepped inside the darkened space. The curtains drawn tight blotted out nearly all light with the exception of a small sliver that shone through a crack in the brocade fabric. He closed the door with a soft click. He laid his back against the panel and stared about her chambers, allowing the memory of her to assail him.

Skimming his gaze over the immaculate room, he searched for a hint or sign of her, but it was as though she'd never been. Cedric walked slowly over to the chaise where they'd sketched together on the night of their wedding and he sank onto the edge.

...I expect you have said that to any number of women...

He dragged a hand over his face. Even in those shared, special moments between them, she'd easily seen the life he lived. She'd seen herself as no different than any woman to come before, when all along she was unlike any he ever had or would know. Cedric sucked in a shuddery breath and pushed restlessly to his feet. Clasping his hands at his back, he rocked on his heels.

Just as he'd had no right to go to Clarisse seeking absolution, he had even less so, going to Genevieve and asking for another chance at them. She'd been clear her last night here that she wanted no part of him, that she regretted having ever entered that library. His chest throbbed, like a weight was being pressed on him, cutting off airflow.

From the corner of his eye, a flash of white caught his eye and he turned. Drawn to that crumpled page; the one out of place in this room, Cedric moved with wooden steps. Desperate for even a hint of her, he picked up the page and unwrinkled it. The small babe, with Cedric's eyes and hair, grinned back. His fingers curled at the edges of the sheet, rumpling it. Pain speared his heart and sucked the life from his legs. Numb, he slid onto the edge of the mattress.

Realizing immediately what he did, he quickly loosened his grip. He ran his palm over the creased surface and forced himself to accept all that he'd lost. Genevieve and a child. A child she'd rightly said he'd never wanted. For he hadn't.

Only…his throat worked…looking at this child that would have been, he accepted a truth he'd never known—until now.

He'd hated the prospect of sharing his blood and proving to be the same, miserable excuse of a man his own sire had been. He'd hated the idea of a child of his blood, because he'd spent years hating himself.

Only, to look at this child and realize—this babe would have never been an extension of the Duke of Ravenscourt but rather an extension of Genevieve and him. It would have been a girl with her mother's smile and strawberry curls. A child that loved to sketch like them. A girl who would have gardened beside her mother and…

He rested his elbows on his knees and buried his head in his hands, further wrinkling that discarded image. A sob tore from his throat. He allowed the page to slip from his fingers and gave in to the tears. He let them fall unchecked; great, gasping sobs that tore from his chest, emotion long buried. He cried for the man he'd allowed himself to become. He cried for having realized too late that Genevieve and their child were the only gifts he'd ever wanted and needed in life. He cried for the aching void of emptiness that would never, ever be filled unless she was there.

And at last, when the tears were gone, he drew in a juddering breath. *She is gone.* Cedric rescued the sketch. He'd not changed for her, as she'd stated before she left him and stole all his happiness. He'd changed because of her. He stilled. And mayhap, even if he professed his love and promised her all of him, she'd still choose a life apart…but he needed her to know.

Footsteps sounded outside the door and for a sliver of a moment, hope hung suspended. Then there was a faint rap. "My lord, His Grace is asking to see you…" Avis hadn't even finished speaking before the duke threw the door open.

"There you are," his father said coldly. "I am here to speak with you about your wife. I—"

"I have no intention of discussing my wife or my responsibilities with you," he said quietly, cutting into his father's lecture. How many times had his father stormed into his home with some form of ducal directive? Only now, Cedric's words were not meant to taunt or bait.

"I beg your pardon?" his father barked, stamping his cane. Then, he narrowed his gaze. "Have you been crying?" he spoke with the same horror as if he'd uncovered his son's plot to overthrow the king.

"I am no longer a child," he said. Even as he'd lived a life without responsibility, he would take ownership of who he was, *now*. "Do not come here and lecture me. Do not come here and speak to me about my wife or my responsibilities. I am going to my wife." Triumph lit the duke's eyes and Cedric felt none of the old familiar hatred. He smiled sadly. "I am not going to Genevieve because you command it or even wish it, Father. I am going because I need to. Because I love my wife." Sketch in hand, Cedric strode over to the door and past his father. "If you'll excuse me." He had a wife to win back.

CHAPTER 28

SHE MISSED HIM.

Oh, the day she'd boarded his carriage and made the long journey from London, she'd had no doubt she would miss him. She'd just made the erroneous assumption that time would dull the love and all the hurt and anger of their last days together would prove strongest.

It hadn't.

The ache inside was just as jagged now as it was since her world had fallen apart. Reflexively, she touched a hand to her belly, the pain of that loss brought her closed. She would have been nearly four months along. Her heart wrenched.

"I never thought I'd see you more miserable than the day you showed up five years ago, Genevieve Grace, until I see you now."

Seated at the windowseat that overlooked the vast Kent countryside, that gravelly, aged voice shifted her attention from the serene view to the ancient, wizened earl she'd once feared. She smiled for his benefit. "I am not miserable." How could she be? In the month since she'd returned to his residence, she'd slipped so very easily into the routine she'd once known—gardening, walking the countryside and collecting flowers, sketching. Why, these were all the activities she'd always so loved. The enjoyments she'd always taken pleasure in.

Her smile dipped and she looked out the lead windowpane.

Except, time had changed her. Nay, Cedric had changed her so much that she'd come to find the enjoyments she'd found did not bring the same joy and fulfillment of being in love. Grief scraped at her still ragged heart. Even if it was a one-sided love.

"This is about your husband?" her grandfather interjected and heat infused her cheeks at his unerring accuracy. She opened her mouth to form a half-hearted protest, but he quelled her with a look. "There is no point in denying otherwise. I've read the papers." She cringed, shame assailing her. Oh, the words printed in those gossip columns; about Cedric, about her, about them. Did her grandfather even know about that scandalous affair she'd arrived at like a naïve fool? "Are you ready to speak of him?"

All the hurt and humiliation of that night came rushing back, as fresh now as it had been. "There is nothing really to speak about," she murmured. Nothing beyond a failed marriage, a lost child, and a gaping hole in one's heart.

Restless, Genevieve shoved to her feet and strode over to the floor-length windows that opened out to the back portion of her grandfather's vast estate. The rolling green hills and cloudless blue skies were a beauty that she could never manage to capture on canvas. Yet, there was none of the calming peace she'd once known in this place.

"Isn't there?" the earl's voice rumbled at her back.

She absently touched her fingertips to the windowpane warmed by the summer sun. "No. There really isn't." Genevieve lifted her shoulders in a small shrug. "My father would have wed me off to one of his old friends and Cedric," the muscles of her stomach contracted at even breathing his name again. "My husband," she amended, "offered me a marriage of convenience. He'd have his freedom and I would have mine." And how simple he'd made it all sound. Only there had been nothing simple about any part of their union.

Her grandfather snorted. "And you agreed to that because your father wished to wed you to one of his miserable cronies?" The thick skepticism coating that inquiry painted her for the liar she was. "You'd have never married one of my miserable son-in-law's picks for any reason under the sun. And you'd most assuredly known you had a home here for as long as you needed it."

His words aligned so very clearly with Gillian's accusations weeks ago that she sighed. "Yes, I knew as much," she conceded. Even if she hadn't admitted as much to herself. Genevieve swiped a forgotten volume of artwork and fanned the pages. "He was..." She grimaced. "Is a rake. I made the mistake of falling in love with him."

A low growl rattled from his chest and he then dissolved into a fit of coughing. Genevieve took a step toward him but he waved her off. He pulled a white kerchief from his jacket and coughed into it, glaring over the fabric when she made to come over. She stopped. The earl had long been a proud man who'd never accept, nor welcome, such displays of concern. "The gossip is true about him, then."

As his was more statement than question, she remained silent. She pressed her fingernails into her palms so tightly she left crescent marks on her skin. All the agony, rage, and humiliation blended into a maelstrom of emotion.

"There is no accounting for love is there?" her grandfather said from where he sat in his old, familiar, leather winged back chair.

She shook her head and looked distractedly down at the page she'd stopped on. Francois Boucher's work stared back and she promptly closed it.

"You haven't returned to Kent to keep me company."

"You would be wrong," she said. Crossing over to him, she claimed the seat nearest his. She'd needed his reassuring presence as much as he, no doubt, needed hers. Perhaps more. "I haven't been comfortable in London in too many years. I hardly welcome the company of people who are cold and emotionless." But for her sister and Francesca, there had been nothing but icy rigidity in all the peerage Genevieve had the ill-fortune of seeing. How could she have failed to realize how very different she and Cedric were? They could have never been happy, together—not forever. Not with his *interests* what they were.

Her grandfather shifted in his chair. "You're nothing like your mother." She would have wagered her every sketchpad that he muttered "thank God" under his breath. "Though she never had sense like you do, girl." He waggled his bushy, white eyebrows. "Her marriage to your father is proof of that."

A small laugh burst from her lips. Through the years, her grandfather had made little effort to hide his annoyance with her parents.

"Such sense that I married a rake who'd never love me?"

He tightened his mouth. "Of course he loves you. How could he not?"

She looked down at her interlocked fingers. "I do not doubt he cares," she said softly, recalling him that last day, when she'd sent him away and he'd acquiesced. "But caring is not love." Nor could it ever be enough—not for her. She'd wanted all of him.

"Enough of that," her grandfather barked. "As much as I am enjoying your company, I want you to go."

She cocked her head.

"Outside. Traipsing across the countryside. Riding. Gardening. As long as you're not hiding away in my library. You need to find your smile again, girl." He snorted again. "And you're assuredly not going to find it with my miserable company."

She made a sound of protest. "You're not—"

"Save your breath, gel, and go." He thumped his palm on the arm of his chair. "I've need of a nap now, anyway."

Genevieve hesitated and passed a concerned gaze over his slender frame. His wrinkled face hinted at a fatigue. His skin was slightly pallid. Worry turned in her breast. Though he was approaching his eightieth year, she'd never allowed herself to think of him as nearing the end of his life. He'd been so much to her and for her for so long. "Are you unwell? Should we call for—"

"I've limited time enough on this earth, Genevieve. I don't have a mind to spend it with a doctor." Then, in a moment, the blustery show was gone as he gentled his tone. "I'm tired, nothing more. I've no plans to die any time soon."

She hesitated. "You're certain you—?"

"I'm certain." He banged his hand once more and that firm thump brought her to her feet. Genevieve leaned down and dropped a kiss on his weathered cheek. "Gah, go, girl," he said, gruffly.

With her book in hand, Genevieve made her way from the library. She paused outside the room a moment to study the aging earl. He closed his eyes and, within a moment, his snores carried over to the door. Gently pulling the door closed with a soft click, she continued through the long, hardwood halls. She made her way outside to the gardens she'd spent so many years working in alongside her grandfather. How quickly time changed a man. The earl showed the signs of his age and, yet, how little a person could truly change.

The memory of her husband's visage slipped forward. This time she didn't thrust his rogue's smile to the far recess of her mind but, instead, accepted that memory. In their last exchange, he'd spoken of a desire to begin again, a willingness to put aside the rakish lifestyle and be a true husband to her. In the moment, she'd been so consumed by her own agony and resentment that she'd not even considered that he possibly meant those words. How could he, a man who'd proudly worn the title of rake? Since her parting, the tumult of emotions that had assailed her through the loss of their child, the remote, but ever-there possibility crept in: what if he'd meant those professions? What if he truly loved her and wanted a life with her in every way that mattered?

Yes, she'd been a pawn of sorts in a matter of revenge against his father, but her intentions in marrying Cedric hadn't been truly honest either to Genevieve or him. With his offer of marriage, she'd thought of her security and freedom from her father's influence and the *ton's* presence. He'd dangled the prospect of sketching and gardening before her and she'd grasped it—not acknowledging until much later that her acceptance had come from deep inside, to the part of her soul that had loved him from their first meeting in the library.

Reaching the back of her grandfather's sprawling manor, she collected a basket in the conservatory, along with her scissors, and made for the glass door that emptied into the gardens. Genevieve dropped her scissors inside her basket. Shifting the bundle in her arms, she pressed the handle and stepped outside. The summer sun immediately slapped her face in with gentle warmth and she closed her eyes a moment, tipping her face up to those soft rays.

Starting forward, she picked her way through the expertly cared for rose bushes interspersed with boxwood topiaries and elaborate watering fountains. As beautiful as this space had forever been, she'd secretly dreamed of a less deliberately manicured garden. Rather, one that belonged in its natural setting and less a testament to a man's grandiose power over nature.

Genevieve stopped beside the bluebells that blanketed the earth and dropped to a knee. Fishing around her basket, she withdrew a small shovel and set to work gently digging about the base of a

plant. The sun beat down on her bent head and perspiration trickled down her neck, dampening her brow. She paused to brush the
sheen from her brow, a healthy exhilaration going through her at
her freedom. Carefully unearthing the roots, separating it, she lay
it inside the basket, and moved to the next.

Except, even as she found peace and solace outside working
in the gardens, her mind harkened back to an overgrown space
walled in by bricks, with a too-charming rake soaking up the sun's
warmth beside her.

HE LOOKED LIKE HELL. HE'D not needed the horror wreathing
the butler of the vast Kent manor to indicate as much. Cedric had
known from the scratch of two days' worth of growth on his face
and the rumpled fabric of his garments.

As such, the old servant had left him waiting in the foyer while
he went to see whether his employer was, in fact, receiving visitors. The man gone, Cedric surveyed the mural painted on the
high ceiling. A storm raged with streaks of lightning, with a single
crimson rose bush in an ominous display. It was hardly the inviting
warmth one would expect for welcoming guests.

He imagined Genevieve as she would have been, an eighteen-
year-old young lady, betrayed by her betrothed, sent away by her
family to this expansive estate. What terror would she have known
at her banishment and in the cold entryway to her new home?
She'd been robbed of so much happiness and Cedric was among
those thieves. Pressure weighted his chest. An aching need to see
her, once more.

Just as he'd no place visiting his sister, he had even less place
coming here. But he was that selfish, because he needed to see her.
He needed to, at least, offer her his worthless heart, for then he'd
know.

Then, what? *What if she turns me away, anyway?* His throat closed
tightly.

"His Lordship will see you."

He spun, having been so absorbed in his musings he'd failed to
hear the old servant's slow, shuffling approach. With a slight nod,
he followed the other man. Mahogany side tables etched with

roaring lions continued the ominous motif of the earl's uninviting home. Yet, upon those narrow pieces of furniture were large urns filled to overflowing with colorful blooms.

His chest tightened. It was her. She was everywhere in those small splashes of cheer in an otherwise dark existence. Just as she'd transformed his life, flipping it upside down on him, so she brought an effervescent light wherever she went. *I would have killed it... If she'd remained in London, her light would have no doubt gone out...*

"Here we are," the butler murmured, bringing them to a stop outside an opened door. "His Lordship, the Marquess of St. Albans," he announced loudly.

For a sliver of a heartbeat, Cedric's breath lodged deep as he skimmed the vast library in search of her. Disappointment filled his chest at finding only an ancient and darkly glowering man seated. Either in a testament of the man's age or in a blatant show of disrespect, the earl remained seated, not bothering to rise. Cedric would wager his very life it was the latter. Genevieve's grandfather ran a coolly appraising gaze over him and then peeled his lip back in a sneer.

"So you're the worthless husband then," he spoke with a slowness, the aged tones stretching out each syllable.

Cedric solemnly inclined his head. "The very same," he said quietly. He was deserving of the other man's loathing...and so much more. Pain clutched at him. She'd deserved so much more.

Pursing his lips, the earl said nothing for a long moment. Then he grunted. "Well, I don't expect you rode yourself into a sweat, with a face covered in beard, to hover in my doorway." He jerked his chin. "Get over here, boy."

Boy. For the hell of his own making he'd lived these past four weeks, a faint smile pulled at his lips. He'd never truly thought of himself as a boy. His father had shattered all vestiges of youth when Cedric had bedded that whore in the schoolroom.

"Well, are you going to sit?" Genevieve's grandfather snapped impatiently, motioning to the seat beside him.

And Cedric, a man long accustomed to giving dictates and never so much as receiving orders...sat.

The earl said nothing for a long, long while. Instead, he continued to study Cedric in that assessing way. The old man's piercing green eyes bore through him and he had no doubt the man could see inside to his every sin, every crime, he was guilty of. Not for the first time since Genevieve had stumbled into Montfort's ballroom and saw the world he was part of, shame filled him. It was fast becoming a familiar, deserved sentiment. He shifted in his seat and broke the silence.

"I've come to see my wife," he said quietly.

"And it only took you four weeks." There was a firm reproach in that statement that sent heat spiraling up Cedric's neck. The earl didn't allow him a chance to respond. "If you were deserving of her, you would have been here the day she arrived." He snorted. "In fact, if you deserved her, she would have never reached my doors."

His throat worked spasmodically. Yes, the man was right on so many scores; the loathing in his eyes, the reproach in his words. Nonetheless… "I am not deserving of her. I never was," he said, more to himself. He held his palms up. "But I love her, my lord. I love her as I've never loved a person, and I need her."

By the unyielding lines of his face, the earl was wholly unimpressed with Cedric's short speech. "And what about what *she* needs?" He folded his arms at his sunken chest and lifted an eyebrow.

Cedric flinched, as the man's words struck their appropriate mark. What she needed…well, it surely wasn't him. "I believe…" He looked beyond the man's shoulder to a rose-inlaid table stacked neatly with leather books. Wordlessly, he climbed to his feet and strode over to them, coming to a stop beside the pile of sketchpads. Pulling off his gloves, he absently stuffed them inside his jacket and then brushed his palm over the surface of the top book. A shock of heat met his touch and filled every corner of him that had been previously cold with her leaving. She'd caressed these pages. While his life had continued to crumble about him with her departure, she'd loved these sheets and transformed them. A hungering filled him to flip through the pages and steal a glimpse into the daily thoughts of her world as it had existed without him. Except, he didn't have the right to be a voyeur on her thoughts. "She deserves more than me," he said finally, turning slowly back to find the earl still intently studying him. "I hurt her," he said, forcing those words out into existence.

The earl tightened his mouth again. "You certainly did." Agony lanced Cedric's heart. "But Genevieve is a strong girl. It would take more than a shiftless rake to destroy her."

"Indeed," he automatically agreed, as memories assailed him. Genevieve tossing her glass of water in the face of the first man who'd wronged her in a public display of beautiful fury. Genevieve slipping away from a ballroom and removing her slippers in her host's home. He turned his palms up. "But I want to begin again with her. I want to have a real marriage with your granddaughter."

"And your wicked parties?"

He winced. The man was relentless but it was just another jab Cedric deserved. "I've grown weary of them." How had he ever found pleasure at those crude, soulless affairs?

"What happens when you crave them again?"

Most husbands would take umbrage with another interfering in his marriage. By the laws, a wife belonged to and with her husband. Cedric, however, would never have Genevieve in that way. He'd not force her to him. And any person, man or woman, who'd so protect her, had his unending gratitude. "I can give you my assurances that there will never be another beyond her. But what reason have I given you," or more importantly, Genevieve, "to trust me?" Shame spread through him. "I have not lived an honorable existence," he said, after he'd found proper words. "I have drunk too much and wagered even more." That brought the other man's eyebrows snapping together. "I enjoyed scandalous affairs, no respectable man or woman should even know about."

The earl scrutinized him with hard, relentless eyes.

Cedric held his hands out. "But then I met your granddaughter. She stepped inside my father's library and in that moment, she forever transformed me, even as I did not recognize it at the time, and even as I did not allow myself to accept that...until I lost her." Memories of her laughter, her smile, her teasing words whispered around his mind, so tangible, so very real, it gutted him, making it impossible to drag forth words. Unnerved by the intensity of the earl's probing stare, Cedric moved over to the floor-length window that overlooked the rolling Kent countryside.

...The sky is bluer and when you lay on the grass and stare up at the sky you see nothing but an endless blue, so that you think you can stretch your fingers up and touch the heavens...

His gaze snagged on the slender figure. Her head was bent over a blanket of bluish-purple flowers and his heart tripped a beat. He leaned forward; a starving man hungering for the first glimpse of her. "I love her," he said again, his voice hoarse. Cedric pressed his brow against the warm lead pane as Genevieve continued to work. "And I will not lie and say I will ever be deserving of her, because I won't. But if she'll let me, I will fill her life with love."

Silence met his profession and he forced his gaze away from Genevieve to look back at the earl.

The old man cracked his first smile. It was a faint, but genuine, expression. "Then, what are you doing with me, boy? Go find your wife."

CHAPTER 29

GENEVIEVE BENT OVER THE EARTH, digging a small hole. Working as she'd been without interruption so long the sun had made its high climb to the sky above, the muscles of her lower back screamed in protest. She straightened and paused to rub the dull ache, before returning to her task of splitting and replanting the bulbs.

She set to work digging the next home for the blooms, when a shadow fell over her. Ever faithful Delores who came to assist each day. "Will you hand me another bluebell from the basket, Delores," she called, as she finished making the next hole. Genevieve held her palm out. At her maid's silence, she looked back, and froze.

With a bluebell held in his large, tanned fingers, Cedric studied her in an inscrutable manner.

The world froze in this peculiar moment that dreams were made of. For all that had come to pass between them, not a day had gone where she'd not thought of him and ached to see him. His garments rumpled, his eyes bloodshot, and a thick set of stubble on his chiseled cheeks, he was somehow even more splendid in his masculine perfection. *Why is he here?* The shovel slipped forgotten from her fingers.

Her husband inclined his head. "I suppose I might say hello."

Oh, God. Those words, some of the first she'd ever uttered to him, brought her eyes momentarily closed. They harkened to a time when she'd still secretly clung to fairytales and the hope of love. Those dreams had long since been slayed—by him. "Why are you here?" she asked, when she trusted herself to speak.

Cedric flexed a hand. "I came to see you," he said flatly.

After he'd shattered her world, did he expect she'd greet him with arms flung about his neck? Genevieve climbed to her feet. Following his betrayal, and their loss…nay, her loss, she'd lost herself in enough tears to fill the Thames. In the recent weeks, she'd managed to wake without feeling her heart was being slowly whittled away with a dull knife. Now, in being here, he'd kick out the shaky foundation of a new world she'd begun to build for herself. "For what purpose?" she asked tiredly.

He caressed her face with a warm gaze. "How can you not know when you left, you took my heart and very reason for being?"

Her lower lip shook and she caught it hard between her teeth to stop that faint tremble. How very beautiful those words were. And at one time she would have sold her soul on Sunday to have them from him. Then there had always been beautiful words between them…just never substance. "I…" she searched her mind, "appreciate you coming here, Cedric. Too much has come to pass for there to be anything more between us." She hated that truth, but she'd come to, at least, accept it.

Shock contorted his face and he shook his head. "I don't believe that."

Tears filled her eyes. "But you wouldn't, would you? Because that child was nothing to you. To me, he…" or she "was. And beautiful words will never be able to take back the pain of all I lost." The air lodged painfully in her chest as all the agony of that loss assaulted her senses.

Cedric pressed his palm to his mouth and then he let his arm fall faltering to his side. Rocking on the balls of his feet, he glanced around the garden. "I never wanted children," he spoke so matter-of-fact that grief scissored through her. Odd how that admission should still shred her. A sad, humorless grin turned his firm lips. "Why should I want a child? He would be an extension of me."

Genevieve hugged her arms close. How peculiar, she had wanted a babe from him, for that very reason.

Cedric wandered over to the pink roses in bloom and studied the satiny petals as though they contained the answer to life. "That child would have been an extension of me, just as I am an extension of my father."

Then his words registered. And with them, the most revealing ones he'd ever shared in the course of their rushed meeting and marriage. *It is too late for more with him... It is too late for more...* She trailed the tip of her tongue over her lower lip. "Is that why you didn't wish to have a child? Because you saw your father in yourself?"

"I spent my whole life believing I was my father," he said quietly. "That I allowed myself to become him."

An agonized groan climbed up her throat. The man who'd entered their home, a man who'd so manipulated his son, was nothing like the humbled man before her now. "That is not true."

"Isn't it?" he said, giving her another sad look. "Even with my being here, when you do not wish to see me, I prove myself a selfish bastard."

A protest sprung to her lips but then, in that gentle caress that was so patently his, Cedric brushed his knuckles up and down her cheek. How wrong he was. How could he not know her happiness had been so beautifully linked to him? "But I needed to see you." His throat muscles moved. "Every day you've been gone, I've thought about what I would say if...when, I saw you again."

A vise-like pressure squeezed about Genevieve's heart as she sought to resurrect the fortress she'd built these past weeks. But with his every word and gesture, he toppled those walls.

He looked to her and so much love blazed from within the fathomless blue of his irises, it robbed her of words. "I didn't want to love. I didn't want a wife. And I certainly didn't want a child." His voice cracked and he let his arm fall to his side. Agony wrapped her heart in a familiar vise with the mention of the babe that had almost been. He gave a jerky nod. "And my life was moving along in a splendidly predictable way, just as I wanted, as I liked. I didn't want anything more from life."

She again folded her arms, hugging herself in a lonely embrace.

"Until you," he said hoarsely. He closed the space between them, his boots noisily crunching the earth. Cedric captured her chin and tipped her gaze up to his. "I never realized everything my life was missing until you were gone from it. You opened my eyes to the person I was and he was a man I didn't much like. You made me see that I want so much more…with you."

"Cedric," she pleaded. Because with every utterance, he made her long for things she'd managed to convince herself would never be.

He was relentless, battering at her defenses. "I want to lay beside you looking at the country sky you described." Her husband tilted his head back and took in the crisp blue above, with bilious, white clouds floating by. "Because I forgot how beautiful it is." A frantic laugh spilled from his lips. "No doubt, because I'd never taken the time to appreciate it…" He returned his gaze to her. "Until you. I want it all. I want a family." His words were a ragged plea.

She clutched at her throat. He was a master of words. He'd proven that since their first meeting. "I do not want you to want a child because you believe that is the only way I'll be yours."

Cedric drifted closer and dropped his brow atop hers. "I want a child with you because she'll be a brave, beautiful girl in her mother's image and she'll have been made in love." Oh, God. "I want to sit in a garden and sketch, not because you want me to change, but because I *have* changed." He stepped away and dragged his hand through his hair, tousling those too-long locks all the more. With a jerky movement, he fished around the front of his jacket and withdrew a gold chain. The ruby heart pendant glimmered bright in the afternoon sun.

The column of his throat worked. "It was my mother's. My sister said it was a gift, given in love. She shared it with me, to share with you." He extended that precious treasure to her.

A shuddery sob built in her throat and she pressed her fingertips to her lips.

"Will you not say something?" he asked hoarsely, letting his faltering hand fall to his side. The chain twisted and danced in a slight circle.

Genevieve flung her arms around him with such ferocity that he stumbled backward and toppled to the ground, her form coming down hard over him. "I love you," she rasped, taking his face between her hands. "I want all of that with you, too."

"Oomph." His breath came fast from the force she'd knocked into him. He closed his eyes a moment and then rolled her under him. "Oh, God, I have missed you," he whispered. That forever errant, golden curl tumbled over his brow.

A whispery half-laugh, half-sob spilled from her lips. "From the moment you slid my slippers on my feet, I was hopelessly and irrevocably yours." Her mouth quivered in a smile as she brushed the loose strand behind his ear. "The lure of a rake is a strong one."

His lips turned up in that charming half-grin that altered the beat of her heart. He lowered his mouth close to hers. "But not nearly as powerful as the lure of a lady."

Cedric claimed her lips in a kiss that promised forever.

THE END

OTHER BOOKS BY
CHRISTI CALDWELL

TO ENCHANT A WICKED DUKE
Book 13 in the "Heart of a Duke" Series by Christi Caldwell

A Devil in Disguise

Years ago, when Nick Tallings, the recent Duke of Huntly, watched his family destroyed at the hands of a merciless nobleman, he vowed revenge. But his efforts had been futile, as his enemy, Lord Rutland is without weakness.

Until now…

With his rival finally happily married, Nick is able to set his ruthless scheme into motion. His plot hinges upon Lord Rutland's innocent, empty-headed sister-in-law, Justina Barrett. Nick will ruin her, marry her, and then leave her brokenhearted.

A Lady Dreaming of Love

From the moment Justina Barrett makes her Come Out, she is labeled a Diamond. Even with her ruthless father determined to sell her off to the highest bidder, Justina never gives up on her hope for a good, honorable gentleman who values her wit more than her looks.

A Not-So-Chance Meeting

Nick's ploy to ensnare Justina falls neatly into place in the streets of London. With each carefully orchestrated encounter, he slips further and further inside the lady's heart, never anticipating that Justina, with her quick wit and strength, will break down his own defenses. As Nick's plans begins to unravel, he's left to determine which is more important—Justina's love or his vow for vengeance. But can Justina ever forgive the duke who deceived her?

ONE WINTER WITH A BARON
Book 12 in the "Heart of a Duke" Series by Christi Caldwell

A clever spinster:

Content with her spinster lifestyle, Miss Sybil Cunning wants to prove that a future as an unmarried woman is the only life for her. As a bluestocking who values hard, empirical data, Sybil needs help with her research. Nolan Pratt, Baron Webb, one of society's most scandalous rakes, is the perfect gentleman to help her. After all, he inspires fear in proper mothers and desire within their daughters.

A notorious rake:

Society may be aware of Nolan Pratt, Baron's Webb's wicked ways, but what he has carefully hidden is his miserable handling of his family's finances. When Sybil presents him the opportunity to earn much-needed funds, he can't refuse.

A winter to remember:

However, what begins as a business arrangement becomes something more and with every meeting, Sybil slips inside his heart. Can this clever woman look beneath the veneer of a coldhearted rake to see the man Nolan truly is?

TO REDEEM A RAKE
Book 11 in the "Heart of a Duke" Series by Christi Caldwell

He's spent years scandalizing society.
Now, this rake must change his ways.

Society's most infamous scoundrel, Daniel Winterbourne, the Earl of Montfort, has been promised a small fortune if he can relinquish his wayward, carousing lifestyle. And behaving means he must also help find a respectable companion for his youngest sister—someone who will guide her and whom she can emulate. However, Daniel knows no such woman. But when he encounters a childhood friend, Daniel believes she may just be the answer to all of his problems.

Having been secretly humiliated by an unscrupulous blackguard years earlier, Miss Daphne Smith dreams of finding work at Ladies of Hope, an institution that provides an education for disabled women. With her sordid past and a disfigured leg, few opportunities arise for a woman such as she. Knowing Daniel's history, she wishes to avoid him, but working for his sister is exactly the stepping stone she needs.

Their attraction intensifies as Daniel and Daphne grow closer, preparing his sister for the London Season. But Daniel must resist his desire for a woman tarnished by scandal while Daphne is reminded of the boy she once knew. Can society's most notorious rake redeem his reputation and become the man Daphne deserves?

TO WOO A WIDOW
Book 10 in the "Heart of a Duke" Series by Christi Caldwell

They see a brokenhearted widow.
She's far from shattered.

Lady Philippa Winston is never marrying again. After her late husband's cruelty that she kept so well hidden, she has no desire to search for love.

Years ago, Miles Brookfield, the Marquess of Guilford, made a frivolous vow he never thought would come to fruition—he promised to marry his mother's goddaughter if he was unwed by the age of thirty. Now, to his dismay, he's faced with honoring that pledge. But when he encounters the beautiful and intriguing Lady Philippa, Miles knows his true path in life. It's up to him to break down every belief Philippa carries about gentlemen, proving that not only is love real, but that he is the man deserving of her sheltered heart.

Will Philippa let down her guard and allow Miles to woo a widow in desperate need of his love?

THE LURE OF A RAKE
Book 9 in the "Heart of a Duke" Series by Christi Caldwell

A Lady Dreaming of Love

Lady Genevieve Farendale has a scandalous past. Jilted at the altar years earlier and exiled by her family, she's now returned to London to prove she can be a proper lady. Even though she's not given up on the hope of marrying for love, she's wary of trusting again. Then she meets Cedric Falcot, the Marquess of St. Albans whose seductive ways set her heart aflutter. But with her sordid history, Genevieve knows a rake can also easily destroy her.

An Unlikely Pairing

What begins as a chance encounter between Cedric and Genevieve becomes something more. As they continue to meet, passions stir. But with Genevieve's hope for true love, she fears Cedric will be unable to give up his wayward lifestyle. After all, Cedric has spent years protecting his heart, and keeping everyone out. Slowly, she chips away at all the walls he's built, but when he falters, Genevieve can't offer him redemption. Now, it's up to Cedric to prove to Genevieve that the love of a man is far more powerful than the lure of a rake.

TO TRUST A ROGUE
Book 8 in the "Heart of a Duke" Series by Christi Caldwell

A rogue

Marcus, the Viscount Wessex has carefully crafted the image of rogue and charmer for Polite Society. Under that façade, however, dwells a man whose dreams were shattered almost eight years earlier by a young lady who captured his heart, pledged her love, and then left him, with nothing more than a curt note.

A widow

Eight years earlier, faced with no other choice, Mrs. Eleanor Collins, fled London and the only man she ever loved, Marcus, Viscount Wessex. She has now returned to serve as a companion for her elderly aunt with a daughter in tow. Even though they're next door neighbors, there is little reason for her to move in the same circles as Marcus, just in case, she vows to avoid him, for he reminds her of all she lost when she left.

Reunited

As their paths continue to cross, Marcus finds his desire for Eleanor just as strong, but he learned long ago she's not to be trusted. He will offer her a place in his bed, but not anything more. Only, Eleanor has no interest in this new, roguish man. The more time they spend together, the protective wall they've constructed to keep the other out, begin to break. With all the betrayals and secrets between them, Marcus has to open his heart again. And Eleanor must decide if it's ever safe to trust a rogue.

To Wed His Christmas Lady
Book 7 in the "Heart of a Duke" Series by Christi Caldwell

She's longing to be loved:

Lady Cara Falcot has only served one purpose to her loathsome father—to increase his power through a marriage to the future Duke of Billingsley. As such, she's built protective walls about her heart, and presents an icy facade to the world around her. Journeying home from her finishing school for the Christmas holidays, Cara's carriage is stranded during a winter storm. She's forced to tarry at a ramshackle inn, where she immediately antagonizes another patron—William.

He's avoiding his duty in favor of one last adventure:

William Hargrove, the Marquess of Grafton has wanted only one thing in life—to avoid the future match his parents would have him make to a cold, duke's daughter. He's returning home from a blissful eight years of traveling the world to see to his responsibilities. But when a winter storm interrupts his trip and lands him at a falling-down inn, he's forced to share company with a commanding Lady Cara who initially reminds him exactly of the woman he so desperately wants to avoid.

A Christmas snowstorm ushers in the spirit of the season:

At the holiday time, these two people who despise each other due to first perceptions are offered renewed beginnings and fresh starts. As this gruff stranger breaks down the walls she's built about herself, Cara has to determine whether she can truly open her heart to trusting that any man is capable of good and that she herself is capable of love. And William has to set aside all previous thoughts he's carried of the polished ladies like Cara, to be the man to show her that love.

THE HEART OF A SCOUNDREL
Book 6 in the "Heart of a Duke" Series by Christi Caldwell

Ruthless, wicked, and dark, the Marquess of Rutland rouses terror in the breast of ladies and nobleman alike. All Edmund wants in life is power. After he was publically humiliated by his one love Lady Margaret, he vowed vengeance, using Margaret's niece, as his pawn. Except, he's thwarted by another, more enticing target—Miss Phoebe Barrett.

Miss Phoebe Barrett knows precisely the shame she's been born to. Because her father is a shocking letch she's learned to form her own opinions on a person's worth. After a chance meeting with the Marquess of Rutland, she is captivated by the mysterious man. He, too, is a victim of society's scorn, but the more encounters she has with Edmund, the more she knows there is powerful depth and emotion to the jaded marquess.

The lady wreaks havoc on Edmund's plans for revenge and he finds he wants Phoebe, at all costs. As she's drawn into the darkness of his world, Phoebe risks being destroyed by Edmund's ruthlessness. And Phoebe who desires love at all costs, has to determine if she can ever truly trust the heart of a scoundrel.

To Love a Lord
Book 5 in the "Heart of a Duke" Series by Christi Caldwell

All she wants is security:

The last place finishing school instructor Mrs. Jane Munroe belongs, is in polite Society. Vowing to never wed, she's been scuttled around from post to post. Now she finds herself in the Marquess of Waverly's household. She's never met a nobleman she liked, and when she meets the pompous, arrogant marquess, she remembers why. But soon, she discovers Gabriel is unlike any gentleman she's ever known.

All he wants is a companion for his sister:

What Gabriel finds himself with instead, is a fiery spirited, bespectacled woman who entices him at every corner and challenges his age-old vow to never trust his heart to a woman. But... there is something suspicious about his sister's companion. And he is determined to find out just what it is.

All they need is each other:

As Gabriel and Jane confront the truth of their feelings, the lies and secrets between them begin to unravel. And Jane is left to decide whether or not it is ever truly safe to love a lord.

Loved By a Duke
Book 4 in the "Heart of a Duke" Series by Christi Caldwell

For ten years, Lady Daisy Meadows has been in love with Auric, the Duke of Crawford. Ever since his gallant rescue years earlier, Daisy knew she was destined to be his Duchess. Unfortunately, Auric sees her as his best friend's sister and nothing more. But perhaps, if she can manage to find the fabled heart of a duke pendant, she will win over the heart of her duke.

Auric, the Duke of Crawford enjoys Daisy's company. The last thing he is interested in however, is pursuing a romance with a woman he's known since she was in leading strings. This season, Daisy is turning up in the oddest places and he cannot help but notice that she is no longer a girl. But Auric wouldn't do something as foolhardy as to fall in love with Daisy. He couldn't. Not with the guilt he carries over his past sins… Not when he has no right to her heart…But perhaps, just perhaps, she can forgive the past and trust that he'd forever cherish her heart—but will she let him?

The Love of a Rogue
Book 3 in the "Heart of a Duke" Series by Christi Caldwell

Lady Imogen Moore hasn't had an easy time of it since she made her Come Out. With her betrothed, a powerful duke breaking it off to wed her sister, she's become the *tons* favorite piece of gossip. Never again wanting to experience the pain of a broken heart, she's resolved to make a match with a polite, respectable gentleman. The last thing she wants is another reckless rogue.

Lord Alex Edgerton has a problem. His brother, tired of Alex's carousing has charged him with chaperoning their remaining, unwed sister about *ton* events. Shopping? No, thank you. Attending the theatre? He'd rather be at Forbidden Pleasures with a scantily clad beauty upon his lap. The task of *chaperone* becomes even more of a bother when his sister drags along her dearest friend, Lady Imogen to social functions. The last thing he wants in his life is a young, innocent English miss.

Except, as Alex and Imogen are thrown together, passions flare and Alex comes to find he not only wants Imogen in his bed, but also in his heart. Yet now he must convince Imogen to risk all, on the heart of a rogue.

MORE THAN A DUKE
Book 2 in the "Heart of a Duke" Series by Christi Caldwell

Polite Society doesn't take Lady Anne Adamson seriously. However, Anne isn't just another pretty young miss. When she discovers her father betrayed her mother's love and her family descended into poverty, Anne comes up with a plan to marry a respectable, powerful, and honorable gentleman—a man nothing like her philandering father.

Armed with the heart of a duke pendant, fabled to land the wearer a duke's heart, she decides to enlist the aid of the notorious Harry, 6th Earl of Stanhope. A scoundrel with a scandalous past, he is the last gentleman she'd ever wed…however, his reputation marks him the perfect man to school her in the art of seduction so she might ensnare the illustrious Duke of Crawford.

Harry, the Earl of Stanhope is a jaded, cynical rogue who lives for his own pleasures. Having been thrown over by the only woman he ever loved so she could wed a duke, he's not at all surprised when Lady Anne approaches him with her scheme to capture another duke's affection. He's come to appreciate that all women are in fact greedy, title-grasping, self-indulgent creatures. And with Anne's history of grating on his every last nerve, she is the last woman he'd ever agree to school in the art of seduction. Only his friendship with the lady's sister compels him to help.

What begins as a pretend courtship, born of lessons on seduction, becomes something more leaving Anne to decide if she can give her heart to a reckless rogue, and Harry must decide if he's willing to again trust in a lady's love.

FOR LOVE OF THE DUKE
First Full-Length Book in the "Heart of a Duke" Series
by Christi Caldwell

After the tragic death of his wife, Jasper, the 8th Duke of Bainbridge buried himself away in the dark cold walls of his home, Castle Blackwood. When he's coaxed out of his self-imposed exile to attend the amusements of the Frost Fair, his life is irrevocably changed by his fateful meeting with Lady Katherine Adamson.

With her tight brown ringlets and silly white-ruffled gowns, Lady Katherine Adamson has found her dance card empty for two Seasons. After her father's passing, Katherine learned the unreliability of men, and is determined to depend on no one, except herself. Until she meets Jasper…

In a desperate bid to avoid a match arranged by her family, Katherine makes the Duke of Bainbridge a shocking proposition—one that he accepts.

Only, as Katherine begins to love Jasper, she finds the arrangement agreed upon is not enough. And Jasper is left to decide if protecting his heart is more important than fighting for Katherine's love.

IN NEED OF A DUKE
A Prequel Novella to "The Heart of a Duke" Series
by Christi Caldwell

In Need of a Duke: (Author's Note: This is a prequel novella to "The Heart of a Duke" series by Christi Caldwell. It was originally available in "The Heart of a Duke" Collection and is now being published as an individual novella.

~★~

It features a new prologue and epilogue.

Years earlier, a gypsy woman passed to Lady Aldora Adamson and her friends a heart pendant that promised them each the heart of a duke.

Now, a young lady, with her family facing ruin and scandal, Lady Aldora doesn't have time for mythical stories about cheap baubles. She needs to save her sisters and brother by marrying a titled gentleman with wealth and power to his name. She sets her bespectacled sights upon the Marquess of St. James.

Turned out by his father after a tragic scandal, Lord Michael Knightly has grown into a powerful, but self-made man. With the whispers and stares that still follow him, he would rather be anywhere but London…

Until he meets Lady Aldora, a young woman who mistakes him for his brother, the Marquess of St. James. The connection between Aldora and Michael is immediate and as they come to know one another, Aldora's feelings for Michael war with her sisterly responsibilities. With her family's dire situation, a man of Michael's scandalous past will never do.

Ultimately, Aldora must choose between her responsibilities as a sister and her love for Michael.

ONCE A WALLFLOWER, AT LAST HIS LOVE
Book 6 in the Scandalous Seasons Series

Responsible, practical Miss Hermione Rogers, has been crafting stories as the notorious Mr. Michael Michaelmas and selling them for a meager wage to support her siblings. The only real way to ensure her family's ruinous debts are paid, however, is to marry. Tall, thin, and plain, she has no expectation of success. In London for her first Season she seizes the chance to write the tale of a brooding duke. In her research, she finds Sebastian Fitzhugh, the 5th Duke of Mallen, who unfortunately is perfectly affable, charming, and so nicely… configured… he takes her breath away. He lacks all the character traits she needs for her story, but alas, any duke will have to do.

Sebastian Fitzhugh, the 5th Duke of Mallen has been deceived so many times during the high-stakes game of courtship, he's lost faith in Society women. Yet, after a chance encounter with Hermione, he finds himself intrigued. Not a woman he'd normally consider beautiful, the young lady's practical bent, her forthright nature and her tendency to turn up in the oddest places has his interests… roused. He'd like to trust her, he'd like to do a whole lot more with her too, but should he?

A Marquess for Christmas
Book 5 in the Scandalous Seasons Series

Lady Patrina Tidemore gave up on the ridiculous notion of true love after having her heart shattered and her trust destroyed by a black-hearted cad. Used as a pawn in a game of revenge against her brother, Patrina returns to London from a failed elopement with a tattered reputation and little hope for a respectable match. The only peace she finds is in her solitude on the cold winter days at Hyde Park. And even that is yanked from her by two little hellions who just happen to have a devastatingly handsome, but coldly aloof father, the Marquess of Beaufort. Something about the lord stirs the dreams she'd once carried for an honorable gentleman's love.

Weston Aldridge, the 4th Marquess of Beaufort was deceived and betrayed by his late wife. In her faithlessness, he's come to view women as self-serving, indulgent creatures. Except, after a series of chance encounters with Patrina, he comes to appreciate how uniquely different she is than all women he's ever known.

At the Christmastide season, a time of hope and new beginnings, Patrina and Weston, unexpectedly learn true love in one another. However, as Patrina's scandalous past threatens their future and the happiness of his children, they are both left to determine if love is enough.

ALWAYS A ROGUE, FOREVER HER LOVE
Book 4 in the Scandalous Seasons Series

Miss Juliet Marshville is spitting mad. With one guardian missing, and the other singularly uninterested in her fate, she is at the mercy of her wastrel brother who loses her beloved childhood home to a man known as Sin. Determined to reclaim control of Rosecliff Cottage and her own fate, Juliet arranges a meeting with the notorious rogue and demands the return of her property.

Jonathan Tidemore, 5th Earl of Sinclair, known to the *ton* as Sin, is exceptionally lucky in life and at the gaming tables. He has just one problem. Well…four, really. His incorrigible sisters have driven off yet another governess. This time, however, his mother demands he find an appropriate replacement.

When Miss Juliet Marshville boldly demands the return of her precious cottage, he takes advantage of his sudden good fortune and puts an offer to her; turn his sisters into proper English ladies, and he'll return Rosecliff Cottage to Juliet's possession.

Jonathan comes to appreciate Juliet's spirit, courage, and clever wit, and decides to claim the fiery beauty as his mistress. Juliet, however, will be mistress for no man. Nor could she ever love a man who callously stole her home in a game of cards. As Jonathan begins to see Juliet as more than a spirited beauty to warm his bed, he realizes she could be a lady he could love the rest of his life, if only he can convince the proud Juliet that he's worthy of her hand and heart.

ALWAYS PROPER, SUDDENLY SCANDALOUS
Book 3 in the Scandalous Seasons Series

Geoffrey Winters, Viscount Redbrooke was not always the hard, unrelenting lord driven by propriety. After a tragic mistake, he resolved to honor his responsibility to the Redbrooke line and live a life, free of scandal. Knowing his duty is to wed a proper, respectable English miss, he selects Lady Beatrice Dennington, daughter of the Duke of Somerset, the perfect woman for him. Until he meets Miss Abigail Stone...

To distance herself from a personal scandal, Abigail Stone flees America to visit her uncle, the Duke of Somerset. Determined to never trust a man again, she is helplessly intrigued by the hard, too-proper Geoffrey. With his strict appreciation for decorum and order, he is nothing like the man' she's always dreamed of.

Abigail is everything Geoffrey does not need. She upends his carefully ordered world at every encounter. As they begin to care for one another, Abigail carefully guards the secret that resulted in her journey to England.

Only, if Geoffrey learns the truth about Abigail, he must decide which he holds most dear: his place in Society or Abigail's place in his heart.

NEVER COURTED, SUDDENLY WED
Book 2 in the Scandalous Seasons Series

Christopher Ansley, Earl of Waxham, has constructed a perfect image for the *ton*—the ladies love him and his company is desired by all. Only two people know the truth about Waxham's secret. Unfortunately, one of them is Miss Sophie Winters.

Sophie Winters has known Christopher since she was in leading strings. As children, they delighted in tormenting each other. Now at two and twenty, she still has a tendency to find herself in scrapes, and her marital prospects are slim.

When his father threatens to expose his shame to the *ton*, unless he weds Sophie for her dowry, Christopher concocts a plan to remain a bachelor. What he didn't plan on was falling in love with the lively, impetuous Sophie. As secrets are exposed, will Christopher's love be enough when she discovers his role in his father's scheme?

FOREVER BETROTHED, NEVER THE BRIDE
Book 1 in the Scandalous Seasons Series

Hopeless romantic Lady Emmaline Fitzhugh is tired of sitting with the wallflowers, waiting for her betrothed to come to his senses and marry her. When Emmaline reads one too many reports of his scandalous liaisons in the gossip rags, she takes matters into her own hands.

War-torn veteran Lord Drake devotes himself to forgetting his days on the Peninsula through an endless round of meaning-less associations. He no longer wants to feel anything, but Lady Emmaline is making it hard to maintain a state of numbness. With her zest for life, she awakens his passion and desire for love.

The one woman Drake has spent the better part of his life avoid-ing is now the only woman he needs, but he is no longer a man worthy of his Emmaline. It is up to her to show him the healing power of love.

A SEASON OF HOPE
A Danby Novella

Five years ago when her love, Marcus Wheatley, failed to return from fighting Napoleon's forces, Lady Olivia Foster buried her heart. Unable to betray Marcus's memory, Olivia has gone out of her way to run off prospective suitors. At three and twenty she considers herself firmly on the shelf. Her father, however, disagrees and accepts an offer for Olivia's hand in marriage. Yet it's Christ-mas, when anything can happen…

Olivia receives a well-timed summons from her grandfather, the Duke of Danby, and eagerly embraces the reprieve from her betrothal.

Only, when Olivia arrives at Danby Castle she realizes the Christ-mas season represents hope, second chances, and even miracles.

"Winning a Lady's Heart"
A Danby Novella

Author's Note: This is a novella that was originally available in A Summons From The Castle (The Regency Christmas Summons Collection). It is being published as an individual novella.

~★~

For Lady Alexandra, being the source of a cold, calculated wager is bad enough…but when it is waged by Nathaniel Michael Winters, 5th Earl of Pembroke, the man she's in love with, it results in a broken heart, the scandal of the season, and a summons from her grandfather – the Duke of Danby.

To escape Society's gossip, she hurries to her meeting with the duke, determined to put memories of the earl far behind. Except the duke has other plans for Alexandra…plans which include the 5th Earl of Pembroke!

"Tempted by a Lady's Smile"
Book 4 in the "Lords of Honor" Series

Richard Jonas has loved but one woman—a woman who belongs to his brother. Refusing to suffer any longer, he evades his family in order to barricade his heart from unrequited love. While attending a friend's summer party, Richard's approach to love is changed after sharing a passionate and life-altering kiss with a vibrant and mysterious woman. Believing he was incapable of loving again, Richard finds himself tempted by a young lady determined to marry his best friend.

Gemma Reed has not been treated kindly by the *ton*. Often disregarded for her appearance and interests unlike those of a proper lady, Gemma heads to house party to win the heart of Lord Westfield, the man she's loved for years. But her plan is set off course by the tempting and intriguing, Richard Jonas.

A chance meeting creates a new path for Richard and Gemma to forage—but can two people, scorned and shunned by those they've loved from afar, let down their guards to find true happiness?

"RESCUED BY A LADY'S LOVE"
Book 3 in the "Lords of Honor" Series

Destitute and determined to finally be free of any man's shackles, Lily Benedict sets out to salvage her honor. With no choice but to commit a crime that will save her from her past, she enters the home of the recluse, Derek Winters, the new Duke of Blackthorne. But entering the "Beast of Blackthorne's" lair proves more threatening than she ever imagined.

With half a face and a mangled leg, Derek—once rugged and charming—only exists within the confines of his home. Shunned by society, Derek is leery of the hauntingly beautiful Lily Benedict. As time passes, she slips past his defenses, reminding him how to live again. But when Lily's sordid past comes back, threatening her life, it's up to Derek to find the strength to become the hero he once was. Can they overcome the darkness of their sins to find a life of love and redemption?

CAPTIVATED BY A LADY'S CHARM
Book 2 in the "Lords of Honor" Series

In need of a wife…

Christian Villiers, the Marquess of St. Cyr, despises the role he's been cast into as fortune hunter but requires the funds to keep his marquisate solvent. Yet, the sins of his past cloud his future, preventing him from seeing beyond his fateful actions at the Battle of Toulouse. For he knows inevitably it will catch up with him, and everyone will remember his actions on the battlefield that cost so many so much—particularly his best friend.

In want of a husband…

Lady Prudence Tidemore's life is plagued by familial scandals, which makes her own marital prospects rather grim. Surely there is one gentleman of the ton who can look past her family and see just her and all she has to offer?

When Prudence runs into Christian on a London street, the charming, roguish gentleman immediately captures her attention. But then a chance meeting becomes a waltz, and now…

A Perfect Match…

All she must do is convince Christian to forget the cold requirements he has for his future marchioness. But the demons in his past prevent him from turning himself over to love. One thing is certain—Prudence wants the marquess and is determined to have him in her life, now and forever. It's just a matter of convincing Christian he wants the same.

SEDUCED BY A LADY'S HEART
Book 1 in the "Lords of Honor" Series

You met Lieutenant Lucien Jones in "Forever Betrothed, Never the Bride" when he was a broken soldier returned from fighting Boney's forces. This is his story of triumph and happily-ever-after!

~★~

Lieutenant Lucien Jones, son of a viscount, returned from war, to find his wife and child dead. Blaming his father for the commission that sent him off to fight Boney's forces, he was content to languish at London Hospital… until offered employment on the Marquess of Drake's staff. Through his position, Lucien found purpose in life and is content to keep his past buried.

Lady Eloise Yardley has loved Lucien since they were children. Having long ago given up on the dream of him, she married another. Years later, she is a young, lonely widow who does not fit in with the ton. When Lucien's family enlists her aid to reunite father and son, she leaps at the opportunity to not only aid her former friend, but to also escape London.

Lucien doesn't know what scheme Eloise has concocted, but

knowing her as he does, when she pays a visit to his employer, he knows she's up to something. The last thing he wants is the temptation that this new, older, mature Eloise presents; a tantalizing reminder of happier times and peace.

Yet Eloise is determined to win Lucien's love once and for all... if only Lucien can set aside the pain of his past and risk all on a lady's heart.

ONLY FOR THEIR LOVE
Book 3 in the "The Theodosia Sword" Series

Miss Carol Cresswall bore witness to her parents' loveless union and is determined to avoid that same miserable fate. Her mother has altogether different plans—plans that include a match between Carol and Lord Gregory Renshaw. Despite his wealth and power, Carol has no interest in marrying a pompous man who goes out of his way to ignore her. Now, with their families coming together for the Christmastide season it's her mother's last-ditch effort to get them together. And Carol plans to avoid Gregory at all costs.

Lord Gregory Renshaw has no intentions of falling prey to his mother's schemes to marry him off to a proper debutante she's picked out. Over the years, he has carefully sidestepped all endeavors to be matched with any of the grasping ladies.

But a sudden Christmastide Scandal has the potential show Carol and Gregory that they've spent years running from the one thing they've always needed.

ᴏNLY ꜰᴏʀ ʜᴇʀ ʜᴏNᴏʀ
Book 2 in the "The Theodosia Sword" Series

A wounded soldier:

When Captain Lucas Rayne returned from fighting Boney's forces, he was a shell of a man. A recluse who doesn't leave his family's estate, he's content to shut himself away. Until he meets Eve…

A woman alone in the world:

Eve Ormond spent most of her life following the drum alongside her late father. When his shameful actions bring death and pain to English soldiers, Eve is forced back to England, an outcast. With no family or marital prospects she needs employment and finds it in Captain Lucas Rayne's home. A man whose life was ruined by her father, Eve has no place inside his household. With few options available, however, Eve takes the post. What she never anticipates is how with their every meeting, this honorable, hurting soldier slips inside her heart.

The Secrets Between Them:

The more time Lucas spends with Eve, he remembers what it is to be alive and he lets the walls protecting his heart down. When the secrets between them come to light will their love be enough? Or are they two destined for heartbreak?

ᴏNLY ꜰᴏʀ ʜɪS ʟᴀᴅʏ
Book 1 in the "The Theodosia Sword" Series

A curse. A sword. And the thief who stole her heart.

The Rayne family is trapped in a rut of bad luck. And now, it's up to Lady Theodosia Rayne to steal back the Theodosia sword, a gladius that was pilfered by the rival, loathed Renshaw family. Hopefully, recovering the stolen sword will break the cycle and reverse her family's fate.

Damian Renshaw, the Duke of Devlin, is feared by all—all, that is, except Lady Theodosia, the brazen spitfire who enters his home and wrestles an ancient relic from his wall. Intrigued by the vivacious woman, Devlin has no intentions of relinquishing the sword to her.

As Theodosia and Damian battle for ownership, passion ignites. Now, they are torn between their age-old feud and the fire that burns between them. Can two forbidden lovers find a way to make amends before their families' war tears them apart?

My Lady of Deception
Book 1 in the "Brethren of the Lords" Series

This dark, sweeping Regency novel was previously only offered as part of the limited edition box sets: "From the Ballroom and Beyond", "Romancing the Rogue", and "Dark Deceptions". Now, available for the first time on its own, exclusively through Amazon is "My Lady of Deception".

~★~

Everybody has a secret. Some are more dangerous than others.

For Georgina Wilcox, only child of the notorious traitor known as "The Fox", there are too many secrets to count. However, after her interference results in great tragedy, she resolves to never help another... until she meets Adam Markham.

Lord Adam Markham is captured by The Fox. Imprisoned, Adam loses everything he holds dear. As his days in captivity grow, he finds himself fascinated by the young maid, Georgina, who cares for him.

When the carefully crafted lies she's built between them begin to crumble, Georgina realizes she will do anything to prove her love and loyalty to Adam—even it means at the expense of her own life.

NON-FICTION WORKS BY
CHRISTI CALDWELL

**Uninterrupted Joy: Memoir: My Journey through
Infertility, Pregnancy, and Special Needs**

The following journey was never intended for publication.
It was written from a mother, to her unborn child. The words
detailed her struggle through infertility and the joy of finally being
pregnant. A stunning revelation at her son's birth opened a world
of both fear and discovery. This is the story of one mother's love
and hope and…her quest for uninterrupted joy.

BIOGRAPHY

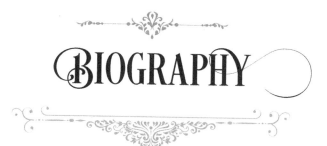

Christi Caldwell is the bestselling author of historical romance novels set in the Regency era. Christi blames Judith McNaught's "Whitney, My Love," for luring her into the world of historical romance. While sitting in her graduate school apartment at the University of Connecticut, Christi decided to set aside her notes and try her hand at writing romance. She believes the most perfect heroes and heroines have imperfections and rather enjoys tormenting them before crafting a well-deserved happily ever after!

When Christi isn't writing the stories of flawed heroes and heroines, she can be found in her Southern Connecticut home chasing around her eight-year-old son, and caring for twin princesses-in-training!

Visit *www.christicaldwellauthor.com* to learn more about what Christi is working on, or join her on Facebook at Christi Caldwell Author, and Twitter *@ChristiCaldwell*